SCRATCHING
the
Seven-Month
ITCH

J. L. Salter

Amanda Moore or Less
A screwball romantic comedy
Prequel to *Curing the Uncommon Man-Cold*

δ

Dingbat Publishing

Humble, Texas

SCRATCHING THE SEVEN-MONTH ITCH
Copyright © 2014 by Jeffrey L. Salter
ISBN 978-1-940520-18-6

Published by Dingbat Publishing
Humble, Texas

Pottery Barn by Williams-Sonoma, Inc.

PowerPoint by Microsoft Corporation

Prada by Prada S.A.

Saks Fifth Avenue by Hudson's Bay Company

SeaWorld by SeaWorld Entertainment, a division of The Blackstone Group L.P.

Smith & Wesson by Smith & Wesson Holding Corporation

Star Trek by CBS Broadcasting, Inc. (Westinghouse CBS Holding Company, Inc.) and Paramount Pictures Corporation (Viacom, Inc.)

Super Bowl by National Football League

Taser by TASER International, Inc.

Telemundo by NBCUniversal Television Group, a division of NBCUniversal, Inc.

Televisa by Grupo Televisa, S.A.B.

Tennessee Titans, a franchise of the National Football League

Twister by the Milton Bradley Company, a wholly owned subsidiary of Hasbro, Inc.

Viagra by Pfizer, Inc.

Wendy's International by The Wendy's Company

Wiki (Wikipedia) by Wikimedia Foundation

Also, the author has made free use of several well-known names from popular culture. Such usage is not intended in any defamatory manner, nor to imply any approval from these individuals for this book nor for any of the actions contained therein.

Dr. Phil McGraw

Oprah Winfrey

Dedication

Not due to the *theme* or *content* of this screwball comedy, but because she taught me so much about writing, research, and literature — I dedicate this novel to my senior English teacher at Covington [LA] High School, **Earlene Howser Ward**, currently of Magnolia AR.

SCRATCHING

the

Seven-Month

ITCH

Chapter 1

Friday, May 22, 2009

Amanda Moore knew from the *Maneater* ringtone which friend was calling: the older, bossy, impetuous one. "Hello?"

"Not sure how to tell you this, but... he's cheating." It came out so easily that Christine Powers must have practiced. A rather startling announcement, considering she didn't even say hello.

"Okay, *who's* cheating?"

Christine's tense silence provided the answer.

"Jason? No way!"

"I wouldn't have said anything, but the evidence is overwhelming."

"That's insane! Jason?" Amanda's voice quavered. "Who the heck with?"

"Not certain... yet."

"Exactly how reliable is this evidence if you don't even know who she is?"

"Overwhelming." Christine always sounded certain.

"Well, spit it out! And quick. My *perfect* sister Kaye will be here any minute!"

"Oh. Maybe we should wait 'til you're not in such a rush."

"Yeah, well, thanks a bunch for getting me all riled up when I don't have time to talk." Amanda scanned her duplex as she struggled to process two domestic emergencies on top of a new crisis at work. "Look, I know Jason's not playing around. But this is very important — Kaye canNOT know ANYthing about this!"

"Mum's the word." Christine probably thought Mum was a deodorant. "Call me later and I'll give you the rest of my intel. Bye."

Amanda flicked her phone shut without reply. Her honey brown hair framed an attractive face which barely avoided being beautiful. Her bright blue eyes could make someone melt or cause them a chill, depending on the person and circumstances. Right now they were icy. Christine, Kaye… and Jason were all ganging up on her.

She checked the kitchen clock — about two minutes until Hurricane Kaye's arrival. Though distinctly skeptical of this sudden accusation, Amanda worried anyway. She knew Jason Stewart better than she'd known any other man, but significant gaps remained. In fact, maybe they didn't really know each other all that well. After getting comfortable within their relationship, Amanda had stopped trying so hard to "learn" him. And probably vice versa.

But even if Jason were taking her for granted, it didn't mean he was playing around. "Jason wouldn't cheat on me. Why would he?" *But if he IS boffing someone else, he's a dead man.* Amanda examined her short, unpainted fingernails. *Might need something else to claw that slut's eyeballs… whoever she is.*

Outside the apartment, a car door slammed — her elder sister was literally seconds away. Amanda sucked in a quick breath. *Remember, keep a hard shell so Kaye won't find any weak spot to probe. And not a word about this Jason mess, because she will immediately tell Mom and Dad that I've lost another one.*

Amanda glanced down at her work heels and smoothed her skirt. Her only ace in the sibling race — she had even prettier legs than perfect Kaye.

The doorbell rang. *She's ba-aacckk!*

Amanda's hand trembled slightly when she turned the knob. "Hi, Kaye!" There wasn't time to invite her inside because Kaye Moore-Smith was already lunging forward. They hugged awkwardly, with noticeable space between them. *No bags?* "I didn't have time to move much since you called yesterday, but there's still room to sleep and that single bed is pretty comfortable." Amanda pointed down the short hallway. It had been about two years since she'd seen Kaye and they didn't talk much on the phone, either. "Come have a look."

When Kaye had toured shortly after Amanda moved in, she'd acted like nobody could survive in less than 2,000 square feet. Now Kaye assessed everything as though she wore white gloves. With higher grades, fuller bosom, better hair (dyed blonde, of course), Kaye had always seemed the favorite daughter. Growing up, she'd been bossy and rather cold... and eight years older. She'd married right after college, moved to an upscale Indianapolis neighborhood, and quickly produced a child... a big plus. With her looks and ability to role play, Kaye could sell anything; currently she represented high-end office equipment. But their parents ignored the facts: Kaye was separated with a pending divorce and her thirteen-year-old daughter was a witchy brat.

And Kaye was finally developing a belly! Amanda hid her glee.

When Kaye peeked into the cluttered guestroom, which Amanda used as an ad hoc storage depot, she wrinkled her nose and delivered a short speech (which sounded rehearsed) about needing space to spread out, so she would find suitable lodgings in Nashville, about 25 miles west. She'd be in the area for most of four days, Kaye had said, so perhaps her company was covering the hotel costs.

"You hear anything much from Mom and Dad?" In their predictable e-mail-and-Facebook sibling conversations, this was Kaye's opening move.

Amanda sighed. "Mom forwards nearly every e-mail she gets, especially the ones telling you to send it to ten people in the next minute so you'll have good luck."

Kaye nodded without replying. Evidently she received the same.

"But she rarely sends anything about herself."

"And Dad?" Kaye asked.

"He still won't use a computer." Amanda smiled, rather tentatively.

"Well, he doesn't use phones much either, as I recall. Unless Mom slaps it to his ear."

They laughed together — the first time in many years. Amanda thawed a bit. Perhaps this visit would be different; maybe they could be more than estranged sisters. Probably not friends, but it would be nice to share something more than coolish civility.

Funny, how Kaye always seemed to be looking for something better. *Must have been tough on her soon-to-be-ex-husband.*

"So, how are things with your, uh... legal proceedings?" Amanda didn't know if her sister wanted to discuss this.

"The divorce? Oh, it's dragging out, but the lawyers prefer it that way. Tom and I had mostly agreed on all the big issues, but they keep finding wrinkles that supposedly have to be documented up the ying-yang." Kaye frowned. "More fees for them, of course." Without warning, she blurted out, "He cheated on me." Then she clamped her lips shut and looked away.

Amanda felt her jaw dropping. That was the first divorce detail Kaye had volunteered. "Oh, Kaye, I'm sorry…"

"Son of a gun was diddling somebody at work." Kaye's eyes reddened. "You want to know how I found out?"

Amanda *did* want to know… intensely. But — unlike celebrity breakups — with her perfect sister being the topic, it felt like prying. "No, you don't have to…"

"She left her nasty panties in Tom's glove compartment!"

They'd used his expensive BMW? *Shocking*. Her sibling was on the verge of tears and normally such pain would give Amanda a tiny bit of pleasure. But she just felt compassion, possibly for the first time since she'd been ten and Kaye had finally left for college eighteen years ago. "Your daughter… how's she adjusting?"

Kaye held her hand vertically. *Don't go there*. She and her witchy daughter had been at odds since Chelsea was nine, almost four years ago. Obviously the trip to Nashville was also an excuse for a beleaguered mom to just get away. Kaye shook her head. "I should leave. My reservation…"

Since she'd never intended to stay, why hadn't Kaye said so last night when she'd called? Nearly two hours of cleaning and straightening… Amanda shrugged. *Same old disapproving, resentful, competitive Kaye.* Maybe that was normal between sisters. *But it shouldn't be.*

By the time Kaye had used the bathroom and emerged with her nose wrinkled, only about twenty minutes had elapsed since her arrival. It was their longest visit in Amanda couldn't remember how long.

Amanda watched her depart. Kaye's home metropolis was much larger and finer — better stores, more culture, and supposedly fewer hicks. But Amanda would rather live with hicks than pretentious snobs. Besides, small town friendliness — underrated by most big city dwellers — was dependable and comforting.

"So Kaye is too refined to stay here overnight." *Fine.* Kaye's presence would have complicated the newly-launched crisis management effort... in case Jason the creep *was* playing around. Amanda inhaled deeply and put on her game face — she had a dinner date with Jason the cheater.

Chapter 2

What to talk about?

The country-casual restaurant bustled around their table. Without looking up, Amanda toyed with the gravy-soused noodles on her plate. Jason seemed different, and not merely because of Christine's shocking announcement. He was definitely acting funny, like he wished he were somewhere else. *Or would he rather be WITH someone else?* He seemed, well… guilty. Antsy and guilty.

Usually he talked about his current team or sports in general, but tonight he was mostly silent. *Guilty people either chatter non-stop… or they don't speak at all.*

Uncertain what to say, Amanda defaulted to shop-talk. "Louis dumped a new assignment on me today."

Jason looked up but continued chewing. His features had not actually *changed* in the past two days, yet they seemed different. He looked like a cheater.

"I don't have particulars yet, but it's his pet department that miraculously gets a grant almost every cycle. Somebody in

Public Works has completely dropped the ball on their evaluations and King Louie's screaming bloody murder." Her boss typically assumed the worst, rarely made any legitimate queries, and went off half-cocked without any real investigation whatsoever. "I hate people who jump straight to the battle stations klaxon at the first radar blip." Most of Amanda's military imagery came from war movies she'd watched with her father as a child. It had been one of her few refuges from domineering Kaye.

Jason just nodded and swallowed at the same time. *Awkward.* He'd been so uncomplicated and lovable... before this evening. But all of her high hopes for their future now seemed as limp and extraneous as the gristle he'd briskly trimmed off his roast beef slab.

Amanda nibbled on beef tips and sipped her iced tea before continuing. "Plus somehow or other Louis makes that my fault." Her job was reviewing and assessing applications from every Greene County agency seeking federal money. She was also responsible for collecting external evaluations at the end of the grant period, but she'd had no part in conducting them until now. "He wants me personally involved in their evals so this gets cleaned up quickly."

Jason didn't appear interested in anything except his buffet platter, but he'd repeatedly established eye contact as he ate. His blue eyes were at times bright with zeal but occasionally dark and soulful. They glazed slightly when Amanda talked shop. "So Monday you get thrown into the shark tank and have to evaluate their lack of effectiveness in spending Uncle Sam's money?" He scooted back his chair and stood.

She was surprised by Jason's perceptive feedback. "Tuesday, actually. We're closed Monday for Memorial..." Amanda broke off when Jason grabbed his plate and headed back to the buffet. *That was rude...* leaving in the middle of her reply! When had he started acting like that? Did rudeness go along with cheating? She fumed while Jason grazed at the seafood section. Friday evening's unrestricted portions and a dollar off the regular price made the restaurant a huge draw for Jason, among hundreds of other buffet fanatics. While she understood that, Amanda preferred smaller places with candlelight and atmosphere.

Finally he returned to his seat with a full plate and two desserts. "We don't have to talk about your work problems. Ruins the digestion." Jason smiled but it seemed strained.

Usually Amanda could smile back, but not after Christine's allegations. If she didn't talk about her job, the only logical subjects were sister Kaye or cheater Jason.

"Is anything else bothering you?" He appeared to struggle for the right words. "You seem... tense."

Amanda wanted to ask outright if he was playing around, but she hadn't even heard Christine's so-called evidence. She also fought the urge to search his glove compartment for someone else's panties. "Well, that dang New Year's Eve photo keeps coming up."

Jason almost grinned, but stopped. "I know that bothers you, but it doesn't really show anything. I mean, yeah, the view is up your short skirt while you're on a ten-foot ladder, but you had, uh, skivvies on. And pantyhose, right? So that's more clothes than you'd have at the pool."

She didn't feel like explaining why it mattered that photos of her underpinnings were circulating as attachments in e-mails and Facebook postings. Any woman would understand. That picture made it even more frustrating to deal with all the county and city departments. Because of Amanda's attractiveness, the most cynical co-workers assumed she'd gotten her important position for reasons other than work ethic and ability. That unfortunate photo only reinforced such views. *Views — hmm.*

****

Jason could tell she was upset but didn't know why. On the scale of Amanda's usual body language, it was more than the grant problem and worse than being reminded of that embarrassing photo. And it wasn't just her boss, because Louis was always a bully. So whatever was eating her was something distinctly different — larger, deeper, and more sinister. But what? He couldn't imagine. It was obvious from her fixed stare at the ketchup bottle that Amanda had zoned out on him, so Jason continued his meal.

In the middle of his chewing, Amanda suddenly resumed. "Oh, my sister finally told me why she and Tom are getting divorced."

He listened with only half an ear to this topical detour.

"Turns out Tommy-boy was *cheating* on her." It was weird, the way she stared at his face... like she was searching for a blemish.

Jason checked his watch. "Guess I have time for another quick dessert or two." Despite being often reminded of his predilection for beer, breaded and pan-fried meats, junk food, and frequent snacks, he was still fast and agile on the ball fields, with commendable endurance.

Amanda exhaled considerable air with extra sound. "I'm going to the powder room." She rose abruptly and stalked away.

Jason watched her leave — sexy view even when she was angry. Why would Kaye's divorce news bother Amanda? Normally she seemed secretly pleased when her elder sibling suffered any indignity.

Oh, well. He had his own fish to fry (besides what he'd consumed at the buffet). The softball season schedule was screwing with his work shifts, their team "manager" couldn't coach his way through Little League practice, and not enough players were available for the big holiday tournament that coming weekend. Jason let a mouthful of artificial ice cream dissolve slightly before he swallowed. Plus, his fantasy league needed a baseball commissioner and so far nobody had volunteered to handle it. During supper he hadn't even wanted to think about his consultant problems at Greene County Electric Co-op. (The power company was known mainly by its initials, GCEC, which everyone pronounced Gee-keck.)

On top of everything else awry in Jason-Land, his friend Kevin Haywood had been regaling him with torrid tales of frequent alley-catting. It was bothersome that Kevin would try to bed a different woman nearly every night, but it worried Jason even more that he was vicariously titillated by the details. In fact, it made him feel a little guilty.

****

Amanda emerged from the restroom and lingered near the buffet's multiple desserts. She was strongly tempted, but managed to refrain by lacing her fingers together in front of her trim waist.

How could Jason be so insensitive? Couldn't he tell she was confused, worried, and furious? Didn't he *sense* that she'd been alerted to his indiscretion and was supremely ticked? How could he wolf down the equivalent of two complete meals while she felt like skinning him alive?

As she resumed her seat, she said, "You sure seem antsy tonight."

He appeared surprised that she'd noticed. "It's the MLB fantasy league draft at Roger Hardeman's apartment. If I get there late, Roger will mangle my picks in the first few rounds."

"Oh, I see," she replied. As an avid competitor in basketball, softball, soccer, and flag football, Jason sometimes seemed to value sports more than their relationship.

"Where is your sister, anyway? I'd thought she might join us."

Amanda eyed him suspiciously. Jason didn't do all that much thinking and when he did, it made him look guilty. "Oh, Kaye doesn't eat at these buffets… thinks they're too common. Plus she was huffy about staying in my guestroom. Evidently has a thing about boxes. Didn't say where she went, but most likely the same place as the company's meetings and exhibits. Probably downtown Nashville."

The evening had not gone well. Jason looked troubled and guilty of something, and she was pretty sure what it was.

She waited while he wiped his mouth with two napkins. While he paid the bill, she crossed her arms tightly and gazed through the window at the parking lot. Outside, Jason neglected to open his truck's passenger door for her. *Another slight! Taking up with floozies AND being rude!*

The short drive was silent and chilly despite the warm May evening. When they reached Amanda's duplex, Jason only said, "Late for the fantasy draft…" with a lame shrug. He actually moved toward her as if for a kiss, but Amanda stiffened and leaned away. She did not want any cheating lips on her face!

After he drove away, Amanda shut her apartment door and slumped into the nearest chair. Too much strain from too many sources… she needed some relief. She reached up and banged on the front wall a few times. It would have been more satisfying to pound the wall she shared with her new neighbor, the yodeling one, but Amanda was too exhausted to get up.

She couldn't stop thinking about it. Jason, a cheater? Most of their time together had been nice… some had been excellent. But in truth, some aspects were quite unsatisfactory. Sex was still good, but there wasn't much measurable *romance*. Amanda had chalked this deficit to Jason's lack of sophistication. If he'd had more enlightening life experiences than commuting to

Tennessee State University in West Nashville, she assumed he would automatically be more romantic. But maybe there were other reasons.

Her eyes half-closed, Amanda thought farther back, over those previous months they'd dated, off and on, non-exclusively. Jason had not been easy to catch. Lots of unattached women flocked around the team sports fields. It had been tricky to maneuver herself into his path and she'd had to elbow several others out of the way. Fortunately, Southern girls developed sharp elbows at an early age. It had been quite a competition to become Jason's girlfriend and Amanda had approached that challenge as vigorously as she had all her other obstacles in life.

Obstacles. A friend had phoned that morning and recited Amanda's Aries horoscope. What was it? She'd transcribed it word for word because it had seemed so important to kooky Sunny Cannon. These were not the normal few lines seen in most newspapers — it was a full-scale "horoscopic work-up" from Sunny's in-depth website search.

Where were those notes? Purse? No, briefcase. First flap inside the lid. *Uhh.* Two distinct sections:

> *Look deeply into your relationship... it's a good*
> *time for you to pick up a few new clues from your sweetie.*
> *Deeply explore your moods, because you're in a really*
> *good position to make a seriously positive change. Be*
> *more willing to get rid of what you don't need.*
>
> *A big decision today, but the more you think about*
> *it, the murkier it gets. Really pore over the details of a big*
> *project to see if they all add up. Just let your intuition*
> *make the call. Once you're settled, it's time to move out*
> *quickly. Step up and enlist the aid of those who are*
> *sympathetic to your cause. Your emotions are leading you*
> *in a good direction, so even if things get weird, you need*

to press on righteously.

It was typical mumbo jumbo to Amanda — vague but insinuated specificity. If all the horoscopes had been inadvertently scrambled by the website's layout crew, this one was general enough that any of the others might equally pertain to her. It could apply to work, finances, relatives, friendships — just about any aspect of life.

But this one mentioned relationships in the first sentence.

Chapter 3

Christine Powers set her chin and looked again at her notes about Jason's indiscretions. Dates, times, descriptions… yeah, she was certain. *Well, pretty sure.*

She really resented Amanda's sister interrupting her big announcement. Such news deserved a special reading, not just a rushed headline. Though they'd never met, Christine assumed she would not like Kaye at all. Way too bossy.

Divorced for four years, Christine was financially secure because of her lucrative alimony settlement. Frankly, she had too much free time on her hands. Brunette Christine had lots of urges and followed up on them so often that people said she behaved more like a volatile redhead.

She pressed Amanda's number on speed-dial and waited. The triggered Hall and Oates ringtone was a good match for Christine. Some people thought of her as a cougar and she did little to discourage that image.

Amanda answered.

"You home?" Rhetorical. Christine had just watched Jason drive away.

"Barely." Amanda sighed. "Just put down my purse and haven't taken off my shoes."

"Well, don't lock the door yet. I'm right outside in your parking lot."

****

Amanda opened the door with a resigned sigh. It was 8:30 and she'd been going all day long. The guest made herself comfortable on the loveseat while the reluctant hostess stalked to her bedroom.

Within five minutes, Amanda returned in cut-offs, T-shirt, and flip-flops — standard apparel for Verdeville's excellent weather at the end of May. She pulled two lite beers from the fridge. "I don't think ice tea has the right horsepower to handle this conversation." She sighed and handed over a bottle. "So what's all this cheating crud?" Amanda plopped down on the wooden rocker. "And thanks a whole bunch for putting me in a panic right before Kaye arrived!"

A few inches shorter, Christine made up for it with additional inches across her implanted bust. At forty, she was a dozen years older. She presently carried fifteen extra pounds — fortunately, they formed very well-proportioned curves. Except for wardrobe and hairstyle, Amanda thought she rather resembled Elizabeth Taylor in her prime.

"Sorry. I'd forgotten your sister was in town. It's not like she visits every month or anything." Christine waved her richly tanned hand. In the body language of a manic individual, that meant *the conversation has changed, so jump on board and fasten your seatbelt.* "Well, like I said on the phone, I hate to be the one to tell you…"

Amanda fought the urge to roll her eyes. *No, you don't.*

Her domineering friend loved bearing bad news.

"...but your athletic boyfriend is like most other men after about seven months of exclusivity. He's got the itch and only a different woman can scratch it."

"What's this seven month business? I've seen Marilyn Monroe's movie, of course, but that guy's itch took seven *years* of *marriage* to develop. That's a big difference." She and Jason had begun sleeping together right after last year's Halloween party.

Christine was already shaking her head. "A lot has changed, girl. Things are hyper-speed now. Jason's friend Kevin is divorced twice in his mid-thirties. Your sister is bailing out of her disaster with what's-his-name. My dreamy lawyer is about ready to dump that neurotic witch he married in law school."

"I don't care..." Amanda tried to squeeze in a word.

But Christine plowed ahead. "I'm just saying it's a different world. If it used to take seven years to realize your relationship was drying up, the national average is now about seven months."

"You just made that up. There's no such statistic for break-ups."

Christine nodded vigorously. "Doctor Phil. Oprah. Everybody knows. Except you, I mean." She looked gravely to the floor. "That's why I felt responsible to clue you in. In fact, I'm a little surprised you haven't felt the itch yourself. You know, after seven months of the same old sex..."

"It's not the same old sex, thank you very much! And it's none of your business anyway. Our sex life is just fine." She retrieved some mental images. "Well, it's not cutting edge stuff that would go in a paperback romance, but we do very well." But on Wednesday night Jason had seemed so distracted. "At least, it's okay."

Christine seemed to absorb every word. "Okay, good.

You're already aware that it's basically over, but you just haven't bothered to admit it yet. Not a problem. By the time you hear what Jason's been up to, you'll be plenty ready to close the book on this bum."

"He's not a bum. We love each other, however many months it's been." She took a long swig of her beer. "And we're going to be together for a long time!"

Christine leaned back on the loveseat. This must not be what she'd scripted. She'd probably hoped Amanda would be clamoring for the evidence.

"Now, if that's all your persuasive, meddling arguments, I just want to go to bed." Amanda gripped the rocker's arms and started to rise. "I've had a completely rotten week at work and my sister makes me crazy. I don't need any invented problems to pile on top."

Christine's manicured fingernails tapped the slim folder resting in her lap. "Okay, I understand." *Tap.* "Doctor Phil says denial is one of the early steps." *Tap.* "Just forget I mentioned it." *Tap.* "We'll chalk it up to a case of—" *tap* "—bad timing or something."

Amanda sat back down. The tapping was hypnotic and she couldn't look away. How many more taps before she launched herself onto the small couch and ripped the file out of those elegant hands? Only by gripping the chair arms could she control herself. *It's just a folder.*

Self-control was not remotely present in Christine's manic persona, however. With a knowing smile, the guest paused. "So what's the deal with your sister?" *Tap.* "You two still don't get along?" *Tap.*

"She's always been so bossy. She'd never let me make my own decisions. Until Kaye went off to college, I couldn't take a breath of air without her involvement."

Tap. Christine had a slightly blank look. *Tap.* She didn't appear to see the problem. *Tap.*

"Plus, she has a hyphen, for crying out loud — Moore-Smith. Don't you think that's pretentious?"

"I had my hyphen 'til I was seventeen." *Tap.* Christine rose like she was leaving, but instead dropped her folder. A scientist releasing that same file sixty times might succeed only once in getting the papers to fan out properly. Christine must have rehearsed the maneuver at home because the pages spread out in a neat sequence ending right at Amanda's flip-flops. "Oh, sorry. Slipped."

Amanda was drawn to them like a spy to Top Secret weapon plans. She crouched. Before actually touching anything, she digested what she could by reading upside-down. Apparently, Christine had not practiced orienting the sheets correctly.

Neither had taken a breath since the folder hit the floor.

Amanda finally inhaled, scooped the papers together, and rose. She held out the file. "This supposedly proves Jason's cheating on me?"

****

Christine shrugged. Her initial approach had been much too aggressive, so she'd play it more neutrally. "Nobody's been photo'd nekkid. Maybe it's just a mistake."

"Well, let's see what kind of mistakes he's been making." Amanda sat again on the rocker, oriented the pages, and quickly scanned them. "Places, dates, times, and some scribbles I can't read." She tossed the folder to the loveseat's empty cushion, her expression dismissive.

But she had to realize — deep down — those details represented something significant involving Jason. Christine picked up the folder. "My handwriting was a little rough because I didn't want Jason to see me following." It was the perfect comeback, neither accusatory nor confrontational.

"You were *following* Jason?" Amanda's eyebrows arched toward her hairline. "Where? And you witnessed it personally?"

"One at the mall and one at the grocery." When Christine patted the adjacent seat cushion, Amanda sat solemnly.

Amanda squeezed her eyes shut. It must have been disorienting to ingest such data about her lover. "He's having an affair at the Verdeville Mall? That's totally sick!" She moaned. "What did the woman look like?"

"Not sure."

"What do you mean, not sure? You've got Jason bedding down a retail tramp and you don't know what she looks like?"

Christine shrugged. "I couldn't see very well."

"Where the heck were you?" Amanda's voice was shrill.

"I ducked into Bath and Beauty when I saw Jason."

"So where was Jason and his mall skank? Next door at the video place?"

"Uh, no." There had to be an effective way of phrasing it. "A bit further," replied Christine. "Actually, down at the food court."

"Food court!" Amanda pointed as though it were in view. "That's five stores away! And one of those is Dillards! That's a whole city block, Christine! How on earth can you be sure it was even Jason?"

"Walked right by me."

"Then you *did* see the floozy up close!"

Christine shook her head. "No, not her. Saw Jason, then I ducked back. He walked right past me. Then I peeked around the corner. When he got to the food area, he started talking to that woman."

"Oh, shoot! From that distance, Jason could have been talking with Santa's home-bound, gray-haired wife!"

"Only if Mrs. Claus wears a tailored suit and power shoes. Heels that high." Christine spaced her fingers five inches apart. "Plus dark hose and lots of leg showing."

Amanda shook her head as if trying to clear it. "Jason was alone when he passed you. So when he got to the food court, this woman with stilettos was already there. They didn't arrive together, each just happened to go to the same place."

"You never arrive together when you're cheating." Her information about philandering didn't come exclusively from the personal pain of her own divorce. Christine read supermarket tabloids — veritable textbooks into a male's behavior and psyche.

"Just because your Daniel diddled a bimbo doesn't mean that every man cheats on his wife or girlfriend. Jason wouldn't run around on me." Amanda's pause dragged for too long. "He wouldn't dare. I'd kill him."

Christine nodded wisely. "There are worse punishments than death."

****

Worse punishments? It sounded portentous but Amanda didn't inquire. She assumed her friend referred to her lucrative settlement and steep alimony provisions. But there was an edge of something even more punitive than mere finances in Christine's smug smile. "Look… the more I think about this, I'm sure Jason simply had lunch at the mall — he eats there a lot — and this high-heeled vulture just happened to be hungry at the same time. Bingo. Two strangers in the same general place."

"But she wasn't hungry."

"How could you know that from so far away?"

"I moved closer. But, anyway, she didn't eat." Dramatic pause. "And that's not all." Christine lowered her voice again. "She touched him."

"That tailored-suit tramp groped my Jason in the middle

of the food court?"

"Well, not actually groped. More like fingertips."

"Where?" Amanda's voice nearly squeaked with intensity.

"Right in front of the chicken place."

"Christine! You're killing me!"

"Oh, sorry. Just below his elbow." Christine pointed to her own tanned forearm.

What a horrid roller-coaster ride. Guilty, then innocent, then guilty, then innocent! "So Jason dropped some chicken crust on his arm and this overdressed stranger brushed it off. Everything has a simple explanation." Amanda tried to look hopeful.

But Christine's head was already moving sideways. "Sorry. Jason also *gave* her something."

"That scumbag! What the heck did he give her? Necklace? Bracelet? The engagement ring he should be buying for me? What?"

"Couldn't see. Looked flat."

Deflated again, Amanda heaved a sigh. "His card! He just gave her one of his office cards so she can challenge her bill at Gee-keck. See? Completely innocent."

Christine shook her head again. "Looked like a regular size envelope."

"What comes in envelopes?" *Hopefully not an engagement ring.*

"Don't know. But it almost doesn't matter." Another dramatic pause. "Because they left to-ge-ther." Christine's pronunciation was distinctly ominous. "She led the way and he followed." Her fingers demonstrated. "Well, they were nearly side by side... all the way out the doors toward the parking lot. And she was walking fast, especially for those heels."

"There's got to be a more logical explanation." Amanda strained to come up with one. "Okay. This person could be his insurance agent. Uh... his truck! Maybe Jason's hubcaps got stolen..."

"I don't think Jason's rattletrap heap even has hubcaps."

"Because they've been stolen!" Amanda eagerly returned to her storyline. "And the adjustor had to see his pickup before the claim could be finalized. They'd kept missing each other because of Jason's ballgames and work shifts. Both realized they'd be near the mall, so Jason — always being hungry — picked the food court." Amanda had a detailed imagination.

Christine shook her head during Amanda's entire spiel. "What does *your* insurance agent normally wear?"

"Hmm. He usually has scruffy shoes, wrinkled khakis, and a coffee-stained golf shirt. Why?"

"Well, I told you what Madame X was wearing. Does that say Greene County insurance to you?"

It didn't. "Okay. Maybe she's not the regular person. The full-time adjustor's in the hospital and they're backlogged, so attractive female agents in stilettos are out doing double duty."

****

Christine decided to let the prosecution rest. Her naïve friend would soon realize the shakiness of that elaborate alibi.

It was just that Christine didn't have enough to *do*. For a time, her energy had been expended helping the Ace Detective Agency catch Daniel *en flagrante delicto*. But after the legal proceedings had ended, she found herself with too little purpose. Christine didn't need a salary and certainly did not *want* to work. She had no real hobbies and her interests tended to flit about with her moods as she moved up and down the scale of not-quite-clinical manic mode. Actually, she'd been chronically bored until she realized Amanda's life needed so much help... and Christine was only too happy to assist. Some people accused her of being overly domineering but she viewed herself as a good facilitator.

Managing friends' lives was art, not science. Sunny Cannon was kind of addlebrained and Maria Perry was too grounded. But Amanda possessed the perfect blend of intelligence, optimism, practicality, and creativity. So she was fertile territory for an inspired facilitator to come in and set down roots. Plus, Amanda had been previously trained by an older sister to function well under external management. The trick, then, was to use a deft touch. Whenever Christine crossed that line, Amanda would bristle and call her *Kaye*.

Convinced of her evidence and determined to protect her less worldly friend from further humiliation, Christine chose her words carefully. "It's not the first time."

Amanda grimaced. "Okay, yeah. I saw two reports in your file. Two times he's spoken to a woman you don't know and you're yanking my chain… trying to get me crazy."

"Two women. *Different* women."

****

"Together?" Amanda imagined a kinky three-way and shook her head vigorously.

"No. Different times… uh, days. Different women on different days."

"Look, Christine, you'd better spit it out. I'm getting really upset here. This grocery store encounter — where exactly?"

"Snack aisle."

"That's one of Jason's favorite spots in Verdeville. If he's not at my place or his — or out eating a meal — he's on that snack aisle. Hardly the place for a tryst. Even tackier than the food court." No way would Christine get away with this charge. "So how close were you this time?"

"Two aisles over." Christine stopped to think. "With the

bread."

"I'm guessing you can't identify this alleged second woman either."

Christine shook her head. "Seemed vaguely familiar, but I couldn't place her. But they were definitely to-ge-ther."

"Doing exactly what?" Not too many possibilities in the snack aisle.

"Talking too softly." She hushed her own voice.

"Hold on. You saw Jason speaking with a woman you don't know, and you're sitting here telling me that he's messing around?" Amanda jumped from the loveseat to keep from shrieking. Her boss was hounding her at work, her sister was hovering nearby on a sudden visit, and her close friend was inventing problems with Jason's fidelity. Plus, she had a yodeler for a new duplex neighbor, a woman she hadn't even seen yet.

"Remember, Amanda, there was contact involved."

"Okay, the mall woman touched his forearm. Not one of the top ten erogenous zones for most men. What was his contact from this grocery trollop?"

"Jason touched *her*."

"Where?"

Christine leaned a bit closer. "Right near the barbecue chips."

"Christine!"

Christine jumped slightly. "Oh, sorry." She leaned in again. "He *cupped* her."

"Jason cupped a strange woman's boobs right in the snack aisle? I'll kill him!"

"No, no! Her elbow! Now you've got me rattled. I meant he cupped her elbow."

"This is insane! You're ready to have Jason arrested for polygamy and your only so-called evidence is a food court woman touches his forearm and he fingers a female elbow in

the grocery. He might have been examining her tennis injury."
A man could have lots of reasons to touch a feminine
olecranon. "She's probably a co-worker at Gee-keck... or
maybe even a customer."

"He wouldn't stand that close to a customer."

Amanda thought of a new tack. "She could be the wife of
one of his teammates. He's on some kind of team practically all
year long. Probably has thirty married teammates in one sport
or another." She paused, trying to convince herself. But the
more she thought about it, the less certain she was. After all,
Jason was acting edgy and distracted. Was that related to the
itch? Plus he'd been uncommonly rude at supper, walking
toward the desserts while she'd still been talking. *What else
could it be?*

****

Christine couldn't believe how much that girl was
blocking the obvious. "But these two women are just the ones I
happened to be there for."

Amanda frowned silently.

"Look, cheaters are a lot like icebergs. Only the top
twenty per cent is visible. The rest is hidden from view."

"So now you're saying Jason's messing around with a
total of ten bimbos?"

Christine nodded sagely. "Probably... at least." Christine
had the uncanny ability to make the most preposterous
statements sound like researched and verified facts. "Maybe
more. The itch is a very powerful urge for men, especially after
seven months with the same woman." There had to be
something she could say as a convincing closing argument.
"Picture a man with a lifelong nicotine addiction. Suddenly
he's expected to give up smoking. So he tries real hard and for
the first month he gets by with one nicotine patch every day.

But it's extremely difficult, so by the second month he wears two patches a day. Well, as you can imagine, by the *seventh* month, he's daily covered head to toe in nicotine patches, but he still craves a smoke."

"And so after seven months, he can't stand it any more and finally he sneaks off and just lights one up!" Amanda finished the allegory. "That scumbag!" She looked like she was about to start crying as she clutched her friend's wrist. "Remember, Kaye cannot hear a whisper of this!"

Christine understood and nodded. Her young friend had cast Jason as Sir Galahad. But the *gala* was long over and apparently now she'd been *had*.

It took a few moments for Amanda to compose herself. "So what did this one look like? At the grocery?"

Uncomfortable, Christine shrugged.

"Don't tell me you didn't get a good look at her, either."

"I saw her, all right."

"And...?"

"Well, I'd rather not say."

****

Amanda had to know. "You can't put the brakes on there. My motor's running too fast because of your half-baked detective work."

Christine shook her head sadly.

"Younger than me?"

Christine nodded.

"Prettier?"

"I've already said too much."

That doesn't usually stop her. Amanda clutched her wrist again, harder this time. "How much prettier?" Her voice had an edge on it.

"Maybe I should go."

Amanda let *prettier* ride for the moment. "And Jason cupped her elbow?"

Another nod.

"I'll kill him. And when I find that younger, prettier elbow witch, I'll deal with her too!" Amanda choked back a sob. "What was this grocery tramp wearing?"

"You sure you want to know?"

Amanda nodded.

"High-heeled sandals and tailored, impossibly tight jeans that really defined her very nice butt." Christine licked her lips; she probably wished she could wear jeans like that. "And a tight, low-cut camo pattern tank top that barely covered her push-up brassiere."

"Camo?"

"You know how guys are turned on by camouflage stuff."

Amanda was thoroughly demoralized. "I didn't know Jason liked camo tanks and tight jeans."

"Actually, it seemed kind of nineties to me, but nobody asked my fashion opinion. I'll bet she wears jeans to hide those bony long legs."

"How do you know they're bony?"

"You have gorgeous legs, Amanda." It was rare to have legs which looked gorgeous in anything from elegant heels to scruffy slippers. "You'd never have to wear jeans or slacks unless it's too cold for hose. But imagine what life would be like if you had scrawny, bony legs — you'd have to find a hundred ways to cover up those terrible twigs."

"Are you trying to make me feel sorry for this grocery floozy? It sounds like you want to help her out with a fund-raising telethon."

"I'm just saying she probably has awful legs. Hence the jeans at the end of May. I know Jason's a leg man, so he's probably just diddling her out of pity."

"Christine! Jason only touched her stinking elbow! That's

a far cry from diddling, whether it's for pity or not."

****

Uncharacteristically, the words hit home. Christine paused. Was she making too much of that encounter? *How torrid is a man's casual cupping of a woman's elbow in front of the barbecue chips?* The moment didn't last long. *My man could touch Aunt Hazel's elbow in front of me, but don't dare touch the arm of a hussy in heels and a camo tank top.*

Serene again, Christine waved her hand. *New subject.* "You realize the next step, don't you?"

"I strangle Jason and flatten both bimbos with a bulldozer?"

"Seriously. The next step is…" she paused and looked to both sides, even though they were alone, "…in-ves-ti-ga-tion." Christine nodded to reinforce the pronouncement.

"I'm not investigating anything. I'll just sit Jason down and make him tell me who he was talking to, at both places."

"No, you can't!"

"Exactly why not?"

"If you confront a cheater," Christine nodded sagely, "he just gets even more devious."

Amanda stared. "Christine, I'm real sorry you and Daniel broke up and I know he was playing around on you. I'm certain that hurts all the way down to your bone marrow. But that does not mean every man who looks in the direction of another woman is doing the same thing. Not every man does that."

"They all have the same instincts… and lusts."

"But they don't all act on those urges."

Such a Pollyanna. "Amanda, you owe it to yourself to check him out. Just a little watching here, asking questions there. Investigation. It's pretty much expected. In fact, he's probably wondering why you haven't already started the program."

"Program?"

"Surveillance. With my help and some other discreet friends…"

"I don't have any discreet friends!" Amanda sputtered. "They're all like you!"

Well, THAT hurt.

"Sorry, it came out wrong. I just meant that none of my friends really comprehend subtlety or discretion."

That didn't help. But Christine understood — Amanda deflected the emotional trauma by lashing out at others. "You can't just leave this dangling. If Jason's innocent, as you keep blindly insisting, then prove it. Have him followed."

"But that's so extreme… too much like a soap opera."

"Life *is* a soap opera. Where do you think they get all their story lines?"

Amanda shook her head slowly. "No." The word was barely audible, but her lower lip remained extended, much like the determined expression of a child resisting instruction.

"You can't just stick your head in the sand and pretend…" Christine saw she wasn't getting anywhere so she exaggerated her shrug. *Sometimes it's up to friends to handle things for hesitant victims incapacitated by naïve gullibility.* Her mission was confirmed.

Amanda stared toward the duplex's back door and eased the wooden rocker back and forth as Christine rose from the loveseat, collected her belongings, and left. She locked the door on her way out.

****

On her way home, Christine lowered the window of her sparkling white Lexus SC-10 convertible, though she left the ragtop up. *What to do?* She would not let Amanda become a victim simply because she was in denial or indecisive. But Maria and Sunny were not exactly the dream team of investigatory surveillance. In a flash of inspiration, she had a back-up plan. "We're going to need some professional help on this case." At the first stoplight, she grabbed her phone and pressed a speed dial number for her dreamy lawyer, Bruce Townsend.

Tall, tanned, and slender, Bruce was handsome enough to make women weak in the knees. The call went to voicemail, so she left a message about hiring the detective agency he'd used for her divorce four years ago. She indicated it was for a small but urgent project and did not reveal specifics. Too many cell phone hackers out there.

After hanging up, she checked her watch. 10:45 p.m. Well, if Bruce waited until morning, that might be okay. What was tomorrow? Saturday. *Good grief!* "Why do weekends keep popping up and ruining all my mission momentum?"

Chapter 4

Finally Amanda had a moment to herself. To distract her hands from the urge to inflict multiple stab wounds on the hussies trying to steal Jason, she checked e-mail. But the compulsion to sharpen knives remained stronger than the desire to open messages from friends, even those from Maria and Sunny. She'd read those later when she wasn't so stressed and confused.

But scarcely ten minutes later the doorbell rang. She put down her notebook computer, the keyboard damp with tears, and checked the peephole. *Maria Perry.*

Amanda cracked the door open. "Maria, I'm really bushed. Can this wait? I've had a really, really horrid day." It was nearly eleven o'clock.

"But I hurried right over."

Heavy sigh. "Why?" She was nearly afraid to ask.

"Christine's e-mail."

A few years younger, Maria had lush black hair and a beautiful dusky complexion. Her mother had been born and raised in Mexico City; her father was a career U.S. Air Force officer. She'd attended five different public schools before enrolling at East Tennessee State University in Johnson City.

Tonight she wore jeans and sneakers with a short-sleeved buttoned blouse. She looked like she'd just thrown her clothes on before rushing over.

"Christine just left here twenty minutes ago. What e-mail? I was just in my mailbox. Christine didn't send me anything."

"I don't recall seeing your name in the address block." Maria cleared her throat and glanced back as if she expected someone to sneak up on them. She had no trace of an accent unless she wanted to use one for whatever reason. Her lovely mother had been a *Televisa* star in Mexico before appearing in some of the American-based *Telemundo* productions. "She probably didn't want you to see it."

Amanda was bone weary — physically and emotionally. "Oh, shoot, come on in and explain. But if I fall into an exhaustion coma, just lock the door when you leave."

Amanda turned, led the way into the living room, and grabbed some new tissues. "So what's this about Christine's e-mail?"

****

"I'm so sorry, Amanda." Maria explained that Christine's e-mail had ordered them to be on the lookout for Jason's comings and goings. They'd been instructed to ask discreet questions of others but not to reveal the reason for their queries. Plus they'd been told to be subtle.

It was bad enough that Christine had pulled them into this disaster, but it would not have been fair to keep Amanda in the dark. However, Maria was inexperienced in helping peers cope with crises. It was far easier to deal with the comparatively innocent dramas of elementary kids slighting one another on the playground. She was wonderful with her second graders and deeply hoped one day to have a boy and a girl of her own. Unfortunately, their targeted future father, the luscious fireman Roger Hardeman, was either clueless about marriage or deliberately dense about Maria's intense interest.

Despite her tears, Amanda's voice was sharp. "How dare Christine air all that out in cyberspace! It's only two very innocent — probably accidental — encounters with two female persons Jason barely knows… if he knows them at all."

Sex with strangers. Even worse than she'd imagined. "Christine's evidently told you more than she spilled in the e-mail. Can you fill me in? I'm dying for details."

"I'm not some splashy story in a supermarket tabloid! This is my private relationship that Christine's broadcasting and meddling in!" Briefly, Amanda's sobs halted her ability to speak. "We're talking about my *life*."

Maria placed a consoling arm over her shoulder, but it felt clumsy and unnatural. They'd first met in college at ETSU when she'd been Amanda's little sister in Gamma Omega. A few senior sorority sisters had bristled at admitting someone with lineage half Mexican and were particularly harsh on Maria during initiation; Amanda had risked her own sorority membership to protect her freshman friend.

"Do you want some hot tea? In a lot of books I've read, upset people usually drink tea."

When Amanda shook her head, tears flew off to the sides.

"Good. Let's have some good old-fashioned booze instead. I never understood that hot tea thing anyhow. You still have those margarita mixes?"

Amanda dabbed her face with a tissue. "Look, I appreciate that you rushed over here to console me…"

True, that was part of Maria's motive. "Uh, Amanda, I think you should know, Christine's e-mail triggered something else. I haven't told her yet." Maria searched the cabinets for margarita makings. Nothing. She gave up and sat back down. "Anyhow, I figure you should know first."

"What? When? Where? Who's the skank in this episode?"

"Now, slow down. I didn't know how to characterize it when I heard it and I'm not completely sure about that now." Teacher talk. "But when I read Christine's e-mail during supper tonight..."

****

Amanda fumed. So Christine had contacted their mutual friends before she'd even showed all her so-called evidence to the injured party!

Maria wouldn't meet her eyes but kept going. "...anyway, I realized my little story seemed to fit right in."

Amanda's hand signaled for the little story to begin... quickly. "Will you please get to the point?"

She cleared her throat. "Now, you know that Roger and I both like Jason a lot. Well, Roger came home from ball practice last night and he was chuckling about something. So I asked him what was so funny. He said, 'Nothing.' I hate it when guys do that. If it's funny enough to make him laugh, it's obviously something... and I want to hear it."

A nod. *Most women would agree.*

"So I finally got him to tell me."

"I'll bet it wasn't funny, was it?"

Maria sighed. "Not at all. Some of the guys on the team were razzing Jason about a woman at work who keeps calling him, leaving messages, and going by his desk area."

Amanda's mouth hung wide open and she wasn't certain she'd be able to breathe. "Wha-aatt?"

Maria nodded. "So I asked Roger who that intriguing woman was. He just shrugged and said he didn't know. I said, 'Weren't you the least bit curious?' You know what Roger said?"

Not a clue.

"He said 'Just somebody pestering Jason at work. What's to know?' At least he could've gotten a name or description… or something. Anyway, like I said, it sounded odd, but I didn't know what to make of it until I got Christine's e-mail this evening. Then it clicked. She said to look for unusual behavior." Maria folded her arms. "Seems pretty darn unusual for a woman to stalk Jason!"

Amanda's expression soured.

"Uh, that didn't come out quite right."

Amanda shook her head: *never mind.* "Did Christine's e-mail state what she suspects?"

She nodded reluctantly. "That Jason's stepping out on you." Maria's eyes flooded.

Both recovered in a few minutes; Maria was first. "Roger once told me he'd worried that Kevin might rub off on Jason. Looks like he was right. Do you know what they say about Kevin?"

"Jason doesn't tell me much, except that Kevin's an alley cat. I guess that's the reason I was so certain Christine was wrong about all this. Jason seems to disapprove of what Kevin's doing. It doesn't make sense that he'd sink to that level himself."

"He's a man. They've got all those extra hormones bouncing around in their britches. Roger says that Kevin even has love nests."

"I'm almost afraid to ask, but what does he mean by love nest? I thought Kevin did all his loving at hotel happy hours. Ought to be plenty of available nests in hotels."

Maria shrugged. "Not completely sure. I just assumed it was different places to take his conquests. Don't know why he'd need them."

"Well, I know Kevin's had two messy divorces. Maybe he

has people following him."

"Speaking of following." Maria looked over both shoulders, even though they were alone. Evidently there was an epidemic of paranoia. "Christine's e-mail also said something about surveillance efforts. She wants our help tracking Jason."

Amanda groaned as she sat back in the rocker. "Don't you think that's awfully melodramatic?" She paused to arrive at the right image. "It sounds like the plot of an old screwball comedy from 1930s Hollywood. Somebody suspects something but they won't just confront the person and get it all straightened out. Instead they skulk around and get into all manner of bizarre situations. In the end, there was nothing done wrong — or almost nothing — but they've spent the whole movie stumbling around it."

"Yeah, I've seen those. You sit there thinking, 'Why didn't she just ask him?' Or whatever the case was." Maria was the most level-headed of Amanda's friends, though that wasn't saying much because friend number three was Sunny Cannon. Amanda didn't have a very long buddy list — she buried herself in her job and her relationships were mostly acquaintances in her office or within the other county-city government divisions "So why don't you do that? Just ask Jason directly... about these, uh, unusual circumstances."

"That's what I told Christine I wanted to do and she nearly jumped down my throat. She said that just makes it harder to flush them out. Or something like that."

"So you're going to leave it there?"

"Well, Christine does have a lot more experience at this." Amanda rubbed her neck. Jason spent a lot of time at games and practices. So did all the sports chickies hanging around the teams. How could she tell if they were watching Jason versus any of the other sweaty guys? Would she have to resume attending his many practices? *Grizzled gonads!* Now her brain churned with visions of a mysterious, possibly glamorous female at Jason's workplace — following, calling, leaving messages, and who knows what else.

On the sofa, Maria watched silently.

"Maria, I'm wondering." Amanda huddled closer, over the rocking chair's arm. "You think Roger's holding back anything? Maybe he really does know who this woman is, but he just doesn't want to spill it. Some kind of man-code or something."

****

"Gosh, I don't know." Maria paused. "I asked a direct question and his answer was indirect. He pretty much deflected my query. Maybe he does know something more." She inched nearer and lowered her voice. "What are you thinking?"

"I'm wondering if you put your mind to it, could you elicit information from Roger that he really doesn't want to reveal."

"Like spies?"

"Yeah. But I'm thinking more specifically... *female* spies." Amanda looked over her shoulder quickly. "You follow?"

For an instant, Maria's brain stayed blank, and then it clicked. "Let me get this straight. You're asking me to seduce my own boyfriend and while we're, uh, passionate, I'm supposed to pump him for information about the woman stalking Jason." The more she thought about it, the more she liked that plan. "Oooh, that's so sexy!"

Amanda nodded. It was.

"Uh, one thing. Won't Roger be suspicious if I start asking questions while we're making love?"

"In my own experience — as limited as it may be — men's brains are pretty much disconnected while they're having sex. I mean, you could ask him what month it is and he might say 'Tuesday'... and that would seem about right to him at the moment."

Maria licked her lips. "And when we're through being passionate, he probably wouldn't even remember the conversation. Right?"

"That's the way I figure it."

"How can we be sure he won't just answer something like 'Greta Garbo' when I ask about the mystery woman?"

"All his defenses are down. He'll likely say the first thing that comes to mind. I doubt Garbo would be in that grouping."

"So there's a chance his answer won't match... like *month* and *Tuesday*."

****

Amanda nodded. "True. So that's why you have to ask the same question again, but phrase it differently." She closed her eyes. "Like, 'Jason told me that woman at work was a real pest... what was her name?'"

"Okay. And if Roger's really revved up, I might have time to ask the question three times." She smiled slyly.

"So, are you willing to take this mission?"

"For my good friend, yes... I'm even willing to sacrifice my body to Roger." Maria giggled, certain she'd enjoy the assignment.

Amanda sat back in her rocker. "Any final questions?"

"When we're making love, sometimes I get all goofy, too. Wonder if I'll remember the questions."

"Ah, you'll do fine. Just remember you're a spy."

"Okay, but Mata Hari never had Roger the fireman in her arms. He's a hunk."

Amanda smiled. Her first smile that entire Friday. She just hoped Maria would remember Roger's answers.

Chapter 5

Saturday, May 23

Empty cup poised, Amanda was reaching for the coffee pot when her cell phone rang on the nearby table. Normally she wouldn't jump that high and drop the cup, but her nerves were fried from the incredibly awful Friday she'd barely survived. She grabbed the phone and checked the incoming number. Louis!

Amanda's boss, Louis Erie — known as King Louie in their division — made her life miserable in too many ways to enumerate. One of those miseries was his propensity for calling her at home during her supposed time off.

"Hello."

"Have you worked up a fix for that sandbag grant problem yet?" Louis could never be bothered to offer any pleasantry or apology for intruding on Amanda's personal weekend time; as usual, he just launched into blustering instructions or recriminations. He was director of the county-city division called Coordination of Supplemental Funding. Its unofficial abbreviation was Coor Sup Fun, which made it sound like a perpetual beer party.

"Louis, like I told you yesterday, evaluations are the responsibility of the agency that got the money. Their progress and effectiveness must be assessed objectively by a person or entity with expertise in that field."

Of course, he'd tuned her out. "Well, they don't have any progress evaluations in yet for the first calendar quarter and this is the end of May. We're going to need to check this out from the inside."

We. Once again, he was making a mountain out of a molehill. Or in this case: a dune out of several thousand sandbags.

"That's not our department's job." Amanda sighed. "If they're failing to administer these funds properly, then freeze their funds. You can even withdraw some of the money they've already received, or confiscate the resources they purchased."

"We don't need 48,000 pre-filled sandbags."

Which was why she'd recommended *not* funding their application. But she refrained from reminding him.

"We can't freeze anything." Louis continued to bluster. "We just need to fix it. We just need to get them back on track."

We. "That's crazy. It can't be our department. They're supposed to use someone completely outside the county-city government, for objectivity." She could already feel the weight of the project being dumped in her lap.

Louis pre-empted her next objection. "That gives you something to work on while we're closed Monday."

"Monday's a holiday, Louis — federal, state, county, city. Except for fire and police, labor law says we don't have to work holidays, unless it's an emergency and then it requires overtime pay."

"You're an exempt, administrative, salaried employee. Overtime doesn't apply to you."

He had her stymied on that point. Louis was technically correct, though only because of a few extra words he'd inserted in her position description... after she was hired. Amanda should have been classified with the other non-exempt employees in the Coor Sup Fun section. The only truly exempt job in that division was the position held down by the enormous Yankee butt of King Louie.

"Unless it's an emergency I'm not coming in on a holiday, Louis. And this evaluation problem is not an emergency."

"Then you can write it at home on Monday."

She felt like a kettle's wheezing rumbles in those final seconds before whistling steam bursts out. "I'm taking Monday off, like almost everybody else. And I'm not working from home on this non-emergency evaluation problem." There was a razor-thin line to walk when refusing a supervisor's improper assignment or instructions. Amanda had lots of cuts and scars on her feet from walking that line.

When King Louie didn't get his way, he tended to either bluster about demoting her or simply repeat the basic problem as though they hadn't already discussed it to death. He went with Option Two. "Well, that grant's going terribly. We've got to get in there and fix it."

He must be getting heat from some higher-up. Amanda put the phone down as silently as possible, retrieved another cup from the cabinet, and poured her coffee. She took a quiet sip and let it burn all the way down. Then she picked up the phone in her other hand. She hadn't likely missed anything.

Louis was still ranting: "...and they're part of the problem. They're looking the other way. That's why we need to go in there and straighten it out."

We. "Hey, I don't implement these grants. I don't even approve them. I just read, score, rank, and recommend. Then you pick and choose the ones you like anyway. In this case, you once again funded an agency's application that I did *not* recommend because I thought its premise was flimsy, they didn't demonstrate true need, and the portion of Cumberland River that affects our county has not reached flood stage in nearly ninety years. Plus, they didn't seem to have the other resources in place to properly store or adequately distribute those requested sandbags, and their evaluation process seemed like it was thrown together with maybes and hopefuls."

As was typical, Louis ignored both her analysis and that shift in blame. "You need to fix this, Amanda."

Me. No longer *we.* Typical. "Louis, just notify the feds to confiscate those resources acquired by that grant!"

"Can't."

"Why?"

Louis' voice seemed hesitant. "The public works manager."

"Are you afraid of Harry Harrison?"

"He's got the ear of the Mayor-President."

Louis must have the M-P's butt. Ha. Amanda groaned. "Let me get this straight. Our own county-city public works department manager received 48,000 pre-filled sandbags from the feds. But instead of rattling Harrison's cage about not monitoring their storage, distribution, and usage, you're breathing on me like it's my responsibility to straighten all this out."

"It is now. It'll make us look bad if there's a big hoo-rah about these federal funds being wasted. You've got to fix it... and quick."

"Louis, I'm going to eat my breakfast and try to enjoy what's left of a rare three-day holiday weekend. When I come in on Tuesday, we can continue this discussion. However, I will state, for the record, that it's a terrible mistake to involve our division in the inner workings of an agency which is not effectively evaluating their use of the granted federal funds. Our involvement at this point should only be to alert the feds."

It was a nice speech. She'd have to remember some of it for her formal memo objecting to the improper use of division resources.

King Louie sputtered. "You mean you're not going to work on this fix until Tuesday?"

Wow. She'd gotten through his thick skull for a change. "Correct. Not until Tuesday at the earliest."

Click. Louis ended the call without another syllable.

Oh, yeah, he was angry. Not enough to deal with the matter himself, but livid at Amanda. King Louie couldn't stand it when her logic trumped his fly-by-the-seat-of-his-pants "management" practices. Come Tuesday, Amanda would pay for her defiant stance. But for the next few moments… it might just be worth it.

Chapter 6

After a sip of latte, Christine jumped right into the agenda. "You're probably wondering why Amanda isn't here." Her text message had instructed the amateur detective team to meet at the new coffee shop at ten. Nobody else sat near enough to their table to overhear, and Sunny and Maria hung appropriately on her every word. Hardly anything pumps female blood more rampantly than catching a cheater. Or trying to. "It's because she doesn't know what we're about to do. At least, not exactly."

"Uh, small change," Maria interrupted. "I told Amanda about the e-mail you sent yesterday evening. So she knows you've assigned us to sniff around."

Christine waved her hand. "No matter. I pretty well told her as much when we spoke right after supper. Problem is, she still thinks Jason is innocent. Amanda doesn't believe any of our evidence."

"Um, another small change." Maria again. "I think she believed what Roger heard from those guys razzing Jason, about the woman at his workplace."

Though she did not like being interrupted, Christine nodded. Maria's e-mail had been the break she'd hoped for — independent corroboration that something distinctly fishy was going on with Jason and other women. The new story's tramp apparently worked with him! That made at least three illicits confirmed. "Good. Then Amanda's already on board. Roger's intel confirms my personal reconnoitering. And men always spill their guts in locker rooms."

"Well, there aren't any locker rooms." Maria used her second grade teacher voice. "On the softball league, all the guys dress at home and show up at the field in playing clothes."

"Whatever. Whenever men sweat, they also brag. Your Roger already knows some other dirt on Jason, mark my words. He just hasn't told you yet." Christine leaned toward Maria. "Can you figure a way to squeeze more info out of him?"

Maria's cheeks reddened. "Amanda gave me some suggestions last night and I'm working on it." She didn't elaborate.

"But Jason's only suspected at this point, not convicted yet." Sunny Cannon occupied the other side of their corner table. Her mom had formerly worked for a Tennessee affiliate of the ACLU.

Sunny was twenty-six and hardly over five feet tall. She wore her long blonde hair very straight — clean, but never set. Her face was pleasant and could have been rather attractive with a little makeup, but she minimized her figure with cotton sports bras and oversized blouses. She chose not to shave her legs and typically wore long shapeless peasant skirts. Flat sandals were her normal footwear and she'd never been seen in heels. Sunny was the kind of friend who got highjacked for those TV surprise makeover shows and it turned into a three-part episode.

"Where there's smoke, there's fire. And Jason's definitely smoking." Christine waved away that objection, too. "But anyway, we're her closest friends and it's up to us to make these difficult decisions for her. Amanda's too incapacitated to think for herself — grief and confusion and whatever." She decided not to mention how dense and naïve Amanda was being about these matters. *Good thing she has me to provide resources and assistance.*

Sunny looked rather blank, but that was normal for her. The nickname Sunny was short for Sunshine — her parents had been devout hippies more than a decade after it was already passé. To counter the "militaristic" sound of the Cannon family name, they'd given their children nature names — Sunshine, a brother named River, and a sister named Breeze.

Christine sipped her coffee and consulted a small tablet in front of her on the table. "So what else do we have besides my two encounters and Maria's confirmation from Roger?"

"Well, I have a friend who works at Gee-keck, but in a different section from Jason." Sunny seemed glad to put something on the table. "I can check with her."

"Good. Call her today."

"On Saturday?"

"Can't waste any time." Christine pumped authority into her voice. "Amanda doesn't have a minute to spare. Every passing hour holds another opportunity for Jason to sneak around and boink some different floozy."

"Every hour?" Sunny cocked her head slightly. "Do you really think he's doing all that boinking?"

"Do you have any reason to believe he's *not*?" Christine the litigator, with inescapable logic. *Mustn't preen.*

Sunny shook her blonde head slowly.

Christine smiled deep inside, but her lips did not betray it. Her allies were enlisted, even if not completely sold on the premise. The important thing was to save Amanda. To do so, they had to catch Jason. *We have to destroy the village to save it.* Where had she heard that?

Christine took another sip of coffee and pointed to her notepad again. "I hope you both comprehend the importance of this next phase."

Sunny nodded solemnly even though her blank expression suggested she had no idea.

"We step up our surveillance?" Maria scored.

Christine nodded and clasped Maria's hand. "Exactly!" She leaned across the small table but her bosom blocked her progress. "Now, it's going to be pretty labor intensive."

Maria also leaned forward, with considerably less interference, and her eyes gleamed. The notion of catching a cheater was instinctive and contagious. "So what's the next step?"

"Tailing, monitoring, and stakeouts."

"But Jason will spot us!" Sometimes Sunny had a practical side.

"Well, then, enlist other folks — friends, relatives, whoever. We'll use people Jason doesn't know."

"Like *Cagney and Lacy* reruns." Maria smiled, then pursed her lips. "But Amanda's not going to want the whole world to know that Jason's cheating on her."

"True." Christine's long pause made the other two lean even closer. "But to make an omelet, you have to crack some eggs."

****

Christine led the conspirators out to the parking lot.

Beside her, Maria suddenly pointed toward a faded forest green Ford F-150 pickup, missing at least the two hubcaps which would have been in view, zooming past on the nearby interstate. "Speak of the devil!" The truck took the exit ramp.

Christine squealed. "Jason! Coming from somewhere east of here." She jutted out her jaw and squinted back the way he'd come. "Caught in the act! Sneaking back into town on a Saturday morning after an all-nighter with some trailer park trash." Amazing, how much detail she could discern from a brief glimpse of a profiled face in a fleeing truck.

Sunny was still looking where they'd both pointed, though Jason had long since sped away.

"Well, we don't know for sure what he was doing. Just that he came from the east," Maria was probably more successful interjecting some reason into her second grade kids.

"Nobody goes east of Verdeville for anything except trouble." Christine spoke with grim assurance. She'd heard that from someone somewhere, at some point in time.

Sunny nodded. "I've heard people get into lots of trouble east of here." She probably just made that up, simply to feel included.

"He sure had a hungry look about him." Christine wrote a short note on her small tablet. "Like an alley cat that's been out all night boinking the available females." Yeah, it was graphic imagery, but she was totally certain she'd just spotted Jason fleeing a nefarious encounter. "And we have three witnesses this time!" She trotted toward her white convertible.

"Where are you running off to?" Maria.

"I'm following that ugly green truck!"

"Shoot a monkey!" Sunny said, one of her favorite expressions.

****

Maria had heard Sunny say that line often. "What the heck does that mean?"

Sunny shrugged.

Of the four friends, Maria most often indulged Sunny's

idiosyncrasies. *Maybe as a child she was frightened by lower primates.* Whatever. Her own cursing was limited to euphemisms like "snap," because she spent so much time around second graders.

And for now, she'd keep her dissenting opinion to herself.

****

Sitting at her kitchen table, Amanda totaled up her problems in a monolog of sorts. Had it been spoken by Hamlet, it would have been a soliloquy.

> *King Louie's on the warpath about a grant he insisted on approving over my objections, and now I've got to dive in to fix the resulting glitches. Plus, I really ticked him off during his call this morning. Probably get fired at 8:30 on Tuesday.*
>
> *The older sister I can't get along with is in town for a conference and she evidently wants to pretend to make nice for a couple of days. What's up with that?*
>
> *My boyfriend is supposedly fooling around with un-numbered, un-named hussies, and I'm apparently the last one to know.*
>
> *Christine now suggests — or demands — that Jason be "investigated" by a bunch of noodle-headed amateurs who couldn't find popcorn in a movie theater.*
>
> *I don't — can't — believe that Jason has been cheating, but he HAS been acting very edgy, stressed, preoccupied, whatever. Whatever we did Wednesday night that passed for lovemaking had to be our worst ever. Plus, Friday at supper he looked and acted so guilty!*
>
> *On top of everything else, last night I actually convinced Maria to do some undercover Mata Hari work on Roger to elicit more information about Jason.*

How could I have sunk this low?
How could my life spin so far out of control?
What else can possibly happen?

Chapter 7

As Christine raced to follow Jason's pickup, her phone rang. "What the heck!" Her first time handling a phone during a high-speed pursuit, so she weaved slightly on the north-bound ramp from I-40. Her foot eased up as she retrieved her phone and flipped it open. *Lawyer calling back.* On a Saturday!

"Hi, Bruce, glad you called. If it seems like we get cut off, it's because the phone might be in my lap. I'm going to need two hands on some of these turns."

"What turns? What are you doing?"

"Driving. Well, following, actually."

Bruce paused. "Is this by any chance related to your cryptic message about a detective?"

"In one sense, yes. But it's more complicated than this particular chase."

"Chase? Uh, Christine, are you by any chance… speeding?" Bruce's internal brain monitor probably activated the unstated default lawyer alarm signal: *I don't want to know if you're breaking the law.*

"It depends how you define it. Some of these speed limit signs were put up by the city fathers when this Verde-burg was just a few gnarly ox trails."

"Christine, slow down. Better yet, pull over. Let's talk about whatever this detective business is. But if you keep doing what I think you're doing, I'll have to come downtown to bail you out."

"You've spoiled my momentum, Bruce. My perp got the last piece of that yellow light. Dang!" Christine slowed, crossed a traffic lane without looking behind her, and cut off a purple-haired teen with rings in his nose and lips. She pulled into the Mighty Dollar parking lot and left the engine on with the A/C running. She'd worked up a sweat. "Okay. I'm stopped."

"Good. This is my first chance to call. Now, why do you need an investigator? Things are moving along nicely with your ex in the renegotiations. We know he's scared and he knows we know it."

"No, not Daniel. This is about my friend Amanda. You remember her?"

"Was she the one up on the ladder at that New Year's Eve party?"

Christine sighed. "Yeah, that's her."

"She's got beautiful legs and a lovely, uh… derrière. Were you aware that at least one photo of that, um, situation is circulating in cyberspace?"

"I know, I've seen it, too." She tired of that story and the stupid photo, and not entirely out of protectiveness. Sometimes Christine wished it had been *her* up on that ladder. "Amanda's new boyfriend has the seven-month itch… and he's scratching."

"Hold on, Christine." Bruce covered the mouthpiece of his phone and muttered something to someone evidently near his desk before returning his attention to Christine. "Is that who you were chasing when I called? Your friend's boyfriend?"

"As a matter of fact, yes. Jason Stewart. Know him?"

"Not that I can recall. Should I?" Bruce didn't wait for her reply. "So you want an investigator to help you follow this Stewart guy? And he's your girlfriend's lover?"

"Yeah."

"And neither one of them's married to anybody else at the moment?"

"Uh, no." Christine examined her nails. She didn't like the direction he was headed.

"No investigator's going to take a case like that. There's no standing involved. They've got no legal ties."

"Well, she needs proof and I can't be everywhere. Plus, as I just found out, I can't give good pursuit if my phone rings."

"You really ought to stay out of this, Christine. Some things are better left alone. Whatever it is, they can either work it out or they can split up. But they don't need any interference."

"Why does everybody keep telling me to stay out of things?" The obvious answer eluded her.

Bruce paused. It was probably clear he wouldn't be able to convince her and a busy lawyer wouldn't want to waste more billable minutes on the matter. "Well, I did check with Ace's Detective Agency before I called you. Frank's drowning already. Can't even discuss handling another case right now."

"Not even some drive-by recon?"

"Nada. Zip. But Frank said he does have a new apprentice, or whatever they're called. No license yet."

"I'll get him vaccinated. Who is it?"

Paper rustled. "Somebody named Cheney. Don't know if that's a last name or first."

"He's Fido to me. You know anything about him?"

"Not a thing. But Frank said Cheney blends into the background really well. How did he say it? Oh, yeah. He said

Cheney hides in plain sight."

"Invisible; even better. I'll take him. Here's what I want Cheney to do." She explained in detail.

His pencil-type scratching sounds suggested Bruce took extensive notes. "Christine, Ace Detective Agency is going to bill this to you directly. I've got your phone numbers, address, and e-mail on file here. I'll give all that to Frank to forward to Cheney with these instructions."

"How soon should I hear from this apprentice?"

"I'll tell Frank to relay whatever date you give me."

"This afternoon."

"Can't promise that soon." Bruce sighed. "I don't guess it'd do any good to repeat that this is a terrible idea. That's my professional opinion and my strong personal advice."

Christine didn't want either. "Look, Bruce, this case is a slam dunk. I just need some more manpower to wrap it up quick, before my friend suffers any further embarrassment."

"Okay, I'll reluctantly forward the info and you'll be in direct contact with this agency apprentice. I'm out of this loop completely. And that means legally out of it, too. You understand what I'm saying?"

She understood — he was washing his hands. "Yes."

"You know I'll stand on my head to work on our legitimate case with your ex. But this thing you're meddling in should not involve a detective... and should not involve a friend, either. In fact, it's the very kind of thing that can blow up a friendship." Bruce's heavy sigh indicated he knew he was wasting his breath. "Okay, I've got to go. More briefs to read and motions to write before lunch. Bye."

The connection broke before she could reply.

A tiny voice in the back of Christine's head whispered something about "fools rushing in where angels fear to tread." But she'd never understood that old saw.

Chapter 8

By late-morning Saturday, Jason was working on a bad attitude. He sat in his truck at a railroad crossing, watched the slow blur of the barely moving train, and contemplated his state of affairs.

He'd just driven over twelve miles to take care of some urgent, delicious business out of town, only to be disappointed.

Not only had he the rotten luck to pull a GCEC shift on a holiday weekend, it was for six hours beginning at noon. Taking the rotational Saturday afternoon shift on a regular weekend was bad enough, but this... he was truly getting the Gee-keck shaft.

After that tense dinner with Amanda, he'd gotten to Roger's apartment for the fantasy league draft and discovered he'd been saddled with second and third choices in almost every key position. Jason couldn't discern if it was incompetence or sabotage, but either way it screwed up his fantasy baseball season.

Plus he had errands to run before his shift began. And he

was hungry.

I sure had a lot less stress before those stress trainers came to town.

A group of consultants from Alabama had conducted a mandatory Customer Service and Stress workshop at GCEC all day on Thursday. Each GCEC attendee was required to have a private follow-up session with one of the trainers, some sort of assessment. Apparently they wanted to cut open his skull and poke around in his brain with sharp mental instruments. At the very thought, he shuddered.

The one assigned to Jason, Erin Chester, had tried to reach him but he'd repeatedly ducked her. Not merely a trainer, she was also a certified counselor — distinctly relentless and atypically appealing. Especially her legs. Jason looked at the small stack of messages on the truck seat beside him. Embarrassing that he didn't want to face her one on one, and that made him also feel a little guilty.

And unfortunately, his reticence had caused unintended consequences. Ms. Chester had begun asking around about him. Some of the other employees had proved themselves only too pleased to spill whatever they knew or suspected. It seemed the result had been a hodge-podge of anecdotes, gripes, and compliments. He'd heard that one coworker even showed her the Internet photo of Amanda on the ladder at the big party. Doubly unfortunately, Ms. Chester now seemed even more intrigued by Jason, as if his absence made the mystery grow fonder.

But Ms. Chester had finally contacted his supervisor, Mrs. Grunion. Grunion gave Jason an ultimatum: 'If you don't take this required meeting, it goes in your folder and screws up your standings for potential promotion.' *Leave it to Grunion to poison the water.*

Well, maybe he was required to meet this consultant, but that didn't mean he'd like it and it didn't mean he'd make it easy for her. Jason hoped he could keep stalling and re-scheduling long enough that the consultants would depart without his session.

And if all that weren't enough, he was sure he'd seen Christine spying on him at the Verde Grocery when he'd dashed in several days ago for some desperately needed snacks.

And on top of all that... Amanda.

Amanda had acted strangely over supper. What was that all about? She'd been a wonderful girlfriend — and seemed a nearly perfect match for him — up until a few days ago. He was beginning to wonder how things would be if he'd just let somebody else get her down from that ladder at the fancy party. That way they never would've met, Amanda never would've begun following his sports activity... and they never would've become a couple. Dating her and *winning* her affection had been the best year of his life. But where was that affection now, when he really needed it?

Maybe they weren't such a good pairing after all.

****

In her Lexus convertible, Christine was pumped. She'd been certain she'd lost Jason when she'd had to pull over for Bruce's call. But because of this twenty-mile-long train, she'd ended up about six vehicles behind Jason's truck on Main Street. Where the heck was he going?

****

In his rearview mirror, Jason thought he saw Christine's distinctive dazzling white SC-10. Thoughts whirled around in his head as he parked the truck. Had she really been spying on him at the grocery? Was she following him to the cable company's office? Where else might she have seen him?

Trying to seem nonchalant, he exited his truck slowly, attempting to see over his shoulder without actually turning. Couldn't. So he pretended to spot something near his left rear tire. He took three steps that direction and crouched, running his hand over the worn tread. Meanwhile he glanced toward the white Lexus. It *was* Christine.

Was she stalking him? What on earth for? He dropped the pretense of the tire and took his bill to the drop slot near the locked front door. *How to play this?* He decided to do the opposite of what he thought was appropriate, so he looked toward the convertible and waved… then smiled.

Even from that distance, he could see Christine was flustered. She grabbed something from the seat and unfolded a napkin with a fast-food logo, as though pretending it was a road map. As if Christine Powers would need a map to find her way anywhere in Verdeville.

Jason got back in his truck and smiled into his rearview mirror. He didn't figure Christine saw his grin because she was still posing as a busty, lost tourist.

There were only two reasons a woman would follow a man, and both involved his body. One — she wanted to kill him. He'd often suspected Christine disliked and resented him, but so far hadn't believed she wanted him dead. At least not badly enough to do it herself. Two — she wanted his body alive, in the sack. It had never crossed his mind that Christine might be interested in him, but why else would she spy on him? And what would it be like to see her augmented bosom completely naked?

A man's natural vanity can persuade him that just about any woman is potentially interested in him, given the right circumstances.

Jason's surly mood had dramatically improved in the course of three minutes. As he exited the parking lot and headed to his shift at GCEC, he found himself humming *Maneater*.

But what if Amanda finds out her best friend is hot for me?

****

Christine squeezed the napkin into a tiny wad and tossed it to the floorboard. *That smart-aleck Jason spotted me!* And he'd waved. Her cover was blown despite her being as subtle as she knew how. Maybe a bright white convertible wasn't the best vehicle for discreet reconnaissance. Perhaps she should borrow something common, like the vehicles of her friends. *Or not.* Even amateur detectives needed some luxury.

Being spotted so early in the game intensified Christine's need to get Apprentice Investigator Cheney on the case ASAP. *That guy better call me soon.*

She heard a warning beep. Low battery. She'd have to plug in her phone as soon as she got home.

Chapter 9

Sitting by the phone in an otherwise empty room full of cubicles on a slow Saturday afternoon gave Jason extra time to think. But thinking was not his strong suit, so it became more of a headache than anything else. He was good at his job, handling the electric co-op's phone customers, but sometimes Jason viewed himself as the anonymous *Press Six for Billing Complaints* rather than an individual with actual identity.

Imagine that busty forty-year-old being interested in me. In the dark screen of the monitor with the empty log sheet (ready for billing-related calls that were not coming in), Jason could see a faint reflection of himself. "Not so bad looking."

"Who's not bad looking?" Kevin Haywood appeared suddenly. "Are you using the Gee-keck computer to download porn again?"

"That wasn't me and you know it." It had been Luther, the scrawny geek who kept GCEC's computers working. In that case, however, Luther'd had them running a bit too *hot*.

Kevin was Jason's closest friend who was not on any of

his ball teams. Nearly two years older, he was already divorced twice and both splits had been costly and bitter. No kids from either marriage, fortunately. He was about average height and weight, in good condition for a man approaching 34. Not movie star handsome, but good-looking enough and he knew it. His vivid green eyes were the first feature women noticed. He had a full head of dark hair, combed straight back, and usually not a follicle out of place. As a modern day Don Juan, he knew a large spectrum of contemporary females ate it up.

"You got time to hit the break room for a minute?" he asked.

Jason sighed. "Can't. Grunion passed a new federal law. We'll be executed if we leave the phones except for a three-minute bathroom break every two hours. I practically have to start peeing in the hallway to get finished in three minutes."

Kevin looked over his shoulder and slid into the room.

"If you get busted by Grunion, it's your own butt. I heard Feeney was keel-hauled for taking his break in here and chatting up his girlfriend."

"Well, I ain't your girlfriend and Grunion's not even in my section." Kevin grinned, showing bright white, even teeth. Not his high-wattage smile that practically smoldered with restrained lust — that was reserved for hunting.

"Well, stand over there so nobody sees you." Jason pointed to a spot along the wall, a few feet from his workstation. "Who's manning the power outage calls while you're in here pestering me?"

"I got a remote which signals me if a call comes in." Kevin patted his pants pocket. "Luther rigged it for me in exchange for me forgetting that I saw him in a chat room with a *Penthouse* centerfold on a Gee-keck computer during work hours."

"Nice trade."

"Only problem is, it vibrates like crazy when a call comes in. No belt clip, so that thing's down in my pocket. When it goes off, I'm jumping for the light fixture."

"I can see how that'd be jolting."

Kevin glanced toward the open door. "Listen, I got a favor to ask you, ole buddy."

Jason's phone rang and startled them both. "Hold that thought a sec. I've actually got a call."

****

During the four minutes and twenty seconds of that call — so said the integral timer on the automated log — Kevin amused himself by trying to access the Internet at each of the other computers. They were all known to be blocked but that didn't stop him from trying. When Jason's billing call ended, Kevin returned to his standing position beside the door.

Jason growled. "That idiot doesn't pay his bill 'til his power's cut off and then he whines over a reconnect fee. Just pay the dang bill, sport!"

Not what he wanted to discuss. "So, anyway, this favor…"

"Hey, it's lucky you barged in here today, because I've got problems, dude, big problems."

Usually Kevin brushed aside other people's problems when he needed a favor, but the expression on Jason's face made him pause. Something here seemed potentially juicy. So he decided to listen. Kevin hooked a rolling chair with his foot and pulled it to the wall where he wouldn't be seen if anyone passed by the doorway. Then he sat. "So talk to Doctor Kevin."

"You know Christine Powers, don't you?"

"Big knockers." Kevin sighed. "Bossy, but pretty durn attractive. Looks like Liz Taylor in old movies."

"You think maybe she, uh, *likes* me?"

Kevin scoffed. "Are you nuts? Christine hates your guts." It rhymed.

"I thought so, too, but not so sure any more." Jason glanced at the open doorway. "I think she's been following me."

"No way. Following you? Where?"

"A few days ago, I saw her at the grocery, but she didn't wave or say hi. She just hung back an aisle or two and seemed to believe I didn't see her."

"Hard to miss Christine, especially with those blouses she wears sometimes." Kevin whistled a muted note.

Both paused to retrieve that image.

Kevin broke free first. "That was Christine *looking*. You said following. Where?"

"Once was today when I stopped off to pay my cable bill. She parked about fifty feet away and watched, but acted like she didn't see me." Jason shook his head. "Seems to think the only white convertible in town makes her invisible."

"What did you do?"

"Waved and smiled. Wanted her to know I saw her watching me."

"Hmm. That's weird, all right. But you figure that means Christine's interested in you? That's nuts, man." Kevin paused, considering other possibilities. "I don't know what she's doing, or thinks she's doing, but it's definitely not any romantic interest in you."

"What's so awful about me?"

"No offense, ole buddy, but you're not her type." Kevin lowered his voice. "Christine's what they call a cougar... and cougars like young cubs they can use up and then devour."

"I'm not exactly an old man. Thirty-two isn't over the hill."

"But you've been around the block a few times. Christine's the kind who'd latch on to a young hard-bodied guy for, oh, maybe six or seven months. Then she'd get tired of him and toss him out on the curb."

"Seven months, huh? I've heard something said about seven months. Can't recall where." Jason checked the doorway again, his expression falling as if depressed.

"Look, Sad Sack, I didn't mean to bust your bubble. Let's back up. Just suppose Christine really is interested in you. What do you figure to do about it?"

"Not sure. Maybe I should ask Amanda."

"No! Absolutely not!" Kevin jumped from his rolling chair and clutched Jason's arm.

Jason tried to shake loose. "What? Let go! What the heck?"

Kevin loosened his grip. "Under no circumstances do you ever, ever tell your girlfriend that you think *her* girlfriend has the hots for you. Never, ever!" He finally let go.

Jason rubbed his forearm. "You want to tell me why I should never ever whatever?"

Kevin shook his head. "It's death warmed over. Eighty per cent definite to break up their friendship and ninety per cent certain that they'll both hate you."

"I'd think Amanda would want to know that her best friend is acting like she's interested in me." Jason's statement sounded like a plaintive question.

More head shaking. "I cannot emphasize this enough, Jason. This is radioactive. You handle this stuff and everybody dies. Slow, agonizing death. Stay away. Act like you never saw Christine do whatever you thought you saw. If Christine *is* interested in you, that secret goes to your grave."

"Don't you think I should discuss it with Christine?"

"Have you got brain fever?" Too loud. Kevin eased off. "Ab-so-lute-ly not! Don't you realize anything you tell one woman, she'll immediately tell her best friend?"

"Immediately?"

"Well, there's something like a tape delay, but quick enough."

****

Jason thought through the advice. Kevin was twice divorced, so he was probably wiser in such matters. "Okay, maybe you're right about not telling Amanda. But it's got me all confused and I need to talk to somebody."

"You could always tell one of those counselors when you have your private interview." Kevin chuckled and then eyed him. "Hey, you're not turning into a woman, are you?

"No! But it's bothering me."

"Suck it up, buddy. Walk it off. Besides, you'd know it if a cougar has her claws in you. She'd be all over you, rubbing up to you, whispering in your ear, acting all sweet and nice."

"Doesn't sound all that awful." Jason controlled a smile.

"Until she has you trapped in your own confused desires. Then she devours you and leaves your jagged bones at the edge of the jungle."

"I don't follow all your imagery, but I get the drift."

"Disaster's written all over it." Kevin slapped the corner of the desk with his palm. "But if you *are* selected as Christine's new pup, let me know how it works out. I want lots of details on her rack." Kevin paused. "Hold on. You're not actually attracted to Christine, are you? I mean, besides her rack."

Jason sputtered.

"Don't tell me you've been thinking about doing the big mambo with busty Christine!"

"Well, not like I'd *do* it. But, yeah, I've thought about it. She's shapely, pretty, and Amanda says she has a good sense of humor."

"Rodney Dangerfield was funny, but you don't want to wake up in his bed." Kevin grabbed Jason's shoulder. "When Christine's in hyper-drive, she'll mow you down, son!" He sometimes mangled his metaphors. "She's a UXB — unexploded bomb. Just walk around it and move away fast."

****

Satisfied with his lecture, Doctor Kevin sat back down. He'd come to this side of the building to speak with Jason for some reason, but could no longer remember it.

Jason fiddled with the phone cord. "You know those trainers that were here on Thursday?"

"Yep, consultants from Alabama, the whole dang day. What about them?"

"You happen to notice the tall blonde one?"

He nodded. "She'd be a hottie if her face was a bit softer. Uh, Miss Chesty, I think."

"It's Ches-TER. Has she been pestering you for a one-on-one interview?"

"No, I got her sidekick for my private session. Skinny guy with buck teeth. Like he's going to help me."

"What do they want to talk about?"

"He just asked a lot of stupid questions about stress. I told him I'm hardly ever stressed unless I'm running from a jealous husband. Ha."

"Did he realize you weren't kidding?"

Kevin grinned but didn't answer.

"Was stress all you talked about?"

"Well, coping with stress, handling the customer, any meltdowns… you know, following up from the group session. It was a waste of time, but it's a breeze."

Jason scowled with anxiety.

Kevin lifted his eyebrows. "What's the problem? You don't want a leggy blonde interrogating you? Sweating you for secrets? Probing you for information?" He chuckled.

"Har har." Jason groaned. "It's just I've got a lot on my mind right now and I don't want some woman with sharp heels walking around inside my head."

"Aw, it's like going to the dentist, you big wuss. Just go in and get it over with."

****

Jason didn't feel as if his problems had been solved, but at least they'd been aired.

Kevin scooted his chair closer. "So, anyhow, let me tell you about the honey I had last night at the Nashvillage." It was the largest of several hotels on Fourth Avenue in downtown Nashville. He spent ten minutes reliving the full hour of passion with his latest happy hour conquest. At least he said it lasted an hour. Jason guessed ten minutes was more likely.

He wished a call would come in. Maybe his screen was dead. Jason tapped a key. It wasn't.

Kevin suddenly snapped his fingers. "You remember that dark night when I saved your butt?"

Okay. Here it comes. Kevin always brought that up when he was about to ask a big favor. Jason nodded. "Three drunks jumped me at that liquor store north of Nashville and beat the crud out of me."

"Well, I pulled off one of them, and he was a mean son of a gun, too."

"True, it was the other two who stomped me." That seventy-five bucks he owed Kevin for filling his truck's tank; the favor had to be about money. Well, I did thank you, after my face healed up enough to talk."

"You know, I risked my life for you."

A bit more drama than it deserved. "You smashed a brick on his head. That's not exactly life-risking."

"Would've been if he'd turned around and seen me. I guess you'd rather have *three* guys kicking your butt…"

"Okay, okay. So I owe you. What's the fav…"

Before Jason could finish his sentence, the high-powered buzzer vibrated inside Kevin's jeans and he jumped from the chair like it was on fire. "Got to run. Somebody's stupid breaker probably flipped." Kevin dashed down the hall, struggling to retrieve the buzzing device from his tight pocket. He looked a lot like someone trying to squeeze a five-minute bathroom visit into the three minutes allowed.

Chapter 10

Finally back home Saturday evening — after watching the GCEC building for two solid hours in the warm afternoon — Christine was peeved. The apprentice investigator had not called her back. When she plugged her dead phone into the charger, the red message light flashed on. *Hmm... don't remember hearing it ring.* She flipped it open; a new text from D. Cheney. *Excellent.*

She pressed the button and read.

> *tried 2 call, no answer. had questions. chck email.*

She'd missed Cheney's call because of her battery. *Dang.* Christine hurriedly logged on to e-mail. Three spams, including someone wanting to sell imported generic Viagra. E-mails from her brother in Ohio, one from Amanda, another from Maria. She read Cheney's:

> *Ms Powers:*
> *First off, I'm required to inform you that I do not have my license requirements complete yet, so technically*

I'm still an apprentice. However, I've studied criminal justice in college, I have over 2 years in military law enforcement and 3 years of other investigative experience (including undercover) with Clarksville P.D., so (to me) the license is just a technicality. I expect to have it by the end of this year.

I've been assigned your case and need clarification on a few things:

1. Do you want fairly "casual" surveillance where I basically try to pick up the target if / when he leaves his apartment in the evenings? Or do you want him monitored practically all day as well?

2. Rates for evening work are higher, so are you prepared to pay a substantial amount?

3: How many days of surveillance do you figure on? Frank seemed to think this was open-ended, but I was doubtful.

4. I work alone. Frank said you liked personal involvement in the cases he's handled for you previously. That will directly interfere with my job and will also likely tip off the target. So I need to know if this presents a problem for you to stay away from the target and let me conduct this investigation solo.

5. I prefer to communicate with e-mails and texts, even when I don't have laryngitis, as I do now.

6. Do you have any questions for me?

D. Cheney.

P.S. I have schedules & addresses you provided for target's work & apartment... please send current photo.

Brassy buck. Christine would need to meet this private dick.

She went to her bedroom to change into pajamas and slippers, then got some low-calorie fruit juice from the fridge, and returned to the computer. Looking through her Facebook albums, she found a picture of Jason and Amanda together after a basketball tournament, and made a copy.

Christine then replied with e-mail:

> *D. Cheney:*
> *Understand your current status. No problem.*
> *1. Full court press*
> *2. Price not a problem*
> *3. Till we catch the SOB*
> *4-A. Frank obviously neglected to tell you how much I ASSISTED that investigation.*
> *4-B. Understand your solo preference. Whatever.*
> *5. Phone is easier for me, but whatever.*
> *6. When do we meet? How often?*
> *Christine P.*
> *P.S. Photo attached as .jpg. Target is not always that sweaty.*

Christine chose not to argue with Cheney about question number four, because she fully intended to keep her own investigation going full bore. Now that Christine had her own surveillance team briefed and primed, it would be a disappointing waste to call them off.

She sat back and tried to picture D. Cheney. The 'D' probably stood for Derek. Ex-military. Probably a Marine... or maybe Special Forces. Probably had a scar on his cheek from a sniper bullet. She wondered how young he was. A young, hard-body ex-military investigator apprentice might be just the tonic Christine needed.

Chapter 11

Jason opened the door a crack. "Kevin! What are you doing here this late?" It was after ten o'clock.

Kevin elbowed his way inside. "Need a place to land, ole buddy." With his overly tight pants, extra starched shirt, and too much cologne, he had obviously just left his date of the evening. "I knew you were alone since I didn't see Amanda's car out there."

"What if she'd found a different parking place and we were in here playing nekkid Twister?"

Kevin dismissed that possibility with a shrug.

"I'm in my skivvies, dude. Go home, or go confiscate a cardboard box from some drunk." Jason pointed to the door, still slightly open.

Kevin closed it. "Better not let the cool air out." He sighed. "Besides, I can't go home yet."

"Another irate husband on your tail?"

"No. Can't let the neighbor lady see me drive up."

"I don't even want to know…"

"Well, since you asked, she's still real good buddies with my ex," he spit theatrically, "and she reports my comings and goings to Tiff."

"Tiffany's wife number one or number two?"

Kevin held up two fingers.

"Why would she care what time you get home? And what business is it of the neighbor's?"

"I'm just trying to keep the next door witch off balance, so I wait 'til she goes to bed," Kevin checked his watch, "which is about now, I guess. And then I sneak in real quiet so she can't tell Tiff when I got in."

Jason rolled his eyes. "Talk about manufactured drama. What stinking difference does it make?"

"Tiff's lawyer has my butt in a crack on the settlement, which is *still* dragging on. My lawyer says they're trying to get extra leverage to sweeten her deal. So they're looking for something to impress the judge with."

Jason couldn't imagine why a judge would care about Kevin's arrivals, departures, or anything else, since there were no children involved. But his uninvited guest scanned the front room like he was looking for something. "Why are you prowling around? Sit down already."

Kevin raised his eyebrows as if surprised his activity had been noticed. "Oh, just thought I might've left something in your apartment… last time I was here."

"You haven't been over here since the Sweet Sixteen tournament. March Madness. I would've seen it by now. Relax."

"Yeah. Whatever." Kevin lifted a cushion slightly before he sat on the loveseat.

"Dude, it's late. This is weird, me sitting here in my skivvies. If you don't leave, I'm gonna have to put some britches on."

Kevin's gaze focused on other portions of the apartment's

interior. "Huh? Oh, yeah. Go ahead and grab some pants. I'm gonna be here a few minutes yet."

Jason sighed so heavily he launched flecks of spittle. He got up and stomped to his bedroom — though it's difficult to stomp barefoot on patterned tufted nylon carpet — grabbed a pair of sweat pants, and hauled them on.

"You got any brewskis in here?" Containers clinked and scraped as Kevin foraged in the fridge. Two cold beers sat on the table by the time Jason returned.

He took one and sat down. "This is about your post-happy-hour date, isn't it?"

Kevin smiled broadly. "Let me tell you about the honey I had tonight."

Jason was tired and a little bored, yet titillated enough to listen. "Not another cocktail waitress. What does this one do?"

"Deals with numbers. Uh, spreadsheets and stuff. Budget analyst maybe. She computes stuff — trends, projections, other stuff. Spots areas of over-runs, shortages, delays and stuff. She computes to keep negative stuff from happening."

She evidently dealt with a lot of *stuff*. "Local girl?"

Kevin shook his head. "Nah, northern Georgia. Five chicks from that same area."

"You talked to her buddies, too?" This sounded like a new tactic.

"Sure, I sort of checked 'em all out. That's how I learned her nickname, The Computer."

"So you compared, contrasted, calculated odds, projected probabilities of failure and success."

Kevin nodded.

"You analyzed the possible victims — uh, winners — and selected the smartest of the lot? Seems unusual for you. I would've thought you'd pick the dumbest — no offense."

Not easily offended, Kevin smiled lamely. "Well, we ought to define *dumb* — I don't go for the total idiots, unless they're really stacked. Then it doesn't matter. But normally I'd just as soon enjoy the company of a woman with a head on her shoulders."

"I didn't think you spent much time looking above their shoulders. And I'm surprised they didn't see you coming a mile away."

"Maybe they did and liked what they saw." At times Kevin's matter-of-factness sounded like vanity.

Jason already had his watch off, so he checked the flashing clock on the DVD player. But he couldn't remember if he'd set it correctly — it couldn't already be precisely midnight. "Okay, so how did you end up with the smart one, The Computer?"

"Well, two of the other girls were cut out of the herd by some other guys." Kevin whispered, "Poachers. They usually hang out at a different hotel."

"Okay, three left." Jason didn't try to hide his yawn.

"Well, I was leaning toward her anyway. Turns out she had a sense of humor."

"I can see where that would be an advantage if she planned to spend time with you."

Kevin just stared back blankly. Apparently he didn't register the dig.

"Which joke did you tell? Not the one about the drunk grave digger, I hope."

"No jokes."

"So what humorous schpiel did you use to get this computer woman to *boot up*?"

"I sat on a chair and said, 'If you're a computer, would you be a laptop?' Then I patted the top of my thighs."

"I'm surprised she didn't slap your face." Jason checked for marks. "What happened?"

"Well, she'd already had a couple drinks by then…"

"Oh, so her analysis of the risk-benefit ratio was

impaired."

Kevin grinned. "Plus her companions egged her on."

"And…"

"She sat on my lap! Right there." Kevin pointed. "It was awesome."

"Wow." Clearly he was in the presence of a maestro. "I can't believe she fell for it."

"Well there was another wrinkle. She kissed me on the mouth — no tongue, however — and then whispered in my ear."

"Stock quotes? Harvest forecasts?"

Kevin shook his head. "She said the kiss was to shock her companions. Said she knew I was trouble."

This smart woman was evidently also wise. "I hope you didn't give her the sob story about your ex-girlfriend being in prison."

"Nah, I've stopped using that one. So anyway, I tell her, 'Yeah, I'm trouble, but I'm the kind of trouble that's worth the trouble.'"

"Don't tell me she fell for that baloney."

"Naw, she saw right through me." Curiously, that awareness didn't seem to bother Kevin. "Then she moved back and forth a bit…"

"A lap dance? Right in the middle of hotel happy hour? You dawg!"

He smiled broadly "So her two companions giggled and acted shocked."

"Maybe they weren't acting."

It apparently went over Kevin's head, because he didn't even blink. "Then they suddenly vamoosed. So the computer lady looked at me and said, 'You really think you're worth the trouble?' And I said, 'I love the taste of women, and you're a flavor I've never tried.'" Kevin winked.

"Wow, great line."

"Heck, I didn't even know what I was saying. Something about this smart, pretty woman sitting on my lap just got my brain all fired up."

"Among other body areas, I'm sure." Jason had to admit, his buddy was the emperor of happy hours.

"So she kissed my cheek and whispered in my ear, 'My flavor is amaretto.'"

"What flavor is that? Sounds like a liqueur."

"Not sure. I don't know any Spanish." Kevin shrugged. "I thought Amaretto was a famous stripper."

****

Kevin warmed as his account totally captivated his host. Retelling these conquests made them seem even more intense. "So anyway, then Amaretto stood up, looked down at my lap and smiled. Then she reached for my hand and led me to the parking garage."

"Whoa! You left the hotel? For ten whole minutes?"

Kevin ignored the obvious dig. "She didn't have her own room and her traveling companion already had their room occupied, if you know what I mean." Jason couldn't know all the etiquette involved in pro-level alley-catting.

"So your place?"

"Nope. Couldn't. That nosy neighbor witch sees me bring a woman home and she's calling the Ex-Wife Hotline to tell Tiff."

Jason's slow and cynical headshake indicated he wondered why it mattered to Tiffany. "So where'd you go?"

"Went to my buddy Walter's place."

"His *house*?" Walter was a GCEC coworker. "He's married and has kids!"

"No. Beyond his garage, there's a metal building. He runs a little mower repair shop. But upstairs is a little office with a vinyl couch."

"So Walter lets you use his mower repair office as a trysting place for your spillover bimbos from happy hour who either don't have their own hotel rooms or can't get into them because another tryst is going on inside?"

He nodded. *That about covered it.* Except for a small detail Kevin didn't plan to mention — Walter was not aware of the goings-on.

****

Jason whistled through his teeth. "I'm still amazed you managed to bag an intelligent woman."

"Me, too. And let me tell you, this computer vixen was a laptop, a desktop, and a couch top, plus an iPod."

"iPod? That makes me hot and I don't even know why." Jason slugged his friend's shoulder in slow motion. "You absolutely amaze me! If I wasn't in a serious relationship, you'd be my mentor!"

Kevin beamed.

"But back up to why you're telling me all this. Usually you just report your conquests and sometimes give me a current tally if you can remember the number."

"I want you to meet her."

"Amaretto? Meet *me*?" Jason squinted. "Why?"

"So I can prove that a brainy woman could be interested in me."

"You don't need to prove it to anybody but yourself. Besides, where on earth would I meet her? I can't go prowling around the happy hours — Amanda would find out somehow and get the wrong idea."

"Dude, be a man. You can't let women tell you where you can't go."

Jason just shrugged. His twice-divorced friend had to be

the expert on such matters.

Chapter 12

Sunday, May 24

Early Sunday morning, Kaye looked up a phone number in her day planner because it wasn't stored on her cell phone. It rang nine times before Amanda answered, yawning.

"Hi, it's Kaye. I wondered if you wanted to join me at the hotel for their complimentary hot breakfast. My colleagues say it's pretty good. Waffle machine and everything."

"Who?" Amanda noisily cleared her throat. "Kaye? What the heck time is it?"

"Uh, eight something. Aren't you awake yet?"

"I am now."

She'd done it again. It was just that they fought so much these days. Back home, they'd gotten along fairly well. Amanda had been a stubborn little brat, but with proper management, she'd developed into a tolerable baby sister. But after she'd finished high school, their dynamic had drastically altered. And at this point in their lives, they scarcely had anything to talk about. Amanda seemed actually to *like* the rural people and small town ways which made Kaye cringe. Kaye was barely able to endure Indianapolis, the literal and figurative center of Indiana, and that area was considerably more sophisticated than a Tennessee hamlet hovering near Nashville.

"Well, anyway, we don't have any meetings or events until late morning. So I'm going to grab a waffle and then I thought maybe I'd come over and visit for a little bit."

"Uh, sure. I'll put some coffee on." Amanda yawned again. "What time you figure to get here?"

"About 9:15 or so. That okay?"

"Uh, yeah. See you then, Kaye. Bye."

****

Amanda had only enough time to shower, dress, and drink one cup of coffee before the expected knock sounded on her door. She waved Kaye in and led her to the kitchen. "Coffee?"

"Got any creamer?"

"Just milk. That okay?"

Kaye wrinkled her nose. "Sure."

"Let's sit at the table. I'm going to make some toast or something. You want any?"

"No, thanks. I did the waffle thing at the hotel. Nasty syrup."

Amanda shrugged.

"How long has it been?" She smoothed the front elastic panel of her slacks. "Since we've had a chat?"

Amanda paused with the bread half out of the pantry. *Good question.* "Not sure. Why?"

"Just wondered. It seems like we hardly ever have any time together. And then when we are together..."

"We don't know what to talk about." Amanda finished it.

Kaye sighed. "Exactly. Have you ever wondered how we got this far apart?"

Amanda knew precisely how and why — she'd only been able to take her own breaths after Kaye left for college. She started to state that clarification for the sibling record, but something held her back.

"Me neither." Kaye evidently mistook sisterly silence for no answer. "But I've spent lots of time thinking about it. We went different directions — that's one thing."

Kaye likely meant geographically, but there were many other differences in their direction. Amanda sensed that narrow focus and fought the urge to expound. She didn't feel like fighting this morning. If she didn't do something with her hands, Amanda felt she might scream. So she manhandled the toast while Kaye drifted around the duplex, examining photos and knick-knacks.

Kaye sniffed noisily. "Do you have a cat?"

"Former renters did, I'm told. Huge, neutered thing named Diabla."

Kaye wrinkled her nose again.

Strike two.

Suddenly Kaye covered her ears. "What's that awful racket?"

No need to listen closely. "Oh, that's my new neighbor. Kind of keeps to herself."

"Wish she'd keep *that* to herself. Is somebody torturing her?"

When the acrid smell of burning toast seeped through the kitchen, Amanda tugged the handle and popped it up. Maybe perfect Kaye wouldn't notice through her audial agony. "Hard to tell from this particular sequence, but I think she's learning how to yodel. I suppose the early phases do sound like someone begging for mercy."

"Well, give me a baseball bat and I'll end her misery."

Kaye always had preferred the direct approach.

"You can't kill my neighbor yet. I've never even met her."

"Let's fix everything right now. You come introduce yourself and then I'll bludgeon her to death."

Just like Kaye.

Amanda battled the urge to ask her sister what she wanted to talk about, but she was doing her level best to refrain from uttering anything that could be construed as confrontational. So she ground her teeth on the lightly buttered partly burned toast and waited.

Finally, after touching some dozen different knick-knacks and wiping her fingertips on her slacks each time, Kaye began again. "How's Jason doing these days? He still plays, uh... sports? Is he still an electrician?"

"He's not an electrician." Amanda swallowed a growing lump in her throat. "Jason works at the power company, our electric co-op — Gee-keck. He handles customers inquiring about their bills."

"Oh. And you two are...?" Her fingers wiggled with a motion evidently intended to suggest the concept of a couple... though it didn't.

"Yeah. We've been together for some time." Amanda tried to smile.

"All the time since that New Year's Eve party? Nice photo, by the way."

Amanda moaned. There was always a dig. *So glad you brought that up.* She pushed the rest of her toast aside. "Not that long. Only since Halloween last year." She dropped onto the loveseat.

Kaye joined her, though more primly. "I'm surprised it took you that long to hook him."

Ordinarily Amanda could have rolled with a crack like that and possibly even joked about it. *But not today.*

****

Seeing the tears, Kaye recoiled initially. Consolation had not been in her skill set for a long time. Then something compassionate stirred deep inside. "What on earth is wrong, Amanda?" She moved closer and touched her sister's shoulder.

Amanda continued to sob.

"What's happened?"

Sometimes, the fewest words, even separated by gulps and sobs, can express things sufficiently for any woman to understand the problem. "I... don't... know... if... we're... still... together." Amanda collapsed onto her sister's side.

"You're breaking up?" Kaye temporarily ignored the salty stains on her neatly pressed slacks and softly smoothed her sister's hair.

Amanda's nod streaked the tears even more.

"He's found some other woman?" She knew telepathically. "He's running around on you?"

More sobs. More salty stains. Kaye patted her sister's shoulder as she tried to squirm her thigh from underneath the tear target zone. "Men! Ought to shoot them all!" That seemed to express it sufficiently.

It took some time for Amanda to settle down.

Kaye snuck a quick look at her slacks and discreetly rubbed at the stain. Despite genuine sympathy, it was strangely gratifying that Amanda's partner was as much a scumbag as her own. "When did you find out?"

"Uh, two days ago... Friday night." Her crying jag over, Amanda's lips thinned and she looked away, as if embarrassed by her breakdown.

"He confessed?" Kaye was astonished.

"No, Jason hasn't said a word. Not one word. That's one of the things that hurts so bad."

"So you spotted him with the other woman?"

"Not me. My girlfriend Christine saw him."

Kaye had never met Christine. "She caught them red-handed?"

"Well, she didn't actually catch them doing anything. She just saw Jason *with* them."

"Them?" Kaye edged closer. "How many are there?"

Amanda teared up again. "We're still counting. Christine saw him talking to two different women and Maria's boyfriend says a woman's been stalking him at work."

"Hmm. At least three. With men, three trees means a forest."

"That's what Christine said, but she talked about icebergs."

Icebergs in a forest? Kaye shrugged. *Can't picture it.* "Uh, one thing puzzles me. Exactly how much physical hanky-panky did your friends observe?"

"Well, that's one of the most frustrating parts. Everything they've seen or heard about seems innocent to me. Well, relatively innocent if you figure he's got no business cupping that bimbo in the snacks."

"He copped a feel of her *snacks*?" Kaye fluttered her hands for the right dramatization.

"No, he cupped her elbow!"

"Oh. I pictured something else." Kaye exhaled. "So what were the other encounters like?"

Amanda provided a sketchy version of a mall incident and a woman at GCEC.

"I don't get the thing with the woman stalking him at work. Most workplaces have pretty serious policies about that kind of stuff. Jason might need to file a harassment complaint about that." Though Kaye doubted any further rational explanations would help, her instinctive sisterly concern overruled. "Uh, Amanda. What you've described is not exactly running around. Cheating usually involves panties in the glovebox, like my tacky Tom so callously forgot. Cheating is checking into shoddy motels or dirty dancing in disreputable lounges at the edge of town. What your friends have seen amounts to Jason can't keep his hands to himself. At least in that one case."

Amanda's expression brightened. "That's what I told them. But they seem so certain." She paused and eyed her sister. "You know, I thought you might gloat a bit when you heard this news."

Kaye had warned her about getting serious with a jock. "No. No gloating." *Not now, anyway.* "But I do have some sisterly advice, if you're willing to listen."

Amanda visibly braced herself. "Okay."

"Don't rush to judgment on this, at least not on the basis of what I've heard so far. Jason might not have done anything beyond some chatting and flirting… though I don't know what to make of that elbow thing. But that's completely different from playing around."

"Wonder why my friends seem so convinced?" Amanda shook her head. "My buddy Christine wants to conduct some sort of investigation and surveillance."

Kaye shrugged. Girlfriends could overplay their hands out of zealous concern. But such misguided protectiveness could easily backfire. "Let me put it this way. If Jason's really running around, there'll be more to go on than malls and groceries. You catch him in some girl's room, then we'll nail him to the wall." She glanced around her sister's crowded apartment and felt a pang of space pity. "In fact, I'll even help you nail him. If Jason is playing around, he'll slip up, sooner or later. And it'll be a lot more obvious than touching elbows near the snacks."

"But you just said you thought he might be innocent."

"It's statistically possible. But men are usually guilty of something. It's mostly a matter of figuring out whether what they've done wrong is significant enough to make him pay."

"Pay?"

"Figuratively speaking." Then Kaye closed her eyes. "Unless you're legally married. Then it's literal."

****

Amanda contemplated that distinction. Strange, how Kaye would try to comfort her after all those years.

"You know, I've never even met Jason. What's he look like?"

Amanda trudged to her bedroom and returned with a small photo of Jason looking like he'd just run a marathon and was dragging himself to the paramedics' truck.

Kaye wrinkled her nose. "Is he always that sweaty?"

"They'd played three basketball games in one afternoon. Why are you so down on jocks?"

Kaye peered up at the dated popcorn ceiling texturing and frowned. "You remember the county fairs back when we were little?"

Amanda nodded. "They let school out on the Fridays." And Kaye had bossed her around the entire time.

"They had those awful hotdogs — large, robust, and meaty, in the sense of unmentionable animal parts, that is. But they were also greasy and dirty."

"Dirty?"

"Duh. They soaked in nasty fairgrounds water all day and rolled around on carts in the muddy midway. Dirty, believe me."

"Oh." A little dirt had never bothered her.

"So, anyhow, you've had a full day of rides and exhibits and walking around, and you're starving. Naturally, you grab one of those terrible boiled franks and wolf it down. It fills you up, but you're thinking, 'If only I could grill it properly, season it enough, dress it a bit, swap the cheap bun for some quality whole wheat.... maybe it would taste halfway decent.'"

Remembering how she'd enjoyed those state fair franks, Amanda started to interrupt.

But Kaye continued. "Every girl has an expectation of excitement, glamour, and romance... maybe even adventure."

That yearning sounded familiar. *When do I get some peak experiences?* So far it had been molehills — reading and evaluating grant proposals all day and dining at two-star buffets most evenings.

"One way or another, we all occasionally hunger for an elegant five-course meal featuring some truly delicious specialty like Beef Wellington. Well, you can't satisfy that craving with a midway frank, no matter how embellished or transformed."

"So why do we women keep buying those hotdogs?"

Kaye faced her, chin up. "Because they're readily available and, at times, we're simply starving." She paused as if letting some cosmic significance sink in. "But at the end of the day, it's just a wiener."

Amanda winced at the metaphor. "So you equate small town athletic men with county fair franks."

"Think about it."

She did. Many of the Greene County men she knew were likeable, but none made her feel warm inside. "So how well did you do with your selection of Thomas Smith from the fine city of Richmond?" It sounded more sarcastic than she'd intended.

Kaye didn't seem to notice, because she was already phrasing the appropriate image. "Tom was more like a cocktail wiener — a little bit of elegance, but still basically piggish... and left a lot to be desired."

Amanda laughed — couldn't help it. Kaye joined in. It was the first time they'd laughed together in neither could remember how long. *Kind of incredible, actually.* Kaye hadn't gloated, they hadn't fought, they'd actually laughed, and even cried together. *Who is that woman and what did she do with Kaye?*

But if Kaye and Christine ever got together, it would be like two asteroids colliding in outer space. The impact would probably create a new black hole somewhere, likely in Amanda's personal universe. And she'd have to strangle them both. *Ha, dream on.*

Chapter 13

As Jason sat in his living room staring at his computer, the sudden sound of Barry Manilow's soulful singing startled him. It took him a moment to recognize it as one of his cell phone's ringtones. *Amanda.*

"Hey. What're you doing?"

Sounded almost accusatory. "Ah, trying to get my head screwed back on."

"What do you mean?" she asked.

"I might get stuck being commissioner of the fantasy league, we don't have enough players for tomorrow's tournament, they're leaning on me at work, and, uh… other stuff."

"What other stuff? Anything I can help with?"

Jason felt minor panic. The three topics she definitely could *not* help with were his ongoing worries about Kevin, new concerns over Christine, and the problems with Amanda herself. "Uh… no, not really. Just stuff to work out."

Amanda paused. Perhaps she'd sensed an opening in the

Jason wall, but he'd quickly slammed the gate shut and latched its heavy bolt. "Well, I was wondering if you wanted to come over this evening and watch a movie. I rented the new Bond flick."

He did want to. They often watched DVDs together, because it was a good excuse for them to be together after dark, when things naturally moved down the short hallway to her bedroom. But with all those problems, he couldn't. Well, wouldn't. If he went over there and she was still acting weird, it would make him act odd and he feared it would be like Friday night when everything seemed to come out wrong. It was better to stay away until this — whatever it was — blew over. "Uh, sorry. Can't. Got some calls to make."

"Calls?"

Wrong excuse. She knew he didn't call anybody. In fact, he considered the phone to be a device of torture and didn't hide his opinion. But his brain disengaged and his mouth repeated, "Yeah, calls."

"Well, okay." Disappointment darkened her voice. "We can hold off on the flick. But maybe we could still grab a bite."

Tempting. Food nearly always hooked him. But that would still put him there after dark. And being alone with her would feel weird while she was acting so odd and moody. "Um, no. Don't think I'm really hungry." A lie; he was always hungry.

"What?" She sputtered. "Jason, are you feeling okay?"

"No. I mean, yeah, I feel okay. Just not really hungry. Maybe I'll eat a few chips later." Or a bag. Or two.

"I could bring you something. How about pizza?"

Jason's mouth watered. "Hmm. Nah, maybe tomorrow. After the tournament and stuff."

"We haven't seen each other since Friday evening. You sure you don't want to hang out or something?" They hadn't made love since Wednesday night, the day before the awful work seminar. It had been the kind of disaster he'd only seen in movies… and he felt like moving to a shack on the river.

"Nah, I think I'll just rest up for the tournament. You know, make my calls."

Amanda could not conceal the disappointed intensity in her terse closure. "Okay, bye."

Jason sat there looking at his phone. He should have just explained he had to call the entire team roster to confirm the ones who'd said they would show up for tomorrow's softball tournament and to coerce those who'd said they couldn't. Amanda had practically begged him to come over and he'd stubbornly refused. Usually that shoe was on the other foot. *What the heck is going on?*

****

At her apartment, Amanda's tears fell onto the phone in her lap. She'd practically thrown herself at him and he couldn't be bothered to interact at all. Not even to *eat*! And that was Jason's second favorite activity!

If anything could prove he was having an affair, surely this was the smoking gun.

****

Apprentice Investigator Cheney had arrived at Jason's apartment about an hour earlier in a nondescript beige Ford Bronco and parked in the complex's larger street-side lot. With binoculars, the target was easily visible through the large window as he sat at his computer in the combined living-dining space.

This would be a tedious assignment. "This Jason schmuck probably doesn't do anything worse than check out an occasional porn site." Cheney looked around, as if anyone might have overheard that observation. Nothing nearby but empty parked vehicles.

Cheney checked visible license plates against the printout from the Ace Detective Agency. Jason's F-150 pickup was in the smaller lot, close to his apartment door and open window. *This could be tricky.*

Waiting until Jason left the front room — possibly for the kitchen or bathroom — Cheney ambled along the curving Walkway B through the complex's green space and affixed a sophisticated tracking device to the inside of the target's truck bumper, on the side opposite the exhaust pipe. This tracker would transmit to Cheney's handheld GPS device and simultaneously to the main computer at the Agency office.

Cheney hurried back to the Bronco. Time to update the client. Cheney drafted a short text to Ms Powers.

Sun. morn -- Target alone in own apt

A waste of time, but easy money. Cheney rolled down the passenger window to catch a late May cross breeze. The pads of Cheney's fingertips drummed against the bottom part of the Bronco's steering wheel. *Some people lead such boring lives.*

Chapter 14

Jason looked beyond his uninvited guest, halfway expecting — and completely hoping — that Amanda was also present. *Nope.* "Uh, hi, Christine." His heart started pounding against his ribs.

"Aren't you going to invite me in?" She squeezed past him in the doorway, her fulsome bosom brushing against him.

Jason's sensory receptors experienced a two-pronged attack: the tangible electricity at the instant of their contact... and the power of her perfume. It would have been pleasant — possibly intoxicating — from six feet away, but during that pithy moment of nearness, the aroma was overwhelming. A weaker man might have swooned, but he merely gulped. "So what's up?" He left the door partway open.

But Christine pressed it shut with a loud clack of the latch. She sashayed past his computer and made herself comfortable on the two-person couch.

His apartment felt much smaller with Christine inside it. He didn't know what to do with his hands and had trouble redirecting his eyes from her abundantly displayed bosom. He couldn't tell whether his increased respiration was due to excitement or panic.

She crossed her legs. "If you offered me some sweet tea, I couldn't turn it down."

It wasn't that no human had ever visited him before, but Christine's particular presence was disconcerting. "Uh, sure. I mean, no, don't have any tea. But I've got cola, root beer, and beer-beer, of course."

"Of course. Any diet colas, by chance?"

He shook his head. "No diet drinks, just the real stuff. Want one?"

"Um, better not. Got to watch my figure." She waggled her torso ever so slightly, as though there were a chance an adult male had not yet noticed it. "How about a sip of cool water?"

****

While Jason was in his kitchen, Christine looked down and adjusted the microphone in the front of her brassiere. The battery and transmitter fit at the lowest part of her back, below the waistband of her slacks. With the tight skirts she usually wore, it would show too obviously; its bottom portion touched the top of the cleft between her nether cheeks. The wire ran along her left hip and up her left side, inside the brassiere under her left breast. The tiny microphone was concealed in the heavy front panel of fabric and stitching which held together her bra's two sturdy D cups. She'd tested the arrangement enough to know she'd have to position the microphone no farther than three feet from the subject if she wanted a clear recording.

And she wanted it very clear.

She was juiced with anticipation. Detective work might

become a good new hobby. But that wire insisted on riding up, so she wiggled her hips to settle it back into position. If Jason had peered around his kitchen doorframe, he might have imagined she was dealing with a wedgie.

A visibly rattled Jason returned with the water, his hand trembling when he extended the glass, barely half full.

"You're probably wondering what brings me out here on a Sunday afternoon." She eyed him and gauged the distance. Too far away. "Come sit down," she patted the adjacent cushion, "and I'll explain."

Jason glanced around as though he wished there were a dozen other seats to choose from. But the loveseat was his only sit-able furnishing. His feet dragging en route, he sat gingerly beside her, as far away as he could lean.

"You know, we seldom have any time together… to get to know each other." Her voice purred.

Cougar. He nodded and gulped again.

"And since we're both so important to Amanda, it's probably good for us to get comfortable around each other, since it's been, oh, how long that you've been together?"

Since he stared blankly toward her chest as he blinked repeatedly, it apparently took him a second to realize her sentence had included a question. "Uh, since Halloween… six months or so."

"Seven months, to be exact." She nearly spit it out. Then Christine checked herself and returned to the soothing voice. She edged over just a skosh. "So we should be able to relax around each other since you and Amanda obviously have a long future together." She'd provided a perfect cue.

Jason looked as reluctant to speak as if he had a chronic stutter.

Christine could not tolerate being ignored. "Us being more relaxed around each other would be for Amanda's sake, of course. You know, less strain on her if you and I get along reasonably well."

****

This was sounding more and more like she wanted Jason's body… alive. *Alive and in the sack.* Gazing at the lovely, healthy flesh visible above her low-cut blouse, he figured he could warm to that notion. But there was something unnatural about the encounter — it somehow felt scripted. Not able put his finger on that feeling, Jason did not reply.

"And since we're going to be, uh, friends, we should feel comfortable enough with each other to share little secrets." That word lingered on her lips. "As part of us developing mutual trust, of course."

He didn't trust Christine any farther than he could toss her in the air. "W-what k-kind of s-secrets?"

"Oh, you know, fantasies, passions… indiscretions."

She knows I've been listening to Kevin's conquest stories. He blushed.

"There, I'll bet that was one in your mind just now. Why don't you share that little secret with me."

He shook his head and tried to will the blood to drain back from his cheeks and neck.

"Well, then, maybe you can think of a different secret to share. Perhaps something else you don't want Amanda to know."

There were lots of things he didn't want Amanda to know. Jason hadn't told her his GCEC performance evaluation was in jeopardy because he'd been ducking the leggy trainer from Alabama. He hadn't revealed that he was tired of hearing her yak about all the work problems with King Louie. No need for Amanda to know he found her best friend's bosom visually irresistible.

"Now it happens I specialize in men…"

I bet you do.

"...and I can tell when a man is holding back. Shall I guess what your secrets are, Jason?" She leaned closer and arched her back until her... *chest* couldn't get much closer.

He shook his head to loosen the new cobwebs.

"Well, let me try anyhow. Let's see. I think there's some unresolved issues between you and me that're keeping us apart. Don't you agree we should resolve them?"

She had to mean how she'd been following him recently. But right that moment there were only two things between them, as closely as she was leaning over. He began sweating but he still didn't reply.

****

She wasn't getting very far. In order to entice Jason to say something incriminating, Christine needed to steer him onto more specific topics like luscious ladies in movies, pretty women in the community, attractive workers at the office, et cetera. So far, all she had on tape were the infinitely faint sounds of him sweating and drooling.

She sipped the water and watched his eyes as she let her tongue's tip linger on the edge of the glass. "You know, Jason, a nice looking athletic guy like you... I imagine you've enjoyed the company of lots of young ladies. I bet they're attracted to your muscles." When Christine touched Jason's bicep with her manicured fingertips, he jerked like she was a 240-volt live circuit. "Oooh, a bit jumpy, aren't we? So tell me again about those girls you've been acquainted with — I'd guess there's a lot."

He shook his head. Didn't reveal a number, but suggested a low total.

"Well, tell me about things at your office. I've heard some of Verdeville's finest young women work at Gee-keck. I bet they can hardly keep their hands off you."

He shook his head again.

This will be a boring tape. Christine paused to formulate another tack. "I believe I know one of your secrets."

His eyes widened.

"Some little treat east of Verdeville."

Jason relaxed enough to grin. "Oh, yeah. Juiciest I've ever had, too!"

Finally, a full confession!

"And it's not all that far. Six miles out and six miles back. I can zip over there, enjoy a quick one, and be back in town within forty-five minutes." Another smile. He even licked his lips.

Not only a confession, but so brazen! "And this little side business is a complete secret from Amanda, isn't it?"

Jason blinked, probably without realizing it. "I've been trying to take her with me, but our schedules aren't quite in sync. She goes to work for eight and I don't usually start 'til ten-thirty." He paused. "I like it better in the mornings."

A lot of men do. Christine was horrified. As firmly convinced as she'd been that Jason had a honey east of town, she'd never imagined he would try to work Amanda into a perverted threesome. "Well, I don't blame her for not going." Oops, her tone shifted again. Christine modulated her breathing and tried to think what else she needed on tape.

Jason wouldn't look her in the eyes. He had to be guilty.

****

Jason kept squirming. Christine was trying to seduce him. She'd gotten him alone on a flimsy pretext — *men don't exchange secrets with their girlfriend's girlfriend* — and was now practically rubbing her chest in his face. And he couldn't retreat much further on the tiny loveseat.

Christine squeezed in. In a bad movie, she'd be recording his answers somehow. "Of course, we wouldn't want to bother Amanda with any of this, would we?"

"Ab-bout what?"

"This little discussion we're having. My afternoon visit. Us getting to know each other a bit better."

"N-no. G-guess n-not." He wondered where his new stammer came from.

"In fact, we wouldn't want anyone to know we even had this discussion today, would we?"

He knew exactly what she meant. *No, we wouldn't.*

BEEP BEEP BEEP BEEP

The harsh bleating alarm of construction equipment in reverse. Jason jumped two feet straight up, whirling around in search of a bulldozer headed his way. Christine leaped back and nearly knocked the lamp from the end table.

Wait. *Telephone.* That was his buddy's ringtone. Kevin had programmed it as a joke and Jason didn't know how to change it.

"Kev?" Jason's adrenalin-filled voice shook. "What the crud, man?"

"Hey, buddy. I need you right now at the mall." No introductory pleasantries. "How quick can you get here?"

That $75 he owed Kevin; it couldn't be anything else. He did not want to go to the mall and definitely didn't want to see Kevin right then, but he reluctantly agreed. Nearly anything was better than being stuck in his own apartment with a quirky cougar — a woman he couldn't actually *have* because she was Amanda's best friend.

Flipping his phone shut, Jason grabbed his wallet and keys and abandoned his uninvited guest, sitting on the loveseat with her mouth part-way open. "Gotta go, Christine." He clumsily waved goodbye. "Uh, lock the door behind you." Then he left.

****

Christine watched him flee. Jason's hasty, and decidedly guilty-looking, departure gave her unexpected time alone in his apartment. *Where's the material evidence?*

She started in the bedroom. "Let's see who else has been in here besides Jason." She narrated to her mic like a seasoned operative from a comic book. "Nothing beneath the bed but dust bunnies. Doesn't keep a clean house, this boy. Let's see what secrets his dresser drawers hold. Oh! Didn't know Amanda liked the fancy condoms. Naughty girl." The condoms meant nothing, however, because Christine knew Amanda was not on the pill.

Beside the bed was a small night table with a single drawer, which Christine opened gingerly. A heavy, metal-bodied LCD flashlight and a stainless steel revolver. She picked up the firearm carefully. "Smith and Wesson .357 magnum. Nice choice." Almost every man in that part of Tennessee had some kind of handgun in his nightstand. She moved the thumb latch and swung out the cylinder. Loaded. *He'll have to change a few things if he ever has any kids around.* She closed the latch until it clicked and replaced the revolver in the drawer.

In the closet was a small stack of adult magazines on the top shelf. "I'll bet he reads the articles, too. Ha." She looked at the centerfolds in the top three magazines. Then she twisted closer to the microphone in her bra. "I think you two girls hold up pretty well compared to these airbrushed twenty-year-old models." Then she put the issues back.

Christine continued a muttering commentary during her sweep of Jason's bedroom and adjacent bathroom, sounding '*Aha!*' toward her microphone whenever she found something intriguing.

Instinct made her spend more time in the living room space than anywhere else. But she also stopped to inspect

Jason's refrigerator — she'd seen *9½ Weeks*.

"Hope they didn't do anything on this kitchen table. Yuck." Christine found a plastic trash bag in the tiny pantry. Into it went everything incriminating, except the magazines.

****

Still monitoring the situation from a too-warm and dusty Bronco, apprentice investigator Cheney had observed an unidentified woman enter Jason's apartment about 25 minutes earlier and later watched Jason depart. Though not in view, the female had to be inside still; Cheney noted the time on a small tablet. It would be helpful to know who that woman was, but Cheney had forgotten to bring an agency camera with a telephoto lens. *Can't hang around here — have to follow the target.*

Cheney waited a few moments for Jason's truck to pass and then started the Bronco. *Just drive and watch... and wait. Blend into the background.*

Cheney switched on the GPS device and squinted into the smallish screen. "Target heading south toward the interstate."

Things were finally getting interesting.

Chapter 15

As he took the turn into the mall parking lot, Jason glanced again over his shoulder. He had the eerie feeling Christine was following him again. But no sign of a sparkling white convertible. In fact, hardly any vehicles heading his way, except a few which turned off and an older beige Ford Bronco. It was nearly a quarter mile back. Couldn't see a face.

Approaching the food court, Jason spotted Kevin near a small group of kiosks beside a cluster of benches. Not many stationary people nearby except an attractive female, back a ways, trying on sunglasses.

No greetings. "Why'd you drag me out here, Kev? I don't have any cash on me."

"It's not about the money, which I still need back, of course. I want you to meet Amaretto before she leaves town."

The good-looking woman trying on sunglasses turned from the kiosk, a puzzled line between her eyebrows.

"Why? You've never paraded any of your other conquests." Jason's head pounded with the extra stress.

"She's special. Besides, I want to prove I wasn't lying about her being smart."

"Just mail me a copy of her IQ test! What you don't seem to get, Kevin, is that I don't care who you pick up!"

The woman's puzzled expression vanished. She returned the sunglasses to the display and approached. "Hi, I'm Paula, but Kevin's been calling me Amaretto."

Wonder if she was close enough to hear everything I said? "He told me. Like the liqueur?"

"No, like the goddess. Spelled with an o rather than an a. Amoretto."

Whatever.

Kevin finally spoke. "This is my buddy, Jason."

Somebody ought to explain. "Uh, Kevin called and asked me to come over. I owe him some money."

Paula squinted. "I don't think so."

So she *was* smart: no money had changed hands.

Kevin cleared his throat.

Jason shrugged. "Well, he was impressed with you and wanted me to meet you."

"So what is your impression?" Paula could have struck a pose, but she didn't.

Nobody spoke for at least ten seconds, which seemed like half an hour. *This would be a good time to take off running.* Kevin, grinning smugly, was no help whatsoever.

Finally Jason shrugged. "Uh… I'm kinda committed, so it's trouble if I do too much noticing."

"Well, hey, while you two are catching up, I need to see a man about a horse. Be right back." Kevin trotted away along the mall's long corridor.

Paula watched him leave. "He must want us to be alone so we can talk."

But he didn't have anything to say to Kevin's newest companion; he just wanted out! Hopefully Christine would be gone from his apartment by the time he returned home.

Again Paula broke the ice. "That Kevin's a piece of work. What's he really like? I mean, when he's not cruising the happy hours."

Jason grimaced. "Kevin has rather limited interests. He's basically a good buddy. But if you don't watch him, he has no compunction about imposing himself on you."

****

Apprentice Investigator Cheney had followed Jason into the mall — at a discreet distance, of course — and milled around until the target stopped near the benches and began speaking first with the unidentified man and then with the unidentified woman.

The detective sat at the food court table closest to those benches, facing away. It had been a while since Cheney ate a corn dog, so that delicacy was a useful prop. After decorating it with ketchup, the investigator began munching.

Cheney glanced over each shoulder occasionally, pretending to be waiting on someone, and dabbed errant ketchup from lips and chin. Too bad the benches weren't closer to these tables so some of the target's conversation could be overheard.

Then the unidentified man left. Puzzling. Cheney finished the corndog, deposited trash in the nearby bin, and sauntered toward a nearby kiosk.

Leather goods, purses, wallets, coin pouches, cell phone covers, plus gaudy beads strung on thongs as necklaces and bracelets. A visibly bored teenaged girl sat at the register; her thumbs flew over the miniature keyboard of her cell phone. She looked up as Cheney began browsing the merchandise, but the detective waved a hand in the universal sign of *just looking*.

The clerk resumed her texting.

****

Paula studied Jason's face, wondering what, if anything, was in his head. "You're probably curious about last night — why I didn't just toss my drink in his face and move on."

If he was puzzled, Jason didn't say so. He just waited.

"I know his type of trouble and normally I steer clear of lounge lizards. But I've just ended something that I'd thought was really special. Seemed great at first, but turned into garbage. Turns out I didn't know him after all."

Jason nodded as though he felt the same way.

"So when I realized I'd been taken for a six-month ride, I decided to use this Nashville conference to redefine myself."

"What's your definition now?"

Good question. Paula considered. "More daring, not as fearful. Willing to take the initiative."

"So you knew what you were getting into with Kevin."

"You know, he is nice-looking… in a cocky kind of way." Paula grinned slyly. "I knew he was trouble and trouble was exactly what I felt like having."

Jason's expression suggested there were several things he could say. He settled for, "Well, you really bowled him over."

Good. "My brains or body?"

"Like I said, I'm not supposed to notice your, uh, physical features." But Jason's grin betrayed his assessment. "But Kevin went gaga over your intellect."

"Oh, I don't think so. Kevin may believe that, but he didn't spend enough time with me to assess my mental attributes. What he interpreted as intelligence was my directness. I felt like having a tumble with the kind of man I've always stayed away from, and he was the one I picked." She grinned. "Kevin thought he picked me because he thinks I'm smart. Actually, I picked him because I figured I knew how to push his buttons."

Jason's eyebrows shot up.

"Does my directness surprise you?" Paula let that sink in. "Picture the way guys like Kevin operate, week after week. He's probably got a sad story for the compassionate women and a different gimmick for the wild ones. You know, designs his strategy to conquer that particular prey. All I did was turn the tables. I decided to ride a spirited stallion and I picked one I knew I could handle."

"So he was right... you *are* smart."

"Funny thing is, you wouldn't think a guy like Kevin would care if a woman had any mental activity at all."

Jason smiled, which likely meant, *Usually he doesn't.* "You represent a new dimension for him."

****

Jason looked again for Kevin. The sometimes irritating buddy stepped from the crowd, still several stores distant, in the direction of the mall's public restrooms.

Her voice turned him back around. "So, your significant other — what's she like?"

"Somewhat like you. Beautiful, smart." Jason couldn't meet her eyes. "But she doesn't rub my nose in it."

Paula nodded like she understood that importance. "Well, thanks for not treating me like a leper."

"What do you mean?"

"I'm not really a trashy traveling tramp. In my normal existence, I'm pretty conservative and usually stay inside the lines." Paula touched Jason's upper arm, just below the shoulder. "This weekend was a one-time thing. Just so I'd know what it's like to ride the wild stallion." She squeezed his biceps. "Anyway, thank you." The final syllable remained visible on Paula's lips and her fingertips remained on Jason's arm.

Kevin arrived with a big grin, as though pleased they'd hit it off. "I'm back. You guys didn't kill each other, I see."

Odd thing to say.

"Well, you weren't gone long enough." Paula checked her watch and peered down the mall's concourse. "I've got a stop to make. Jason, nice meeting you. Take care of your significant other." She touched Kevin's chest with her fingertips. "Kevin, I'll be back in fifteen." She disappeared among the geriatric exercise walkers, middle-aged window shoppers, and the oddly dressed teens desperate to be noticed.

Kevin stared after her. "So what do you think?"

Very impressive, actually. "Well, she's definitely not typical of the conquests you've previously described. And, I agree, she does seem intelligent." Not sure how much his buddy wanted to know. "She's not desperate and not low in self-esteem."

"I think she might even be a manager in her department."

Jason heaved a sigh. "Okay, she's smart and pretty. I believe you. Now can I go?"

"What's your rush? Got a hot date?" Kevin peered at him more closely. "What are you keeping from Uncle Kevin?"

Jason hated having such a transparent face. He reluctantly explained about Christine's surprise visit.

"Oh, you're back to that business about her wanting to jump your bones. What could she possibly do that would make you think she's got a thing for you?"

"Well, for one, she stands and sits real close and stares at me."

"Christine stands real close to all men under the age of eighty and over twenty. She's got that great rack and she loves to let men drool over it."

"No, this is different." *Why can't anybody comprehend?* "It's like she's peering into my soul, like she wants to know more about me. Like she's, uh, interested in me."

"Any interest Christine has in you, my deluded buddy, is

more like a quirky grad student doing a complicated science experiment."

"What do you mean?"

Kevin paused and thrust out his lower lip as he considered. "Like attaching electrodes to different parts to your body and seeing what twitches when she flips certain switches."

"That's pretty graphic... and it rhymes."

"You asked."

"And you don't think it's remotely possible she has any interest in me at all?" Demoralized as he was, Jason's voice was plaintive.

Kevin shook his head. "Nothing except a twisted science experiment, ole buddy."

****

Absent-mindedly fingering a small leather jewelry box at the nearby kiosk, Cheney had watched the woman squeeze Jason's arm. *Surely they already know each other. You don't get that touchy with someone you just met.* But the trio's voices were still too low to be overheard, even at the kiosk's closer distance.

As soon as the detective found an opportunity to write, the small note pad page would be filling up.

Cheney watched Jason leave and — after a suitable interval — discreetly followed. The target made a slow circuit past most of the food court vendors. Then he looked as if an idea had suddenly hit him like a microscopic lightning bolt. He changed direction and his pace quickened as he exited the mall and got into his green pickup truck.

Cheney hurried to the Bronco, turned the key, and start backing out.

Thump thump thump — flat tire!

Disgusting. Cheney scribbled the necessary case notes

and then pulled out the agency-issued BlackBerry.

****

Back inside the mall, Kevin watched as Paula returned with a tiny pink bag from the lingerie store and a big smile. "One more night in town before I head back home."

Kevin eyed the bag appreciatively and tried to peer inside. But Paula moved it behind her back. "You'll have to wait 'til I'm wearing it."

"Is it edible?" He grinned.

She didn't answer, so it might be. He couldn't quit grinning. "So what did you think of my buddy Jason?"

"Well, Jason seems like a typical small town good ole boy. The kind of guy you could count on for help when nobody else would bother. I figure he's a person whose hospitality you shouldn't impose upon."

"What did he tell you?" Guilt crowded out Kevin's smugness.

"Nothing specific. But I got the impression you may have overstepped your boundary in some way."

Wonder if Jason knows which boundary.

****

Cheney flipped on the GPS device and watched as the target's blip merged with the interstate and headed east. The stationary Bronco's insides were distinctly uncomfortable in late May's afternoon heat. While watching that little screen, Cheney phoned the auto club hotline and provided the necessary information about account number and location. The wait would be at least an hour.

It took roughly seven minutes for the blip representing Jason's truck to come to rest about six miles east of town.

The detective didn't like the BlackBerry's tiny keyboard, but it was better to compose and transmit an e-mail while data was still fresh in mind.

> *Sun afternoon*
> *Target active*
> *Un-ID female arrived his apt*
> *Target left 1st un-ID female @ his apt & raced away*
> *2 mall*
> *Target met 2nd un-ID female & un-ID male @ mall*
> *Male left briefly; target talked w female*
> *Male ret'd later & female left*
> *Target left shortly*
>
> *Tracked target 2 GPS point approx 6 mi. E;*
> *destination unknown*
> *More later when known*

Cheney wondered if another corn dog could be consumed in what remained of the hour before the tow truck would arrive.

Chapter 16

The *Maneater* ringtone startled Amanda from what could have become a much-needed nap. "Hi, Christine, what is it now? Is Jason also guilty of treason and tax evasion?"

"You'll change your tune when you see what I found at his apartment."

"What were you doing at Jason's apartment?"

"Long story. I'm coming over with the ev-i-dence."

Amanda wanted to beat her head against the wall, the one vibrating with vocal monstrosities. Besides all her other problems, she already detested her new neighbor. Quiet as a retired mouse for her first three weeks, then she'd begun incessant yodeling practice. Usually it was faint, but at times it came right through their shared duplex wall. *Isn't yodeling against the law?*

There had to be someplace she could anonymously bury three bodies — Kaye, Christine, and the yodeler. *And toss in Jason to make it four!* Maybe in the dumpster behind her complex?

If that weren't enough, within fifteen minutes, Christine entered without knocking and began her briefing. "He put it in the slot."

"He *what*?"

"I followed him to the cable company yesterday." Without even a greeting, it was a rather breathless report. "He stuck his payment in the drop slot."

"I thought you meant he'd nailed a bimbo at the cable company!" That didn't sound like particularly astute detective work.

"Then he went to Gee-keck on a Saturday!"

"He works there, Christine."

"Whatever."

Amanda stood in the doorway; maybe that would halt Christine. "I believe you need to call off this effort. I don't think Jason's doing anything wrong. My sister even agrees, and she'd usually be the one calling for his head on a rusty plate."

"You told Kaye?" Christine stepped around her, sputtering. "You made me swear on Aunt Tilly's grave that I wouldn't spill the beans. It was top secret from your sister. Why on earth did you tell her?"

"She tricked it out of me. But get this — Kaye wants to help."

"Help what?"

"Help us determine whether Jason's messing around."

Christine scoffed. Clearly she was long past that question; to her, it was simply a matter of catching him in the act. "You think she can follow orders?"

"Are you kidding? Kaye doesn't listen to anybody!"

"Well, we certainly don't need any prima donnas on this case."

Yeah, one Christine is enough. Amanda had a sense of *déjà vu*, but shook it off. "So explain what you were doing at Jason's apartment."

"I told you the investigation had commenced." Christine shrugged away the question. "I was simply interrogating him."

Amanda pictured glaring lights and a rubber hose, Christine with a whip and high-heeled boots. "You and Jason alone in his apartment?" Amanda shook her head. "I don't like the sound of that."

"Relax." Christine headed toward the dining space. "We just needed to be alone so I could get down to his secrets."

"I don't want you in his secrets." Amanda did a double-take. "What secrets?"

"For one — Jason admitted to the little side dish he visits six miles east of town."

"Huh? There's nothing out there but a gas station and some beat-up trailers."

"Exactly! Perfect spot to stash a side piece."

Amanda stood in stunned silence. "Jason admitted it?"

"It's all on tape."

"You taped this?" Amanda sputtered. "He just sat there and spoke into a microphone?"

"Well, it's not like he knew about the mic, but he did say it, all right."

"Illegal taping of conversations? What next, Christine? Searching body cavities?"

Christine ignored the hyperbole, though she likely wouldn't rule out that procedure. She waved her hand. *Subject shift.* "You've been waiting for us to find a smoking gun. It's right here."

"Where?"

"Well, somewhere in this assortment of stuff from his apartment. Put down a few newspapers — some of it might be dirty."

****

Christine rummaged beneath the sink for dishwashing gloves; she came up with one blue and one yellow. With considerable drama, she lifted her cotton recyclable Verde Grocery bag to the tabletop, which Amanda covered with a week-old newspaper spread open. "Item one, female scarf." She held it up. "Obviously not your color."

"I'm pretty sure that belongs to his mom. I'm certain she's visited Jason's place at least once, if only to clean."

Christine waved her hand. "Item two, small comb with strands of unusually-colored hair." She sniffed it gingerly. "Likely traces of peroxide. And I think this particular woman has dandruff."

Amanda grabbed it. "That's Jason's lost pocket comb! Where'd you find it? He spent most of last week griping about that."

"In between the couch cushions, where all traces of unseemly trysts usually collect." Disappointing that her carefully collected evidence was not as persuasive as she'd imagined.

Amanda smelled the comb. "No peroxide. That's what hard rubber combs smell like. And it's not a weird color hair. Jason has sandy highlights in isolated places."

Her enthusiasm undampened, Christine pulled item three — a small jar of cherries — from the bag with a flourish. "Tah-dah! Right out of Mickey Roarke's hands and Kim Bassinger's mouth."

"You stole Jason's cherries? He's going to freak. He loves those! I've watched him put away half a jar of these at a time. I had to convince him that eating more than six at a sitting would poison him!" Amanda put them in her fridge.

"Would seven cherries really poison you?"

"Don't know. I heard it somewhere."

Christine waved her yellow gloved hand. *New subject.* Three pieces of her carefully procured evidence had been explained away. Only two remained, but she'd saved the most convincing exhibits for last. "Item four, a nearly brand new tube of ChapStick," she paused for extra drama, "with traces of lipstick on it!" She held it up proudly.

"Let me see that!" Amanda snatched it away and held it up as she carefully removed the cap. "It *is* lipstick!" Her face clouded. She sniffed as though her nostrils could identify the user's DNA. No clue, but definitely female.

"I doubt Jason's mother wears that particular shade of scarlet." Finally Christine had scored.

Amanda kept staring at the ChapStick. "Where did you find this?"

"On the side of the little sink, in the half bath off the short hall."

Amanda thumped into her rocker. "Okay, I don't like that ChapStick at all. The rest I can explain, to my own satisfaction, at least. But not these traces of red lipstick."

"Well, wait 'til you see my final item — people's exhibit number five." Christine pulled it out — a single piece of knee-high hosiery, black with serpentine stitching on one side.

Amanda blanched. "That better not have been in his bedroom."

"On the loveseat, between the cushion and the arm, tucked against the side part." Christine motioned with her gloved hands. "Way down, almost completely underneath the cushion."

"You only found one of the pair?"

Christine nodded.

"I don't wear knee-highs. Never have."

"I know. But if you had scrawny legs like I bet that grocery tramp has, you'd wear these under the slacks you'd always have on."

"You think the snack aisle woman left these at Jason's apartment?"

"It's a mathematical possibility. Of course, I guess it could be just about anybody who wears them... for whatever reason."

Amanda's eyes flooded. "Well, I'll tell you one thing. If I ever find a woman wearing a single black knee-high, I'm going to rip it off her foot and strangle her with it!" She burst out crying. "I'll probably sharpen that comb and use it to stab Jason!"

Poor Amanda. But Christine felt — deep down — she'd performed a valuable service.

The only thing left was to catch that slimeball in the act.

Chapter 17

Monday, May 25 (Memorial Day)

Cheney phoned the Ace Detective Agency office and a sleepy voice answered.

"Beau, it's Cheney. Need a favor." The detective glanced over the succinct case notes spread across the small dining room table. What had at first seemed like a no-brainer assignment, with probably an innocent target, had yesterday developed into a perplexing mix of unusual activity and unidentified players.

Elvis Beauregard had been named for two heroes of the Confederacy. At least that's the way many Tennesseans felt about it. He was the agency's computer wonk who could do wonders with both hardware and software. "Hi, Cheney. What's wrong with your voice?"

"A touch of laryngitis, I think. Probably just a summer cold." Cheney's hoarse voice had to be difficult to hear. "I uploaded some GPS coordinates to the main computer last night. Did you get them?"

"Haven't checked. Hold on." Beauregard yawned. "Okay. Got them."

"Wondered if you'd check them against some of your satellite maps or something. All I could get was that it's six miles east of Verdeville, which would be mile marker 248."

"Six miles out? Why didn't you just follow the target and see for yourself?"

"Tried to, but I got a flat."

"That's what you get for driving your heap with bald tires, Cheney."

"They're not bald and maybe I'll get new tires when I'm paid for this case." Cheney coughed. "My target rushed away from the mall yesterday before supper time and I tracked him 'til he stopped. Didn't appear to veer off I-40. I can't recall anything out that way and my maps don't show much besides a dot that could be anything… or nothing." It might even be a speck of chocolate. Cheney poured another cup of coffee and took a sip; it burned against tender throat tissue. "So can you hook into a satellite image or something?"

"Well, in some areas of a full-fledged city, I could access photos of individual houses on a street-by-street basis. But out in the boondocks of I-40 east, we'll be lucky if anything pops up besides some forestry charts or topo maps. Uh, let's see." Beauregard's fingertips rattled what sounded like hundreds of keys. "Nope. Hold on." More key strokes. A long pause. "Bingo!"

"What'd you find, Beau?"

"Okay, hold onto to your chair, because this is a real *destination*." Beauregard yawned again. "It's just a big ole gas station. No. Wait. Must be a truck stop. Yeah, truck stop, with lots of big rigs parked to the north side… I guess that's the rear. The main building looks pretty typical. You know, the kind with restrooms, showers, a little store and maybe a chicken counter or something off to one side."

"Chicken counter?"

"I'm just guessing, Cheney... can't read the signs. The sat pix don't take me inside the place. But the truck stops I've been to sometimes sell food off to the side — you know, pizza or sandwiches, Or something."

"Whatever. But that's the only thing out there?"

More key strokes. "Nothing on the south but woods, as best I can tell. That exit only feeds to the service road on the north side. Uh, looks like a few dirt roads leading from that access road. Hmm. There's several dots at the end of those dirt trails — could be small residences, I guess."

"Houses?"

"Well, judging from those pitiful roads, I'd guess something on the order of shacks or maybe old-style trailers. Might even be abandoned." Another agency phone rang in the background. "Does that fix you for now?"

"Yeah. Thanks, Beau. I owe you." The detective disconnected.

Cheney looked over the notes scrawled during the conversation with Beauregard. Truck stop. Lots of vehicles. Facility large enough for showers and food outlet. Nothing around it but dirt roads and a few shacks or trailers. "Doesn't sound like a place I'd rush to after I finished talking with two people at the mall." *Unless I was meeting somebody else.*

Chapter 18

Amanda couldn't look away from the ChapStick and knee-high. She'd thrown out the newspaper and tried to put Christine's evidence in a drawer — *out of sight, out of mind* — but all she'd succeeded in doing was crumpling them together atop the kitchen table. The knee-high, in a snakelike coil, partly covered the ChapStick, and she couldn't quit staring. They'd begun to resemble some sort of avant-garde centerpiece.

Ordinarily on a holiday, Amanda would be somewhere with Jason, even if only watching him run around a ball field like a big kid. She didn't really like attending his games, but she enjoyed watching Jason. Or she used to. Normally she'd go just to keep the chickies at bay. Flocks of bouncy, perky girls clustered around the single players (and some of the married ones). It would be easy for one to turn the head of a red-blooded Tennessean like Jason. And he was quite red-blooded… at least until last Wednesday night.

She still couldn't figure out what had gone wrong that evening. Other than Jason being apprehensive about the next

130

day's seminar and whining about an interview with a trainer, what had gone through his head? Christine seemed certain Jason's distraction was a clear sign of waywardness, though Amanda still had doubts. But so many other things had fallen into place, especially that single knee high and lipstick-covered ChapStick. Plus all those sightings and suspicious behavior. Jason was doing something! The question remained, what was it? Or, the better question, *who* was it?

She checked her e-mail and updated her status on Facebook: *Why do people suddenly start acting weird... with no explanation?*

Maybe that was what she needed right then — a blend of sympathy, questions, and sarcasm. In other words, Facebook.

****

Jason scanned the bleachers near his team's dugout. Amanda hadn't made any of his practices in a good while, but she usually tried to attend games and was nearly always at tournaments unless they were out of town. No Amanda. *Must still be mad about whatever.*

The huge Greene County Slow Pitch Softball Memorial Day Tournament had finally arrived and Jason figured he'd rather watch it on TV. Normally he was psyched about playing and often his team did reasonably well, beating the poorer teams and giving good fights to the better ones. But today he was in such a state about everything going on in his life that he didn't even feel like playing softball. Besides, they'd be at least one player short, despite all of his calls yesterday. If next year's slow pitch team was as unenthusiastic as this one, he might jump to another squad or quit softball altogether.

The GCEC Transformers' first game was against the Verdeville Police Department. They played aggressively because they couldn't stand to lose. *Cops act like it's a major league game.* The catcher was a big ugly guy who physically blocked the plate so you had to knock him down to score. Nobody even tried to. *Probably carries a 9 mm pistol under his chest pad.*

The police squad didn't even have a team name. They just wore their regular yellow T-shirts with *POLICE* emblazoned front and back. It worked. The umpires gave them the benefit of the doubt in close calls. Perhaps they figured to hedge against future speeding tickets. Or perhaps they *were* just blind.

He searched for Amanda again during the seventh inning stretch. Nope. But there was Erin Chester, the GCEC trainer, in the stands near his team's dugout. She wore tight white shorts which revealed a rather thick waist and a decidedly flat posterior. Despite those flaws, she looked very good — her legs were fantastic as far as the eye could see. The other trainer, buck-toothed Dexter Something, also wore shorts, but shouldn't have. He had ghastly pale legs, with almost no remaining hair, and knees so knobby and loose they looked like they'd been assembled without instructions.

Erin came over to the fence behind the Transformers' dugout and spoke with some of the other GCEC employees while they waited to bat, but she initiated no direct interaction with Jason. However, Jason watched her carefully, and he was certain Erin kept watching him. When he finally got to bat, he was so rattled he swung on the first pitch — which he never did — and flew out to right field. *Swung too late.* He *never* did that.

"Maybe that goes in her report, too," he muttered. The burly catcher cop looked distinctly pleased and the blind umpire asked Jason what he'd said. Umpires are quite sensitive to anything verbal which might conceivably be criticism.

The Transformers lost, 7–2, and immediately fell into the loser's bracket of the double elimination tournament.

Not enough time between games to go anywhere or do

anything; since Amanda wasn't there, Jason felt bereft. They'd spent little time together since Wednesday night and none since their tense and awkward supper Friday evening. It felt like their longest separation since they'd become a couple.

The whole day felt off. The entire team had played poorly, and despite all those hated telephone calls, some players hadn't shown. Jason went to the parking lot, lowered his pickup's tailgate, and lay down in the truck bed. Then he put his glove over his face and tried to take a catnap.

Too many vehicles and people going by. Too hot. No breeze. Not enough shade. Jason moped.

The Transformers' second game was against the Junk Yard Dogs, Verdeville's sanitation workers. He wrinkled his nose. *Funny how the stink never completely gets off a man who works forty-hour weeks on a garbage truck.*

With two outs in the fifth inning, Jason beat out the throw to first on a dribble to shortstop and advanced to second on a sacrifice fly to center. Then Big Ernie hit a double. Jason's pulse leaped at the bat's crack and he took off running. But he tripped on the third base bag and stumbled toward home, then sprawled on his face in the loose dust twelve feet from the plate. He tried crawling the rest of the way in, and the Junk Yard Dog catcher strode over and tagged him out on the ground. Big Ernie died on base.

Covered in dirt and ribs aching, Jason limped back to the dugout and again peered into the stands. A little comfort from his girlfriend would have been nice, but Amanda still hadn't appeared.

But someone was staring at him. Jason blinked. Erin didn't. *She probably thinks I'm looking at her.* Actually, he was — her legs, anyway.

They lost to the Dogs, 6–3. Jason was almost glad the Transformers were out of the tournament. After playing two matches minus their roving short fielder, Jason was bushed, busted up, and broiled from the sun. Everything hurt.

He headed home.

****

In the shade of the concession stand awning, where half a dozen littered and dusty picnic tables were anchored to a blacktop slab, Cheney watched the target scanning the nearest bleachers several times. Maybe his gaze was directed toward the unidentified tall blonde with nice legs and tight white shorts. No direct interaction, but they seemed to lock eyes briefly. That could be consistent with two involved people trying to be circumspect — no overt communication, but lots of eye contact.

Jason lost both games. But at least he made a nice play for the highlight reel when he rounded third base and ate four pounds of loose dirt. He looked more than dazed, dusty, and embarrassed, however. Jason seemed to be breathing with difficulty. *Might've cracked a rib.* That ought to slow down his extra-coupular activity.

Nothing to report to Ms Powers, at least not until Cheney identified the thick-waisted blonde and ascertained whether they'd exchanged anything besides glances. That unidentified female left the ball field soon after the target, but she seemed to be in the company of a homely buck-toothed man with possibly the scrawniest legs ever displayed by a member of the male species. And that was saying a *lot*.

Cheney tossed away a partly melted chocolate bar and, at a discreet distance, followed Jason to his apartment.

Chapter 19

After her Facebook post, Amanda waited for comments to roll in. Three friends liked her post, which didn't even make sense, one wrote, 'Sorry, hon,' and another asked, 'What's up?' The inevitable wise-cracks were, 'Thing are tough all over' and 'Pull up your big girl panties and deal with it.' Not the kind of support she'd hoped for.

So Amanda shifted to Jason's profile page, not looking for anything in particular. He didn't have all that many Facebook friends, about four dozen. His two older brothers, his mother Margaret, Kevin and an assortment of other GCEC coworkers, plus Big Ernie and other teammates from various sports. Several names she didn't recognize. *Maybe high school friends.* Doubtful if Jason had made many friends during his five scattered semesters of college, but it was certainly possible.

One friend had a profile photo of a teenaged girl. That didn't necessarily mean it was her current picture — people who played on Facebook a lot often switched their profile photos. But who was this child named Noreen Spender? And why was she friends with Jason? This didn't look good.

And Karen! *Whoa! What the heck is SHE doing on his friend list?* It was Karen What's-Her-Face, Jason's college fiancée who'd called off the engagement two months before their scheduled wedding.

Amanda clicked on Karen's name for more information. *Nope.* Blocked from general viewers. A person would have to already be a friend to see her profile info. Amanda had no intention of friending Karen, though she had from time to time considered hiring a hit man to pay a visit.

None of Jason's recent posts appeared to include any interaction with Karen. *Dead end.* But Amanda wondered how long ago Jason and Karen had reestablished contact. And why? Maybe Karen had commented on a thread from one of Jason's friends. Or vice versa. Then possibly they'd chatted: "Hey, how you doing? Long time. Blah blah." *Whatever.* This was not a good sign, either.

Then she checked out Jason's photo albums, mostly shots of him playing ball or holding trophies. One snapshot — evidently taken by a coworker — showed Jason at the phone bank with his headset on, wistfully glancing out the window and clearly wishing he was outside playing ball instead.

She clicked on an album entitled "Mandy" — her nickname when Jason was passionate. Several photos of them together. She got distinctly misty. No, Jason couldn't possibly be messing around.

But she couldn't forget Wednesday night. Jason had not called her Mandy. In fact, he'd barely spoken at all during their un-intimate intimacy.

Amanda again studied the ChapStick and knee-high on her table… and re-lit her fuming.

****

Dusty, sweaty, and thirsty — each ragged breath pierced his chest like a hot poker. By the time Jason had driven home, stood in the shower for fifteen minutes, and changed into gym shorts and T-shirt, he was ready to stay in the rest of the evening. It was three o'clock and he hadn't even eaten lunch.

He popped a couple of ibuprofen (although inadvisable on an empty stomach) and opened a cold beer, though it hurt his ribs to swallow. Exhaustion, however, was overcoming pain or hunger as his chief concern. Jason barely remained awake enough to check his e-mail. A few spams, something from Roger about the finalized fantasy league draft, one from Big Ernie asking why Jason hadn't scored on Ernie's good double — *Thanks for the sympathy, man!* One from Jason's middle brother whining about something and another from oldest sibling warning Jason that middle bro was in whiny mode. *Like that's news.* And a rare e-mail from Kevin, probably about the money Jason owed him or concerning the big favor that Kevin still hadn't spit out. *Have to wait. Too tired for more drama.*

Jason turned off his PC and eased himself into bed. He couldn't lie on his left side because of the ribs, but rolling over nearly made him scream.

****

Christine's phone rang. *Blue Spanish Eyes.* Maria Perry's ringtone.

"Hi, girl. You off school today?"

"Not only off school but finished for the semester, except I have to show up a few more days to post grades and straighten out my supply cabinets."

"So, what's up?" Christine didn't get many calls from Maria, who seemed to think she needed to protect Amanda from her. *As if that were necessary.* Not a likeable trait, that. Still, she'd been sitting, alone and bored; it was someone to talk to.

In the four years since Daniel's departure, Christine had actually been fairly lonely at times. She'd considered getting a pet, but they require regular, ongoing care, not just attention when she felt like it.

"Well, you said somebody told you something about a truck stop east of here. Remember?"

"The one Jason apparently visits. What about it?"

"Well, I heard about some fight out at that establishment. It's around exit 248, isn't it?"

"Yeah, that'd be right: just over six miles out." Christine nodded into the phone. "So what did you hear?"

"No details, but police hinted that two truckers scuffled over which one was going to drive a particular female east toward Knoxville. She'd climbed up on one rig and then changed her mind and got in a different cab with some other driver."

"Hmm. Sounds like the kind of girl Jason's been visiting."

"You don't know that, Christine."

"Well, we haven't caught them together, but I've got a gut feeling."

"Whatever." Maria usually rolled her eyes when she said that. Another unlikeable trait. Really, Maria wasn't her favorite of their little group. "Anyhow, I thought you'd like to know."

Christine took notes. "How'd you hear this?"

"The guys at the fire station get all the lowdown from local cops that you never hear on the news."

"So Roger has been more forthcoming with salacious information about folks of his own gender?"

It took a few seconds even for a school teacher to translate that question. Then Maria's voice indicated she was smiling. "Oh, yeah, he's been a real chatterbox lately. I've been practicing my detective skills."

Puzzling remark. But as long as her Stealth Team members were collecting reliable intel, she didn't care how they got it.

****

It was well after six o'clock and the target appeared to be in for the night.

Cheney, sitting in the Bronco in the larger parking lot outside Jason's apartment, was exhausted and dirty. All that dust at the ball field surely wouldn't help a summer cold's laryngitis. If the hourly pay weren't so good, the detective would have thrown the assignment back in Ms Powers' face. That poor schmuck wasn't at all the classic philanderer — he didn't do anything but work and play ball. Well, and dash off to the mall and then out of town six miles east.

At least the detective had a newer model phone with a full slide-out keyboard for texting. That way the ailing voice could be saved and might recover faster.

Cheney sent a text message to Ms Powers.

> *target looks bedded down 4 night… alone*
> *figure 2 call off surveil unless U say other*
> *pls reply if other*

After waiting fifteen minutes, Cheney started to text Ms Powers again when the client's message came through.

> *wondered where U were*
> *if sure JS is down, leave OK*
> *chk N'village H. downtown N'VL*
> *JS buddy hangs out @ HH*
> *possbl lead n case*

Well, everybody who knew anything about regional night life knew the Nashvillage had the best happy hour on Fourth Avenue. But, good grief. *Looks like a rabbit trail.*

> *on way 2 N'village*
> *need name & descr 4 JS buddy*

Cheney watched in the Bronco's rearview mirror while

leaving the target's apartment parking lot. "Wonder if this guy has actually done anything wrong?" Cheney had an uneasy feeling the whole case was hollow. But something was definitely going on which *related* to the target. "Wonder if this Jason Stewart has any idea what's swirling around him?"

****

BEEP BEEP BEEP BEEP

Jason jerked awake. He started to leap out of bed, glancing around for the heavy equipment about to back over him, but two things stopped him: one, he remembered that was Kevin Haywood's blankety blanking ringtone; and two, spasms of pain shot from his ribs to his toes and fingers. Without moving anything more than absolutely necessary, he fumbled for the cell phone.

"Okay, Kevin. Thanks a whole bunch for waking me up."

"Dude, you sound like death warmed over." It was likely more observation than an expression of concern.

"Uh, got banged up at the tournament. Plus we lost..."

Kevin cut him off. "Yeah, yeah. So anyway, here's the deal. You know that seventy-five bucks you owe me?"

Still groggy, Jason forced himself upright. It took a lot of effort and caused much pain. The alarm clock by the bed said it was just after seven o'clock. "Now?"

"I'm in a bind."

"Look, every time I've tried to give you that money, you wave me off, but when I'm practically dead from injury and exhaustion, you want me to pay up!"

"So, are you coming or what?"

Jason grimaced. To Kevin, loaning money to a friend was like having a small, mobile bank account — *you leave it in the bank until you need it.* Now he needed it. "What the creepin' crud is this big emergency?"

Kevin lowered his voice. "I bet this girl fifty bucks that she couldn't feel my crotch."

"Let me guess, she felt your crotch."

"Yeah, but it took her a minute to figure it out. She's not a rocket scientist."

"And you're gonna pay up?" Jason started to shake his head, but his ribs screamed too much.

"After you bring my money."

"Where the heck are you?"

"Nashvillage lobby. Happy hour." Kevin sounded surprised that Jason even asked.

"That's at least a half hour drive from here!" Jason sputtered, but that hurt, too. "You guarantee this is a real emergency and not just some other girl you want me to look at?"

"Bona fide emergency. This girl is ready to par-tee, if you know what I mean. But she's a stickler for me paying up on our bet. Says she's never won anything before."

"Do you realize that if you've sunk to paying women fifty bucks to feel your crotch, you're only one step away from hiring a hooker?"

"Nah. Completely different. These ladies are classy."

Jason sighed. That hurt, too. "Rubbing her hand on your privates to win a bet. That's real class."

"Are you bringing my money or not?"

"Okay. But I've got to wake up enough to get moving. Sure wish you'd loaned that seventy-five bucks to somebody else."

"Then you would've run out of gas that night, good buddy. It was me to the rescue then. Now you." *Click.*

Jason closed his phone. He'd have to put on street clothes, and that kind of movement would make his ribs scream. Well, if he was going to get dressed anyway, he might as well try to hook up with Amanda. *Take a chance on her being in a tolerable mood.*

He called. No answer, so he left voicemail:

> *"Want to meet for supper at the Steakhouse Buffet?*
> *Mondays they have ribs. After I get some clothes on, I*
> *have a quick errand first. How about eight?"*

In his exhaustion, pain, grogginess, and aggravation, Jason lost track of a most fundamental time-space continuum tenet — driving to downtown Nashville and back was not a quick errand.

Chapter 20

Kaye sat back in a surprisingly comfortable stuffed chair and watched the people milling about. Work pressures, home matters, her poor sister... she needed a break. Not that this happy hour looked like much. There was a line at the cash bar, another for the complimentary boxed wine and kegged no-name beer, and two waiters circulating with trays of half-filled plastic cups. Self-service Kaye wasn't, nor could she drum up any enthusiasm for cheap booze. Sitting felt good, but it emphasized the belly she'd tried unsuccessfully to hide with dressy dark gray slacks. Her burgeoning abdomen was her ex's fault; she'd never lost a grip on her eating until foreign panties appeared in Tom's Beemer.

Suddenly, out of the corner of her eye, Kaye saw a man entering who looked a bit like the photograph of Jason. She monitored him closely. It *was* Jason! *Well, maybe.* He was muscular, nice-looking, and his hair ought to be combed the other way. Slight belly. *Has to be him.*

She instinctively thought she should hide, but realized

Jason had never met her and probably hadn't even seen a picture. So she openly watched him from her comfortable chair.

The man-who-must-be-Jason looked around, then approached a cocky-looking guy with combed-back hair. They talked animatedly. The Jason-person seemed angry or out of sorts, and even seemed to be limping. Well, not really limping, but maybe it hurt when he walked.

Kaye rose and moved closer.

****

Standing quietly against a column in the Nashvillage lobby, Apprentice Investigator Cheney discreetly watched the numerous faces and grabbed a half cup of beer when the waiter zipped by. Still no word back from client Powers with a description of Jason's lounge lizard buddy.

But there was a man who looked exactly like the unidentified male at the mall on Sunday afternoon. Didn't spot that same unidentified female, however, though there were plenty of other women present.

Some females were just relaxing with friends, dressed down in jeans and sneakers. But some were obviously on the prowl, wanting some action. Same with the men — most just hanging out and watching the ladies, others clearly players. The un-ID'd male from yesterday was obviously a player and looking for a new playmate.

Cheney kept one eye on him and another eye on the front door and elevator. It was 7:45, early enough that people were still arriving, from upstairs hotel rooms and from the street.

Cheney tossed the watery beer and got a cola from the open bar. Shouldn't have alcohol while on duty anyway. The investigatory eyes picked up Cheney's target when Jason walked in from the street. *Thought he was home in bed! Maybe there's more to this Jason guy than meets the eye. Hey, that rhymes.*

Not only was the target's sudden appearance suspicious, but Cheney also noticed an unidentified blond female in tight dressy slacks seemingly stalking Jason. *She bears monitoring.*

****

Kaye was not tall enough to see over most of the men milling around, so she did a lot of darting back and forth. The agitated verbal exchange she'd previously witnessed suddenly calmed and the man she was certain was her sister's lover produced a wad of cash from deep in his pocket. Kaye couldn't see how much, but it was several bills and they didn't look like ones.

The operator pointed, less than discreetly, toward a woman nearby and the man-who-must-be-Jason sized her up and nodded. That woman had seen the cash transfer and looked eager; she even edged closer, though not near enough to join their conversation. *What a meat market!*

Abruptly, the-man-who-must-be-Jason turned and strode out the same doors he'd just entered a few moments before. When the nearby woman approached the operator and held out her hand, he handed her most of the cash!

Wow! What a flagrant encounter — agitated conversation and money changing hands twice! Kaye didn't need to strain to make sense of it. That oily-looking jerk was a pimp and Jason had just paid for a prostitute! Couldn't be anything else!

The woman-who-must-be-a-hooker smiled and then walked away. Kaye didn't see where she went, but she'd headed in the direction of the restroom.

She'd learn no more by simply hovering nearby. Sometimes an agent has to go in undercover and consort with the enemy. She took a deep breath and walked toward the slime-bucket Jason had just paid off. Kaye deliberately bumped into him. "Oh, sorry. Didn't see you."

The man she-didn't-know-was-Kevin eyed her appreciatively. "No problem. I've never had a lovelier collision."

Ooh, he's a smooth-talking devil! Kaye smiled. She was actually charmed and it shook her. She had to focus on her mission, obtaining information about the cash exchange she'd just witnessed. So she started chatting.

****

A sudden vibration in the detective's pocket nearly spilled the flat cola. Discreetly, Cheney slipped out the phone and read the text from Ms Powers.

> *Kevin Haywood*
> *ave ht & wt*
> *good-looking & knows it*
> *dk hr comb bk*
> *grn eyes*
> *Don Juan & women eat it up*

Dark hair combed back. *So that's Jason's buddy.* Things were falling into place. When the target raced to the mall on Sunday he was meeting his friend Kevin, though the woman with him that day remained a mystery. So despite seeming to be in for the night, Jason had rushed 25 miles to this hotel lobby to give Kevin a handful of cash.

But who was the nice-looking dyed blonde in gray slacks now seeming to hang on Kevin's every word? And who was the eager looking woman who had stood nearby until she got her money?

****

Kevin appraised the shapely blonde in tight pants as she chatted about her convention for office equipment. Then she drew a breath, sipped her drink noiselessly, and apparently waited for his comeback. He glanced toward the restroom area where his intended conquest had last been seen. Disappointing that the bet winner hadn't come back, but oh, well. It was her loss.

He focused again on the blonde in the hand and calculated which lie might impress her most. "Oh, I'm a lawyer, in town from Memphis for a deposition."

She cocked her head. "So, that guy who just paid you. Was he the plaintiff?"

Whoa. Kevin grew flustered. *Didn't realize anyone had witnessed that transfer.* But he had to keep the lie going. "Oh, that guy? No, he's the valet. I'd given him a hundred dollar bill to park my Ferrari where it wouldn't get dinged, and he just brought me back some change."

"Never heard of a valet giving change." Kaye smiled thinly.

"Well, sometimes I have a twenty on hand." He eyed her more closely. "You're mighty curious for someone in copier sales."

Her smile broadened cynically. "Where was he going so fast? This valet-who's-not-really-a-valet?"

Kevin sensed trouble. "Well, I can't discuss an ongoing legal case — Hippocritic Oath." That sounded about right, so he simply backed away. Since this blonde was asking so many questions about Jason, she had to be the stalker he'd heard about through the grapevine — the one pestering Jason at work. He eased over to one of the young attendants behind the free bar. "Are y'all letting hookers in here now?"

The hotel employee shrugged. Not his job to distinguish between hookers and bank examiners.

Chapter 21

At the Steakhouse Buffet, Amanda was hungry and fuming.

Jason was 45 minutes late for the supper meeting he'd booked at the last minute. And why wouldn't he be already clothed at seven o'clock?

She'd waited inside the buffet for the first twenty minutes and then went back to her Mini Cooper, where she sat for another fifteen minutes trying to decide whether Jason was even worth the trouble. Then another ten minutes pondering whether to give him the satisfaction of calling to see what had caused his delay.

Just about the time she was ready to drive away, she spotted Jason's green Ford pickup, taking the corner a little too fast.

Apparently without seeing her or her car, Jason hustled inside the buffet, though not too speedily because he seemed to be limping. Well, not exactly a limp, but something affected his gait.

His turn to wait a few minutes. She leaned back in the seat and hoped he'd fume, too.

After five more minutes, Amanda opened the car door and swung out one leg. But before she could exit completely, Jason rushed from the buffet with his phone to his ear, jumped back into his truck, screamed as though he'd been stabbed, and then sped away.

What? Over half an hour late for a date and then he breaks it completely! And what was that scream all about?

She decided to wait a bit longer. Maybe he'd come back.

Five minutes later, Amanda's phone rang with Linda Ronstadt's *Desperado* — Jason's ringtone. Should she answer? By the time she reached for the phone, the music stopped. "Blistered butt-rash!"

Should she call him back? Amanda's brain flooded with uncertainty. Why was he so late? Why hadn't he called? Well, he did call, but she didn't answer because he didn't let it ring long enough. Why did he dash into the buffet, wait a few minutes, and then high-tail it back out? Why did he scream? Where was he heading so fast?

Amanda did not notice the dusty beige Bronco which pulled into traffic two cars behind Jason's truck.

****

Cheney guided the Bronco into traffic and settled in behind the target, several cars behind. The logical assumption was that Jason had arranged to meet a different woman at the buffet, but there'd been a last minute change in location. Might have been to a happy hour, perhaps a motel, or maybe even a truck stop six miles out of town.

A phone beep startled the investigator. Cheney fumbled with it.

What U found @ trk stp 6 mi E?

Cheney waited until a traffic light and then replied, *no chance 2 chk yet*.

Client: *maybe I shd chk*.

It was several minutes before Cheney could answer, *no! client not meddle N case*. Besides, a busy truck stop at night in the middle of nowhere was no place for a lady.

The meddlesome client texted again. *what R U doing?*

At the next light, Cheney responded, *follwng target - nu activity*.

That likely made the hair rise on the back of the client's neck, because she texted, *rept ASAP*.

Cheney could read the text, but couldn't respond while driving, so the client would have to wait for a report. Right now the trick was to keep the target in view without being spotted.

****

She was being silly. Amanda tamped down her uncertainty and grabbed the phone. She called Jason back.

But it went straight to voicemail. With so many unanswered questions, she wasn't about to leave a message. She didn't know if she'd been stood up or if Jason had driven himself to the E.R. because of a terrible injury — like an irate, spurned woman stabbing him with a sharpened comb. If so, the attacker had beaten Amanda to it.

As she drove home, Amanda cried at all the red lights.

She was just driving into her apartment's parking lot when her phone rang. No distinctive tone, just a generic ring. The first three numbers were 317 — an Indiana area code. *Big sister.* "Hi, Kaye. Are you still in town?"

"Yeah, my last night supposedly, but I don't think I can leave yet. Wait 'til you hear what I saw this evening, right in my very own hotel."

Amanda checked her watch; 8:05 p.m. "I give up already. A drunk salesman?" She was in no mood for guessing.

"No. Your Jason at this happy hour, paying for some fast flesh."

"Paying for what?" She'd never heard that euphemism. "No, that's ridiculous! When?"

"Tonight. This evening. Right here in the lobby." Kaye's voice was breathless. "He dashed in, looking very suspicious, and handed some cash to a slimy-looking man — obviously the pimp. I even saw the girl Jason paid for — not very impressive. She must have been a real slut, because he didn't produce much money."

"A hooker?" Amanda's eyes filled with angry tears. "His big errand was a quickie with a hotel hooker?" It was so incredible she had to repeat it. "Jason paid for a hooker right there in the lobby?" Something about it didn't sound right.

Kaye tsked into the phone. "And I talked with the pimp later."

"You did what?"

"The pimp. After Jason dashed off to connect with his hooker, I talked with the pimp. I asked who was the guy that just hustled off. He said that was the hotel valet bringing him back change. You ever seen a valet give change? And this pimp pretended to be a lawyer from Memphis. As if. The closest he's been to a lawyer is his call to a law school dropout when he can't post bail for his pandering arrests." When Kaye embellished an impression, she went all the way.

"Let me see if I've got this right." Amanda's right temple throbbed. The case had become a preponderance of evidence. "Jason calls me to meet him, then he dashes off to a prominent Nashville hotel to give money to a pimp who claims to be a Memphis lawyer. And the pimp says Jason is the hotel valet." Her eyes filled again. "Then Jason rushes off for his quickie with the hooker. And that's why he stood me up for supper at the steakhouse."

"I didn't know about the supper," replied Kaye, "but a man does get hungry after a quickie."

The phone buzzed, signaling another incoming call. Jason's number, but she didn't put Kaye on hold to take it. She had no intention of speaking with him — not now or ever. Jason could just talk with his hooker friend — see what level of conversation she's capable of.

Amanda closed the phone and pressed her forehead against the Cooper's steering wheel. Tears dropped onto her thighs. No sign of cheating Jason or his ratty old truck in her parking lot.

After sucking in a deep breath, she exited her car as Christine's white convertible suddenly rolled into the adjacent parking space.

She wasn't sure she could contend with Christine right now. But over the next five minutes, she told Christine everything she'd learned from Kaye about Jason's hotel hooker. Christine looked jazzed. Well, at least her investigation was coming together, even if Amanda's relationship was coming apart.

Chapter 22

After racing away from the buffet, Jason drove to his own apartment, thinking Amanda might have misunderstood and tried to meet him there. On the way, he called a few times but she didn't answer. *Better not leave voicemail since I don't know how mad she is.* If he apologized too much, it might make him seem guilty of something serious, like a husband suddenly producing flowers for his frazzled wife.

But her vehicle was not in either parking lot at his place, so he sped to hers, hoping she was home. It was already 8:15, over an hour after he was supposed to have met her at the buffet. On the way, he tried to call again. Busy signal.

There — Amanda's Mini, parked in her complex's parking lot. And Christine's convertible. *What is she doing here?* He almost turned to leave. But somewhere deep inside, a tiny voice suggested it was better to face this boiling kettle right now rather than let it steam and whistle overnight.

With considerable apprehension and several groans because of chest pain, Jason approached and knocked on the door. Amanda noisily looked through the peep hole, then paused before opening the door. She stood well back out of the way. No greeting. Her face was a mess of streaked mascara.

And the normally talkative Christine went stony silent. Not good.

That creates a spooky feeling even when a man's not already in trouble. "Uh, sorry I was late..." She probably wouldn't care about his excuse but he launched it anyway. "Didn't realize how long it would take and then I rushed around checking for you at the steakhouse and then went to my place in case you were there and here I am. Sorry. Um, it was an emergency I had to deal with." He would have been breathing heavily from that speech alone, but his ribs hurt too much.

"Emergency? Some woman stab you with a sharpened comb?"

"Huh?" Puzzling image. And alarming. "No, it was... uh, well, something I had to do."

"Where? Must've been a long way off."

"Well, over in Nashville, actually. I thought I could get there and back quicker than it took." He cleared his throat. "Forgot how far it was... not used to driving it at night." He shifted position and groaned.

"I'll bet." Christine punctuated her contribution with a stern stare. "So, how much is a hotel quickie these days?"

What? "Uh, did I interrupt something?" He pointed in Christine's direction.

"Actually, I'm just leaving." Christine walked so near Jason that she practically stepped on his toes. "Amanda, call me if you need to talk, after you run him off." She also (accidentally-on-purpose) brushed an elbow against his sore ribs as she passed.

Jason yelped.

Amanda didn't manifest any concern. Probably too angry.

Finally they were alone together, for the first time since

Friday evening. But Amanda still glared. Maybe he should have left with Christine.

He wanted to tell Amanda everything: about the awful seminar, the trainer hounding him at work, his horrible fantasy league draft results, Christine's bizarre visit in his apartment, the odd meeting arranged by Kevin to meet Paula / Amoretto, having to play in the tournament with one man short, bruising his ribs, having to dash away to the hotel to pay back the debt so Kevin would have another salacious story to tell. Et cetera. But he didn't.

He wanted to hold her — to embrace her and kiss her. He wanted them to return to a point where words were not involved and to wipe the slate clean of the past four days.

But instead he stood awkwardly, groaning as he hugged his side, and unable to look Amanda in the eyes, because he knew he was withholding all that (and more). And he could see that she knew — it was written all over her face. He kept one eye on the door; he might need to exit in a hurry.

From the direction of the duplex neighbor's apartment, Jason heard a noise so awful he wanted to pound his ears. As he scrunched his face — the only defense — he identified the faint sounds of amateur yodeling. *Is Amanda being punished for something?*

Apparently ignoring the racket, Amanda silently sat on her rocker and stared toward the blank TV screen. Jason followed tentatively and eased onto the loveseat. Neither spoke for so long it seemed each might explode from the tension.

"So, where were you earlier this evening while I'm waiting in the buffet like a pitiful gawky girl watching for a prom date who isn't going to show? And you didn't even call for the first forty-five minutes."

That seemed a trap question with no correct answer. Jason didn't want to explain about repaying the $75 or stopping off at happy hour. He had a fundamental choice — appear seedy with the truth, seem guilty with no answer, or try to hedge his way out of answering directly.

Finally he answered, "An emergency." Sadly, the third option made him appear seedy and guilty *and* evasive. It was also repetitive, but he shrugged in spite of the pain and left his words hanging in the cold silence.

"I suppose you also don't feel like explaining the woman you groped at the grocery store, or the other tramp that fondled you in the mall." Angry tears rolled down her soft cheeks.

He reached for her instinctively. *Tears always do that.* But he'd turned too suddenly. Yelping, he clutched his side.

She recoiled even farther.

"Wait. What was that about the grocery? The mall? A tramp? Huh?"

"Yeah, go with that look of complete ignorance, you and your seven-month itch." Her voice radiated the heat. "Act like you have no idea what I'm talking about."

Didn't ring any bells. Shrugging would have hurt, so he sat there desperately perplexed. Maybe he should return to her first question, about standing her up, and answer differently this time. Then perhaps they could pretend she hadn't even mentioned all that other baffling stuff.

Too late. Amanda shot from the rocker. "Seven months and *boom!*... It's over?" Without waiting for a reply, she hurried to her bedroom and slammed the door.

Jason gulped. No precedent for this. He wondered what would happen next in a romance novel. But he didn't know, since he didn't read. Of course, he did watch movies. What would Brad Pitt do? *Not sure.* Maybe there'd be clues in earlier movies. What would Harrison Ford do? *Nope, still a blank.* Maybe farther back. What would Errol Flynn do?

He couldn't be positive, but his best guess was that all three of those film heroes would simply smash open the bedroom door, sweep the crying woman off her feet, and urgently make love to her. Just the right touch of Hollywood splash. But screenplay impulses never seemed to work in real life for ordinary people. Plus he had bruised ribs to contend with and Amanda would probably call 9-1-1 and make Jason pay for the broken doorframe.

What Jason wanted to do was knock softly on her door and embrace her. Apologize again. Then explain, face to face, everything on his plate right now, including why he'd been late tonight. *But I don't think Amanda would believe me.* Even if he could assemble the words necessary to convey his complex explanation.

Besides, how could he respond to those other bizarre accusations? Something about someone groping somebody in the mall and the grocery, and some kind of rare allergy itch. *What's that all about?*

Jason lingered in the hallway, staring at Amanda's bedroom door. "Over? Seven months with this woman and it's over?" Then he sighed, despite the pain. Instead of responding like a Hollywood he-man, he settled on what Pee Wee Herman would do — he wimped out. Locking Amanda's front door behind him, he departed.

It had been a very memorable Memorial Day. The sooner it was over, the better.

Chapter 23

With all the driving around, Jason had never eaten supper. Starving, he stopped at a busy fast-food joint and ordered the largest sandwich on the menu board. Then he sat by himself at the only four-seat table still vacant and started eating.

Shortly a woman approached. "Crowded tonight. Mind I have the other half of this table?" Though the dining area was noisy, she only whispered.

Intriguing. Jason couldn't speak because of the huge burger chunk he'd just bitten off, but he waved his concurrence. Waving hurt his ribs, too.

She sat on the opposite corner. Attractive in an athletic-looking way with nice proportions, she wore dark Dockers, comfortable black shoes, and a six-button Henley with both sleeves pushed up. Probably in her early to mid thirties, a light tan darkened her forearms. She held a steaming cup.

Jason hurriedly chewed and swallowed. "If I drank coffee this late," he pointed to her cup, "I'd be awake all night."

"Half decaf." She smiled, still whispering. "Just enough buzz to keep me going for now, but not enough to bother my sleep later." She also held a small notepad, though he couldn't see what was on it.

"Are you writing a book? Lots of frustrated authors out there." He shook his head. "Better stick with a solid day job."

"This? Oh, just a shopping list. Never remember what I need once I get to the store." She unhurriedly put it away.

Jason felt like reaching over and twisting her volume knob. *Ha, that'd be trouble.*

"So what kind of day job do you think is solid? I might be interested." She spoke like she didn't want anyone to overhear her remarks.

He considered as he chewed. "Oh, I don't know." He wouldn't recommend GCEC. Based on all of Amanda's problems, he couldn't recommend a local government job. "Maybe the military?"

Although she didn't reply, her smile suggested she knew a little about the military. *Probably an Army wife.* No, no ring. *Or Army divorcee.*

"Ever tried sales?"

Her eyes rolled dramatically.

"On second thought, maybe book writing *is* a better idea. There's certainly enough nutty people out there to make very interesting characters."

"But for a good novel, you'd need a plausible plot," she whispered. "Readers demand believability. If the plot is too absurd or improbable, agents won't touch it, so it never gets published."

Must be an English professor. "I wouldn't know about that. But most of the people I'm acquainted with are pretty unbelievable." He could have added *absurd* and *improbable.*

She smiled. The dark circles beneath her eyes made her seem tired, but her expression held warmth.

"I'm Jason. I don't normally eat supper this late, but I had… uh, several problems this evening."

She sipped her coffee. "Wendy."

"Like the red-haired girl in the logo?" Jason grinned as he pointed toward the menu board.

"No, like the girl Peter Pan loves but can't actually have." A wistful whisper.

Definitely a lit professor. "You live around here?"

"Only passing through." Wendy nodded toward her coffee. "Just needed a little pick-me-up before I get back on the road."

Jason eyed her again. Here he was trying to wolf down a late meal when the process of swallowing hurt his ribs, and intriguing strangers were hitting on him with seductive whispers. Could he be that irresistible? If this Wendy stranger was as athletic as she seemed, perhaps she had a lot in common with Jason. That would be nice, for a change, instead of a girlfriend who wouldn't even show up for his tournament and had offered no TLC for his painful injury.

Wendy took a long sip of coffee and wiped her lips with a napkin. She looked into his face and shrugged, which seemed to say more than *finished my coffee… I'm outta here*. Her expression seemed almost sympathetic. Surely it wasn't so obvious that he was confused, demoralized, and just-broken-up with his girlfriend. Or maybe it was.

Wendy stood and offered an abbreviated wave. Then she turned and dropped her empty cup in the trash near the door as she exited.

Jason's final word didn't completely form until after Wendy was already out of earshot. "Bye."

Chapter 24

Tuesday, May 26

At 6:45 a.m., Amanda felt like a ten-wheeled, tri-axled dump truck had dropped thirteen tons on top of her... and it all smelled like fertilizer. Physically exhausted, mentally stressed, and emotionally stretched to the limit, she had nothing left to offer the *Coor Sup Fun* division today. King Louie would have a cow, but she reset her alarm for another hour. *Not going in today.*

After a coffee to strengthen her resolve, Amanda phoned her supervisor's direct line. When Louis answered, she gave him the news.

"On the morning after a three-day weekend?"

"If I'm sick, I'm sick. I don't select times for my body to collapse."

"Exactly how sick are you?" Louis was ever the comforter.

"I can barely move, I can't think straight, my heart is pounding, and I have a strong urge to strangle someone." All true, but none would impress King Louie. "Plus I might have fever and there's mucous to contend with." That was a bald-faced lie, but she knew Louis wouldn't want any mucosa near his empire.

"But I need you over at Public Works kicking some butts and getting their crud straightened out."

The danged grant's evaluation requirements! "I'll have to kick butts tomorrow or Thursday, if I'm able to function by then."

A brief silence while Louis' bird-sized brain processed that. "Oh, I get it. This is your attempt at payback because I called you over the weekend." He'd gone immediately to bullying mode. "You're faking."

In earlier years, Amanda had quietly endured his hectoring. Not any more. "That's insulting!"

"Well, you have to come in." Though not visible on the phone, his third chin was certainly twitching.

"Everybody else gets sick days when they need one. It's absurd and unfair that you act like I'm not allowed to be ill."

It still caught Louis off guard when his underlings dared speak up. "I don't even believe you're sick."

He was possibly correct in a hair-splitting legalistic sense. But Amanda was definitely incapacitated, so she shifted to that tack. "On the very rare occasion I'm unable to work for whatever reason — and the policy manual has broad definitions, by the way — I'm not required to endure a supervisor's allegations or abuse. This borders on harassment, unless it's already over that line."

The H word usually shut him up.

Louis muttered some curse words she hadn't heard recently. When he was that ticked, he'd have Amanda arrested if he thought it would get her on his assigned task. "I want a notarized doctor's excuse on my desk in the morning." *Click.*

So like King Louie to chastise the very person whose skill sets could undo his bungling. Amanda flipped shut her phone and struggled to hold back tears. With everything else going on in her life, she'd very possibly just jeopardized her job. King Louie was *not* a forgiving despot — he would hold this against her for the remainder of her career.

She needed a strategy. She needed a *life*! But first, more coffee.

Amanda washed her face and changed from PJs into lounging wear that wouldn't shock the mailman. Then she nibbled on a Pop-Tart and turned off the TV.

"Let's get to the bottom of this fiasco, instead of operating on King Louie's rash presumptions and inflamed worries." She verbalized as if she were chairing an impromptu crisis management meeting. "Why don't people communicate any more these days? It would save a lot of blow-ups and melt-downs."

From her briefcase she retrieved notes from her Friday discussion with Louis. "Just what I thought…" Then she dialed the cell phone of "Harry" Harrison, chief of Public Works. His office phone might ring off the hook, but he answered his cell on the second ring. "Yeah."

"Harry? This is Amanda Moore at Funding. Got a couple of questions about that sandbag grant…"

Chapter 25

Following the directions she'd gotten from a gas station near Exit 242, Kaye easily found the Greene County Electric Co-op less than a mile west of downtown Verdeville. It had the typical flat roof and pale brick of office buildings constructed in the 1970s — plain, functional, and already crowded. Kaye parked and entered, trying to remember any details which might clue her in concerning Jason's whereabouts.

Finished with her convention, she had that entire day to return home to Indianapolis. Her daughter was staying with friends and Kaye hoped they'd still be friends by the time she got home and relieved them of Chelsea. Surely there was enough time for her to take a peek at her sister's wayward lover in his small town workplace.

An immense counter dominated the front of a huge room. On the entrance side were several short metal posts for theater ropes if enough customers ever appeared at the same time. The ropes had been stored years ago and nobody admitted having seen them lately; however, the empty posts remained. To either end of the main counter were employee doors to the inner sanctum.

The counter area was divided into thirds and the portion on the far left was marked for *New Accounts / Start Service.* On the far right the sign was equally clear: *Bills / Pay Here.* The center portion, not presently staffed, appeared to be anyone's guess since it had no visible signage.

Not wanting either of the two known options, Kaye stood at the middle window. She cleared her throat, shifted from foot to foot, and even tried signaling as one would when ignored by an inconsiderate waiter. However, no employee moved in the direction of the middle window. The GCEC staff were obviously content with their routine and signage, and willing to wait until the customer made up her mind.

"Excuse me! Does anybody work here?"

Bad move. Those words were less a request for assistance than akin to a battle cry. A gray-haired lady stood, smoothed the wrinkles down the front of her longish skirt, and sauntered over. Wordlessly, she pointed to a tiny sign: *Next window please.*

The sign's presence might have held up in a court of law, but it did nothing to improve Kaye's prickly temper. Citizens of Indianapolis were not accustomed to being treated this way by Tennessee Volunteers. "So you don't intend to assist me?"

The employee's lips twitched. "Next window, please."

It's difficult to make much noise stomping on the wiry industrial plastic mats used in places where public feet meet institutional tile flooring, but Kaye stomped over toward the line marked: *Bills / Pay Here.* A large woman with a sleeveless buttoned shirt and no brassiere edged herself in line a split second before Kaye arrived. Had she been less concerned about stomping, Kaye might have beaten her there.

It cannot be verified, but many would assume some curious employee counted the number of times Kaye rolled her eyes as she waited for the hefty woman to pay her bill and stuff the small purse back into the large, cluttered bag hanging from her fleshy shoulder. Finally that customer departed.

"Next."

Kaye stomped the additional thirty inches to the window. "I'm here to see Jason Stewart."

"This is the bill window. Do you have an account?"

Kaye hesitated and then shook her head sideways. Once.

"Well, Mister Stewart only handles billing problems on existing accounts. Next."

"No, not *next*. I'm not finished. I want to see Mister Stewart."

"If you need to establish electrical service, please wait in that line." The clerk pointed to her right.

"You mean I'm not allowed to speak with one of your employees?"

"The person who handles new accounts will be happy to deal with you."

Their brief — and increasingly brittle — conversation went circularly, a bit like a snippet from *Who's on First?* with Abbot and Costello.

"I don't want to speak to," Kaye glared in the direction indicated, "*her*, and I don't need a new account. I want to talk with Jason Stewart."

"Ma'am, do you have electrical service with Gee-keck?"

"Well, I have electricity where I live, but I'm sure it's different than what you have way out here."

The employee stiffened as if those were fighting words. "Where might that be, ma'am?"

Kaye sighed. "Back in Indianapolis."

The dutiful clerk checked a list. "They're not in our co-op."

"What a surprise," Kaye muttered.

"I think you'll need to make local contact when you return to, ah, Indiana." The tiniest smile. "Next."

Two customers had collected behind Kaye; if any more stacked up, GCEC might finally need to locate those velvet ropes.

"Let's give this another try, shall we?" Kaye cleared her throat theatrically. "I'm not a customer of *your* electricity, so I don't want new service here and I don't have a bill to pay in this little town. But I *am* a citizen and I want to see one of your employees."

"Would that citizenship of yours belong to Indiana, by any chance?"

"Well, of course." Kaye could feel steam rising from her ears. "But public citizenship applies just as much in middle Tennessee as anywhere else."

"I wouldn't know about that, ma'am. Here, we mainly deal with electric service. All the citizenship issues are handled over in the courthouse. At that other window is a box of maps that our Chamber of Commerce leaves here for new customers." She pointed to a spot near the *New Accounts* window. "Next."

"No, *not* next. I'm still here. Tell you what, let me start over." Kaye hauled in a deep breath. "Suppose I'm a friend of Jason's and I'm just passing though town. Haven't seen him for a long time but don't remember where in this building he works. Other than these two available windows and the one in the middle that's poorly marked but definitely not in service, how could such a person locate said Jason Stewart?"

Kaye's awkward interrogatory construction likely lost the employee on its exact content, because she appeared to mentally diagram the sentence, without success. But she was game to respond anyway. "If I know the nature of your customer inquiry, I can direct you to the correct department."

"There *is* no inquiry. I'm not a customer. I just want to see Jason!"

At this point, one of GCEC's assistant managers (said his

name tag) strode over and motioned Kaye to the middle window. He carefully removed the *Next window please* sign. "What's your business with the employee in question?"

"He's my brother-in-law… kind of. Except they're not married." *There went another topic for the local courthouse.*

"We can't have any more loud disturbance in this customer lobby. Dial this main number," he handed her a business card and pointed, "and when you get to the third menu, press six for billing complaints. Mister Stewart is one of the employees on that phone bank."

"You mean he's somewhere in this building but you won't let me see him?" She'd watched a movie where someone in a similar situation just screamed the name of the person being sought until that individual finally appeared. Kaye briefly considered that ploy but decided it wasn't worth it. "Let me tell you something. If I *did* live here, I wouldn't buy my electricity from your cruddy outfit."

The assistant manager smiled contentedly. "Ma'am, in Greene County, we're the only electric."

****

Mabel Scott watched the irate visitor turn on her heel and stomp upon the heavy mats. Her sympathy was entirely with her GCEC coworkers. When the hostile intruder was safely gone, the manager carefully replaced the tiny *Next window please* sign in the middle window, turned to Mabel, and said simply, "Hoosier." It explained everything.

Mabel waited until the manager retreated to his office space and then remarked to her co-worker at the next desk, "Did ya see the belly on that bitty? She's preggers!" Then she pressed 9 for an outside line. At the tone, she punched in Sunny Cannon's phone number. "Sunny! It's Mabel." She lowered her voice to a whisper. "Know how you'uns wanted to know if anything funny happens around Jason Stewart? Well, let me tell ya…"

Chapter 26

Kevin found Jason in the far corner of the break room. "Oh, there you are. Been looking for you. There was a big buzz about you a few minutes ago out front."

"I'm hiding." Plus, it looked like his ribs still hurt.

"Good thing, too. From what I hear, some irate woman was just in here looking to kill you."

"I seem to have that effect on females these days," Jason sighed dramatically, "they either want my body... or my blood."

"So you don't know anything about that woman just now?"

"Only what you just told me — she's a homicidal maniac who knows my name. What's she look like?"

"No idea, old buddy. Wasn't there. I just heard about it from that new assistant manager."

"Weiner?"

"Ha. No, Werner. But some of the girls say... You're a funny dude for somebody in hideout mode." Kevin paused.

"So why are you hiding if it's not about the maniac out front?"

"I'm steering clear of that counselor." Word around the office said Erin Chester had issued an ultimatum to Jason's supervisor; his personnel folder would be marked as ineligible for promotion unless he came in from the cold. After the crazy holiday weekend, more than ever, he didn't want any counselor in his head.

Kevin blew that off. *Whatever.* It wasn't a matter of not being a good pal, just that he didn't care about anybody's problems but his own. "Glad we finally have a chance to talk. I've been trying to ask you a favor since early May."

"Okay, but shoot fast. I'm on the run." Jason glanced around and winced from the continuing pain. "No telling who else wants me dead or dissected."

"Well, since you have a minute, let me tell you about last night."

"I already know about last night. I'm in big trouble with Amanda because I had to run over to Nashville to give you money so that ignorant woman could feel your crotch some more."

Kevin paused, his eyebrows wrinkling. "Oh, no, not that girl. She split as soon as I gave her the fifty bucks."

"So she was smarter than she looked."

"I was going to tell you about who I met after that."

****

To Jason, it was a too familiar tale — Kevin spotted a probable victim and closed in. He got her another drink and quickly assessed which buttons to push. Last night's individual would likely respond best to the sympathy buttons, so he dusted off his old stand-by — the Dear John letter.

In this fabrication, Kevin was an Army officer just home from the Middle East; his girlfriend had written him a Dear

John letter and shacked up with another man before Kevin got orders back. He usually managed to squeeze out a thin tear by that point in the tale. He was only a shell of a man — blah, blah, blah — and didn't think he could ever feel close to a woman again.

She'd melted, of course, and after a third drink, they'd gone up to her room.

Jason had heard variations before, a lot. He tuned out.

Kevin inserted some bare details of physical description. "Then we got busted."

"Busted?"

"Well, turns out it wasn't her room."

"Huh?" Jason tuned back in. "How could she take you to the wrong room?"

"She'd just borrowed a key from one of her companions so she'd have a safe place to leave her purse."

"Wait, I'm confused. You left the happy hour and went to this strange woman's room, and it wasn't even her room?"

"Right. Wrong room." The consummate player seemed impatient. "So we're in the middle of some serious business, if you know what I mean, and in comes the woman whose room it is."

"What did you do?"

"Well, if it had been just that other woman, I could've kept going and it might even have been cool to let her watch. Kinky. But she had a guy with her, so we put our clothes back on and hurried out. Went down to her car."

"Her car?"

"Yeah, she was staying at a different hotel — four blocks away." Kevin held up that many fingers as though the spoken numeral hadn't conveyed enough impact. "So we drive clear over to *her* room and then we have a chance to finish things up finally."

"Wow. Who could imagine so much lust and drama lurks

in the happy hours of downtown Nashville? Somebody could write a book about all this stuff."

"Yeah, maybe me. I had to hike back to my car at two in the a.m. So anyway, the favor. I still need..."

"Aha!"

****

Kevin flinched. But it was Mrs. Grunion, Jason's supervisor, entering the break room — not anyone looking for him.

"Jason, get to the conference room." She tapped her foot while Jason struggled up. "I'm tired of hearing complaints from my supervisor that the counselors are having trouble tracking down my people. My entire division works in this single facility. It's not like you're spread out all over the county."

Jason paused in the doorway and gave Kevin a *look.* "We'll talk about this big favor later. But let me tell you something, Kev. I don't care if you killed a whole squadron of bad guys to save my life. When I get around to learning this favor, and assuming I do it for you, we're going to be even forever. Understand?"

Kevin nodded. He wasn't worried even though Jason had not yet heard his big favor request. Surely his good buddy would comply. In fact, he'd practically agreed to it already. *Besides, what could go wrong?*

Chapter 27

Jason trudged along the GCEC hallways, trailed by Mrs. Grunion, whose breath hit his shoulders like poison darts. It felt like he was being marched along the Green Mile to Cold Mountain's electric chair.

Grunion knocked once on the meeting room's open door. "Okay, Miss Chester. Here's the final package, hand delivered." She winked theatrically. "Be gentle; I think it's his first time."

That was pretty embarrassing.

With the tiniest bit of a smirk, Grunion left and closed the door. The distinct click of its latch sounded like the final hammer tap on a hand-forged coffin nail.

****

Less than ten minutes before, Erin Chester had completed her interview with one of the company's linemen, a man who showed classic signs of instability. Not good for a basket case to be handling live power lines which carried everything from 50,000 volts on down to 4,000 volts. She'd just finished up her detailed notes as the elusive final interviewee entered, and she glanced up from her position at the end of the heavy conference table. Each seating place held a small notepad and cheap ballpoint pen, which GCEC supplied free to lobby customers. She set her own pen on the full-size tablet in front of her.

Erin was 27, a year younger than Amanda, and at 5' 7" she was an inch taller. Her skirt was dark purple linen with a slit in the middle, and her white buttoned silk blouse revealed modest contours of the type bosom which some men considered perky. Folded over a nearby chair back was her linen jacket in a complementary shade of lilac. She had blonde hair, clear skin, soft blue eyes, a caring expression, and distinctly Scandinavian facial structure. Not classically beautiful, but appealing in a handsome sort of way.

"At last we meet, Mister Stewart."

"Actually, I saw you at the tournament yesterday. White shorts."

She wrote the word *observation* on her tablet. "Yes. Quite a warm day. Sorry the company Transformers didn't get to advance." She motioned to the seat adjacent hers.

Jason remained standing as though he might make a break for the door at any moment. "We also met at the seminar last week. You called on me to answer a question that had no right answer." He sat at the opposite end of the table with a wince.

It looked as if he'd been hurt in that bizarre incident between third base and home plate. "Ah, yes. My hypothetical situations about irate customers." She rose and moved to Jason's end of the table, took the chair nearest him, and crossed her legs. The modestly-cut skirt was one of her favorites because it disguised her thick waist and looked really good on her. It hit right above her knee while she stood, but rode up a few inches as she sat. "There. Much better." Now she wouldn't be distracted by people walking past the window in the conference room door. Erin wiggled slightly to get comfortable. "Did that bother you?"

****

Yes, Jason was bothered. Beginning at the recent seminar when Erin had perched on the stool to point her laser pen at the PowerPoint slides and her skirt rose up to reveal two very nicely toned legs. Her attractive legs bothered him a lot... but not in the way her question had leaned. "Which part?"

"My question at the seminar."

"Don't like being called on. Never did." No teacher had ever asked Jason anything he knew or had been assumed to know, only stuff they were certain he didn't.

Erin waited expectantly, as though she knew what was in his mind.

"Miss Chester, it's probably obvious enough that I don't want to be here."

"Call me Erin."

"Whatever. Would you mind telling me what this crud is all about? And why my job performance evaluation could be affected by it, one way or the other?"

Erin wrote the word *resistant* on her tablet. "What have you heard about these sessions?"

"Kevin said it was about handling customer meltdowns, coping with stress, and stuff like that." Jason doodled on his small GCEC notepad. "He said it was all just a waste of time." Immediately, Jason wished he hadn't blurted that out. "Of course, he had the skinny guy counselor, not you."

"Of course." She cleared her throat. "We both covered stress coping skills, among many other things."

Jason started to reply but then just shook his head. If this was intended to minimize employee stress, it had achieved the opposite effect in his case. "I wasn't stressed out until the night before your seminar."

"Were you stressed before the seminar or *by* the seminar?"

"Both."

"Why before?"

"Because I knew somebody would call on me and try to embarrass me by asking questions." *Back to childhood school anxieties.*

She wrote *anxious.* "Look, Mister Stewart…"

"Jason."

"Very well. Jason. One of our goals here is to equip customer service employees with skill sets for coping with people who are irate…"

"Or don't have money to pay their bills."

"Let's start there. How does it make you feel to be the hinge pin in a transaction which terminates a customer's power?"

"I know some people really can't afford it. Some have worked hard all their lives and draw maybe seven hundred bucks from Social Security. For lots of them, that's all they've got for paying rent, trying to eat, and staying warm. But other people who never worked a lick are getting even more government money, maybe two or three times more. Yeah, that makes me crazy." Jason doodled some more.

"So how do you handle that stress?"

"I only have three options and some customers get all three. I can give an extension, waive the penalty fee, and give them a contact number for an agency that helps out with utility bills, especially in the winter."

"It sounds like you do everything in your ability to help."

Jason sighed. "But sometimes the *unpaids* go so long that

I'm cut out of the picture. Case gets bumped up to my boss."

"How do you feel about it then? Relieved?"

"You'd think that. But actually I worry that they'll lose their power. I wonder, but I almost never know how it's resolved."

"So how do you cope with that?"

Jason shrugged… with his shoulders and his brain.

****

Erin studied her anxious interviewee. "What do you do to lessen your worry about these unfortunate customers?" She could see Jason still didn't get it. "Some people respond to this type of stress by drinking, or drugs, or other destructive behavior." Erin cleared her throat. "Individuals are at risk of such extremes if they aren't adequately coping with their stresses, at work and home."

"Home?"

"Well, of course I'm not supposed to discuss an employee's personal life, but yes, work stress can spill over and affect family," she noticed his left hand did not have a ring, "or relationships." Erin let that word dangle. "Let's discuss customer interaction."

As they talked further, she realized Jason answered as best he could. And his coping strategy was normal for such organizations — he'd never reported anything because he figured it would be even more stressful to be grilled by the bosses who would parse every syllable spoken in the initial interaction. No reports, therefore, but Jason did grouse about it in the break room.

Erin felt stymied, so she shifted tangents. "I heard a story this very morning about a woman in the lobby demanding to see an employee. One of the managers said she was potentially dangerous. How would you handle that kind of irate customer?"

"Just a random lunatic." Jason shrugged. "We call them full moon customers."

Erin raised an eyebrow.

"Whenever we get several contacts like that clustered together, somebody checks the calendar and sure enough, it's probably a full moon or within a day one way or the other."

Erin wrote *superstitious.*

They'd been talking for 45 minutes and a clearly uneasy Jason had doodled on two pages of the notepad. Yet he remained very much an enigma. Though it was a slight breach of professional protocol, she steered to some general personal questions. "Tell me about your family life. Have you typically received a lot of familial support?"

"My parents went to a lot of my ball games when I was a kid, if that's what you mean."

Well, that was part of the picture. "Any siblings?"

"Brothers."

"No sisters?"

Jason shook his head and Erin wrote Ø *females.*

"Just two older brothers. I'm youngest."

She wrote *youngest.* "As you were growing up, how did you and your siblings handle stress?"

"Not sure I knew what stress was exactly, as a kid. But when things were bothering one of us, he'd act up until one or both of the others pounded him a bit. Then things got back to normal."

Erin winced. It sounded barbaric. "I suppose that's effective in a crude, wolf-pack kind of way. But it's not exactly textbook stress handling."

"Well, it wasn't so much fistfighting as it was tussling… or maybe smacking."

"Most seminars would suggest something more on the order of relaxation breathing, or even aromatherapy."

"You asked what we did."

"Right." She closed her eyes. "Jason, I've covered what I'm required to, but I don't feel like we've really scratched the surface. This may sound unusual, but I'd like to terminate the official part of this interview and ask you a couple of questions that might help you with coping — here and at home." She scooted her chair closer and lowered her voice. "You are not required to discuss any of the following, but I sense you keep your guard up so much that communication might be problematic for you." Erin watched his face for reaction. *None.* "Would you tell me about your current social life?"

Jason sighed. "You mean my girlfriend?"

"If you have one."

"Is this like talking to a priest or psychologist? I mean the privacy stuff."

"Confidentiality. Certainly. Nobody sees my detailed report. All I turn in to your company is a summary sheet indicating you attended, how much you participated in the process, and whether I believe you're using more or less healthy coping measures."

"Confidential."

She nodded.

****

Jason did not like the direction this interview was heading, though it was not because of the individual facing him. But suddenly he found himself spilling his guts, so to speak. "Well, things were great until the middle of last week."

"What happened then?"

"I was stressed about the next day's seminar. So this was Wednesday night. And we were... I mean, I was distracted or something... and, well, it wasn't exactly the best time we've ever been together."

Erin quickly grasped the picture. "Many men experience isolated instances of impotence."

Jason cringed at that word, but continued. "So, I figured when we got together Friday evening, after the seminar was over, that everything would be back to normal, but then *she* was all stressed out about her sister visiting who she can't get along with, and she wanted to yak about her work problems which I'm sick of hearing about, and I was late for the fantasy league draft meeting which I figured Roger would screw up my team which he did, and our fantasy league doesn't even have a commissioner yet and I don't want to get stuck with it again, and I knew we didn't have enough players for the tournament on Monday 'cause some of those guys don't give a crud, and I think my girlfriend's girlfriend has been following me which she has I've since learned."

It all flooded out like a Faulknerian sentence and he'd hardly taken a breath. Jason immediately realized he'd said too much, but it had seemed to spill like water from a knocked-over bucket. He needed to right that bucket and hold it steady.

"Wow." Erin's brain seemed to spasm as she tried to capture the totality of those revelations. "At least seven different issues — some of yours and some of your girlfriend's." Erin wrote *multi-probs.*

"Plus, I didn't get enough to eat at supper, Amanda and I didn't get to get together that night or since, and I've recently learned that yodeling makes me nauseous."

The yodeling was likely a puzzle, but Erin only wrote *girlfriend.*

"And on top of everything else, my best buddy is an alley cat who can't wait to tell me juicy stories about his numerous conquests."

"But you don't have to listen…"

Jason grimaced but didn't reply.

"…unless you actually like hearing your friend's juicy

stories."

He nodded, slowly and sheepishly.

"Pretty normal for a man." Erin wrote *juicy* and then tapped her tablet with the pen. "So how do you let off steam with a plateful of stressors like those?"

"Steam?"

"If a person doesn't have an outlet of some kind, he or she can simply explode with the unprocessed pressure. Your friend seems to let off his steam by conquering women — I suppose *different* women."

"I never thought of it as releasing pressure. I just thought he was horny and had the morals of a billy goat." Jason didn't like talking about Kevin's avocation. It was titillating, vicariously, to hear of such Don Juan escapades, but at heart Jason thought it was tacky.

****

Erin waited for an answer. Surely he had a stress outlet?

"Sports." Jason broke the silence. "Sports is how I let off steam."

"Well, that's a reasonably healthy way to cope with stress." Erin studied Jason's face. He seemed like a lost boy, though in a man-sized body, of course. She rather pitied his simplicity, though she also admired him for it. If she could be with a male this unsophisticated, Jason Stewart was the kind of unsophisticated man she'd want to be with. "Is, uh, Amanda the only girlfriend you've had?"

He shook his head. "I was engaged once, back in college. She was a year older and about to graduate. We were a few months away from the July wedding and she just called it quits."

Erin wrote *break-up*. "What was your reaction to her breaking off the engagement?"

Jason paused. "Honestly, after the surprise wore off, I mean... I think I was kind of relieved."

"Relieved?"

"Yeah. I'm not so sure I wanted to get married to begin with, not back then. I was just kind of carried along with the current. It seemed to be what she wanted and I wanted to make her happy."

Wonder how many marriages began in similar fashion. "Have you had other girlfriends since then?"

"Oh, I've dated a good bit, but I didn't really, uh, love any of them. Until Amanda."

Erin smiled. She loved knowing he was in love with someone. "So, you and Amanda probably *talk.*"

Jason's face blanked. "Talk?"

"Communicate."

"Well, I talk about sports stuff and my work gripes. She yaks about her work and her girlfriends... and weird neighbors."

Erin frowned. "But do you discuss things? You know, what's on your mind, what you're feeling, if you're troubled."

Jason began shaking his head, his expression still blank.

"For example, you said last Wednesday evening you had some anxiety and it made things hard, uh, I mean difficult... to, um, get together. Did you two discuss that? Did you explain you were apprehensive about the next day's seminar?"

"You mean out loud?"

Her eyes widened. "Of course, out loud. A straightforward discussion about things that are bothering you, or her, or even both of you. Communication."

"Well, I figured she'd just know I was nervous about the meetings."

He really is clueless. "Jason, without communicating even the most basic feelings or worries with your girlfriend — and vice versa — you two are setting up a likely disaster of confusion and misunderstanding. Why, the slightest thing might set off a chain of events that could throw each of you into irreconcilable positions."

Completely lost. And still blank.

Maybe an analogy would help. "Let's say you accidently dinged Amanda's car with your door when you parked too close. So, you come inside looking guilty, but you don't ever say anything. Then she wants to go out to eat, but you say, no, let's stay inside. You're thinking you don't want her to see that you dinged her car, but maybe she's thinking you're ashamed of her or don't love her anymore. You see how things can get crazy?"

"How bad did I ding her car?"

"Forget the ding!" Erin calmed the edge in her voice. "I'm saying anything that's on your mind, or whatever's bothering you, should be expressed to your girlfriend. Otherwise she'll pick up signals from your behavior and attach some other significance to it. Do you understand?"

"You're saying I should talk with her about stuff... all stuff."

Erin collapsed back in her chair. "Look, I have an article you need to read. It's about communication between couples. You're not married, but you're a couple in the sense of this article. I don't have a copy with me, but if I get it to you, will you read it? And do you promise to try to apply it to your relationship?"

"I'll look at it." Jason studied her. "Uh, Erin, why do you care? I mean, about whether Amanda and I communicate?"

She thought about how to respond. She could have told a personal anecdote about a man she'd thought she loved, but he wouldn't communicate. After a long pause she finally spoke. "Over time, if not dealt with appropriately when they're current, little disappointments can develop into bitterness, small disagreements can break out into open warfare, and tiny confusions can become horrendous misunderstandings." Erin searched his face to see how much registered. *Not very much.* "Couples who don't communicate with each other will usually go one of three ways. One, they'll find someone else with whom they *do* communicate. Two, they'll break up because there's not enough shared substance to hold them together. Three, they'll just tolerate each other and grow old and bitter as people cohabiting the same living space, but not actually sharing their lives."

Jason likely understood part of that. "But why do you *care*?" His repeated question sounded more plaintive than the words themselves might have conveyed.

She groaned. "It shouldn't have to happen that way, if people would just open up to each other and express their feelings and thoughts. It could clear up lots of confusion, lessen major misunderstandings, and possibly prevent catastrophes."

"But you seem to really care."

"I'd hate to see it happen to you, Jason."

"Why?"

Whack!

The sudden knock startled them and two sets of eyes zoomed to the opening door. Erin fidgeted with her skirt's hem and Jason blanched at the sight of Mrs. Grunion's grim face.

"I need Jason back on the phones," Grunion explained. "It's lunch time for one worker and another went home sick. Waited as long as I could… your interview's been nearly ninety minutes." She looked for Erin's signal that it was all right to reclaim her employee.

Erin nodded concurrence, first to Grunion and then to Jason.

Jason rose with a slight yelp and started to leave. Then he tore his two doodling pages from the notepad and crumpled them up. He waved haphazardly to Erin and tossed the wadded paper in the trash can before he left the room. Perfect shot.

Mrs. Grunion closed the conference room door and followed Jason closely.

Erin slid her bottom forward, leaned back in the chair again, and looked up at the ceiling. She'd like to have had more time with Jason because she thought he was salvageable. He basically seemed like a good, if somewhat ordinary, man who just didn't *get it* about open communication. It was probably quite frustrating for his girlfriend.

She just hoped she'd gotten through to him.

The trash. She walked over and retrieved three wads of paper from the otherwise empty can. One was somebody's shopping list, which she tossed again. Another was a page of her own handwriting — a few words to jog her memory when she'd written her analysis on the employee she'd met prior to Jason. No name or other identifying information, of course, but that individual had been a real basket case, a nervous breakdown or drug-alcohol abuser in the making. She re-crumpled that page, too, and tossed it back in the trash.

The third wad contained Jason's doodlings. Erin took them back to her seat and smoothed out the paper. *Typical.* "Towers. Guys always draw towers, trees, or mountains... or vehicles."

Erin remained at the conference table for about twenty minutes writing detailed notes based on the prompts she'd scratched onto her tablet. Then she read over the notes and made a few insertions. Finally she looked at her original page with eleven brief notations — most were only a single word. "Funny how a person's current life can be summed up with less than a dozen descriptors." She wadded up that page, tossed it — and Jason's doodlings — into the trash can, turned off the light, and exited the meeting room.

Chapter 28

After the closed door interview ended, Mabel Scott ducked into the conference room. None of the other sessions she'd heard about had lasted anywhere near as long as Jason's, and she'd quite purposefully cruised past the door several times, glancing through the window in passing, to monitor the meeting before it was abruptly halted. No broken furniture or any other clues of what they'd talked about.

Nothing on the white board. Nothing on the table but a few scattered notepads. *Notes*. Mabel scanned the floor around the table. Nothing. *Trash!* She checked the can near the door. *Bingo.*

Carefully monitoring the hall for traffic, Mabel retrieved four wads of paper from the can. First were two small pages with some drawings of a tall building. *Toss*. Second was a large page of words, which she counted — eleven terms:

> *observation*
> *resistant*
> *anxious*

> *superstitious*
> *Ø females*
> *youngest*
> *multi-probs*
> *girlfriend*
> *juicy*
> *sports*
> *break-up*

Mabel put that to one side. Third was the beginnings of a shopping list on a small page; somebody needed milk, bread, and eggs — big news. *Toss.* Fourth was another large sheet with eight phrases:

> *critical duties*
> *very jittery*
> *prob. unbalanced*
> *ill-suited for position*
> *fury just beneath surface*
> *danger to self/others*
> *off the wires*
> *high-risk*

Same handwriting as the first page.

Mabel scanned the first sheet again. Still didn't make much sense and the second page wasn't any clearer. But even though she couldn't understand them, Mabel instinctively knew they were important. She smoothed and carefully folded both pieces.

Not wanting to be seen carrying anything out of the conference room, she reached under the front of her skirt and tucked both sheets into the waistband of her panties. Nobody would find them there. *Nobody.*

Before returning to her desk, Mabel used her cell phone to call Sunny Cannon again. Three rings. "Sunny, it's Mabel.

Wait'll ya see what I got from Jason's lo-ong private conf'rence," she explained.

"Well, shoot a monkey," exclaimed Sunny.

****

At home in comfortable slippers during early afternoon, Christine put the phone beside her on the long couch. Sunny's call had come at just the right time. Not counting any updates today from her hired investigator, Christine's stealth team had already collected a wealth of direct observation, second hand reports, and circumstantial evidence. She'd spread all her notes across the custom mahogany dining table and savored them along with a cold diet cola.

Amanda... her friend, the hapless victim. Of course the poor girl was upset and suspicious, but not yet totally convinced of the crimes. She would be once she saw all this evidence.

It was time to repackage the overwhelming weight of this case and deliver it.

Once again, it was up to Christine to take charge. She'd schedule a strategy session with Maria and Sunny at Amanda's apartment.

She stood, placed both hands on the luxurious dining table, surveyed her case materials once again, and called Amanda. "I'm coming over after you get off work. Your place. Six o'clock." Christine ended the call before Amanda could say a word.

Some people called her bossy, but Christine didn't agree. "It's not bossy if you're helping someone who can't help themselves. Or won't."

****

Amanda hadn't been anywhere that day and hadn't even washed her hair. Nor did she after Christine's hurried call.

Visibly startled when the door opened, Christine peered into her face. "What have you been doing all day?"

"Worrying, snacking… crying. If I had any serious booze in the place, I probably would've been drinking, too."

"You need to get a grip, girl. We've nearly got this case settled."

Amanda stared. "It's your stinking case that's made me crazy. I actually told Louis I might murder someone if I came to work today."

"Huh?"

"Well, not those exact words. Not a direct threat to him… but he got the message."

"Amanda, you need to be careful what you say to that cretin. A transplanted New Yorker is liable to call you on it."

"I know. But I was about to lose it because he was acting like he's the one who determines whether an employee is fit for work or not. If that enormous, ignorant Yankee was in charge of work conditions, we'd all be chained to plank benches and rowing a galley ship."

Christine nodded solemnly — she'd worked three years at an insurance office before she married well.

"You know where I can get a doctor's excuse for being unable to work because my friends think my lover's playing around and they're driving me nuts, chasing him all over town?"

Without hesitation Christine replied, "It'd probably be easier to go with murder and get your excuse slip from the police department."

Amanda had hardly slumped to the small couch when the doorbell rang again. "Who the heck is that?"

"Should be Maria and Sunny."

"Who invited them?"

"I did." Christine nodded sagely. "You're not responsible for your own welfare at a time like this, so we're taking care of you."

"You're doing what?"

Christine opened the door, pulled Maria and Sunny inside, stood between them, and linked arms. "Amanda, meet your stealth team." They looked like three distaff musketeers.

"Hi, Amanda." Maria turned to Christine. "I don't want to be a *team*," she said as though she'd given it considerable thought. "Let's be the Stealth *League*."

Chapter 29

The Stealth League.

Christine rolled it around in her head for a moment and nodded. "I like its sound."

"Stealth?" Amanda made no attempt to disguise her skepticism. "You three noodle heads couldn't be discreet if it was a matter of life and death. Your notion of discretion is to blow up a billboard."

Though Maria looked disappointed, she didn't refute the statement.

Christine just shrugged.

Apparently Sunny got stuck on the imagery of noodle heads.

They settled around the living room, like spies in an old movie.

"New info." Christine nodded to Sunny. "You have the floor."

Ever the literalist, Sunny studied Amanda's linoleum flooring with a puzzled expression.

"Just tell her your updates." Christine waved toward the papers in Sunny's hand.

Sunny described the incident with the hoity toity woman demanding to see Jason at GCEC.

"Whoa." Amanda interrupted. "*Who* was demanding to see Jason?"

"Well, I didn't see her, but Mabel said she was bossy and witchy and dyed blonde, plus had a bit of a belly — which everybody figured that woman's a spurned lover and pregnant with Jason's baby."

"Pregnant? It's probably her own husband's baby." Amanda sputtered. "She's local?"

"Mabel said the assistant manager called her a Hoosier. The woman herself admitted being from Indiana." Such admissions were rare in central Tennessee. "She might also be on the run from law enforcement, because she wouldn't go to the courthouse."

"When was this?" Amanda landed in her rocker with too much impact and winced.

"Today sometime. I guess mid-morning. Why? Do you know any Hoosiers?"

Amanda moaned. "Just my sister Kaye. Nobody else could make that negative an impression in just a few minutes."

"Your sister's pregnant by Jason?" Sunny's enthusiasm for the case further neutralized her normally skewed perception.

"No! My sister's not pregnant by anybody. Kaye's in the middle of a divorce and she's started eating again. The first fifteen pounds always goes to her lower belly."

Maria shook her head. "On me it's the hips."

"Butt and boobs." Sunny pointed.

Christine resumed control. Someone had to. "Enough of this Diet Club meeting! How certain can you be that the woman causing that Gee-keck scene was your sister?"

"Well, it might not hold up in court, but Kaye made a big deal about seeing Jason's picture and finding out where he works. Plus, she said she was going to help me solve this case. Had to be Kaye. Who else?"

"How about a traveling skank from Indiana who's carrying Jason's love child?" Christine took pride in her way with words.

Amanda shook her head. "Absolutely not. We might have some evidence somewhere of something Jason's done wrong, but he didn't do this. That woman at Gee-keck had to be Kaye and Jason didn't have means, motive, or opportunity to get her pregnant. Toss that one out. No true bill." She made it sound like the final determination of the local grand jury.

"Okay, cross that one off, Sunny." Christine the moderator. "What about those notes your friend found?"

Amanda looked distinctly interested.

****

Sunny fought to restrain her smile as she unfolded the notes and carefully smoothed them out. Then she wiped her hands on her long, loose skirt. "Physical proof from the closed door session — you could dust it for prints."

"Not any more, you've just smushed them all around… not counting your Gee-keck friend's manhandling." Christine.

Better not mention that Mabel had carried them inside the top of her panties. "Anyway, my friend saw Jason in the conference room with that Alabama trainer lady and was able to swoop in and pull these notes from the trash almost immediately after they left."

"Sounds pretty airtight to me." Christine tucked her chin smugly. "Read them out to us, Sunny."

"Well, they don't read all that well. It's almost like a code or something."

"Oh, let me see one. Teachers are good at puzzles." Maria grabbed the page with eleven words. "Hmm. This is good, even well-organized. Her intro is the word *observation*, clearly setting the stage for her analysis that follows. The analysis itself seems to be, uh, three groups of three words each. The first grouping is *resistant, anxious,* and *superstitious*. Obviously she asked questions relating to his frame of mind and possibly his belief system."

Amanda interrupted. "Jason's not superstitious."

"Doesn't he wear the same shirt for every ball game?" Sunny feared she'd lost the gavel.

"It's a team shirt; they *have* to wear it for the games. What kinds of questions did the trainer ask these people?"

Sunny shrugged. "I dunno, but Mabel said the main point of the interview was helping them cope with stress in their jobs."

Christine waved her hand. *Whatever.* "Go ahead, Maria."

"The next group is Ø *females, youngest,* and *multi-probs.* This could go a lot of ways, but the most obvious is that Jason doesn't like women, prefers young boys, and he's got lots of problems." Maria squinted. "Unless that last word is *probe,* in which case, it's even kinkier than the first interpretation."

Amanda sputtered. "Jason's not gay! He loves women! In fact that's the stupid basis for all your amateur tiptoeing around. But he loves *me!*" She grabbed the page. That's not *probe* — it's clearly *probs* and yeah, Jason does have a lot of problems. Not the least of which is you three — and your other friends, whoever they are — all spying on him every time he belches. I happened to know that his job performance paperwork was partly hinging on this interview."

Christine retrieved the sheet away and handed it back to Maria. "That's a far cry from explaining Ø *females*." She nodded wisely. "Go ahead, Maria."

"Oh, this final grouping could also go different ways. It's

girlfriend, juicy, and *sports.* The most logical solution is even kinkier than multi-probe. I think this trainer discovered that Jason and his juicy girlfriends engage in kinky activity, known on the street as sports."

"That's outrageous! I'm his girlfriend! We don't do anything any kinkier than the next couple. And if this refers to Jason at all, it's perfectly clear that *sports* is sports. Which is just about all he does. Besides…"

****

Christine interrupted. "But what if that comment refers not to his *known* girlfriend, meaning you, but to one of his unknown bimbos? Maybe the one at a trashy truck stop east of here. Somebody needs to listen to my tape again. I think Jason used the word *juicy* to describe whoever was six miles out of town."

Christine reached for the page of eleven words, but Maria stopped her. "Wait, this last term is the conclusion to the entire interview. It helps explain the three groupings we just analyzed."

"What is it?" Amanda frowned.

"I'm sorry, Amanda. The final word is *break-up.*" Tears formed in Maria's eyes as Amanda's shoulders trembled with sobs. Sunny moved over and hugged her.

Christine took the sheet and read back over those words. She could have interpreted each of the groupings differently, but they still wouldn't have cleared Jason from much of anything. He was obviously guilty of something and the final term summarized everything.

Slowly, Amanda regained her composure. "I don't think any of that has anything to do with Jason except maybe *anxious* — anxious about the interview's effect on his raise and promotion possibilities — and *sports.* The rest could be about any employee at Gee-keck. We don't even know where those notes came from."

"Amanda, for the sake of argument, let's say you're right about *that* page. But this other one is even worse." Christine handed it to Maria. She took no pleasure in destroying Jason's image. But somebody had to protect naïve Amanda.

Maria read and gasped before slamming the sheet face-down.

"What does it say?" Amanda groaned.

"No need to analyze that one. It's clear enough already." Maria pushed it over with her fingertips.

"I'll tell you what it says." Sunny had read it twice at Wendy's with Mabel and three times since. "These eight phrases of the trainer's interview notes state very clearly that the employee in question is a dangerous lunatic practically on the verge of mass murder, probably in the Gee-keck workplace."

"Let me see that!" Amanda grabbed the page, flipped it over, read it, and resumed weeping.

All three friends tried to comfort her.

Finally, she wailed, "What the heck has Jason done? I can't believe I didn't have a clue — he seemed so ordinary."

Christine's smile was ever so slight, because *ordinary* had been her analysis of Jason all along.

Chapter 30

Leaving work just after six o'clock, Jason called Amanda's number. No answer. Not wanting to leave a reconciliation message on voicemail, he figured to try back later. Erin Chester had made her point: last night's refusal to explain his delay — because it sounded tawdry — could conceivably have caused Amanda to suspect even seedier reasons.

Jason couldn't have that. Life as a couple was difficult enough without problems based on misconceptions being manufactured out of thin air.

Following up on Erin's groundwork, he'd decided on a course of action which should clear up the entire matter, as far as he understood it. He would get Kevin to explain to Amanda that he'd caused Jason to be late for Monday's supper and he had involved Jason in the Sunday mall incident with Paula.

Once those two matters were resolved, things should be back to normal, except that Amanda's girlfriend had the hots for him. But they could deal with Christine's lust later. One crisis at a time. Jason vowed he'd diligently try to maintain open communication lines.

Unable to reach Amanda, he phoned Kevin's number. No answer there either, so he left voicemail. "Kev, it's Jason. Look, we've been talking about favors and even though you've never actually spit it out what the heck your favor is, consider it done, if it's in my authority to do so. I mean, I can't get you appointed the new ambassador to the Nation of Nubile Women or anything. Ha. Anyway, here's the deal. Now I really need a big favor from you, dude. I need you to clear up some stuff with Amanda..." Time ran out for the message recording. *Creepin' crud!*

Where would Kevin be at 6:45 on Tuesday evening? Happy hour at one of the hotels on Fourth Avenue. Where else? And he kept his phone either on silent ring or turned off completely while he was prowling. It could kill a closing if his phone went off at the crucial moment.

Jason really wanted to settle this quickly. So he'd just have to drive over to the hotel Kevin typically frequented and hope he could arrive before Kevin wrangled his score for the evening.

****

Following discreetly, Apprentice Investigator Cheney arrived at the Nashvillage moments after the surveillance target's dusty green truck rolled into the hotel parking garage.

Cheney wrote the place and time (7:25) on the ever-present notepad and then parked along the short strip of yellow curb at either end of the block directly opposite the Nashvillage. *Hope there aren't any eager beaver cops out writing tickets tonight, while real crimes are being committed within a stone's throw of this intersection.*

Cheney crossed the street, casually entering the hotel's lobby.

****

Kaye Moore-Smith was stepping out of the elevator at 7:30 when she saw Jason hustle into the lobby with a worried (and guilty) look. Maybe he was out of money and looking for the pimp again to beg for a shoddy freebie in some tacky broom closet.

She hung back to watch.

Despite her slight belly, Kaye knew herself to be an attractive woman. Even in a conservative silk blouse, dressy charcoal slacks and low heels, she drew a good bit of male attention. "A refined lady," she'd often told her sister, "will always catch the eye of a gentleman." (It had always sounded to Amanda like a line from Charlotte Brontë... or perhaps Tennessee Williams.)

A heavyset car salesman from Johnson City in East Tennessee approached — everything anyone needed to know about him was on his I.D. tag — and handed Kaye a drink.

"Thanks, uh, Or-ville." She'd made it sound like something to spit.

"Just saw you come down here and I noticed you didn't have anything to drink." Orville nodded as though it needed explanation. "Thought you might be thirsty."

Kaye took a sip, then wrinkled her nose. Should have known it would be boxed wine.

"It's hot in Nashville this time of year."

Kaye ignored Orville's weather observations and refocused on Jason, circulating in the main portion of the happy hour crowd.

"Uh, you want to go find a seat somewhere?"

The big guy hadn't yet caught on. Kaye turned and looked Orville up and down like he had overweight leprosy. "Do... you... mind?" She icily handed back the flimsy plastic cup.

****

Cheney watched Jason and the unidentified dyed blonde also clearly tailing him. It was the same woman who'd spoken with Kevin during the previous night's happy hour.

This Jason dude sure has a lot of women moving in and out of his perimeter.

The stalking blonde was not a professional — she darted around too much, dodging people who were standing, sitting, and milling about. So far she didn't seem to realize she was being monitored. Jason, however, kept looking over his shoulder like he was expecting it.

Hanging back and watching both, Cheney blended into the background with little movement and no intensive stares. The key was to be focused on the target(s) but aware of everybody else — not really looking into any of their faces, but rather scanning them like a computer imaging system.

Target movement! As Jason approached the column where the unidentified stalker leaned, suddenly a tallish, handsome woman with very nice legs appeared from nowhere and grabbed his elbow. Looked like a dressed-up version of the woman in white shorts from Jason's tournament.

Was there no end to the number of women touching this man? Cheney's eyes widened. Yet another unidentified woman in Jason's immediate orbit!

Chapter 31

At the clutch on his elbow, Jason jumped like he'd been goosed with a cattle prod. "Uh, h-hi, Miss Chester."

"Erin, remember?"

Jason glanced around the crowded lobby with an unspoken question.

"Oh, I'm staying here at the Nashvillage while we're in town. Dexter and me both. Different suites, of course." Her manicured fingertips pointed in opposite directions. "It's lovely of this hotel to provide free beverages and a place to unwind."

"Yeah, I guess. Well, I can't rewind right now."

"Is your girlfriend here with you?" Erin looked both ways.

Jason probably looked as guilty as he felt. "No, I'm trying to get over to Amanda's place later, but right now I'm looking for somebody."

"Lots of *somebodies* here tonight. This place is filling up."

"No, somebody in particular."

"Describe. Maybe I've seen your prey." Erin smiled.

"It's just Kevin from work. Kevin had the trainer with buck teeth."

"Dexter." Erin spoke her partner's name as though the very syllables caused irritation. "Oh, yes, the Kevin who cruises happy hours and gratifies lonely women temporarily out of their own element. I'd like to meet your Don Juan buddy."

I should've never told her about Kevin. "Well, I need him first. But after I get through with him, he's all yours."

"Get through with him?"

"Uh… well, I need him for my girlfriend."

Erin's eyebrows arched. "Interesting." She likely pictured something three ways or other kinkiness.

"No, that came out wrong." Jason rose on his toes to survey the crowded, noisy room. Still no Kevin.

Erin had that thoughtful, optimistic expression suggesting she'd identified a teachable moment and still wanted to help, if she could. "Maybe we should sit for a moment and talk about this *situation*. Might help me understand some of the gaps in our interview this morning."

Jason studied her compassionate face. Even though he was distracted by his search for Kevin, he sensed Erin truly wanted to help. He wasn't certain what she thought she could assist *with*, but she seemed sincere. Unfortunately, his radar wasn't very discerning that evening — too many blips and echoes… and phantoms. Simply too much interference. "How long would it take to finish the interview? Fill in your gaps and whatever?"

Erin smiled. "I shouldn't think it would be more than a few minutes if we could find someplace quiet." She peered over her shoulder toward the elevator.

"Oh, you mean here? Tonight? Uh, I thought…"

"I've had all kinds of trouble meeting with you at work. And when I finally did corral you the other day, we had to end before we covered everything. Plus, I have that article to give you. Besides, my co-op contract ends today and tomorrow I'm officially on vacation time. Fate must have brought you here this evening so we could finish up."

Without speaking, Jason found himself being steered toward the elevator.

— —

From her stakeout column, Kaye watched with eyes wide, mouth open, and brain reeling. "He just walked in a couple of minutes ago and he's already going upstairs with a convention camp follower." She hadn't been close enough to eavesdrop, but that aggressive female had *fondled* Jason's arm. And she'd practically dragged him toward the elevator!

Kaye had trained herself to recognize and read women's faces because they were either customer or competition... or enemy. "This bimbo is not here selling copiers."

— —

Also too far away to overhear, Cheney now monitored *three* targets: Jason, the leggy woman clutching his arm, and the wide-eyed dyed blonde who watched them both.

If anyone split off Cheney would, of course, stay on Jason's tail, but it would be vital to keep tabs on all three if possible. Whatever was going on, Jason and Legs were oblivious to the blonde hanging on their every movement.

— —

As he allowed himself to be steered into the elevator, Jason had the brief insight that he was too easily maneuvered by women with attractive legs. Somewhere deep inside, some tiny reservoir of intelligent instinct told him this was the wrong meeting at the wrong place at the wrong time with the wrong person. But when a compassionate woman pulls your arm toward the elevator and you've just had a stupid fight with your girlfriend, you're in an unnaturally weakened condition. On a basketball court, Jason could plant his feet and withstand an oncoming charge from a power forward. But with the gentle-but-firm tug by manicured fingertips on his elbow, he could also be led toward who-knew-what and here-goes-nothing.

— —

Still following, Kaye tried to be discreet, but worried she'd lose them. In her haste, she found herself again headed straight toward Orville, who was already sweating profusely despite the air conditioning.

Orville plastered a surprised, porkish grin on his expansive face and made an unsuccessful effort to suck in his belly.

Kaye very nearly stepped on his fleshy foot as she raced past with absolutely no eye contact.

The staircase. She'd take the stairs and catch this illicit pair for Amanda.

— —

As the unidentified blonde nearly crashed into a large bystander, Cheney approached the front desk. "My friend who just walked by with that gentleman... remind me what room she's in."

The thin young clerk started shaking his head.

Cheney's hand slid back, revealing half of a ten dollar bill.

"Purple business suit and legs to die for?"

Cheney nodded and revealed more of the bill.

The clerk tapped the bill once.

Cheney slid another ten on top but kept finger pressure on both.

"That's Miz Chester, some kinda consultant, from Birmingham, I think. Working over in Greene County this whole week, not sure where. Pretty high maintenance, but she's got a nice disposition. Everybody on staff knows her."

"As I do, but I've forgotten her room number."

The clerk tapped the bills again.

Cheney added a third ten, but then began sliding all three

bills backward.

The clerk's hand was swift. "Your friend's still in Suite 686, as I'm sure you recall now."

"Of course… 686. Momentary lapse." Cheney released the currency and the clerk pocketed it quickly. "Thanks for jogging my memory."

The clerk looked around furtively and cleared his slender throat. When the phone suddenly rang, he jumped a few feet.

— —

After watching Jason and the leggy woman enter the elevator together, Kaye raced up the nearby stairs and listened on every floor for that loud-but-flat elevator ding. Finally, on the fifth floor, she heard it and sagged against the wall, completely out of breath. Racing up stairs was not among her usual activities.

She waited in the stairwell until the uncareful footsteps receded. About midway down the hall, an elbow smacked the wall and a female giggled. A male shushed loudly, bringing on even more laughter from both. *A few too many at happy hour.* After several mirthful attempts, one of the parties was able to unlock the door and they finally entered their trysting room. Kaye couldn't peek around the corner into the hallway without being seen, so she waited for the final loud clack of the heavy door.

Then she scurried down the hall and listened at every door on both sides of the wide hallway. She heard voices in 537 and exhaled, pressing her ear to the door.

The latch suddenly opened and she staggered. Her heart leapt into her throat and danced a jig there. *Please don't let me tumble into a naked body.*

Before she could concoct a reason for being that close to their entrance, a hairy male hand reached around the partly-open door and placed a Do Not Disturb sign over the lever handle. Then the door shut again with the same loud clack.

They had not seen her!

Of course, she hadn't seen them either, except for what was obviously Jason's hand. Her heart still pounding, Kaye listened through the door of Room 537 for fifteen minutes. She took notes on everything she heard... plus a few sweaty details supplied by her own imagination.

Chapter 32

Up one floor in 686, Erin tried to settle Jason on the small couch in her spacious suite as she situated a writing tablet and pen. When she crossed her legs, her purple linen skirt rode up and showed several inches of her thighs, encased in black hosiery. Jason's gaze fastened on them and didn't budge. *Nice to know my dedicated elliptical workouts are paying off but Jason needs to focus on his girlfriend.* She tugged on her skirt and placed the tablet on her lap.

"Now, before we were interrupted today, we were talking about how small things, when not explained properly, can sometimes seem like large matters to the other half of a couple. And I was urging you to make substantial efforts to be proactive."

"And right before Grunion busted in, I was asking why you cared one way or the other."

Hoped he would have forgotten that part. "Correct, that was one of the questions on the table." Erin rolled the top of her pen against her bottom lip. "Suffice it to say that I've seen relationships founder because one of the partners — usually the man, it's true — refuses to communicate." Hopefully that would satisfy his question. "And tonight, when I encountered you downstairs, you again gave me the kind of non-informative, minimal response that I assume you also use with your girlfriend. If so, I worry that just about anything you do could be misconstrued."

"What did I say?"

"I don't recall your exact words, but it was something about looking for Kevin, and that you needed Kevin to do something with Amanda... and it sounded awfully suspicious."

"Well, I just need him to clarify a couple of things — one, that I was late because of Kevin and the other, that somehow Amanda found out about even though I can't figure out how because I don't remember meeting anybody at the mall but we fought about it, I guess it was a fight, because she seemed to be really ticked but I couldn't figure out why and I was feeling guilty because I figure somehow I'm to blame when she's mad and when she asked me to explain both of those things, plus whatever was her beef with the grocery store, I didn't seem to be able to spit out anything that sounded reasonable." He finally inhaled.

Another exhausting Faulknerian sentence. "Well, what you just said — while confusing — did actually go a long way toward explaining things. At least to the point that there were reasons for whatever happened at the mall and for you being late on the other occasion. I'm afraid I don't comprehend the grocery issue. Whether your girlfriend accepts your reasons is another matter. But, Jason, you have to give her the opportunity." She looked into his anxious eyes. "Apparently you freeze up and don't tell her anything. Right?"

Jason slowly nodded. "Some of the stuff that happens to me is unbelievable. So I figure if I tell the truth, it'll sound like

I'm lying. I don't want her to think I'm lying to her."

"So you'd rather say nothing and let her suspect the worst?"

"Well, I don't have any way of guessing what she'd suspect."

Erin closed her eyes. "But what about her concern over something or other at the mall?"

"I'm still trying to figure that out. I mean, I do go to the mall every now and then, but it's more to grab a bite than to shop or whatever. And I don't go there with other women anyhow. I did run over there Sunday evening, but that was to meet Kevin. I didn't get the feeling Amanda was asking about that in particular, but it's the only mall event I can remember."

"And you have no idea about the grocery reference either?"

Jason strained his memory so hard, it looked like sweat beads might appear on his forehead. "Nada. I go to the store when I need stuff. Mostly it's snacks and beer, because I really don't cook."

I can well imagine. "So your girlfriend provided no tangible clues?"

"All she said was that groping and fondling were supposedly involved."

"Well, did you engage in either?"

"I sometimes squeeze chips to be sure the bags are airtight — you know, no holes — because I don't like them stale." Jason's brow wrinkled. "But I've never known Amanda to get upset over that."

"Hmm. The normal context for groping or fondling would tend to involve people rather than chips." *Amazing that distinction needs explanation.* "But you don't recall any encounters where your hands made contact with human bodies?"

"Nothing except what you saw during the tournament.

You know, high fives and butt slaps. Shoulder whacks. The usual."

"But not at the mall or at the grocery?" *Trying my best to get to the bottom of things.* "And Amanda wasn't at any of the games yesterday, was she?"

Jason frowned as he shook his head.

Eureka! "It seems to me that your girlfriend suspects you of, uh, misbehavior... and it sounds like she — possibly with help from a friend — is looking for your confederate."

Jason shook his head. "Not likely, because *her* confederate acts like she's hot for me."

"Oh? Can we explore that tangent?"

"Couldn't possibly explain it. Even Kevin thinks I'm crazy." He studied Erin. "You ever hear of something called a seven-month itch?"

As her eyebrows drew together, Erin scooted closer to her perplexing subject. *This could be interesting.* "Where did you hear that term?"

****

Without any attempt to be discreet, Jason looked at his watch — eight o'clock — and started to rise. *I really need to intercept Kevin and get over to Amanda's.*

But Erin motioned for him to keep his seat. "Look, I understand you're in a hurry. But what you're still missing is that this shouldn't involve your friend at all. If you and Amanda have some misunderstanding, you should just speak with her about it, privately and directly. Clear the air."

"What if she thinks I'm lying?"

"Stay with the truth, no matter how fantastic it sounds. Surely all your circumstances can't be so unbelievable."

"You want to bet?" He sighed. "The deal I just mentioned, at the mall on Sunday, was Kevin wanting me to meet his one-night stand before she left town. No, wait, I think she was a two-nighter."

"Why would he want you to meet her?"

"See? It's not believable, is it?"

"No." She'd have to reconsider. "I mean, if it's the truth, you should stick with it. But did Kevin explain why?"

"Because Paula was smart and Kevin thought I was looking down on his conquests because I supposedly thought they were all empty-headed. But I didn't think about their intellect at all, except maybe to question their judgment." *How to clarify?* "You know, traveling to Nashville for a meeting and hopping into bed with a lounge lizard like Kevin."

"Well, do you look down on Kevin's conquests?"

It was difficult to express, especially to a woman. "I wish he wasn't doing all that running around. It's tacky and it's dangerous — you know, health issues for one thing — and I worry that some of these women go home confused and possibly hurt."

Erin's eyes were misty. "Jason, have you ever told that to Amanda?"

"No, of course not."

"Why not?"

"It sounds all gushy-mushy."

"And that's exactly what Amanda needs to hear from you — word for word, like you just explained it to me. Tell her why you went to the mall Sunday evening, why you were late Monday evening, and then explain how you feel about what Kevin does."

"I can't."

"Why not?"

"When I try to explain serious stuff, it all tumbles out and everything jumps everywhere and some of it probably doesn't even make sense, and when I start talking like that I sound like some accused murderer on a Perry Mason movie after all the evidence proves what a scumbag he is and he tries to justify why he did what he did, but Perry doesn't buy it and Della Street sits there with her sexy legs crossed and looks like she wishes the case would be over pretty quick so she could coo at Perry for a while." He took a breath.

"Well, I do understand what you mean about rambling a bit. That's probably just nerves. But here's the heart of it — if Amanda cares about you, she'll be willing to wade through those long soliloquies and parse out the nuggets. I think I'm already starting to get the hang of it and I've only known you for a few hours." Erin smiled.

****

Cheney waited for the elevator and rode it to the sixth floor. Quick stop at the vending area to pick up a spare ice bucket. One thing apprentices learn quickly is that investigators like to have something contextual in their hands. In an office building it might be a clipboard. When loitering in a hotel hallway for who knows how long, an ice bucket makes a great prop.

Jason and Legs had been in Suite 686 for about four minutes when Cheney began prowling back and forth past the doorway, not veering more than a few feet to either side. When listening through a door, one doesn't want to be stationary if anybody suddenly appears, so a good investigator keeps moving — albeit slowly — and not very far.

Cheney had not heard much from inside the room even when the patrol pattern had an investigatory ear near the door. Whatever they were doing in there was not very noisy. From bits and pieces of the audible dialog, it sounded like they were role-playing. *But playing which roles?*

Chapter 33

Twenty minutes after entering Suite 686, Jason left with a "couples and communication" article in hand.

Feeling guilty for leaving a woman's hotel room at 8:20 on a Tuesday night, he hoped nobody spotted him besides that person walking in the other direction with an ice bucket. *Imagine how it would look to Amanda!* If the story broke, she'd scream "Liar!" and stab him with a sharpened comb or something.

As the elevator descended, Jason took stock.

The interview was over, the consultants were out of the picture, and his GCEC status was stable again. He'd finally paid back Kevin's $75, even though it had caused a big brouhaha with Amanda. He had lobbied some of the fantasy league players to apply pressure and convince Roger to serve as commissioner. So really, the only stress remaining in Jason-World was Amanda acting weird and Christine having the hots for him. No printed article could possibly help with those problems.

Four photocopied pages. He scanned them quickly. The key words were straight off the covers of *Cosmo* and other chick mags: *open, honest, truth, blah, blah, blah.* "Women want to hear what they expect to hear. Women don't want the truth. They can't handle the truth." Paraphrasing an iconic movie character. Good thing nobody else was in the elevator.

— —

The moment Jason entered the elevator, Cheney dropped the empty ice bucket and raced down the stairs to the lobby.

Arriving out of breath just outside the elevator a moment before it opened, Cheney re-acquired the target. For a moment it sounded like Jason was speaking with actor Jack Nicholson. *Nah.* Nobody else on board.

— —

When Jason reached the lobby, it was likely already too late to catch up with Kevin. But he spent a few minutes looking around anyway. *No dice.*

He threw the trainer's useless article in the trash. At 8:30, Jason exited the hotel and walked next door to the parking garage.

— —

Cheney caught the target tossing something into the trash. *Interesting.* Monitoring the bin with one eye, the detective watched as Jason circulated among the thinning crowd in the lobby. After about ten minutes of peering around — looking for someone? — the target left.

With a smooth, discreet motion, the apprentice investigator retrieved the discarded article and then followed Jason from the hotel.

Sitting in the beige Bronco waiting on Jason to leave the garage, Cheney bagged the article without even examining it.

— —

Outside Room 537, Kaye had the seven-*minute* itch, eager to tell her news to Amanda.

She eavesdropped until her feet ached and her neck broke into a sweat. Hearing the muted sounds of love-making through a hotel door was a lot edgier than most of her prior vicarious experiences.

When she could hear no more activity from inside the room, Kaye took the elevator up to her room on the eighth floor.

She could barely wait to give Amanda the lowdown on that scumbag cheater Jason. But a thirty minute drive to Verdeville, deliver the emotional news, then drive a half hour back — no, she was too exhausted. And she was too wired with adrenalin to make much sense on the phone. It would have to be tomorrow.

Right now she needed a drink. Happy hour was over, but maybe the hotel bar would send something up.

— —

Glad to be free of Erin but bummed at not finding Kevin, Jason exited the hotel's parking garage. "No point in trying to explain things to Amanda... again." *Audible. Not good.* He vowed to keep the rest of his reasoning inside his head. Jason drove straight home, but it took longer since his mind wandered and he tended to ease up on the accelerator when he wasn't concentrating.

Every time he tried to explain things, it seemed only to make them worse. Surely the testimony of an objective third party would bring about some resolution.

"Or maybe not." *Audible again.* "Shoot."

Knowing Kevin's wayward reputation, Amanda might not believe anything he said anyway. *Consider the source.* Maybe not finding Kevin had turned out for the better.

But entering his apartment, he remembered something which had bugged him since the weekend. Some of his belongings were missing and others — including several issues of Playboy — were out of place. He couldn't blame the cleaning lady because there wasn't one.

About a week ago, a strange tube of ChapStick had showed up in his hall bath, but then it disappeared. And weirdest of all, his cherries! Missing from the fridge. Completely gone. Somebody'd stolen Jason's cherries. He felt... what was the word? Violated!

Chapter 34

Wednesday, May 27

Heart in her throat, Amanda strode into the office of her Yankee supervisor. "Dock me!"

"What?" Louis had just staggered in and collapsed into his enormous chair.

She handed him the note she'd written a moment before. The only strategy she could think of to foil King Louie and his bullying. *Maybe.* Some time ago, she'd heard the expression — from a noted statesman, a successful military leader, or possible an NFL coach — "the best defense is a strong offense." It had never made much sense to her before.

He squinted and read the note out loud: "Formally request dock time for unauthorized absence on Tuesday, May 26th. Amanda Moore." He sputtered and dropped the page like it was contaminated.

As she'd intended, her aggressive move had upset his momentum. Usually Louis mounted the attack, waddling into her office and badgering her. Now what could he do, besides sputter? Amanda wanted to smile.

She didn't. "I believe that takes care of things, according to the county-city H.R. manual, anyway."

"Well, uh…"

"Of course, I also intend to file a grievance with H.R. to the effect that the practices of the male supervisor in this division are discriminatory and hostile toward female employees."

"Wha…?" Louis hurriedly read the note again. "But you're *asking* to be docked."

"Only because of the harassment I endured yesterday."

"But you acted like you were just in a bad mood or something."

Fortunately he'd forgotten the part where she'd mentioned possibly committing murder. "When I told you I couldn't work, it was your obligation to take my word for it. I've earned that respect. When you didn't and, instead, continued to probe, it created a hostile work environment."

"Because you didn't feel like coming in?"

Amanda rarely played this card at all and had never used it with respect to work. But today she needed a trump. "Cramps."

That was one place even Louis dared not go. It was, in this instance, a fabrication. But let King Louie insist on a doctor's excuse for menstruation — the female members of the County-City Council would nail his hide to the courthouse door!

More sputtering.

Amanda almost felt sorry for him. Well, not really — it honestly felt great to have Louis on defense for a change. She left him staring at the note.

An hour later, Louis tip-toed to Amanda's office. Didn't knock — he never did — but he did pause in her doorway until she acknowledged him. That was a first. Then he came in and thumped his butt into her visitor's chair.

Unlike most of his impromptu visits to her office, he actually got to the point. "Uh, the main thing I needed to discuss with you yesterday was about that grant for the sandbags. We still don't have any evaluation in place and it's required for the second federal fiscal quarter."

Amanda nodded. She already knew that.

No barked-out instructions, no extra-threatening bluster. None of the typical bullying obnoxiousness in his voice or manner. He just sat there civilly with nothing more to say.

"As a matter of fact, I think I've developed a solution to that problem." She paused for effect. "Did you happen to ask Harry why his unit hadn't evaluated the efficacy of the sandbag distribution system?"

"Uh, no. I just rattled his cage."

"Well, if you had asked him why, maybe we could have avoided this unpleasantness." Her finger tapped the top of her portfolio, not yet open. It held the tablet with notes from her phone conversation with "Harry" Harrison yesterday.

Louis stared at it with something approaching amazement. Over the course of their years working together, plans, projects, solutions, and other miracles had emerged from Amanda's leather portfolio. Judging from the awed expression on his face, King Louie wondered why his own office supplies were not that clever.

Now that she had his attention...

"The reason Public Works has not conducted an evaluation is because there's been no need yet for the sandbags and nobody could figure how to assess their distribution without actually handing them out."

Louis nodded, but surprisingly did not interrupt.

"It's still rough, but after I spoke with Harry, I cobbled together a plan. Public Works will have one crunch day of PSAs, advertising free Titans T-shirts."

"T-shirts?"

"Sure. People eat up free Titans stuff. I called the County Fair commissioner to see if he'd donate those thousand T-shirts he'd printed up when he gambled the Titans would win their division last season."

"Uh, they didn't even get a wild card berth."

"Correct. Which makes these even more rare — it commemorates the championship the home team didn't win."

When Louis shook his head, the folds of fat jiggled under his chin.

Amanda held up her hand. "It's win-win. The commissioner unloads the T-shirts — at a loss, but he can write it off his taxes. One thousand citizens get a free Titans shirt. Public Works gets to test both the distribution system and traffic flow at the sandbag distribution site as well as the effectiveness of getting the word out through radio spots and TV crawlers."

Louis stared again at the leather portfolio, his eyebrows rising. He seemed additionally impressed that *it* had been so inventive.

It still rankled Amanda that Louis had approved grant funds to purchase 48,000 pre-filled sandbags. Rainfall had been near record lows for the past two years and the Cumberland River — which formed the northern border of Greene County — had not been a threat to crest its banks since a flood control project in the early 1960s.

"Anyway, that's the mechanism, but we still need assessment. I'm pretty sure Harry can get a neighboring Public Works department to act as the objective judge-evaluator. One of the counties on the north bank of the Cumberland would have a vested interest, because it could conceivably help them down the line, if the river ever does reach flood stage again."

Louis struggled from the chair. As usual, he did not thank her for producing a viable solution. Slowly he tore Amanda's "dock me" note in half and slid it onto her desk. "We don't need to bother Payroll with this, uh, misunderstanding." As he paused, the third fold of his chin twitched slightly. "Or bother H.R. with that other thing."

When an obese man over six feet tall waddles away, his head down, it makes one want to look at something else. Anything else.

Chapter 35

It was midmorning when Jason spotted Kevin leaving the GCEC break room. "Kev, I searched all over for you last night at the Nashvillage. Didn't you get my voicemail?"

Kevin gave him a look. "I don't keep my phone on... thought you knew that."

"Yeah, yeah. So where were you last night, anyway?"

"Two hotels over. Decided to spread the Kevin-wealth around a bit more." He checked over his shoulder, probably out of habit. "So how come you were looking for me?"

"I wanted to get you to come with me to Amanda's to explain about Sunday at the mall and that I was late picking her up Monday evening because I had to run some cash over to you at the hotel."

Kevin frowned. "Yeah... some help, buddy. Once she had that winning bet money in her hand, she took off."

"So the girl you thought you were playing was actually playing you. Ironic."

"Huh?" Kevin didn't get irony, but he did watch Jason's

shallow breathing. "You still hurting? I heard about your injury. Something about running into a truck after you left third base."

"Very funny. I'm laughing so hard it hurts." Jason flattened against the wall to let a secretary walk by. "So how about this evening? Can you come with me to Amanda's?"

"Sorry, prime hunting tonight."

Great buddy. "You mean you won't break off long enough to ride with me to Amanda's so you can explain how come her source spotted me with your bimbo?"

"Amoretto's not a bimbo, she's smart." When Kevin paused, the other part registered. "Spotted? Amanda's following you?"

"Not Amanda herself. Some unnamed source. But, yeah, they're following me."

Kevin shook his head sadly. "Dude, you're toast. This thing with Amanda is all over except for rolling the credits. Once they start the following crud, the we-and-us part has completely ended and it's all about you-versus-them."

"And their posse of buddies and anonymous sources."

"Jase, I can't believe you let Amanda follow you."

"Didn't *let* her. I didn't even know anything about it until Monday night."

The same secretary walked back through the hallway and Kevin intently watched her derrière as she passed. She exaggerated the sashaying motion until she rounded the corner. "When did all this following start?"

Jason sighed and it hurt. His friend had a one-track mind that never switched to the siding. "Not certain. I thought things were going pretty good... you know, since the Halloween party. But Amanda's things are suddenly in a tailspin and somehow I'm the one going down in flames."

"So one day everything's fine with you and Amanda. Next day, sister's in town and you're in the doghouse... with people following you."

"I think that covers it." Jason shrugged. "Complete mystery."

"You'd mentioned before the business about Christine acting funny. You think that cougar has set all this up just so she can jump your bones?"

Jason scrunched up his face as he thought. "She's certainly capable of underhanded stuff, but she wouldn't do that to Amanda. Christine seems to resent me, maybe always has."

"Whoa. A few days ago your story was that Christine has the hots for you. Now she resents you. Which is it?"

"I don't know. Either, neither. Both. Christine's been acting extra screwy lately, and I think you know her regular screwiness is wild enough." Jason sighed so heavily that it seemed he might sink to the floor of the GCEC hallway. "I get the sense she thinks I'm a barrier between her and Amanda."

"That's bizarre. A girl needs her buddies, but girls also need guys."

"And guys need girls. But I'm in the doghouse and don't even know why. Except some baloney about a seven-month itch."

Kevin clutched his friend's elbow. "Wait, you didn't mention that before. What's with the itch stuff?"

"Seven months. Amanda's got herself convinced that after that many months together, I'd have an itch to nail some other woman. I never heard of it 'til our argument Monday night." Jason scratched an itch at his temple. "Erin wonders if Amanda and her buddies might be looking for the woman supposedly scratching my itch."

"Why didn't you say that to start with? This explains everything!" Kevin poked a finger into Jason's bruised ribs. "So who've you been scratching with? Erin the leggy trainer?"

"Ow!"

"Sorry… forgot." Kevin paused. "Hey, did I tell you there was a hooker asking about you at the hotel the other night?"

"Hooker? Asking about *me*?"

"Yeah. Dyed blonde. Kinda cute, but needed a girdle or something. Had a Yankee accent."

"When?"

"Right after you dropped off my money and skedaddled. She came straight over and started asking questions about you."

"Why would a hooker consult you about me?"

"My very question. Maybe she's willing to scratch your itch — for a price."

Jason moaned. "I'm not scratching anything with anybody. But Amanda's evidently determined there has to be some itch."

"Sounds like the only person itching is Amanda. Maybe *she's* got the itch after seven months and she's projecting that onto you." He sounded like a would-be therapist killing time in the neighborhood bar. Still, it was pretty deep, for Kevin.

"Maybe so. Sure can't think of anything else."

They'd been in the hallway so long that Werner, the front section manager, peered around the corner and gave them the thumb signal umpires use to call a man out at home plate.

Kevin ignored Werner. "Have you considered it might be time to dump Amanda?"

"No!" Jason had started returning to his workstation, but stopped short. "Why would you even say that?"

"All this hassle. Couldn't possibly be worth it."

"But… I love her."

Chapter 36

Kaye slid into the seat across from Amanda in the mall's busy food court, their trays bumping. She'd gotten three different dipping sauces with her chicken nuggets. Hopefully one of them would be tolerable.

Amanda poked at her pizza slice and took a sip of diet cola. "I thought you'd headed home yesterday. Why'd you stay over?"

"Well, not to see the sights in Verdeville, that's for sure. They're not worth a day of vacation time." In a rare moment of clarity, Kaye realized that was a cutting remark. "Uh, sorry." Even rarer, she apologized. "Okay, I stayed over because I saw your Jason the other night."

"Yeah, you already told me, hooker in the hotel on Monday." Amanda sighed. "How low can he go?"

Kaye cleared her throat and waited.

"Don't tell me you saw him again?" Amanda clutched her sibling's wrist.

She nodded.

"Where?" Astonishment. "When?"

"Last night, in the hotel lobby again."

"Another hooker on Tuesday?" Too loud. People munching on greasy burgers at a nearby table looked their way and muttered as they dabbed mustard-blotched napkins to their mouths.

Kaye held up her hand. *Gospel.*

"Another cash transaction right there in the middle of happy hour?"

"I didn't see the money this time. Don't know where the pimp was. Probably another hotel. Pimps have to circulate, you know, to keep their stable of girls in line." Kaye nodded with assurance.

A sudden mask of cosmic exhaustion formed on Amanda's face. "So what was Jason doing this time? Robbing the main desk for hooker money?"

"When I first saw him, he was obviously looking for someone. Next thing I know, that someone found him."

"Please let it be his grandmother."

"Only if she has beautiful legs and a purple business suit. Which, by the way, she wears the wrong heels with that skirt."

Amanda silently stared at the cooling cheese of her pizza as though it might hold some answers. "What... hap... pened?"

Kaye looked around to be certain the burger people were otherwise engaged. "She came up on his blind side and clutched his arm, and he jumped nine feet in the air. Then she steered him to the elevator and they went UPPP-staaiirrrs."

Amanda straightened and gripped the edge of the stained table. "And..."

"I raced the elevator upstairs. Nearly killed myself but I got to the fifth floor the very second the elevator clanged. The doors opened and two people got off, laughing."

"Wait, which two people?"

"Well, it had to be Jason and the tall woman with nice

legs and wrong shoes."

"You didn't see them?"

"I watched them get on the elevator, first floor, but I only heard them get off on the fifth." Kaye gave her younger sister a look. "It's not like *Star Trek*. They don't step in the transporter room and get vaporized to another location."

"Okay, okay. You heard them get off. Where were you?"

"Hiding in the stairwell, of course. If they saw me, the jig would be up and they'd pretend they were just picking up her purse or something."

Amanda rolled her hand. *Continue.*

"After I heard their door close, I checked all the rooms until I heard their voices and laughter again. Room 537." Kaye lowered her voice to a whisper. "And I nearly got caught listening."

"What do you mean?"

"My ear's to the door and suddenly it opens!" Kaye put a hand her throat. "If he had opened it just a few more inches, he would've seen me."

"Who?"

"Jason, of course! The guy who got off the elevator with the tall floozy." Kaye patted her heart dramatically. "But all he did was hook his hand around the door and put a Do Not Disturb sign on the outside knob."

"You saw his hand."

Kaye nodded.

"What did it look like? Jason has distinctive hands."

"I don't know! It was a *guy* hand. I didn't take his fingerprints!" She shook her head. "I was about to have a heart attack because if he'd opened the door any wider, I would've fallen into the room." Kaye wiped the chicken grease off her fingers.

Amanda twice banged her head on the table, barely missing the pizza. The burger people looked alarmed and abandoned their table.

"I'm sorry, Amanda. I'm sure there are better ways for you to learn all this distressing news, but I don't know what it is." *Finding strange panties in your husband's glove compartment certainly wasn't any easier.*

Amanda merely moaned.

As her younger sister's head rested on the table near the pizza, Kaye related everything she'd overheard on the fifth floor. She halfway hoped Amanda would ask a few questions because it would be rather edgy to elaborate on certain portions of the account.

But Amanda had obviously heard enough; no need to hash it over.

In the distance, the burger people were talking to a food court vendor and pointing toward the table where Kaye and Amanda sat.

Kaye polished off her chicken nuggets and entertained a possible nibble of Amanda's cooled pizza... but she refrained. *You don't swipe pizza from a scorned sibling.* "Room 537." She thought that a fitting coda.

A smudge of pizza sauce adorned Amanda's forehead. "Why didn't you tell me last night what you'd seen and heard?"

"I'd been on my feet all day in meetings and exhibits and demos; it was late. Didn't feel like an hour or more on the dark highway. Too wired up to tell it calmly on the phone. Besides, it's more believable in person. So I just drank a few Manhattans and went to bed." Better not mention her earlier break from the conference to drive to Verdeville for the unfortunate business at GCEC. She handed her scorned sister a napkin and pointed to the pizza sauce.

****

Amanda dabbed absent-mindedly at her forehead. "What next? What the hairy hell is next?"

Kaye shrugged. She'd delivered her bad news — with relish. She collected her purse and keys.

"Where are you going?"

"I've got to hit the highway and head home. Chelsea, you know." She paused. "All this is exciting, but it's too stressful. I thought I was going to have a heart attack running up all those stairs." Kaye stood. "Uh, I'm sorry my news couldn't have been more…"

Amanda nodded.

"But I figured you'd wouldn't want to be in the dark. In that position, any woman deserves to know."

"I understand."

There was something else to say, but neither knew exactly what it was.

Finally Amanda also rose from the table. "Kaye, I wish we would've had some quiet time together — I mean normal quiet time — you know, to try to straighten things out a bit."

Kaye hugged her. There was still some coolness, but they embraced more closely than before. "We'll have time later. Right now you've got a first-class mess on your hands with that cheating scumbag. I don't know if you two will kill each other or if you'll patch things up, but — either way — you don't need a bossy older sister in your way right now."

That was the nicest gesture Kaye had extended in eighteen years. Amanda hugged her again, tighter.

Chapter 37

While the surveillance target was occupied at work Wednesday afternoon, Cheney used that opportunity for a first-hand look at whatever was six miles east of town. Elvis Beauregard had called it a standard interstate truck stop, but there had to be something special out there. What would attract someone to drive a dozen miles round trip, when gasoline was readily available in and around Verdeville proper?

"If it's not for gas, what would you drive out here for?" The Bronco's tires on I-40 eastbound sang along with Cheney's thoughts. "Maybe you go there to get something. What? Drugs maybe, or something else illegal. Nah, doesn't make sense." The exit was approaching. "If not for something… has to be for some*body*. But who? Why?"

Time to find out. Cheney slowed on the ramp. As Elvis had noted, nothing on the south side of the interstate. The eastbound ramp went straight to a stop sign and a left turn rose over the roadway toward the north. Roughly a mile long, the access road was a blacktopped, abandoned spur to U.S.

Highway 70, which had once been a main thoroughfare.

A sprawling truck stop complex, but not like the newer ones specifically built for interstate traffic. This establishment seemed at one point to have been a regular service station which had expanded. Currently, the gasoline stations were in front with a small parking section for cars and passenger trucks. Two long diesel bays for big rigs stretched along the east side, which had a separate large parking area in back.

The inside had been enhanced as well. Showers at the rear, close to the truck parking area; a separate room for video poker machines. *Maybe that's the attraction — no video poker allowed in Verdeville.* The main retail area had everything from paperbacks and DVDs to touristy souvenirs. A large bank of glass doors encased cold beverages, including plenty of beer selections. Also a small section of grocery-type items, including a huge galvanized bucket with bruised bananas.

Off to the west, apparently the newest part, was a meal counter with several large metal trays kept warm by hot water in the steam table. Cheney took a quick look. Smelled pretty good overall, but the blend of aromas was unusual. It looked to be pizza, rolls, chicken, buns, burgers, and some other meat. A grungy dispenser featured the usual assortment of self-service beverages. Diners could choose from seven small tables or three booths.

A plain-looking employee hustled out and collected the trash left on several tables, and then wiped their surfaces with a greasy rag. Then she hustled back behind the counter and "cleaned" the food area with that same cloth. She took the incomplete step of rinsing her hands, but then dabbed them against the filthy rag to dry them. The proprietor had to be too cheap to buy paper towels. No latex gloves in sight.

Hmm. Nothing out of the ordinary except disgusting health code violations. Cheney went back to the video poker room. A big warning sign admitting no minors. The room was so smoky it was difficult to see and nearly impossible to breathe, so the apprentice investigator made a quick exit.

A walk around back. Some dwellings in the distance, west of the truck parking area and north of the access road. Couldn't tell much, other than they had metal roofs. The primitive roads leading in were narrow and crowded with brush on the sides. They'd needed a new load of gravel at least a decade ago. No evidence of much traffic, if any. None of the structures looked inviting and only two looked conceivably inhabited.

The investigator ventured up the middle lane. After some hundred feet, Cheney was startled by angry barking from a protective dog. Sounded like a large mutt, hopefully at the end of a chain. Nothing in view that resembled a fence.

A few more steps and the barking intensified.

A voice called out, "He's a biter!" Sounded elderly and female, possibly missing her upper dental plate.

"Just looking around," Cheney replied hoarsely, not certain which direction to speak.

"Find ya another place ta sightsee… or I'll turn him loose on ya."

Cheney didn't need a second warning. Nothing down that road to beckon anyone from Verdeville… or anyplace else.

Another quick stroll through the inside retail area. Moderately busy for mid-afternoon on a Wednesday. "Why would a truck stop way out of town have this much traffic? Why not patronize one of the newer places closer to Nashville?"

"Huh?" said a driver with an enormous gut straining his tight T-shirt. Stained cargo shorts revealed pale heavy legs.

"Uh, sorry. Just talking to myself." Cheney moved aside. *Don't stand between a trucker and a restroom.*

No reason to hang around there, so Cheney returned to the Bronco. With engine on and the under-charged A/C running full blast, the investigator took one more look around the complex and then drove the full length of the short access road before returning to the ramp and heading west, back toward Verdeville.

"I sure wouldn't come out here for anything... even if it was free."

Chapter 38

Jason phoned Amanda shortly after 6 p.m. as he sat in the GCEC parking lot. He'd been thinking. Not his strong suit, but the discussions with Erin Chester had convinced him he should at least attempt explaining some things to Amanda before everything got out of hand. If this worked out, he would head to her apartment instead of home. If it didn't, he'd find a bar somewhere.

Her phone would play the *Desperado* ringtone, so she would know it was him. Since it went five full rings, she was probably wondering whether to answer. Finally, "Hi."

Sounds real chilly. "Uh, Amanda, it's Jason. Wondered if you wanted to grab a bite. Well, food, of course, but also thinking maybe we could talk a bit, uh, or should talk because things seem kind of weird somehow but I can't figure out why and somebody told me that stuff goes better if people talk about it so it doesn't become some big magilla or something. So you think you feel up to talking about stuff and maybe we can grab a pizza or something?"

"I had cold pizza for lunch."

It probably froze when she touched it. He'd never heard that much ice in her voice before. "Uh, well, what do you think about getting together so we can talk about stuff, you know hash out whatever seems to be the problem?"

"What seems to be the problem? You want to yak about what seems to be the problem?"

Uh, yeah. Obviously. "Wouldn't that be a good idea?" All the grocery store mags seem to think so. "You know, it's good for couples to talk about stuff before it turns into problems."

"Before it turns into problems? You want to yak about things before they turn into problems?"

She was repeating herself this evening. Jason shook his phone. "Uh, yeah. At least I think so." He was no longer sure. "Don't you?"

"I'll talk about stuff, all right. You were seen with your *new* woman at the mall on Sunday."

"Sunday?" It took a moment to register. "That wasn't *my* woman. Seen by who?" Jason shook his phone again. Had to be a bad connection.

"Doesn't matter who saw you. Who were you with?"

He groaned. "She's one of Kevin's conquests. He bedded down a computer whiz named Amoretto."

"And he dropped her off with you so you could sample the leftovers?"

"She wasn't *with* me."

"Jason, you were seen!"

A flash of insight, finally. "By Christine, I bet. She's been following me."

"Not Christine. But she has a source. Reliable source."

This is outrageous. "Look, Kevin wanted me to meet this person, but not for the reason you seem to think. He wanted to prove she was intelligent."

"I guess she aced that test. She was huddled in the

Verdeville Mall with the best friend of the guy who boinked her. That's brilliant."

He wanted to scream. This was *not* turning out like Erin had given him to understand. At this stage of the communication exercise, the blissful couple was supposed to be calmly enumerating points of agreement.

Amanda didn't wait for an answer. "So why would an allegedly smart woman waste ten minutes of passion on Kevin?"

Jason tried to grasp words which could actually clear this up, but they would merely be more ammunition for Amanda's distorted imagination. His apologetic tip-toeing was about to become angry stomping. Since Christine was stalking him and had already tried to seduce him, Christine's jealousy *had* to be behind all this. He decided to turn the tables, or try to. "Why has Christine been following me?"

"And the rest of the Stealth League."

"The what?" He'd never read that comic book. Maybe he should just extricate himself from this ill-advised conversation. Well, not so much a conversation as a fiery explosion — and everything he contributed merely functioned as more gasoline.

"Never mind." Amanda picked up the pace. "So, why are you hooking up with your old squeeze from college again?"

How'd she know about that? "Karen? That's just on Facebook." He sputtered. "She lives in Florida somewhere. I've said maybe four things to her."

"What about? Moving back in?" Amanda would have been an intense prosecutor.

This is insane! "No! Just catching up. She's married now… has a kid and two pugs."

"Nice cover story. Are you going back to Karen and her nasty pugs?" She paused while the steam traveled through the phone line.

"What the creepin' crud are you talking about?" Jason

was so floored, his righteous indignation couldn't get a foothold. "Where did this new bizarre fantasy come from?"

Amanda ignored the question. "Well, Karen clearly wants another sample of what passes for your charms. But she's apparently only one of the sluts scratching your seven-month itch."

There she goes again. "What itch?"

"*Your* itch. Seven months. That's how long we've been together. Aren't you in touch with anything besides bimbos and balls?"

It took Jason a moment to decipher *balls* in the intended context. Sports; she meant sports. "Look, I don't itch and I'm not scratching anybody. This is all a mistake."

"Yeah, your mistake, hotshot. You got caught. Like your secret meeting behind closed doors with a woman who doesn't even work there. Did you have to sneak her in the back way?"

"Secret? Sneak? What?"

"I have someone on the inside. Your illicit trysts at work are no longer on the sly. I have real-time intel on every woman you diddle."

Have I traded places with Kevin? "Where and when did all this come up? And why?"

Amanda hammered on. "I know where you were, and for how long. And what you talked about is evident from the notes."

"Notes? You mean I supposedly diddled a woman at work and one of us took notes? Don't you see how crazy this is?"

"They all say that when they get caught."

"They... who?"

"Cheaters, that's who. Like you!"

That stung. *So the howling cat was finally out of its flimsy bag.* Tempted to fire back, Jason strained for a handle on the-conversation-that-was-supposed-to-defuse-potential-problems.

He could only think of one angle. "You said Christine was behind some of this alleged info. Well, did she tell you how she was rubbing her boobs all over me Sunday afternoon and trying to seduce me right in the middle of my own living room?"

Amanda ignored that, too. "Attack the credibility of my witnesses. Another standard ploy. Well, in this case, I've got over half a dozen witnesses. They can't all be crazy."

"Christine sure is." *Half a dozen?*

"Besides them, my own sister saw you…"

"I've never even met your sister."

"…pay a pimp for a hooker."

"Pimp? Hooker?" Jason sputtered. "The only pimp I've ever seen is in the movies. Where was *this* alleged incident?"

"Don't remember right this minute. It's all in the file."

"File? I've got a file now? We've been together for seven months and Christine tells you enough lies to start a file on me? Well, start a file on *her*! She's nuts. Plus, she wants my body." *Oops, shouldn't have gone there.*

"Your body? Well, if that's the case, then just drag it outside until she has a chance to run over you with her flashy convertible. And don't bother contacting me to whine about it." The tension in Amanda's voice seemed harsh enough to squeeze the phone.

Jason examined the inside of his truck like he expected someone to open the passenger door and hand him a script correction. "You're dumping me? You're keeping a file about me that's filled with bogus, hare-brained stories from your nutty friends, and now you're dumping me?"

"Y-yes." Her voice sounded hollow and exhausted.

Jason sputtered and then tried counting, but couldn't remember the numbers. *Deep breath.* "Amanda, the reason I called is so we could talk about whatever's bothering you so it wouldn't turn into something ugly. What happened?"

"It was already ugly. You just didn't realize that I already knew it." *Click.*

Jason glared at the phone. "If I *did* have a multi-month itch, *now* would be the time to scratch it!" *When you say that out loud, it has more import.*

What went wrong? Why hadn't the high-paid Alabama consultant's advice saved the day? Why had talking it out only made things worse? Jason was furious and dumbfounded. When Amanda had been perturbed at supper Friday, he'd assumed it was about her irritating sister being in town. On Monday evening, after he'd been late, they'd kept missing each other. They'd argued that night, once he'd tracked her down, but it too had been about things he could barely register — some woman at the mall? At the grocery? Perhaps he could have responded cogently if he'd had some idea what the heck she'd been talking about!

Tonight, he'd anticipated a spirited discussion about Christine's attempted seduction. But Amanda had ignored that vignette completely! Evidently she imagined he was playing around with one or more unnamed hussies? *What's that all about?*

And somehow the alleged trigger — it had been seven months since they'd become lovers. But if anything had actually developed, it was the Seven-Month Insanity... in Amanda.

"What do you do on Wednesday evening when you just got dumped by your girlfriend?" He spoke out loud as he sat in the GCEC parking lot with his windows rolled down. It was nearly 6:30 and the dispatcher team would still be around, though they parked near the far door at the back, close to the loading dock. The main part of the lot was mostly empty.

Lonely, depressed... and his stomach grumbled.

"What do you do at *suppertime* when you just got dumped by your girlfriend?" He could head to a nearby bar, or get his revolver and shoot rats at the Verdeville Dump. Or take a six-pack to the dump and shoot empties. *Nah. Don't mix beer and bullets.*

"Well, there's at least one constant in Jason-World." He started his truck and headed toward the interstate. Hopefully he could find some comfort east of town at Exit 248.

****

In the dusty beige Bronco which had been parked next to the GCEC building, Cheney followed the target at a discreet distance. Once on the interstate, it took hardly five minutes to drive six miles. The truck stop was incredibly crowded, far more vehicles than Cheney had seen during daytime. The apprentice detective watched as Jason took the last parking spot in front. Cheney circled around and finally found a spot in the back with the big rigs.

Once inside, Cheney looked all over for Jason, but the target was nowhere in sight. Not even in the smoky area with video poker machines.

"Lost him! Dang!"

Chapter 39

Thursday, May 28

Amanda hung up the office phone.

"Everything worked out?" Louis waddled in and crammed his immense frame into her visitor chair.

"Yeah, pretty much." Had he been listening to her call? "Just got off the phone with Mister Withers, in fact." He was the Public Works supervisor in the county across the river to the north. "He seems eager to help us out — won't even charge mileage." She looked at her notes and desk calendar. "After a single day of TV crawlers provided gratis by the cable company and massive radio PSAs on June eleventh — uh, Thursday, two weeks from today — Harry will test PW's flood disaster sandbag distribution by having a T-shirt giveaway the next day, Friday."

"How about the evaluation?"

"It's a simple form with a dozen questions or so, plus a page for his narrative assessment and any suggestions he has for improvement of the distribution system." She checked her calendar again. "No reason Withers couldn't have it to you by the end of that week."

Louis nodded. It was rare for him to assent to anything Amanda said. Usually his head moved sideways.

She checked the wall clock. "After I eat lunch, I'll head out there and see what Harry has in mind for traffic flow and signage, and possible extra staffing for the drill itself." Still rattled after her fight with Jason, she could use an hour out of the office.

"You know," his chins shivered as he cleared his throat, "it takes longer to load a dozen sandbags than to stick a rolled-up shirt through the driver's window."

"True. That's why I arranged for Gee-keck to pass out flyers about electrical safety and the gas company to hand out info warning people not to dig in their yards. By the time a driver has interacted with all three distributors, it would be about enough time for two men to load a dozen sandbags." She closed her eyes and visualized two sweaty men loading six bags apiece. Not much more than sixty seconds. She flashed back to a sweaty Jason racing about a dusty infield… and realized she would never witness that again. Yet suddenly she wished she were perched on a splintery bleacher, shading her eyes from the sun. Her heart cramped in her chest. *Nope, I can't watch a cheater play ball.*

Louis looked around like he figured there ought to be something to fuss about. Then he cleared his throat and struggled to get his hips past the arms of the chair. She didn't watch him depart.

****

Christine strode into Amanda's apartment right at 5:30. She loved being precisely on time. "Well, tonight we settle things, one way or the other."

"You aren't going to kill anybody, are you?" Amanda eyed her warily.

"I won't... but *you* might decide to." Her phone beeped. "Oh, a new text from Cheney."

"Who's Cheney?" Amanda attempted to peer over her friend's shoulder.

Oops. Until that very moment, Cheney had been one of Christine's all-time best kept secrets. "Uh, well, there's one little detail I didn't get a chance to tell you about."

"How little?" Amanda grabbed the phone. "Who the heck is Cheney?"

Christine flapped her empty hands. "Now, you'll remember I told you from the very beginning that I was looking out for your interests, because I knew you were in no condition to."

"Who the heck is Cheney?"

"Um, basically, a ringer." A ringer was someone you'd bring into a high-stakes game to tip the scales for your team to win, a professional of some sort. It was a great word and she'd always wanted to use it.

"Ringer?" Amanda tilted her head and thought. "What kind of ringer can help with..." Her eyes opened wide as she stared at Christine's phone screen. "A detective?"

Christine nodded, trying to conceal her pride. She'd been so proactive.

"You hired a private detective to follow me?"

"Not you. Jason! Cheney's been on Jason's tail since Sunday."

Still clearly indignant, Amanda couldn't take her eyes off the screen. "So what did your detective find out?"

Christine explained everything Cheney had told her so far.

"So your mysterious source was a private detective? I can't believe this. You should've checked with me first." Her face was stern. "This is over the line, Christine." She shook the offending phone and then slammed it on the table.

Christine retrieved her phone and examined it for damage. "Look, I'm sorry I didn't ask you, but I figured you'd say no."

"All the more reason *not* to do this!"

"But I knew I couldn't be everywhere at once and I don't like fighting the Nashville traffic at night."

"You still should've asked."

They had so much else to cover, and Amanda focused on that one tangle. "Well, I did apologize and it is for your own good that we settle this. We needed professional assistance. At least let me see what Cheney has to say." Christine refreshed the screen.

> *need 2 meet. important.*
> *Tue nite -*
> *target went to 4th woman room*
> *both followed by 3d woman*

"Well, that's old news that I got free — Kaye told me that yesterday at lunch." Amanda still bristled. "Obviously Kaye is your detective's so-called third woman."

Christine continued:

> *Wed aftrnn*
> *target bck 2 X248*

"He went out there again?" Amanda looked as if somebody had conked her head.

> *went in 4 abt 10 mins*
> *didn't see him lve*

"Ask him what time?"

Christine typed in the question.

Cheney's response: *aftr wrk 6:30.*

"That's right after Jason talked to me on the phone!" Amanda squinted. "Speaking of which, why are you and your private dick texting instead of talking?"

"Laryngitis. He's a wuss with a summer cold." Christine texted: *Still sore throat?*

Cheney replied: *yeh. meet?*

Christine's thumbs moved over her miniature keyboard. *Hows Fri 4 lunch?*

There was a pause on the detective's end. Then: *better sooner.*

Still wounded from being told to butt out of the investigation, Christine asserted her dominance over the hireling: *Fri lunch.* Then she turned to Amanda. "Detectives are so dramatic. They watch too many movies."

"He probably just wants to check out your dang hooters."

Chapter 40

Amanda was stressed, emotionally exhausted, and jumpy with apprehension. Perhaps it should have been comforting that a Stealth League had formed to "assist" with her presumably private domestic problem, but there was something surreal about having three bosom buddies gang up on one's lover. Besides, regardless of the awful things she'd said to Jason over the phone, Amanda still couldn't completely believe he was playing around. Despite the preponderance of evidence and testimony.

She'd changed into jeans and sneakers and a golf shirt. Amanda didn't know what to expect this evening, but wanted to be comfortable. *Only in a movie or bad novel would you run around in heels and short skirt.*

The rest of the Stealth League arrived shortly after six o'clock, and Christine began the meeting. "Amanda and I will watch Jason's apartment. You two are at the hotel where Kevin hangs out."

"Why are we watching for *Kevin*?" When Maria scowled,

Amanda remembered her friend was expecting to hook up with Roger the hunky fireman after second shift.

"We got some valuable intel from Kaye that Jason has been there at least twice this week. Some money changed hands and he's even gone upstairs with a tall blonde in bad shoes." Christine's sympathy seemed focused on the harlot's fashion problems.

"Kaye said she heard them in a room on the f-fifth fl-loor." Amanda covered her face with trembling hands.

"Which hotel?" Sunny.

"Nashvillage, of course." Christine seemed irritated she had to explain.

Sunny's excitement spilled over. "Can we use blackout paint on our faces?"

"Only if you want to be arrested by the NAACP." Christine sighed. "This is not about paratroopers dropping behind enemy lines. You're just two ladies picking up a friend at the hotel."

"Who do we pick up?" Sunny again.

Maria rolled her eyes. "Nobody. That's only our cover if anybody asks. We're just watching the hotel to see if Jason comes out with a bimbo." She turned to Christine. "Right?"

"Correct." Christine beamed.

Despite her well-known skepticism of Christine's bossy plans, Maria seemed pleased to be in sync. "When we get in place, should we split up? One watching the front and the other watching the back?"

"No, you two stay together." Christine connected the forefingers of each hand. "Park where you can see both the hotel entrance and the exit for the parking garage next door. You know Jason's truck?"

"It's a forest green Ford pickup, F-150." Amanda, mostly composed, still dabbed at her eyes with a tissue. "Got a few years on it."

"Big dent in one of the front fenders?" Maria asked.

"Dents in all four fenders, I believe." Christine. "It's not much more than a heap, really."

Amanda nodded and shrugged — at the same time. Hard to do.

"I guess this will sound stupid," said Sunny, "but what if Jason and his date just shack up *inside* the hotel?" She glanced furtively at Amanda. "Sorry."

It felt like a gut punch.

"Good question." Christine the facilitator. "I've got that covered. My other source is staking out the interior."

Maria peered around the room. "Who is this other source of yours?"

"She hired a private detective!" Amanda glared. "You didn't know either?"

Sunny shook her head. "Shoot a monkey."

Maria's nod suggested she had figured some other resource was involved. "I wouldn't have guessed detective."

"Cheney's an apprentice investigator, to be exact." Christine consulted her watch. "Okay, each sub-team needs some prep time before we get into place."

Sunny, often a half step behind, cocked her head. "Why don't we all four surround the hotel? With your detective inside, we're bound to catch Jason."

"But we don't know if he operates from other hotels or if he sometimes finds a slut somewhere else." Christine inhaled suddenly and lowered her eyes from Amanda. "Sorry."

Maria's brow furrowed. "We'll be thirty miles away. We can't race over here to hand you the news. Were you figuring to use text messages or something?"

****

Christine shook her head. But at least Maria was thinking.

As for Sunny... "Texting is too difficult — wastes time and sometimes it's hard to read. Plus you need to keep your eyes peeled."

"Do what?" Sunny likely imagined some form of blinding torture.

"Never mind." She turned back to Maria. "We'll use the radio."

"Radio?" Sunny.

"The phone, doofus." Maria tried to whap Sunny's arm but missed. "You've got her on speed dial. She's got you." They'd experimented with speed dial and ringtones months ago, over some nachos during margarita night at the local Mexican restaurant. The manager had finally asked them to leave.

"Oh. Do we get to say 'out and over'?" Sunny must have had some corny movies in mind.

Maria rolled her eyes again.

"We'll use some standard code language, in case anybody's nearby and could overhear our conversation." Christine didn't actually expect bystanders, however.

"What kind of code? You mean like Tango Delta Red Two?" Maria grinned. "I've heard Roger talk like that and it makes me hot for some reason."

No matter how simplified the code, Sunny would be confused and unable to concentrate. "Here, I wrote down the main expressions." Christine handed it to Sunny. "We're just trying to spot Jason and his honey of the evening."

Amanda cringed yet again.

"Sorry. I mean we're trying to catch him in the act." Christine cleared her throat. "So it's silent surveillance as much as possible. In fact, Amanda and Maria, you both turn your phones off."

"Why?" Amanda looked more baffled than Sunny.

"One communication device per team is plenty. Cuts

down on the possibility of extraneous calls. We keep conversation to a minimum. Just brief transmissions of the facts."

"Just the facts, ma'am." If Maria thought that was clever, she was alone.

"No radio chatter." Christine the mission coordinator.

Sunny was not quite up to speed yet. "Radio?"

"Your cell phone, idiot!" Maria's whap hit pale flesh that time.

"Ow!" Sunny took umbrage. She also read over the code sheet finally. "I can't remember all this."

"Wrap it around your wrist like football quarterbacks do." Christine pointed to her own arm.

Sunny rolled the page and held the ends together. "My wrist isn't eleven inches around. It'll flop all over the place."

Christine groaned. "You'll mostly be sitting in the car. Just wrap it above your knee and you can read it that way. Then both hands are free to take notes and handle the radio."

"Radio?"

"Phone," Maria growled.

"Maria has better eyes, so…" Christine handed her the night vision glasses.

Maria put them on and turned to the window. Since it was still broad daylight, the view probably blinded her. She flinched. "Yikes. Where'd you get these?"

"I kept a lot of Daniel's stuff. Never know when you'll be on a stakeout." She looked over her remaining notes.

One simply cannot launch ships or activate troops without a speech. As the victim of the chicanery which led to this caper, Amanda had that privilege. Christine gave her the floor with a dramatic hand flourish.

Amanda cleared her throat. "I still say Jason isn't cheating. But there's been enough evidence — all circumstantial, of course — that's he's up to something. It might even be illegal."

"Drugs?" Sunny interrupted.

Christine shook her head. "No telling what."

Amanda continued, "But if it brings him into contact with shady characters and changing money and such, it could get ugly. I'm hoping we don't see Jason at all. I say he's home in bed…"

Christine rolled her eyes.

"Alone!" Amanda added quickly. "In bed alone."

Christine sighed. Of course the Stealth League would end the evening with Jason and a nekkid bimbo in their dragnet. (When a person takes a shower, she's naked. But when she's up to something… she's nekkid.)

Chapter 41

At 8:25 p.m., Maria arrived to pick up Sunny at her parent's house. She remained in her Honda Civic with the headlights off but the quiet engine running. Maria rolled down her window and shouted in a whisper, "Sunny! Sunny!"

"What?"

Maria jumped high enough to bump her head on the car ceiling and her elbow hit the horn button. "Snap! Don't sneak up on me! You nearly scared me to death!"

Sunny peered from behind a tree near the curb. "I thought we were being stealthy."

"Yeah, but we blew that when I hit the horn just now." Maria put her hand to her chest as though that might slow her heart rate.

Sunny, already pouting, removed her backpack and placed it gently on the seat between them. She raised her skirt hem and straightened the code cheat sheet, which she'd secured to her left thigh with bright yellow duct tape.

"You taped Christine's list directly to your leg?"

Sunny shrugged. "Just following orders."

"You didn't think this through very far, did you?" *Clueless.* No point in mentioning the obvious conflict between aggressive strips of two-inch tape and thousands of fine blond thigh hairs. Maria simply shook her head and drove away.

She couldn't shake a premonition. Nothing specific, just a definite sense that some degree of chaos would surely attend anything being railroaded by Christine. And Christine's determination to catch Jason cheating was definitely a locomotive of momentum. Though she was also propelled by a certain contagion of excitement, Maria went along with this so-called plan mainly on the hope that she could help protect Amanda from collateral damage. If it was in her power, she'd shield Amanda from being hurt further.

With a tiny penlight on the code sheet, Sunny silently practiced talking on the phone with HQ. She turned to Maria. "What is our call sign again?"

"Bravo. They're Stakeout Alpha and we're Bravo." She'd have preferred Alpha, but, like almost everybody else, Maria deferred to Christine.

"Sounds so courageous." Sunny took a deep breath and resumed her silent practice.

Maria drove on. It was about twenty minutes to the east loop Briley Parkway and then at least another ten to reach the very busy Fourth Avenue in downtown Nashville.

"What on earth is that backpack for?" Maria pointed. "We're on a stakeout! This isn't a sleepover."

"I brought a flashlight, some snacks, and a few Handi Wipes in case we leave fingerprints anywhere."

"Fingerprints? We're not going to *grope* Jason. We're just supposed to follow him *if* we spot him." On the opposite side of the wide avenue, Maria parked in front of an enormous bank building with leased offices, closed that late at night. "At this distance, it'll be a miracle to recognize anybody." She held up the night vision goggles and scanned the large parking garage next to the Nashvillage Hotel. Even though there were few other cars along the street, Maria had still managed to hook her right front tire up on the high curb. The sedan's position placed Sunny several inches higher than her. *Annoying.* "Is that all you brought?"

"Plus a stun gun, in case there's any action." Sunny fumbled around in the knapsack. "It looks exactly like a cell phone, so the bad guys won't know you've got voltage waiting for them. Want to see it?"

"Not now. Save it for when Rambo jumps us." Maria had a second thought. "Be sure it's turned off. You can get a nasty surprise from those stun thingies if you're not careful."

Sunny sighed. "It's on the lowest setting. The instructions say it's a *mild* jolt."

"Well, their definition of mild is probably enough to make you confess to kidnapping the Lindbergh baby."

Sunny had never even met the Lindberghs.

A stun gun. "How'd you get that thing?"

"Oh, it's my dad's. He has a buddy who tinkers with broken things he finds here and there. Recycling is real big with my dad, so he's eager to help out this guy."

"Wait. This man found a discarded stun gun and your dad bought it from him?"

"Well, the buddy tinkered with it first. You know, refurbished. Uh, reconditioned."

Maria gave her the stern teacher look. "You don't know where that's been. Whoever trashed it probably had a reason. It's possibly even defective somehow. You're better off tossing it right back in the trash can where that guy found it."

"Then it goes to the landfill. That's not green, and my dad's into green."

"Electric gizmos that give off volts or amps, or whatever, are not to be messed with. Only factory technicians can overhaul those things." Maria sighed heavily. "Does this guy have any training whatsoever?"

"My dad says he gets all his info from Wiki. You know, they show you how to salsa dance or make baskets from toilet paper."

"Wiki? Well keep that thing away from me. I don't play around with 100,000 volts when the wannabe technician trained on the Internet."

Sunny shrugged. Sometimes there's a price to being green.

Already wishing she was home with Roger, reclining on the couch, Maria yawned. "I don't guess you've got any coffee in there."

"No, but I did bring some bourbon."

"Bourbon?" Maria's eyes widened. "On a stakeout?"

"Just a little bottle like you used to get on airplanes."

"Let me see that." *Could use a little snort about now.*

Sunny unscrewed the cap and handed over the bottle.

Two things happened at precisely the same moment: Maria brought the tiny bottle up to her lips... and inches from her face, a policeman tapped his flashlight on the window.

Sunny shrieked and both jumped. The bottle flew into the air and landed back in Maria's lap, open end down. The bourbon emptied in a split second with scarcely more than a subdued bubble burp.

Neither had seen the flashing lights of the city police cruiser as it quietly slipped in behind them.

Patrolman Jack Blaine motioned for her to roll down the window. In late May she should have already had it all the way down, instead of the three-inch crack at the top. Maria pressed the button, but the window didn't budge. Engine was off.

Blaine kept motioning.

"I'll have to turn on the engine to get the window to work. Don't shoot us."

"Do not start your engine," warned Blaine. "Just switch it to accessories."

"Switch it to what?" Maria started the engine and revved it for good measure.

The patrolman tapped more urgently and his hand covered the pistol's grip. "Turn the engine *off* and lower your window! Now!"

She turned it off.

"Window down. Now!" Pistol in hand.

When Maria reached for the key again, Blaine bellowed, "Accessories!" and unholstered his pistol.

"How am I supposed to know all this junk? I teach second grade — I don't read stupid car manuals!"

Having regained a measure of her own wits, Sunny apparently thought she could assist by shining her flashlight on the ignition switch area. She rustled through her knapsack and produced the cell-phone-looking-stun-gun instead. With her other hand she then retrieved the flashlight.

"Keep your hands where I can see them!" The officer's pistol moved from one woman to the other.

Sunny looked around as though someone lurked behind her.

"Drop your items! Now!" He shone the light directly into Sunny's eyes.

"Oh, this?" Her left hand. "It's just for muggers." Her right hand. "And this—"

"Ma'am, put the device on the floorboard, *now!*"

"Shoot a monkey." Sunny obeyed, taking care not to let the terminals touch her sandaled feet.

"What did she say?" Blaine asked Maria.

"Not important. She says it a lot."

Then, to Sunny again, he barked, "Hands where I can see them."

Sunny placed both hands on Maria's right shoulder.

"Not on me, idiot!" Maria wriggled away. "Put them in your lap."

As the anxious blonde complied, the officer's attention focused on Sunny's raised skirt. He'd likely monitor that area later.

Maria found the accessories position of the ignition switch without the aid of Sunny's flashlight, finally lowered the window, and turned the key back off.

"License and registration." Standard greeting from law enforcement.

Maria momentarily couldn't recall where her purse was.

"Ma'am, is that an open container?" Blaine pointed with the flashlight beam. His breath smelled like stale coffee and old hotdogs.

Maria was rattled, but still sharp. "Well, it's technically just an empty bottle. What little bit of liquid that was formerly inside is now soaking my lap, thanks to you busting down my window."

"Just doing my job. Checking for trouble."

"We're no trouble, officer," Sunny said eagerly.

He frowned. "Assuming there are no other violations," Blaine flicked the light toward the back seat, "you're going to have to move away from this red curb."

Maria hadn't noticed any color. It was nighttime, for Heaven's sake. "Red?"

"This bank facility is a high rise. No parking near any high rise."

"We're not really parked. Technically, we're just waiting." Maria sometimes couldn't turn off her schoolteacher hair-splitting.

"Well, wait somewhere else. Not on a red curb."

Maria mumbled and reached toward the ignition switch.

"Whoa, lady! I still need to see your driver's license."

Maria exhaled. With all this police interference of their

stakeout, Jason would probably sneak right past them with his bimbo. When she undid her seatbelt, turned completely around in the seat, and reached way over the back to retrieve her purse from the floor of the rear seat, a cone of light surrounded her, illuminating the car interior — as if the officer fastened his flashlight beam on her posterior. Of course, in that position, her anatomy was practically in his face.

Sunny's eyes widened. Blaine cleared his throat. "Checking for concealed weapons."

Maria lugged her heavy purse onto the front seat and repositioned herself. "Officer, is this really necessary?"

"If you had moved along when I told you the first time, we would've been done five minutes ago and I'd be sitting in my patrol car finishing a very late supper." Blaine, who exhaled a lot when exasperated and hungry, could really use a breath mint. "But you've obstructed every one of my, uh, requests."

None had been deliberate. Maria inhaled deeply and let it out slowly. "Officer, you ever have one of those days when stuff just goes haywire and then you have to pick up a soft-headed friend and drive downtown? And then things get even worse? But you haven't really done anything wrong? It's just the whole world is out of whack?"

Blaine's expression blanked out partway through her verbiage, but a hint of understanding in his eyes seemed to comprehend Maria was having a bad evening after a hard day.

He flipped the light beam on Sunny, with her hands resting on bare thighs, and then back at Maria. "Okay. If you move off this curb, right now, don't open up any more booze, and promise to read the ignition switch part of your vehicle's manual, I can let you off with a warning."

Maria wondered what type of warning, but wisely only nodded. "All the booze is already gone and I promise I'll read the manual when I get home."

The officer let the beam drift down to her bosom before he extinguished the light and slipped it into the metal loop on his heavy equipment belt.

Sunny's wide eyes had clearly noticed his visual detour, but she didn't mention it.

Maria refastened her seatbelt, started the engine, and looked back at the officer for final take-off clearance.

Chapter 42

At 9:04 Amanda and Christine reached Jason's place. On the way, they'd discussed strategy. Christine's manic plan, though thin on details, was pretty straightforward: hide, watch, and catch. Though Christine talked like she'd been on stakeouts since childhood, Amanda knew this was actually only her third occasion. Christine drove her cousin's sedan; discretion over comfort for stakeouts.

"What's the umbrella for?" Amanda pointed. "Supposed to be clear and warm tonight."

Christine shrugged — she also had a raincoat. "Don't own a billy club and figured if I had my gun I might shoot you by accident."

Amanda's eyes widened.

"Just kidding."

"Which part?"

"I wouldn't shoot you by mistake." Christine's wording seemed too carefully chosen.

"Did you really bring a gun?"

Christine paused. "Thought about it, but didn't. Things can get really messy when lead starts flying."

"Christine, sometimes you scare the beans out of me." Amanda tried to peer into her face, but the darkness interfered. "So why the umbrella?"

"Need something to do with my hands." Christine sighed. "Sometimes I have a bit of excess energy."

"Hadn't noticed."

Now Christine tried to peer into Amanda's face, or at least she seemed to. But the darkness kept Amanda from being certain.

Jason's apartment complex had a lot of green space: trees, bushes, and expanses of grass and flower beds formed a tight frame for the buildings and primary parking area. All the complex's mail sleeves were grouped in front of the central building. His first-floor apartment occupied the west end of the central building in the three-building complex. A small parking strip fronted the buildings, with only a dozen places for each.

Which genius had thought 36 parking spaces for 48 apartments was a good idea?

Christine cruised past the apartments, but Jason's truck wasn't visible. She paused in front of the utilitarian structure with all the mail slots. "Where can we park that we won't be easily seen, but still have a good view of his door and that walkway leading to it?"

Amanda pointed to one of the two short lanes, West Drive and East Drive, which led from the apartments back toward Blackwell Street and a much larger central parking area. "Let's stay back in the big lot, over near the light pole with the burned-out bulb." The larger lot could hold perhaps a hundred vehicles. Posted signs prohibited tractor trailers from using the space.

Christine drove into position and parked. "Whoever laid out this place must have been an idiot." She pointed with irritation. "Two places to enter into this huge stretch of unmarked parking — filled with potholes, by the way — and then two little bitty lanes leading to the apartments and their postage-stamp residents' lots. What were they thinking?"

"Mystery to me. It's not like there's anything in walking distance. People living here need a vehicle to do everything." Amanda looked around the mostly dark larger lot. "Plenty of cars back here. A lot of the residents have to park here and hike down those narrow walks to whichever building they live in."

There were three such walkways, one for each building, all bordered by shrubbery and trees and surrounded by unlit green space.

Amanda checked the time — 9:07. "They sure are cheap about the lighting out here." She'd never spent much time in the back section at night without Jason beside her and for as long as she could recall, it had been eerily dark at night.

"Well, despite being gloomy — and spooky if I was out here by myself — it could play to our advantage tonight, because the cheater and his tramp won't be able to see us."

Headlights flashed as a car drove up. Both sleuths toppled over sideways. Unfortunately, with Christine moving to the right and Amanda to the left, they collided in the middle.

"Spies don't do that." Christine rubbed her head.

"Shh! What's that car doing?"

Christine eased up, peering over the dashboard. "Can't see," she whispered. The newly-arrived vehicle parked thirty feet away.

Voices — a loud man, sounding drunk, and a woman.

"That's not Jason!" Amanda felt unbelievable relief.

"Good thing, too, because the skank with him is definitely trailer trash."

"You don't know that." But Amanda agreed.

They watched as the woman walked unsteadily from the passenger side to the driver side, got in, and drove away. The drunk male didn't even wave good night; he had other urgent business. He stumbled closer, fumbled with his pants, and began urinating on the base of the darkened light pole. He must have been hurting, because his bladder was loaded.

Something about that function evidently rubbed Christine the wrong way. She reached into the dash and flashed the hazard lights. The drunk whirled around like it was a close encounter of the third kind. Without taking time to fasten his trousers, he stumbled in the opposite direction, leaving irregular urine trails in the rough pavement.

"Good riddance."

Amanda's heart pounded and her head hurt from the collision with Christine's skull. "What next?" It was rhetorical.

Christine answered anyway. "We need to get a lot closer." She squirmed in her seat, restarted the vehicle, and drove over near the entrance of Walkway B, the 100-foot paved path between the large and small lot. There she grabbed her flashlight and umbrella and reached for the door handle.

"We're not staying in the car?"

Christine shook her head. "Nope. I didn't realize what this layout was like in the dark. Parked this near the walkway entrance, we'd have to keep our heads ducked all the time."

Amanda didn't reply. She wondered if amateur detectives on stakeout were allowed to use the bathroom of the person being monitored. They exited the sedan and stood a few feet from the darkened green space.

"It's like a frazzling jungle in there." Christine exhaled. "Didn't notice that before. But you know, all those trees and bushes will give us pretty good cover and concealment." She checked the luminous dial of her watch. "Okay, let's go."

Amanda followed her leader. Halfway along Walkway B, Christine examined the trees with her flashlight. "Which one do you want?"

"We're not going to stay together?" Amanda hadn't

figured on that.

"We can't know for certain what direction they'll come from. People who mess around don't walk in straight lines."

Amanda tried to determine if her friend was serious. *Apparently so.* "Okay, I guess I'll hide behind the corner of those mailboxes." She pointed to the structure, fifty feet distant. At least it had a dim bulb in the light fixture bracketed to its roof. Also it was much closer to Jason's bathroom in case she couldn't wait.

"Uh, I'll be behind that big tree to the other side of the lane." Christine pointed with the beam of her light.

"Wait. Before we split up, how do we notify each other if somebody does show up?"

Christine scrunched her face. As usual, her plan was conspicuously short of logistical details. "Improvise." She made her way to the designated tree.

Amanda hurried along the gloomy walk and then leaned against the mailbox structure. The metal box fronts were still warm from hours of afternoon sun.

And they waited. To Amanda it seemed like half an hour, but when she checked her watch, it had been four minutes — 9:12. "Psst!"

No response from Christine, not even visible, though only 35 feet away. Amanda would have phoned, but hers was turned off, as per operational orders. "Pssstt!" More volume and quite a bit of spittle. She dabbed at her chin.

"What?" Christine left the cover of her selected tree and approached the mailboxes. "This isn't the time to chat. We're on a stakeout."

Amanda met her halfway. "I wish that drunk hadn't peed in front us. Now I've got to go."

"You should've gone before we left." Christine sounded like her own mother, thirty-some years ago.

"I had some ice tea before we left. It didn't hit me 'til that drunk expressed himself." A flash of light caught Amanda's eye and she spotted a bony hand parting the curtains in B-20. One of Jason's female neighbors. The gnarly fingers vanished, then her deadbolt clacked loudly.

Christine huffed indignantly. "Well, go tinkle and then let's find different hiding spots. Maybe a bit closer together. I think the neighbors are on to us." Christine flicked her light a few times and headed toward an immense azalea bush, a little nearer than the tree.

Amanda headed inside.

****

Outside, Christine ducked behind the azalea as another car turned in to the large parking area. "That's got to be Jason and Whoever." Only her brain heard. "No time to call for back-up." Due to distance and darkness, all Christine discerned was that a man and a woman had arrived by vehicle and gotten out of their car. Not much to go on, but who else would be coming down the walkway toward Jason's apartment at 9:17 p.m.?

Coming closer. Ahead of the couple on the path, voices drifted, but too low for Christine to hear. She recalled a quote from her schooldays: *Confront first and ask questions later*. Well, close enough. Heart racing, Christine leaped out from behind the bush with the flashlight in her left hand. "Aha!" Her right hand pointed the compact black umbrella.

When a female lunatic leaps from darkness and blinds your eyes with her flashlight, a stubby collapsible umbrella looks precisely like a .45 caliber semi-automatic pistol. The man jumped like a flushed rabbit and the woman promptly collapsed with a whoosh of stale air. For a moment he struggled to clutch her, but then she dropped like a damp towel sliding off the side of an overloaded hamper.

"What the...?" He settled enough to speak amid heavy

breaths, glaring with wild eyes. "I don't have no money!" He pointed back along the darkened walkway. "Take her car if ya want."

How gallant.

Amanda emerged from Jason's apartment and hurried over. "You didn't call me."

"I forgot. Or there wasn't time. Not sure which." Besides, she had the situation under control. Christine watched the intruders and kept the man at bay with her umbrella. Her flashlight beam flicked across their pale faces.

Amanda halted when she could see the victims in the unsteady light. "Who are these people? That's not Jason!"

"I know."

"Why are you accosting complete strangers?" Amanda muttered into her ear. "Need some practice?"

"I was so sure it was him, my instincts took over. Reflexes."

"You don't have reflexes, Christine. You're just hyper and hair-triggered." Amanda likely pictured herself sitting on cuffed wrists in the back of a police car.

The man squinted back and forth between them, perceiving their confusion. "Look, ya two. I don't know what's goin' on, but it cain't be nothing ta do with me."

"That depends." Christine flourished the stubby .45 caliber umbrella.

The man shuddered and dropped to a crouch, out of the probable line of fire.

"Let him go." Amanda clutched her forearm. "We need them gone. They're wrecking our stakeout."

"Are ya guys cops?" He nodded his head toward the woman collapsed beside him. "Look, I didn't know she was married. She never said nothing ta me."

"Relax, Lothario. We're not here for you." Christine decided to keep up the illusion of undercover cops. *Might keep him from reporting an attempted burglary.* "Take your hussy and get out of here before I have to call a squad car."

"Don't think I can carry her." Lothario straightened but kept his knees bent.

"Well, grab her arms and drag her." Christine scowled. "I'll help you toss her in."

"Uh, could you point that somewhere else?" Lothario eyed her weapon.

Why did the umbrella frighten him so? Christine turned her wrist and accidentally pressed the release button. The thin aluminum ribs exploded out with a loud *whoom*.

Lothario stumbled backwards to the ground.

"Get your cheating butt away from my stakeout. Now! And take her, too."

The man struggled to his feet, staggered to the unconscious woman, and poked her with the pointed toe of his cowboy boots. "Git up, Trixie. There's something goin' on an' we gotta be somewheres else. Wake up!" He nudged her again, with more vigor.

Trixie grunted.

Christine glared. "You grab one arm and I'll get the other. But you'll get a bill from the Verdeville PD for this. I'm on duty."

Lothario didn't seem to care about the cost. He just wanted to be gone.

She closed the umbrella and handed it to Amanda. "Cover me."

Together Christine and Lothario dragged unconscious Trixie along the paved walkway to the victim's vehicle. During that rough journey, one of her high-heeled sandals fell off. Leaning over to handle the dead weight, Christine displayed considerable cleavage and even in his frightened and agitated state, Lothario noticed.

Christine saw him looking. "Visually assaulting an officer

while undercover is punishable by fine and time, buster. Keep your nosy eyeballs to yourself."

Lothario looked embarrassed he'd been caught, but didn't seem to regret taking the risk. Maybe he'd never seen a police officer with cleavage. Usually the female bosoms were flattened by Kevlar vests. "Uh, can I see your I.D., officer?"

She reached toward her back pocket. "Sure. And then I'll be forced to look at yours... and call it in... and have them run it. Have you ever picked your feet in Poughkeepsie?"

"Huh?" The line from *French Connection* threw him.

"I said, did you ever pick your feet in Poughkeepsie?" She tried, unconvincingly, to sound like Gene Hackman.

"Where's that? I never left Tennessee, 'cept that one time we slipped across the border into Kentucky."

No doubt that was a big wing-ding. "Well, lucky for you, because if I ever catch that feet-picker, he won't make it alive to the desk sergeant downtown. There will be a series of unfortunate accidents along the way."

"Hey, officer, no offense. Uh, sorry an' all that. I just wanta git outta your, uh, operation here..."

"Better not get her angry, dude." Amanda chimed in. "Everybody in the department is scared of Popeye here, even the guys from Internal Affairs."

Nice touch. Christine nodded.

The shaken man bent back to the task of lifting Trixie. With considerable effort of his own — and limited assistance from Christine — Lothario heaved Trixie into the back seat, slammed the door, and then got in the driver's side.

"Don't even think about having your way with her while she's passed out. In Greene County we call that premeditated date rape."

That notion had possibly not occurred to Lothario, who appeared worried, likely by the loaded umbrella.

Amanda walked over carrying Trixie's abandoned shoe as

Lothario drove away. "High heels and tight jeans. Is that coming back?" She handed over the footwear.

Christine held the tip of the heel as she examined the imitation leather sandal. "Hmm. Cheap floozy, cheap shoe." She tossed it in the bushes to the east of Jason's Walkway B. "Crud! Tugging on that bimbo ripped a seam in my top."

Chapter 43

9:26 p.m.

Thirty miles away in downtown Nashville, less than a minute after the officer departed, Maria cruised around the block, convinced that Stakeout Bravo had already missed Jason.

When Sunny's phone rang, she jumped. "Shoot a monkey!" In her excitement, she nearly grabbed the stun gun by mistake. "Uh, Sunn... I mean, Two Bravos here. What's up?"

"Bravo Two, this is Alpha One. We just opened the wrong package."

Sunny stared at Maria. "They've gone *shopping*!"

Maria rolled her eyes.

Sunny refocused on the phone. "What do you mean, you opened the wrong package?"

"Would you please read your dang code list?" Impatience dripped from Christine's telephonic voice.

"Hang on, Alphie."

"Alpha!" Then Christine's voice mumbled something

away from the phone.

Sunny scanned the sheet taped to her hairy leg. "I don't see code for *open* anywhere."

"Give the phone to Bravo One!" Christine demanded.

"Shoot a monkey!"

Obviously acute disappointment.

"Here," said Sunny, "one of the Alphies wants you."

Maria took the phone while continuing to circle the block opposite the hotel's front. "Okay, this is Bravo One. What?"

"Tell that dimwit what 'opened the wrong package' means."

"Hold on." Maria thought for a moment. *Well, obviously.* "Christine and Amanda accosted a different guy with the wrong bimbo."

Sunny nodded slowly. "Why would they do that?"

"Never mind." Maria turned back to the telephone. "Try to keep the felonies to a minimum, Christine. If all four of us are in jail, there won't be anybody to catch Jason cheating." School teachers could be so practical.

"What do you mean, Bravo?"

"We were just now rousted by Nashville's finest — some fetish about red curbs. You want us to stay here or come back home?"

"Stay at Outpost X-Ray—"

"X-Ray?" Maria sputtered. "We're in downtown Nashville. I thought we were Outpost One!"

"I changed it. All the numbers were confusing."

"Christine, you can't change the codes now. I can barely keep Radar O'Sunny in the right state!"

Sunny glared. She likely did not understand the allusion to *M*A*S*H* but knew they were talking about her.

"Can you just use X-Ray? Please?"

"Whatever. So tell me what happened with those wrong packages."

"It was dark. I'll have to fill you in later. For now, suffice it to say that some local citizens presently believe we're undercover police officers."

"Oh, snap, Christine! Do you have any idea how much trouble...?"

It sounded like Christine spluttered a raspberry. "That guy was banging a married woman. Who's he going to tell?" A whoosh as she sighed into the phone. "Anyway, has there been any sign of the target at Outpost X-Ray?"

"Well, not before the cop got here and not since. But during his harassing visit, a brass band could have gone in or out of the hotel. Unnerving."

Doubtful if Christine had factored in her Bravo team being questioned by police. "Well, don't provoke the cops any more."

"Provoke? We were just sitting here in my car!"

"Okay, whatever. We've adjusted our positions at Ground Zero. Things here are again under control... for now, anyway." Christine paused. "Uh, Alpha out."

"Over and out."

Sunny grabbed the phone. "I wanted to say that!"

Too late.

Sunny mouthed "out and over" and then flipped the phone shut. She started to put it back down where she'd gotten it, but fingered the lookalike stun gun and placed the phone instead near her opposite hip.

Chapter 44

At newly-renamed Outpost X-Ray, Maria had Team Bravo on the move. Remaining near the downtown hub of activity, she repeatedly circled the block of high-rise buildings, always cruising slowly when the hotel was in view across the busy avenue.

"This is ridiculous." Maria slapped the Civic's steering wheel. "We've got almost no chance of catching anybody like this. Plus, I'm burning up a week's worth of gas."

Sunny shrugged blankly. "What else can we do?"

Maria paused short of the corner as she peered along Fourth Avenue. "We're parking again."

Sunny's eyebrows arched. "But..."

"No way Dudley Do-right is still crowding our spot."

"I don't see his patrol car."

"Get out that light and see if you can find part of this curb that's not red." Maria drove as though she were tip-toeing, and unhurriedly turned right for at least the twelfth time.

As they crawled along the avenue opposite the

Nashvillage, Sunny played her light along the curb. "That very first part wasn't red. But everything else is. Go to the other end and let's see how far the red goes."

Maria felt certain that if Jason ever had been inside, he'd already departed and eluded their surveillance net — if not when the officer was haggling, then probably during their endless circling. "This whole thing is totally stupid."

"Okay, the red paint stops close to this end, just like it did at the other end." Sunny pointed. "Right there at the bus sign."

Maria pulled over and twisted her head around. "I can't stop here. The hotel is behind us and the garage is even farther back." She began her series of right turns again. "We'll stop at the other end, before the red paint."

Sunny nodded, certainly preferring to operate within the confines of the law.

After four more turns, they finally got situated at the other end of the block.

Once parked, Maria flapped the air above her jeans, trying to help dry the two ounces of bourbon currently soaking into her panties and beyond. Didn't help much, but it kept her hands occupied until she remembered to scan the massive hotel with her night vision goggles. "I wonder which unfortunate couple was ambushed by Christine and Amanda." She considered the possibilities. "She said they'd shifted their original positions."

Bravo Two shook her head. "They probably stopped off at IHOP for coffee."

"Or maybe they've already been arrested for assault." Maria put the heavy glasses back up to her eyes and scanned the parking garage's exit.

****

Back at Alpha Team's Ground Zero, Amanda was having

second thoughts… for about the tenth time. Deep down, she still felt Jason had to be innocent of scratching his alleged seven-month itch. Yet she was perfectly willing to be present when they caught him cheating. Difficult to reconcile those conflicting emotions. *When you can't make up your own mind, just take instructions from somebody elese with a strong opinion… any opinion.*

But still she had to try sorting it all out. "Christine, this whole thing is bogus. We've been here more than an hour…"

"Less than half that." It was 9:28.

"However long. But besides that nosy neighbor, the only people we've seen is a drunk peeing on a pole and that stupid cowboy dragging Trixie." Amanda exhaled. "Jason's not going to show."

"He has to. This is his apartment."

"I mean, he's not going to show up with some other girl. *I'm* his girl." As she spoke those words, Amanda realized Jason's girlfriend should be *with* him on a Thursday night, not hiding behind bushes trying to catch him *en flagrante delicto*.

Christine was too busy staring to comment.

"Do you seriously think we're going to catch Jason out here tonight doing anything besides coming home alone?"

"What you'll see is what you'll get. Soon." Christine sniffed the air like a lioness, or perhaps a cougaress.

"How long do you intend to stay out here and keep up this charade?" Amanda heard the frustration and exhaustion in her own voice. Plus worry. *What if Jason DID show up with someone?*

Christine gritted her teeth. "Tell you what — you wait inside Jason's place. I'll stand lookout and signal you when they show up."

Amanda started to refute, but changed her mind. She surveyed the dark parking lot, the shadowy green space flanking the gloomy walkway, and then gazed back toward

Jason's apartment. They'd had many good times there — in several rooms. They should be having one now, instead of this fiasco. "Okay, I'll wait inside. When you get tired of this cloak-and-dagger stuff, come join me and I'll have a lite beer ready for you."

No response from ultra-focused Christine.

Amanda hurried through the forested darkness. As she approached the building, the front window curtain shifted again at Apartment B-20.

She flung herself onto the loveseat. "Jason should be here with me."

****

Carping, waffling — *argh!* Christine struggled to keep the correct perspective. *I'm doing this for you.* She could have been angry, but of course Amanda was out of her rational mind with grief and guilt. Jason wouldn't have had to wander if Amanda had kept his itches properly scratched. But there would be time for those discussions later — right now the mission was to catch the crafty cheater.

A breeze put a light chill in the night air, so Christine retrieved the raincoat from her borrowed vehicle before heading back along the gloomy walkway. She didn't need it yet, but might later if the temperature dropped any more.

In the shadows behind a lush cedar tree, she discovered a five-gallon bucket upside-down on the ground. Probably left by the landscapers. Cigarette butts all over the place — a seat for illicit breaks.

Christine placed her folded raincoat on top of the bucket as a modicum of cushioning and to prevent stains on her designer jeans. She sat gingerly, rocked the bucket to level off, and waited, watching the larger parking area seventy feet distant.

Had she been more comfortable, Christine could have nodded off. Minutes passed and then footsteps on pavement, coming from the large parking area — 9:36 p.m. Listening intently, she tried to force her eyes to see through the darkness. Finally she spotted an unidentified woman approaching along the walkway.

Third time lucky?

She needed to signal Amanda. But how?

Chapter 45

Sharp lights flashed behind Outpost X-ray. Maria whipped around. A Nashville P.D. cruiser pulled up even with her Honda and Patrolman Blaine leaned out his window to peer into hers.

Dudley Do-right again. "Snap!"

The officer drove farther up, parked in front of Maria's car, and unfastened the strap on his pistol holster. When Blaine reached the vehicle window, Maria realized she was still waving her hand above her lap. Sunny had her dress hem pulled up as she continued to study the code cheat sheet.

"Still here, I see."

"Actually, officer, we just arrived here. Before, we were way over *there*." Maria pointed.

"Yeah, I'll get back to that." He eyed them suspiciously as his flashlight played over the car's interior. "Are you two looking for a John?"

"No, his name is Jason," offered Bravo Two.

"Hush." To Sunny. Then Maria turned. "No, officer.

We're trying to spot my cousin. She said to meet her here, but I don't know what she looks like since the accident."

"What accident?" A trigger word for police. "Around here?"

"No, down in Mississippi. It was a backyard barbeque. She was cooking a drunk chicken... which exploded. Nobody told her to open the beer can first." Maria closed her eyes somberly. "Two years and they're still doing surgery on her face."

Blaine shook his head sympathetically. Then he looked farther along the street to the place they'd parked previously. A heavy sigh projected more disagreeable breath.

"Officer, why did you stop this time?" Maria motioned toward the sidewalk. "We moved off the red curb like you said."

Blaine leaned down to check. "Yeah, but now you're parked on the yellow part," he drawled. "Didn't you see that sign?"

Maria turned to Sunny, the navigator.

Bravo Two shrugged. "It just marked a spot for the city bus."

Blaine nodded. "And right next to that is a sign which says, basically, *No parking at any time, for any reason whatsoever.*"

"Are you serious? But it's... it's..." She sputtered, trying to see her watch.

"Uh, I've got 9:42." Do-right extended his hairy wrist.

"Whatever. How could we possibly be interfering with anything or anybody by pausing on this allegedly yellow curb this late at night?" Then Maria turned again to Sunny. "Why didn't you say the curbs at the end were painted yellow?"

"You just asked where the red paint stopped."

Maria sighed so heavily that bits of spittle flew onto the dashboard. She felt like scratching Sunny's naïve blue eyes out, and then maybe turning on Do-right. "Snap, snap, snap."

Blaine allowed the tame cursing even though Nashville had an ordinance about public profanity. "So, why the night glasses?" His flashlight beam pointed.

Bravo Two started to speak, but Maria discreetly slugged her arm. *No telling what she'd come up with.* Instead, Maria explained, "I don't have good night vision since the twins were born."

Another sympathetic nod from Blaine. Police don't verbalize their compassion because that could dilute their sense of authority.

"Maria, you don't have…"

Maria whapped Sunny's arm again.

In the distance, someone resembling Jason exited the hotel. Maria put the glasses up to her eyes but Blaine deliberately blocked her line of sight.

Maria craned her neck. "Would you mind scooting over a bit?" *Oops.* Big mistake. And she'd almost had him with the sympathy ploys.

Blaine certainly realized he'd been played. "Listen, ladies." That term dripped with sarcasm. "If you don't drive away from here right now, I might have to take you in." He shone his flashlight in the back seat again.

Maria scoffed silently. Nothing back there but some ungraded spelling quizzes, and in second grade, those were pretty unsophisticated. "For what offense?"

"I can search you and your vehicle on suspicion."

"Suspicion of what?"

"Are you giving me a hard time?" Blaine's hand went to his right side, where hung his pistol and a Taser, slightly farther behind his back.

Sunny clutched at Bravo One. "He's going to shoot you, or zap you, or smack you with his billy club. Let's just go!"

"We haven't done anything wrong. We're just sitting here." Then she turned again to Blaine. "Seriously, officer, what's our crime, so far?"

"Loitering. And after I asked you politely to leave, it became hindering an officer in the, uh, performance of my duty."

Music blared. Both women jumped, and Sunny's dress hem flew even farther up her thighs. Blaine ducked below the level of the car door's open window. When he slowly straightened, his flashlight beam was in Maria's eyes and his Taser was pointed at her torso.

Maneater. Someone's phone. Not hers; she'd have felt the vibration. Sunny's.

Taser in hand, Blaine motioned to Sunny. "You. Take those drug packets off your leg and give me that phone."

Sunny muttered she didn't have any drugs and then exclaimed, "Shoot a monkey!"

The officer ducked instinctively, his Taser aimed toward the ditzy blonde. "Do what?" His voice rose several notes higher.

Bravo Two looked conflicted. She wasn't sure whether to answer Hall and Oates or converse with the cop.

"Like I said before, it's just an expression of hers." Maria tried to calm the officer holding an electronic weapon inches from her face.

"Expression of what?" Blaine was still rattled.

Sunny seemed scarcely aware he was referring to her colorful wording, but her wiggling fingers indicated she was dying to answer the phone. *Maneater* continued to play.

"General, uh, exclamation." Sometimes being a teacher came in handy.

"What did she say?" Blaine pulled the Taser back to a less aggressive pose. "Shoot who?"

"A monkey!" Sunny had caught up. *Self-explanatory.* "Shoot a monkey!"

Maria saw the patrolman flinch. "She means figuratively.

No gun, no bullets. In fact, not even an actual monkey. Just an odd way of not cussing. Think of it as *green* cussing."

The officer was clearly not impressed with the parts he understood.

"Can I answer this now?" Sunny waggled the ringing phone in her right hand.

"Give me that phone." *Maneater* lyrics continued. Blaine shifted his flashlight to the hand holding the Taser and reached with his empty fingers.

Sunny reluctantly handed him the device in her left hand.

It could have happened to anyone.

In a dark environment, the initial sparks might have been seen for perhaps a quarter mile. However, with the garish lights of downtown Nashville, the only way to know Blaine had been zapped by Sunny's phone replica stun gun was his loud roar. Sounded like a lion stepping on a *punji* stick.

Blaine's flashlight and Taser fell from his hands. His bladder also loosed a dribble. Fortunately, rigorous prior NPD training helped him shake loose by smacking his hand against his boot, but he was rattled... and angry. If he'd thought he could dispose of both female bodies and the vehicle, he might have seriously considered execution at the very least.

For everyone concerned, it was fortunate that Sunny had set the device on its lowest voltage. Some really, really tough Navy SEALs might claim that was only a tickle, but Blaine was anything but amused.

Maria wished a tornado would suddenly sweep through downtown Nashville and remove her from this incredibly awkward scene. She'd intuitively known that some disaster would befall them — it always seemed to when Christine was at the helm of a major hare-brained operation. Yet for reasons none of them could articulate, again and again they just went along. *As though we were zombies in a trance.*

In Sunny's case, that description was nearly apt.

Having regained control, Blaine instinctively checked his sides and back, as if there might be other threats nearby. His jaws hurt, so he spoke with difficulty. "One last time, ma'am," to Sunny, "hand me those drug packets taped to your leg."

With a combination of aggravation at the cop and adrenalin from the stun gun demo, Sunny grabbed the code list taped to her hairy thigh and pulled. A corner of tape came free. "Ow, ow, ow, ow. Oh, shoot a monkey!" Sunny finally realized why *tape* and *leg hair* didn't belong in the same sentence. "Ow, ow, ow."

Blaine's expression morphed from peeved to puzzled.

Maria confided in a conspiratorial whisper, "Doesn't shave."

Blaine peered closer.

They needed to end this. Maria reached over, grabbed the single corner of tape Sunny had been ow-ing over, and gave it a good Tennessee yank. Sunny yowled an agonized shriek. Maria's yanking hand crossed her body, flashed over her left shoulder, and smacked into flesh. More specifically, into Blaine's right cheek — he'd stepped in to take that closer look at Sunny's legs. Code sheet taped to his cheekbone, he leaped back.

Well, that would teach Sunny a leg-shaving lesson. And though it had not been deliberate to plaster his cheek with paper and tape, that might teach Officer Do-right not to peek so closely at a lady's crotch.

Blaine whipped the tape and paper away from his face with the back of one hand and holstered his light. Sunny's phone — the real one — suddenly resumed ringing *Maneater*. He reached in the vehicle, grabbed the phone, and flipped it open without any verbal acknowledgement.

"Bravo, we located the package!" Christine's voice was breathless with adrenalin. "Perp not yet in sight, but we located the package."

"Who is this?" Patrolman inflection.

"Uh, sorry… wrong number." *Click*.

"I guess this is a drug deal after all." Blaine glared at the phone. "Your dealer said something about a package."

"She's probably just going shopping again," suggested Maria.

Blaine was on his last half-inch of civility. "Ma'am. Step… out… of… the… vehicle."

Sunny obeyed promptly and shut the car door behind her.

Two ounces of bourbon had soaked into the crotch of her jeans, so Maria remained seated. "Officer, we just got off on the wrong foot here. If you'll let me explain, I think we can satisfy you."

"Satisfy? Is that an attempted bribe?" Blaine's indignant tone would have been good in a bad movie. "Are you really *trying* to get yourself in the jailhouse?"

"Jail?" It was known to be Sunny's second worst nightmare. She'd never revealed the first. "Shoot a monkey." A frantic wail.

Blaine's point became a thrusting motion. "Pick up those drug packets and hand them over."

"It's not drugs." Sunny bent over to the sidewalk and then held out the taped sheet. Hundreds of blonde leg hairs stuck to the tape.

"What *is* this?"

Maria rolled her eyes. *It was just on his face. Didn't he get a good, close look?*

Sunny moved closer. "Code list. I couldn't remember everything."

"Code for what?"

"Officer, it's not about drugs." Maria finally exited the vehicle. "And we're clearly not hookers." She extended both empty hands, as though that gesture confirmed her claim. No change in Blaine's expression. Maria realized it was about time for truth. "We're trying to follow our girlfriend's boyfriend because we think he's cheating on her."

"We're part of the League of Stealthies." Only Sunny could mangle the description so badly.

Blaine shook his head, probably thinking they should have stuck with more believable lies. "You," to Maria, "next to her." Then to both, "Hands on the vehicle. Spread your feet, shoulder width."

"Officer, can we just discuss this?" Maria should have tried whining earlier.

"Do I have to call for backup?"

Maria pictured herself on the TV show *Cops*. Several of Roger's friends watched it religiously. "No, no backup. No cameras. We'll cooperate."

"About time." Blaine began patting her down one-handed, less vigorously than he could have.

Music blared. Everybody jumped. Blaine lurched. His hand struck Maria's crotch, still soaked with bourbon. *Maneater*. Again. Sunny's phone, in Blaine's free hand.

Maria thought fast. "Could you let me talk to her?"

"Is she the dealer or distributor?" Collaring either one would be good for Blaine's record.

"Neither." Maria shook her head. "She's sort of the coordinator for our stakeout."

"Still sticking to that story?" Blaine sighed. "Okay, I'll hold up the phone. You talk just enough to tell her not to hang up. Then me."

Maria nodded. "Press the green button." Then to the phone, she said breathlessly, "Christine, do *not* hang up. Just listen. A policeman's here. He acts like he's going to arrest us. Tell him what we're doing and why — the truth. He thinks it's a drug deal."

****

Christine swallowed hard and whispered, "Okay, put him on, Bravo One."

"What's this all about?" Blaine's voice was loud enough for crowd control.

Christine still murmured. "Our good friend has a cheating, low-life boyfriend and we're trying to catch him in the act."

"Why are you whispering?

Christine sighed in a soft hiss. Difficult to do. "I've got the perp's bimbo in sight and I'm calling in my girls from downtown to get to his place as soon as they can."

Girls from downtown was evidently a regrettable choice of words. "Are you their madam?"

"No, no. Scratch that. Let me start over." Still at minimal volume, she clarified. "I'm here at the perp's apartment, my two helpers are watching the hotel where the perp and his buddy get bimbos at happy hour. I called to tell them we've just spotted the latest tramp but we're waiting on the cheater to show up. I need them here to help."

"Help what?"

Sounds like he'd be a good date for Sunny. Christine's new sigh was louder than before. "To capture the cheater when he shows up. We think their wires are crossed on the time for their tryst, or they came in separate vehicles for sneaking reasons."

"So who is this female you've spotted?" Possibly Blaine worried it was the wife of some important muckety-muck.

"Never seen her. Some trash from out of town, probably here for a conference."

"You know, not everybody attending a Nashville conference is out looking for trouble," recited Blaine. "Some actually go to meetings and exhibits." Likely an observation from the desk sergeant's recent briefing.

"No meetings scheduled at this time of night for the apartment we've staked out in Verdeville. The only exhibit is whatever he'd planned to show her when they got inside." Christine's whispers were more urgent. "Look, officer, we don't have much time. We need to secure this tramp and I need my girls from downtown to help catch the skunk that can't be too far behind."

It took some convincing. Christine name-dropped several officials of Verdeville and Greene County, including the divorce judge who'd given her such a generous settlement. Hearing no immediate reply from Blaine, she figured she had talked their way out of another jam.

****

Blaine did not recognize any of those individuals listed by the frantic whisperer, but he finally relented anyway. By that point of the evening, a few minutes from shift change, he was content for the Stealth League's Bravo Team to leave his Nashville jurisdiction and return to Greene County from whence they'd come.

Shaking his head, Blaine gave the real phone back to the ditzy blonde, who conferred briefly with the crazy whisperer before ending the call. "Out and over." She smiled with genuine gratification.

Blaine re-holstered his Taser, adjusted his equipment belt to try to hide the small urine stain, and let the Bravo Team go with a vague verbal warning. "I'm keeping this alleged code list as evidence."

"Evidence of what?" asked the one who acted like a teacher.

Blaine shrugged as he pulled some of the longer leg hairs off the wide expanse of tape. "Nobody at the station will believe any of this without evidence." In truth, he had not yet decided whether to breathe a word of it. He made his way to the patrol car while brushing at the stain on his upper thigh.

****

Jason ignored the flashing lights of a cop car on the far side of Fourth Avenue, even though two females leaned on the hood of a pulled-over car. *Probaby hookers.* He drove into the garage and entered the main hotel structure through the inside hallway, lined with bolted-down framed prints of Civil War lithographs.

He'd come looking for one person but stumbled into someone else entirely. After about fifteen minutes of conversation, Jason and a female left the hotel lobby together and made their way through the Civil War themed hallway to the parking garage. They stood side by side for a moment while Jason used his phone. He shook his head as he thrust his hand in a pocket for the keys. Then they went to their separate vehicles and both drove east toward Greene County.

Chapter 46

9:51.

Back at Ground Zero, Christine was in a pickle — the suspected bimbo was slowly approaching on the gloomy walkway among the darkened trees and bushes of the complex's green space... and the other half of Team Alpha was inside Jason's apartment cooling her heels.

Might be better to wait until Jason showed up to rejoin his date. No... Christine felt itchy to do something. Almost anything.

Why wasn't that woman moving any faster? She seemed to be lagging on purpose, like she was waiting on her date to catch up. But nobody else was in sight, at least not from Christine's vantage point. She'd read a quote somewhere, sometime, about grasping opportunity before it became regret. Or maybe it was regretting opportunity after you grasped. She couldn't remember, not with adrenaline coursing through her entire body.

It would be nice to have Alpha Two out here helping, but

she could handle this tramp by herself. Christine started to rise from her crouch. Just then the woman in the shadows stopped and turned, looking back toward the large parking lot. Perfect opportunity! Christine shot up, whacked her on the head with the stubby umbrella, and tried to shove her to the ground.

The woman struggled, but succumbed when another umbrella blow landed on the back of her neck. She folded in half and toppled over. She was stunned but not unconscious — not limp enough.

Christine threw her raincoat over the woman and then sat on top to hold her down.

"Psst! Psst! Psssttt!" Christine's call could not conceivably be heard by Amanda, indoors and over ninety feet away.

However, in a stroke of good fortune, Amanda appeared in Jason's doorway not long after that plaintive whisper-cry, cautiously emerging from the apartment. Peering into the darkened distance, she froze and then raced over. "What the heck have you done?" It was not even close to a whisper.

The neighbor's curtain shifted again at B-20.

"Help me with the body!"

"What body?" The word clearly chilled Amanda.

"I found your boyfriend's mystery woman!"

Amanda leaned over as though she could see anything in the dark. "Did you kill her already?"

"Not sure. She dropped like a sack of feed." Something smelled. Smelled awful, like the excrement from a large sick dog. Had she stepped in it? Had she ruined her brand new butt-toning shoes?

Struggling resumed. The captive hadn't remained stunned for long.

"She's alive!" It sounded a bit like the archetypal line from the *Bride of Frankenstein* movie, but Amanda's voice was filled with relief. "What's that on top of her?"

"My raincoat. I didn't have a net."

Amanda stared as though she'd never even met Christine Powers before. "Net?"

"You know, like wild game. Now give me a hand with her!"

"Well, if I help you, I'll be an accessory to attempted murder!"

"You're already an accessory, Amanda. And if you don't help me get her body off this walkway, you'll probably be the only suspect, because I'm taking off."

"Okay, okay. Need to think."

"Think later. Right now, help me drag her inside." Christine started tugging.

"Inside? Take her out back by the trash bins or something."

"That's the first place they look for bodies! Help me!"

More struggling. Christine clubbed her again, but it served more as a warning than an injury. With considerable difficulty, they steered — mostly dragged — the raincoat-covered woman into Jason's apartment. One eye and a shock of permed hair from B-20's window monitored the entire scene.

When they released the captive inside, she crumpled to the floor, still covered by Christine's raincoat. She moaned and tried to peel it off.

"Help me hold her!" Christine sat on her again.

"At least she's still alive. Now it won't be murder, at least."

"But she'll have a pretty good case for battery. Help me tie her up." Christine noticed she had one nice shoe — elegant, with obvious quality. The other of that pair was not visible. "Keep her face covered so she can't see who we are."

"But she's already heard my name, Christine."

"Now she has both our names, idiot!" Alpha One panted from the exertion. "Close the door. Lock it. Draw the curtains." Christine barked orders like she'd kidnapped before.

A phone rang and Team Alpha jumped back like they'd been electrocuted.

"What the…?"

"She's got a phone!" Amanda pointed.

"No kidding!"

"Answer it!"

"You're really new at this kidnapping thing, aren't you?" *Disappointing novice.* "If you answer the victim's phone, the police locators can pinpoint where you are. If it just rings, she could be in Oshkosh."

"You sure about that?"

"I watch *CSI* every week."

"They deal with dead bodies. Ours is still alive." To be certain, Amanda poked the body with the toe of her sneaker.

"For the moment," replied Alpha One. "But if she doesn't stop trying to bite me, that might change in a hurry."

The woman stopped struggling.

"We can't just let it ring."

"Why not?" Christine loosened her grip, but still sat atop the captive.

"It's irritating me. And I need to tinkle again."

"Well, go deal with that and I'll keep her pinned down. But hurry up. I need to, also. Besides, that call will go to voicemail. Eventually."

Amanda left. The woman began struggling again and her phone finally stopped ringing.

Christine called down the hallway. "Hurry up! She's regaining her strength. We still need to tie her up. And gag her, too."

The water cut off and Amanda reentered the front room. "Gag her with what?"

Christine looked around. Typical male room. "Greasy rags, Jason's dirty socks…"

"No! No socks!" She struggled even more.

"Or maybe duck tape."

"Uh, let me see. I'm pretty sure Jason has some tape somewhere." Amanda scurried away. "Hold on, I'll look in the kitchen."

"No taping!"

Amanda returned. "Pretty wrinkled. It was next to the toaster."

"Heat does that. But it's probably got some stick'em left. I'll lift up this raincoat and you reach in and put the tape over her mouth."

"Uh, how about I sit on her and you handle the tape?"

The woman shrieked. "No!"

"She's wiggling too much." Christine grunted with the effort to restrain their captive. "We need to hold her still and I'm stronger than you."

"Just because your chest is bigger doesn't mean you're stronger."

"We can have a brassiere contest later. Right now, stick that tape on her mouth. We've got to keep her from yelling. Jason's neighbors might hear."

That ship already sailed from Pier B-20.

Amanda pulled off a strip of tape five inches long, reached in with one hand, and felt for the woman's face. "Ow! She bit me!"

"Hey! Listen to me!" The captive's first coherent sentences. "If you want a ransom or something, you're out of luck. I'm not worth anything."

"See?" Christine pointed the squirming bundle beneath her. "No self-esteem. The fundamental problem with all bimbos."

"I am not a bimbo!" The captive bimbo.

That line sounded familiar.

"Shut up, tramp!" Christine struggled to hold the woman's head still. "Hurry with that tape!"

Amanda reached in with both hands and firmly affixed the tape, then smoothed it down. Then she sat back on her haunches with the first exhaled breath in the past five frantic minutes. "Done."

"We'll also need a belt or rope or something to tie her up."

"No! No tying!" the woman interrupted. "I've got phobias. One is being tied up. The other's being attacked by two insane women."

"I thought you taped her mouth."

"I did." Amanda demonstrated with her fingers. "You saw me."

"Well, she's not a ventriloquist."

"She missed my mouth. The tape's over my eye and stuck in my hair."

"Great job, Amanda."

"Thanks for giving her my name again, Christine!"

"Okay, we're Thelma and Louise. I'll be Thelma."

"You're older. You should be Louise."

Christine fumed as she tried to remember which character had been played by Geena Davis. "Okay, scratch Thelma and Louise — we're Cagney and Lacy.

"Only if I get to be the Sharon Gless character."

"She's the one I wanted!"

"Look, you can be Starsky and Hutch for all I care," the woman interjected. "Just let me go. I don't know what bank you robbed, but I don't even care about that. Just turn me loose and I won't even remember you. Amanda and Christine are easy names to forget."

"Lacy and Cagney." Christine still couldn't remember which role was played by the prettier actress.

"Whatever. Obviously you're looking for somebody else. I'm not even from around here."

"Suppose we believe you," Christine answered. "What

about this address?"

"Never saw it. I was in a different neighborhood altogether. Aren't we still in the north part of Nashville?"

****

9:51.

Back in downtown Nashville, Team Bravo reentered their vehicle, took a collective deep breath as the officer walked off, and then Maria drove away from Outpost X-ray. "Where did Christine say to meet her?"

"Ground Zero," said Sunny. "But where's that? The cop confiscated my cheat sheet."

"Zero, my dense Bravo partner, is Jason's apartment."

"Well, evidently they've located his bimbo but Jason is still at large." Sunny sighed. "And it'll probably all be over by the time we get there."

Maria weaved among lanes on the combined I-24 / I-40 until she could break out on I-40 itself and make good time. "You know, that's absurd." She gestured eastward, toward Verdeville. "Jason and his date would be together. Doesn't make sense for the slut to be alone."

"What are you thinking?"

"They've got the wrong girl." Maria nodded grimly.

"Shoot a monkey *dead*!" Sometimes Sunny's emphatic variant captured things perfectly.

"Ten to one Christine has pulled the trigger on another hare-brained scheme that's going to backfire in their faces. Our faces, too."

"So why are you breaking every known traffic law to rush over there?"

"Duh." Maria glanced at Bravo Two. "To watch the remainder of this fiasco unfold. I'll bet they've caught the mayor's wife or something."

"I'm sure Christine knows the mayor's wife."

"Well, it could be that skank married to the fire chief. Roger says everybody in Verdeville's fire department knows she's a cougar."

Sunny groaned. "Suddenly everybody's a cougar. Just because you're two years older than some schmuck doesn't mean you're a cougar."

"Just saying." Maria took the ramp too quickly and ice seized her lower belly as she straightened out on I-40 going east. They'd be in Verdeville in about eighteen minutes. Considerably sooner at 90 m.p.h.

****

10:04.

Back at Ground Zero, Amanda helped Alpha One periodically struggle on Jason's apartment floor with the woman still covered by the top-label raincoat, which now had a slit in the back.

"Where the heck are our reinforcements?" Christine couldn't check her watch but time was passing. "When did I call Maria and Sunny?"

She couldn't remember.

"Well, keep the tramp covered for a minute."

"Covered? I don't have a gun."

"You don't have to tell *her* that." Christine's whisper was loud enough. "Shh. I heard something outside the door. Check the window!"

"Look, you two whoevers, this is all a horrible mistake." The captive's voice was plaintive.

Amanda ignored the woman Christine perched upon and peered out the window. "Uh, just some kid. He touched the door and ran away. No, he's getting in a car. Driving up to the next apartment building. Kid getting back out. Stuff in his hands." Amanda turned around. "Flyers! Some kid delivering flyers!"

"At night? That's insane!" Christine paused. "What kind of flyer? If it's Pottery Barn, let me have the coupon."

"You can shop later. Right now we've got a woman in my boyfriend's apartment that you just kidnapped, maybe for no good cause."

"Amanda sounds reasonable," the victim interjected. "You should listen to her, Christine."

"Shut up, you! Besides, it's Cagney and Lacy. And we got plenty of good reasons — we just don't know what they all are yet."

"Hey, let's back up a bit." Amanda tapped her manic friend's shoulder. "I was inside when this person came up. I didn't see the original encounter. Tell me what happened."

The woman began, "I was on a dark sidewalk headed toward this door..."

"Not you! She meant me!" Christine obviously didn't like smart aleck captives.

"Oh. Well, go ahead, I'd like to hear this part, too. All I know is, you jumped me from behind, clubbed me with a crowbar, and dragged me in here with this tent over my head."

"Tent? You really do want to be tied up, don't you? Plus, it was just an umbrella."

"You two stop bickering," said Amanda. "Tell your dang story, Christine."

"It's Cagney. Well, I saw this woman lurking, scurrying, whatever you do when you don't want to be seen."

The woman interrupted, "Amanda, tell your aggressive friend here that I didn't do anything wrong. Walking on a sidewalk at night is not a crime, not even in Tennessee."

"Don't listen to her, Lacy. I've seen this in movies. The hostage tries to drive a wedge between the kidnappers."

"I'm not a kidnapper. Besides, I want to be Cagney."

Christine never liked losing debate points. "We can't both be Cagney."

"It won't matter who we are once we get to prison. Get off of her, let her up, and let's find out who the heck you've just kidnapped."

They slowly let the captive out from under the raincoat. She was a pitiful sight: mascara running, lipstick smudged, a long piece of duct tape over her left eye, another strip beginning at her forehead and disappearing somewhere in her disheveled tresses. Amanda didn't mention the abductee had one really nice shoe.

If standing, the captive would have measured about 5' 3". Her short blonde hair had dark brown roots. Her silk blouse — in the dim light, it was difficult to determine whether the material was off-white or ecru — was wrinkled and streaked with makeup and tears. She wore a short, tight, light brown skirt with sheer hose marred by runs. Probably in her mid-twenties. In a normal state, she could have been considered reasonably attractive, though about twenty pounds over her optimum weight.

With her untaped right eye, the terrified woman studied the door.

Christine discretely blocked that potential exit and flipped the dead bolt with a loud click.

Amanda sucked in a deep breath. The interrogation could proceed without further delay.

Chapter 47

At 10:17 p.m., Maria drove Team Bravo into the large parking lot nearest Blackwell Street; they'd made record time reaching Jason's apartment complex. Turning out her headlights and rolling to a stop, Maria parked as close as possible to the center building's Walkway B and turned off her engine. "Gosh, it's dark out here."

"Which building has Jason's apartment?" Sunny looked around. "I mean Zero Ground."

"Middle one. I think he's on the far left. Bottom floor." Maria pointed even though all they could see were trees and bushes. "I've been here with Roger once to watch a ball game, but that was on a Sunday afternoon. Nothing looks the same after dark."

Bravo Two suddenly hissed. "Who's that lurking around the front of those cars?"

"Don't know. He's surely suspicious, prowling around in the dark like that. Like he's looking for somebody."

"You think we should get him?"

Maria turned, eyebrows up. "What do you mean, *get* him?"

"You know, capture him."

"You and me, catch a grown man? We'd need a big cargo net and some tranquilizer darts."

"I've got my stun thingy." Sunny pointed.

"I still bet that device is faulty. Besides, you can't just zap people walking around at night. You'd better call Christine."

"Oh, yeah. Radio." Sunny put the real phone to her ear. "Wish I still had my code sheet."

— —

Music purred. Christine jumped. Stevie Wonder's voice, crooning *You are the Sunshine of My Life*. "What the frazzle! Uh, this is Alpha One at Ground Zero... over."

"Uh, I'm one of the Bravos. We left X-ray Pole and we're in the apartment lot — I mean we're close to Zero Ground. I guess this is Zero minus one."

"Oh, for crying out loud. Just spit it out, Sunny!"

"We're in the parking lot and we've just spotted Jason. Over."

"You sure it's him?" Christine already felt the adrenaline.

"We're parked right at the little walkway to Jason's place. He's approaching it now. You said you've already got his bimbo. Who else could it be? Over."

It was one of those heat of battle moments when an admiral has no time to hesitate — send in the destroyer or call it back. But no time to confer with the intelligence officer or check those charts again. Had Amanda been flag rank, she would have deferred to fleet command. But not Christine — she always attacked at flank speed. "Grab him!"

— —

"Roger. Out and over." Sunny loved saying that. She grinned at the other half of Bravo Team. "Okay, Maria, the mission is green-light."

"Did she say how a school teacher and flower child are supposed to capture a strong guy who plays every sport known to mankind?"

Sunny shook her head. "I think she wants us to improvise."

Maria seemed skeptical. "Okay. But I'll go talk to him first. You slide over behind the wheel. When I maneuver Jason to where he's facing you, turn the lights on bright and honk the horn."

"Uh, I don't think that will necessarily drop him."

The man, stepping very slowly, loomed in the shadows thirty feet away. He did not appear to notice the vehicle with two women inside.

"We don't have time to debate this, Sunny. While you've got him blinded and startled, I'll jump on his back and subdue him with your stun gun. You jump out and whack him on the head if he's still moving. Bring a grocery sack from my back seat to hood him."

"He'll suffocate with a plastic bag on his head."

"Not plastic, those new reusable cloth bags. Open weave. We use them for craft items at school. I've got several in the back seat."

Sunny hesitated. "Uh…"

"What?" Maria eased out of her car.

"Not sure." Sunny slid over. "Something doesn't sound right, but I can't put my finger on it."

"We can't dither all night. That's our plan. Your part is H-words — headlights, honk, then help. Bring bag and flashlight."

"Wilco." Sunny's new favorite word.

— —

Maria slipped around the side of her car and crept toward the man swiftly, silently. She might have been a jungle predator. His face wasn't visible because of the shadows, but she was certain it was Jason. Who else would be poking around the cheater's place in the dark? "Forgot your address?"

"Huh?" He turned suddenly and stumbled on the edge of a pothole. "Maria?" His voice sounded funny. *Creeps who cheat on their girlfriends often sound different under stress in the dark.*

"We've got a friend of yours waiting inside. You'd better come with me." She motioned.

Incredibly, he took two steps toward her. When she shifted sideways, he turned, too.

Just a moment too soon, Sunny hit the horn and switched on the high beam lights. The confused man flinched, but it also caught Maria's eyes. But she knew where the target was, so she jumped on him. It wasn't his back, however, as her plan had specified — she landed on his front, with her legs around his waist, almost like agile, embracing lovers.

Still couldn't see anything — besides, her bosom was in his face. But she did remember the next step: stun gun. She zapped him somewhere on his shoulder joint.

Properly working stun guns deliver high voltage (but low amperage) electrical charges into the target, on direct contact. They are engineered to negate the fundamental physics of household electric current — namely, conductivity and grounding. But when such a device has been altered, the results can be vastly different.

Between her clutching legs, the grounded target absorbed most of the stun gun's voltage. But the explosion of current zapped Maria, too. Something in her brain screamed *Turn it off!* but her fingers wouldn't or couldn't comply. The accosted man shrieked. Maria tried to shout for help, but her only sounds were variations of "Gnuhhh!" and "Rhreee!"

Good thing it was still set on *low.*

Likely unaware of the conductivity flaw she'd witnessed, Sunny evidently remembered she was supposed to club the perp, so she scurried over with the heavy flashlight and recyclable grocery bag.

As part of the couple writhing in the clumsy and unintended embrace, Maria watched helplessly as Sunny struggled to line up a solid head shot. She swung once and missed entirely. Her second effort whacked the arcing stun gun out of Maria's hand.

Maria gratefully exclaimed, "Gnuhhh!"

The man groaned and collapsed. Maria was barely able to disengage before she would have been trapped beneath him on the cratered pavement of the parking area.

"Are you okay?" Sunny was out of breath.

"Gnuhhh!"

"What are you saying?" Bravo Two leaned closer.

"Bbaaaaggg!" Maria tried to point but her fingers wouldn't straighten.

Sunny evidently understood that word, because she slipped the bag over the cheater's head, face down in a dry pothole. "What happened?"

"Kkoooonnnkk!" Again Maria tried to point.

Sunny shrugged and whacked the hooded head with her flashlight, though without measurable enthusiasm.

"Ccaaaalll." Maria tried to pose a hand near her ear to simulate a phone, but her digits still wouldn't cooperate.

"Call? Call Christine? Yeah. Wilco." Sunny flipped open her real phone and pressed the speed dial for Christine. "The eagle has landed."

— —

Christine was waiting and answered almost before the phone sang. "What?"

"We have the delivery... er, package. Oh, shoot a monkey, the cop took my stinking code sheet. We've got caught Jason outside his apartment, like you said."

"We're inside his apartment." Christine hurried to the window and peeked out. "Where exactly are you?"

"Out in the big parking lot near the middle walkway. Doesn't anyone listen to me?" Sunny sighed. "Maria jumped on him and zapped him with my stun gun. I whacked him with a flashlight and now he's out cold, face down in a pothole with a hood on his head. Bagged and tagged."

"Is he still alive?" Amanda leaned closer, straining to hear Sunny's side of the report. To anyone overhearing only bits and pieces, it would have sounded like a gruesome fatality.

Christine brushed off Amanda's query. "As soon as we re-stabilize this bimbo, we'll be right out." She peered out the window. "I still can't see you."

"Too dark. No moon."

"Wave something, Bravo Two."

Sunny waved the only thing with any volume and looseness, her long skirt. The breeze helped the sting where the tape had yanked a large irregular patch of blonde hairs from her thigh.

Maria tried to roll her eyes, but they paused in the top of their rotation. "Owwww."

"I still don't see you." Christine worried that Bravo might have the wrong apartment complex, or at least the wrong building of this one. "Let me talk to Maria."

"Uh, Bravo Uno's not talking so good right now. Some mix-up with the stun gun. Did you know you can shock yourself if you're holding on to the guy getting zapped?"

"Owwww," added Bravo One.

"That's not what I learned at the self-defense class last year." Christine strained to remember. "Maybe yours is defective. Whatever. Never mind Maria, I still don't see you. Just keep waving whatever you've got and let Maria hold your flashlight with the beam straight in the air. We'll find you in two minutes. On our way." Christine paused. "Don't let him see your faces and don't mention your real names. Maria is Batgirl and you're Robin."

"I don't want to be Robin!"

"Would you rather be Starsky and Hutch?"

In the background near Sunny, Christine heard Maria struggling to speak. "Owwww." *Like her teeth ache.*

Sunny seemed to understand. "So you two already claimed Thelma and Louise?"

Christine nodded into the phone. "We couldn't agree on names. We both wanted Thelma. Never mind, we can assign characters later. Oh, Sunny, if he wakes up, conk him again." *Click.*

Christine grabbed the wrinkled duct tape roll and put two wraps around the woman's wrists, one wrap around her ankles, and a big strip over her mouth. The captive struggled throughout. With tape mostly covering her left eye, she resembled a defeated Cyclops.

Then Christine and Alpha Two both stepped outside to locate Team Bravo and help them bring in the captured cheater.

Chapter 48

Amanda couldn't guess exactly where Team Bravo was, but she knew Jason's apartment complex, so she steered Christine through the small parking area and along the dark walkway lined with bushes and trees. As they neared the large lot near Blackwell Street, she finally spotted the wobbly beam of light. Maria was reasonably vertical, but looked like she might topple over from the flashlight's weight. And there was Sunny, waving her billowing skirt up and down like an addled cheerleader from the 1930s, standing over an inert male body with a fabric grocery hood over his head.

Amanda hurried toward them, but couldn't hear their conversation.

Maria had a nasty headache and a terrible attitude, and while she'd regained more of her senses, her speech hadn't caught up. Her moans were self-explanatory, but efforts to form real words emerged as nearly a different language altogether. In her mind, she said, "Quit flashing the neighborhood. All of Verdeville doesn't need to see your underpinnings." The actual transmission, however, was more like, "Qwee ffllls naaybbrrd uhlv Vvrrddvv zznt neee seeeyrr unnddrrppnngss."

Interestingly, Sunny understood — and acted like a very patient dolphin trainer. She hadn't considered the view from elsewhere. All she could see was her plentiful skirt fabric blowing around. "Oh, you mean like Amanda did at that big party?"

With the arrival of Amanda and Christine, Teams Alpha and Bravo were reunited.

When Maria nodded, the flashlight beam waggled in the dark sky. "Owww. Jaazznn's parrmnn?" She tried to point down the walkway, but her arm jerked away before she could aim.

"What did she say?" Christine peered closely.

"She's asking about the location of Jason's apartment."

"Are you sure?" whispered Christine. "What happened to her, anyway?"

"Zzzzzppppddd." Maria's nod turned to a loopy smile.

"Like I told you on the phone, she zapped herself while her legs were wrapped around the cheater." Sunny pointed down.

An inert male body. Hooded, face down among the potholes. Amanda's eyes burned as she fought two opposite instincts: to throw herself on top and smother him with comforting kisses... or to kick the stuffing out of him. She started to go over to him, but Christine restrained her.

"He could be playing possum. Don't get close enough that he could turn on you."

"Owwww." Maria's teeth still hurt and she wondered if she'd ever regain full speech.

Sunny momentarily ignored her injured dolphin. "I'm a little confused." Her normal state. "We got here after you were already inside with the bimbo. We just saw him walking along the edge of the bushes."

Amanda stared into the darkness — easier than looking at the limp body. "I don't see Jason's truck anywhere."

"Yeah. We never saw a vehicle either," said Sunny. "How come Jason dropped off the tramp, she evidently walked a bit, and then he parked way over somewhere else?"

"Standard procedure for cheaters. Never park where you plan to end up, because vehicles have license plates." Christine beamed, enjoying the role of expert. "When Daniel was cheating with the Chamber of Commerce secretary, he usually parked about a quarter mile from her house. He was getting in pretty good shape from all that extra exercise by the time my detectives finally caught him."

"But Jason's truck belongs here. No reason to worry about someone seeing his plate." Amanda scratched her head. "He wouldn't park somewhere else."

"Before you nailed him, where exactly was he?" Christine monitored the hooded, prone body.

When Maria pointed, her wobbly hand actually reached the aim-spot this time. "Wee naallldd mm awllz waallknng ruuthz sshhaadzz."

"Huh?" Christine whispered again to Sunny, "Is she going to be all right?"

"We nailed him while he was walking through those shadows." Sunny the translator. "Yeah, she'll be fine. She's already speaking much clearer than before."

"Owwwww."

Amanda eased away from Christine and stepped closer to the huddled prone form. "Not only is he cheating, but he bought new shoes to cheat in!" She knew all of Jason's footwear: two pairs of leathers, three pairs of sneakers, and cleats for every outdoor sport.

Sunny pointed toward the traffic on busy Blackwell Street. "I don't think we should stand around a body out here, but how are we going to get him into his apartment?" It was a line one might have expected from the more rational Maria, had she not been so dramatically compromised.

"He only weighs about 195," Amanda replied.

Christine took charge. "Okay, we each grab a limb and carry. That's about fifty pounds apiece."

It didn't sound like much weight except Maria could barely move herself, so the other three hauled closer to 65 pounds apiece. Christine's theory was fine, but in practice, it went badly. They carried the cheater's limbs, but mostly dragged his butt along the potholes of the parking lot — and along Walkway B — before the ungainly entourage reached Jason's front door. The covered captive moaned and grunted, but didn't regain sufficient consciousness to speak or try to resist.

Amanda again unlocked the door of B-17 and they rolled him into the front room with a final heave. He lay face down, motionless, one arm awkwardly trapped beneath him. With the body finally under indoor lighting, the electric pink recyclable grocery bag covering his head looked like a female action figure's accessory from a horror movie.

The captured woman rolled over and tried to scoot away. Her eyes widened in horror at four women dumping another limp body.

All four Stealth Team operatives finally in the same room, their joint attention turned to the securely taped female on the floor.

Christine crouched nearby. "She's the one most awake, so we'll pick back up where we left off a few minutes ago."

The captive's uncovered eye grew larger.

"Why does she have tape in her hair?" Sunny pointed.

"Never mind the tape," replied Christine. "We didn't get very far with her before we had to stop and locate you two. Let's resume the interrogation."

"No water-boarding!" Sunny looked horrified. "That's against the law now."

Maria rolled her eyes, which made a full rotation this time. She'd been silently practicing words and seemed to be pleased with a potential breakthrough in her speech progress.

Amanda pulled from the victim's mouth the single strip of tape, none too gently.

"Ow! I already told you this is all some big mistake. You've got no reason to hold me here."

Amanda realized she was actually correct. The captive was only needed to prove that Jason was cheating. Now that the core issue was resolved to everyone's satisfaction, they didn't require any further corroboration from her.

Christine's brain was visibly whirring. "You know, she's got a point." Christine faced Amanda. "Do you have any questions for her, before we move to Step Two?"

The woman trembled as if imagining the horrors of a *second* step.

"Just a couple." Amanda approached the woman, who had managed to struggle herself into a seated position. "How long have you known him?" She pointed to the hooded body a few feet away.

Practicing her speech self-therapy to one side, Maria paid little attention to the interrogation.

"Just since this evening. A few hours, I guess." With her uncovered right eye, the hostage looked from face to face to see if her answer had made the situation better or worse.

"Where did you meet him?"

"Downtown Nashville, big hotel. I'm not staying there. One of my friends convinced me to go over."

"The Nashvillage?"

"I think so." The woman nodded vigorously. "It's huge. Free drinks."

"Why'd you come back here with him after just meeting

him tonight?"

The captive must have considered lying, but maybe couldn't think of any convincing reasons. In fact, she struggled to think of anything at all. So she shifted to a different topic and lied about that instead. "This is my first time. Honest. I've never done anything like this before. I've been to other conventions in other cities and never done anything but get drunk. My first time, I swear."

It sounded heartfelt in a panicked sort of way, but Amanda didn't buy it. She looked at her Stealth League colleagues and all but Maria shook their heads sideways. *Nope.* Not believable. "Okay, here's what I figure. You've done this before. Maybe not the first few trips out of town, but after a while you saw your friends and other people doing whatever and you thought, 'what the heck'... so you started messing around, too. The only difference is tonight you got caught."

The woman began crying. *Truth hurts.*

"Got caught," Maria enunciated distinctly. She'd tuned back in.

Sunny noticed. "That was wonderful, Maria." She seemed ready to toss a morsel of fish as a reward. "I'm so proud of you."

Maria beamed like a star *SeaWorld* performer.

Chapter 49

Amanda had no real pity for their frightened captive, but realized it was a distinct liability for their evening's atypical activity to have a witness.

"We don't need this tramp any more." Christine had reached the same conclusion. "In fact, we need to get rid of her."

"Is that Step Two? You're going to *kill* me?" The woman sobbed. "Just because I drank too much and took a ride to this guy's place? Murder?" She started wailing.

Christine checked her watch — 10:29. Then she pointed to the source of the noise. "Tape her mouth again."

Maria had also regained her manual dexterity, so she tore off a fresh piece of wrinkled tape and planted it on the woman's mouth, moist from her recent tears. The unfortunate captive still had tape over one eye. "Slut." Everyone recognized that word. Maria smiled. *You don't miss speech until you don't have it.*

Sunny whispered, "You're not really going to kill her, are

you?"

Christine ignored Bravo Two.

Amanda also whispered. "She knows our names and faces. She's going to tell on us." She didn't favor capital punishment for cheating, but was concerned about the repercussions of their kidnapping.

"Would you tell anybody you got captured by four women when you were cheating with Jason?" Maria, the logical teacher, with her newly regained voice.

Sunny hesitated. "Well..."

"Not sure," said Amanda.

Christine bent down. "Look, tramp. I'm going to step to the side and confer with my colleagues here. You keep quiet and maybe we don't have to pull out your fingernails." She started to get up but paused. "Grunt if you understand me."

The captive resumed sobbing. Close enough to a grunt.

Christine backed away and whispered urgently to her stealth team. "We've got to wrap this up and get out of here. This stakeout is a total bust. We were supposed to catch them together and then just chase off the bimbo."

Maria looked over her shoulder at the woman. "So what do we do now?"

"Well, we can't just walk away and leave this slut in Jason's apartment with him passed out on the floor." Amanda felt somebody should state the obvious.

Apparently Christine had considered doing just that. "Okay, here's the deal. Only one way out of this — or we'll all get jail time for battery." She paused for that to sink in and to calculate some way out. "We pretend we're lunatics."

Amanda surveyed the scene and three Stealth League faces. "Not too much of a stretch."

"Okay, speak loud enough that she can hear," Christine whispered, "but act like you don't want her to."

Sunny was good at games. "We'll tell her we're vege-lanties." Almost too loud. "We're tired of the muggings and break-ins, so we're here to even the score."

That sounded pretty loony.

"No, we're not. We're law-abiding citizens commissioned by the Police Auxiliary to help cut down on vice," offered Maria. "What plays in Vegas might stay in Vegas, but sluts coming into Greene County get a phone call to the editor of their hometown newspaper."

"Not crazy enough," Christine whispered. "That's actually a *good* idea."

Maria shrugged.

Christine edged closer to the quaking body on the floor. "Don't listen to them, tramp. We're just out joyriding and looking for scalps. We'll probably just break your legs and carve a scar into your forehead. T for tramp."

More trembling.

"Look, you skanky whatever." Amanda tried to get into character. "I don't know how much sense you've got, but I'll try to hold off these bloodthirsty witches long enough to give you a head start." She poked the captive with a shoe for good measure. Then she yanked off the tape covering her mouth.

"Ow!"

Amanda continued. "You didn't see anybody's face and you didn't hear anybody's names."

"I… don't… even… know… my… own… name."

"Good, keep it that way." Christine looked pleased with how her protégé handled that.

"Roxanne!" the woman exclaimed, blinking her visible eye. "That's my name, Roxanne."

"Figures." Christine looked around the room like she wanted an enormous rag to clean up a really huge mess. She whispered something to Amanda and then raised her voice again. "Uh, we're going to step outside into the shadows and count to thirty, if we can remember all the numbers. You better be gone when we get through."

"Gone? But I came in *his* car. With him." She pointed both taped hands toward the pink-hooded body.

"You can drive, can't you?" Now that her jaw functioned properly again Maria could sneer.

Roxanne was probably too frightened to mention the tape still on her ankles and wrists, and she certainly didn't want to tick them off, but there were some practical considerations. "Keys?"

Christine looked Sunny in the eye and motioned her head toward the male body on the floor. For once, Sunny understood without explanation — *search his pockets for car keys.*

While Sunny groped him, and took her own sweet time in his front pockets, Amanda averted her eyes. *Can't watch my girlfriend fondle my boyfriend.* To shift her focus, she resumed her lecture. "Next time you're out of town and some smooth-tongued devil tries to get you in the sack, remember this night."

Roxanne nodded eagerly. "If I g-get home alive, I'm never leaving my city limits again."

"Where do tramps like you come from?" Christine frowned theatrically.

"Kn-Knoxville."

"Figures." Christine once got a speeding ticket there.

"What are y'all going to do to Kevin?" Roxanne didn't really care at that point, but when crazy people have attacked you it's sometimes good to keep them talking.

Christine rolled her eyes. "You mean Jason."

"I don't know any Jasons except a third cousin in Kentucky," Roxanne answered. "But you can tar-n-feather Kevin if you want. Be my guest."

The bottom dropped out of Amanda's stomach. "Hold on. Say his name again."

Roxanne eyed them cautiously. "Keevv-vviinn."

****

When Christine looked at Amanda, both knew exactly what the other was thinking. Christine inclined her head toward the male body on the floor.

Amanda scurried over and shoved Sunny aside. "Get your hands off Kevin's privates! You don't know where they've been." Amanda yanked away the cloth bag like she was finally uncovering the man in the iron mask. "It *is* Kevin! Grizzled gonads!" She crumpled to her knees.

"Oops... we got the wrong scumbag." Christine. "This might change things a bit."

Amanda's eyes were impossibly large. "What the heck is Kevin doing with this Knoxville woman in Jason's apartment?"

Roxanne could have answered but she was laying low, clearly hoping they'd focus on Kevin and forget about her. Perhaps she could eventually escape these lunatics.

"Well, technically neither of them was *in* Jason's apartment when they were apprehended." Unlike most of the Stealth Team's collective thinking so far, Maria's point was quite logical.

"Let me see those keys." Amanda checked them against hers. "Kevin has a key to Jason's apartment!"

"Shoot a monkey." Sunny blankly stared at her colleagues. "Why do we care who Kevin is banging?"

"We don't." Maria massaged her jaw muscles.

"Then why did you jump on him and zap him with my stun thing?"

"Didn't."

"Did so." Sunny was adamant. "I saw you in the headlights."

Maria shook her head. "Nope. He was Jason then."

"Huh?" Bafflement. "When did he turn into Kevin?"

"As soon as Amanda took off that hood you put on him."

To Maria, that satisfactorily shared the evening's blame, so far.

The man formerly known as Jason stirred. Sunny raised her flashlight with the intention of conking him again.

Maria stayed the execution. "Sunny!"

"Christine said to keep him out."

"That's when he was Jason. But he's Kevin now."

"She's right, Sunny. Better he's awake for a few minutes." Christine pointed elsewhere. "Whack the hussy instead."

Laying low had not helped Knoxville's unfortunate conventioneer.

As she half-heartedly bopped Roxanne's head, Sunny realized that, curiously, she enjoyed it.

Roxanne yelped and slumped over, dazed but not out.

Christine nodded at Maria. "Tape her mouth again."

Maria located the roll of wrinkled duct tape.

"Help me pull Kevin onto the couch." Christine grabbed him and with considerable difficulty, Amanda and Sunny helped wrestle him into position. "Now put the woman next to him."

They did, but Roxanne's head flopped over into Kevin's lap. Normally that would be fine with Kevin, but he was just coming out of a stun-gun-and-flashlight-induced stupor. Even his private parts felt dazed.

Amanda pulled Christine aside. "Forget about Kevin. How are we going to explain all this to *Jason*? You know Kevin's going to tell him everything."

"Simple. Leave it to me." Christine smiled thinly. "I'll use Man Psychology, my major in college."

"No such thing."

"Well, there ought to be. And I could teach it."

Amanda let out a cosmic sigh. "So what's your spin?"

"Just follow my lead."

"All I ever do. And that's exactly how we get into catastrophes like this!"

"This isn't a catastrophe. If that Knoxville woman was dead and we accidently shot Kevin for a mugger — *that's* a catastrophe. This is just a setback." As Christine paused to savor her wording, she wondered what had happened to the semi-conscious woman's missing shoe. But such topics were quite fleeting while Christine's brain churned in hyperdrive.

Maria checked her watch and Sunny eyed the apartment door. The evening's stakeout surveillance had taken a wrong turn onto a dead-end street.

Gazing out the window, Amanda wondered if the apartment's legitimate resident might show up anytime soon. Some people are actually home by 10:38 p.m.

Christine surveyed the two captives on the small couch. Neither was fully conscious yet. *Eureka!* She gripped Amanda's arm. "This, my dear, is a blessing in disguise. Not only do we have Kevin right where we want him, but he's going to help get us clear with Jason."

"How the heck do you figure that?" Amanda sputtered. "Oh, never mind. I'll just follow like usual."

Chapter 50

Christine hustled over where Kevin was perched next to the recumbent Knoxville female.

Groaning as he came to, Kevin eyed her warily, clearly unsure what to expect. Glancing down, he appeared startled to find his evening date bound and gagged on the couch next to him. He likely wondered whether he'd participated. "What happened to Roxanne?"

"She's fainted."

He leaned over, peering more closely. "It sounds like she's coming to."

"Well then, hurry! What's your cover story?" Christine played offense better than defense.

"Huh? I don't need a stinkin' story. Two of your buddies jumped me, zapped me, clubbed me, and stuffed my head in a bag." He scrutinized Roxanne. "Who knows what y'all did to this poor girl."

Christine edged closer. "You kind of left out the part about drugging her drinks and dragging her across county lines."

Kevin sputtered. "I didn't—"

"Not to mention intent to break and enter this apartment. That alone is three months hard time." Christine made up that penalty and paused for dramatic effect. "Four witnesses." She held up as many fingers.

He again attempted protest.

"Kevin, I can help fix this for you. But only if you play ball with us."

Amanda's jaw dropped. Her glance at Christine radiated a new respect. Deserved, of course. How many other people could so quickly shift the onus onto Kevin?

"Whatever." Kevin groaned. "But it better be quick. One of her eyes is moving."

"Okay, here's the real story. Amanda and I were never here at all. Neither were Sunny and Maria. A mugger jumped you both as you got near Jason's stoop." Christine pointed toward the door. "You bravely tried to defend this tramp, but she passed out before she could see the fight you put up."

Kevin began nodding. *Sounds pretty good.*

"It was the third mugging this same evening in these very parking lots," Christine continued. "Your resistance foiled him and the mugger ran away. You're a minor hero in this neighborhood."

Amanda looked on with undisguised admiration. Christine really had majored in Man Psychology.

"Kevin, can you remember all that?" Christine touched his temple.

"Let's see. Never saw you two or them." He nodded at Bravo Team. "Somebody jumped us. Uh, Roxanne fainted, I fought for our lives and chased off two muggers... I mean three big guys. Smashed the nose of one and broke the wrist of another. Third one ran for his life." Kevin's respiration increased, as if he relived his imaginary struggle.

"Exactly as I said it. One more thing." Christine waggled her forefinger. "You never, ever speak to Jason about us being here. Nehv-ver! Got it?"

Kevin nodded until he remembered his head pain.

Christine turned for the door.

****

Amanda clutched her elbow. "Hold on a second. I need some first-hand information before we skedaddle." She turned to Kevin. "How long have you had a key to Jason's place?"

He rubbed his head. "Eight or nine months, I guess. Since last time he had a tournament out of town."

"How many intoxicated bimbos have you brought here?"

Kevin paused, eyes calculating. "Only a couple. Three, maybe. Four, tops."

"Did Jason know about any of this?"

"I kept trying to check with him, but every time I was about to explain my big favor, somebody would interrupt. Didn't exactly want to ask him on a Facebook post, you know."

Amanda understood.

"Didn't figure it'd cause any problems as long as Jason wasn't here. And he was usually with you."

That was true, until the bizarre confusions of these past several days. Amanda's heart ached. *Will we ever get back to how we were?*

Christine crossed her arms. "Did one of your floozies wear black knee-highs with a serpentine pattern?"

"Snakes? Yeah, as a matter of fact, Layla made a big deal about losing one. I even came back and looked for that thing. Where was it? Kitchen?"

Amanda didn't even want to know why he assumed that location.

"Never mind where I found it," Christine interrupted.

"Oh, one more thing… hold out your hands like this." She demonstrated — flat with knuckles facing up.

"Why?"

"If you fought off that squadron of armed goons, you'd better have a few scratches on your knuckles."

Kevin's eyes widened but he complied. Most people obeyed Christine. With her .45 caliber stubby umbrella, she whapped the backs of his hands like she was destroying a deadly six-pound spider on her clean kitchen counter.

"Ow! Ow!" Kevin lacked her enthusiasm for authenticity.

She paused the abuse long enough to examine his reddened knuckles. "That'll do for the swelling and probably some bruising."

Amanda peered closely. "But of course we'll need some abrasion."

Kevin started to pull back. But his mental processes were not as fast as Christine's hands. She raked her sharp manicured nails across his knuckles. Cougars have claws.

"Freakin' heck, Christine!"

Sunny's eyes became saucer-sized.

Amanda leaned over as Christine whispered to her.

When Christine motioned for Sunny and Maria to leave, they didn't need additional instructions.

"One more thing, Kevin," Christine said. "Shut your eyes."

Later Kevin would likely wonder why he had unquestioningly obeyed such a command and vowed next time he'd simply flee. But without thinking, he closed his eyes.

Following Christine's earlier instructions, Amanda backhanded Kevin's face. Hard.

"Owww!"

Then the other side. Without permission, he had been using her boyfriend's apartment to seduce traveling women and his shoddy activity had caused Jason to be suspected of infidelity. Kevin deserved what he got. Amanda felt like delivering a roundhouse blow that would have knocked him over the back of the couch, but she restrained herself. After all, unless they're cornered and outnumbered, Tennessee ladies don't usually punch with a closed fist.

Kevin slumped over like he'd endured the rubber hose treatment of a ruthless 1930s police department.

Amanda tossed Kevin's key ring into his lap. "I'm keeping Jason's key." She squeezed it. "And don't ever set foot in this apartment again unless Jason's hosting a daytime Super Bowl party."

Kevin nodded wearily. "Are you going to tell Jason I've been using his place?"

"No." Amanda considered. "If he ever finds out, it should come from you."

Christine hustled back over. "Now get a damp washcloth and act like you're comforting her as she wakes up."

"Washcloth," he repeated and rose, shuffling toward the bathroom.

In a few moments, Kevin's return to the couch roused Roxanne and he dabbed the cool cloth to her forehead. She seemed groggily grateful for his tender ministrations.

Chapter 51

Amanda stood at Jason's front door and mentally surveyed the bizarre wreckage of the evening. *Ill-conceived, at best.*

Maria, who had been waiting just outside the door, stepped back in and pulled her aside. "You and I go way back."

Puzzled, Amanda nodded.

"I realize I'm just a second grade teacher and don't know very much 'worldly' stuff." Maria's fingers made air quotes.

That wasn't her perspective, but Amanda didn't correct it.

"Well, this has been egging on me since all this Stealth League business got cranked up by our hyper-ized buddy over there." Maria glanced over her shoulder. *Out of earshot, but paying attention.* "I heard you moaning about whether Jason is romantic enough and blah blah blah."

That wording surprised her.

"That's what it is — just blah blah. Fairy-tale stuff that everybody crams down our throats from the time we're toilet trained. But relationships are not constructed solely on romance. Sure, romance leads to the concept of the relationship, but the couple builds on a foundation of love and commitment, not romance. Yeah, the romance is great and if you're lucky, some major threads of that will continue through the relationship."

Amanda opened her mouth to interrupt.

Over at the couch, Kevin removed the tape from Roxanne's ankles and dabbed her face with the washcloth. She was still pretty much out of it.

"Listen, Amanda." Maria gripped her arm. "You don't love Jason solely because he rescued you. That was a fairy-tale moment that most women never get to experience. You're fortunate, really fortunate. But that was just the beginning of the interest that later developed. It was the early concept of the relationship. Not the relationship itself."

Amanda smiled. Funny how her friends could seem so ordinary most of the time, but — out of the blue — one would discern the most significant truths in a given situation. "So if not because of that romantic rescue, why did I fall in love with Jason?"

"He was just a bystander at a big, wild party. But unlike the others, he realized you — a total stranger to him at that point — needed help and he was willing to stick his neck out to provide it. And from what I saw, he nearly got decked by three angry drunks for his trouble."

"Just one drunk, but he was a really big guy."

"Whatever. You love Jason because he cared enough to risk something to help you. And you cared enough to risk something to thank him."

"What did I risk? Other than climbing on the ladder in a short dress, in the first place."

Maria sighed. "Do you really not remember your mindset at that time? Or I guess you could call it your *heartset*."

Christine quit staring and started walking toward them.

Domineering, hyperactive types don't like to wait in the wings while an important conversation is going on center stage.

But for once, Amanda waved her off. "Uh, yeah, Maria, I remember." She did. It was a point in her life where she'd again sworn off men. "Didn't want to be hurt any more."

"Exactly. So you risked that to thank Jason. And the more you and he saw of each other, the more you wanted to know."

"We moved from fairy tale to infatuation."

"But it didn't stay at infatuation; it continued to evolve. Your friends could see it." Maria pointed to herself. "That was the beginnings of your relationship — awareness grew into love."

"Love... including romance, but not exclusively powered by romance."

"I guess that covers it. We all watched it develop over those, uh, ten months between New Year's Eve and Halloween. Most of us couldn't believe it took you so long to realize you were already in love."

Amanda thought back. Some of it had been rocky, but it had taken a long time for them to come together because of how much she'd resisted. "Didn't want the pain again."

"And you *weren't* hurt. This recent stealth business was misguided and poorly informed, even if each of us, myself included, thought we were actually helping you out." Maria's eyes reddened. "We very nearly contributed to breaking you two up." She choked back a sob. "And Jason, apparently, had nothing to do with this apartment business after all."

So it would seem. There were other situations left to be explained, so Jason wasn't completely in the clear. But it was a relief to know the truth about the serpentine knee-high and ChapStick. "Thanks, Maria." Amanda hugged her. Sometimes this elementary teacher seemed distinctly astute.

Christine's hovering finally got the Stealth League moving. Maria hustled back outside, intercepted Sunny, and they both jumped into the Civic. Amanda and Christine grabbed their belongings and scooted out. About halfway down Walkway B, Amanda tripped on Roxanne's missing shoe. "Hold on, I guess I should toss this on the porch. Supposed to be some rain later tonight."

"Let me see that." In the dim light Christine examined it. "Prada. Very nice. This tramp actually has some taste in shoes. Knoxville must have a higher class of hussy than Nashville." She flung it into a cluster of heavy bushes.

"Why'd you do that?"

"That girl in there needs a lesson about leaving happy hour parties with horny divorced men she's just met."

Amanda stared back toward the bushes as they continued walking. "How's losing an expensive shoe going to reinforce that lesson? She's probably got them insured."

"You don't insure heels." Christine screwed up her face as she reconsidered. "At least I don't think you can." She waved her hand. "Anyhow, when she spends over five hundred dollars at the Knoxville Saks to replace those Prada pumps, she'll always remember where she lost half of the original pair."

"Or maybe she'll just start wearing cheaper shoes."

"Women who can afford Prada don't move back down the shoe chain to box stores."

Amanda slumped in Christine's borrowed car and sighed. "Wish I could wear Prada."

"I know how you can get them for half price or less... brand new." Christine winked as she closed the driver's door. "I'm very friendly with a young guy who likes lady's feet and can get fine shoes wholesale." She peered down at Amanda's dirty sneakers. "You're a size seven, right?"

She nodded. "This guy with the foot fetish. Is he icky?"

Christine pursed her lips. "Seems relatively okay to me. He fondles your feet for a few minutes and you save maybe two hundred dollars on really nice shoes. Just wash your feet when you get home."

"I don't know. Sounds sleazy."

"If you want a pedicure, you pay some girl thirty bucks to fiddle with your feet. With this guy, you *save* maybe six times that much and *he* fiddles with your feet. It's win-win."

"Prada's out of my league, anyway." Amanda shook her head. "I think I'll let Jason keep my feet entertained."

****

Inside Jason's apartment, Kevin locked the deadbolt and peeked through the closed curtain. They were gone. *Finally*. He returned to the couch, touched the damp cloth to Roxanne's forehead, and then to each of his own stinging cheeks.

Her eyes fluttered open.

"Hold still, Roxanne. I'm going to peel the tape from your mouth." He did.

Roxanne yelped and gasped, "What the h-heck h-happened?"

Kevin eased the tape from her wrists. "How much do you remember?"

"Not a whole lot after you dropped me off to park." Tears formed. "Some crazy women attacked me..." Roxanne gulped and her right eye glanced frantically around. "They were totally nuts! One said they were vege-lanties. What's that mean?"

"I'm gonna let you get that tape out of your hair. It's liable to yank some roots." He brushed stray strands from her forehead. "Uh, vege-lanties are those militants who don't want you to wear fur or eat meat." *Sounded good.* "Yeah, they were working with the four muggers who jumped me. When I saw you were in trouble, I came rushing over and four guys took me down. Beat the crap out of me before I finally got the upper hand. Thought I'd be killed trying to save you."

"Oh, Kevin, your lip's cut."

He flicked his tongue and tasted a tiny drop of salty blood. He held out his hands, scraped and swelling knuckles showing. "Those guys were built like NFL linemen. We're lucky to be alive."

Roxanne slowly pushed herself up and sat upright for the first time in over an hour. "I don't remember most of that. Must've already been unconscious. I do remember one thing for sure, those women were certifiable crazy!" Her hand felt the tape in her hair. "Ow!" She left it alone for the moment, but finally removed the piece from her left eye.

"So did you get a good look at them?" Kevin asked. "Think you'd recognize them in a lineup?"

She blanched. "Lineup? Are you kidding? They said they'd run an ad in the Knoxville paper if I ever said a word. Besides, when you see four lunatics, you've seen them all."

"Yeah, I don't think I'd recognize those five guys who jumped me, either."

She didn't notice the gang of thugs kept growing. *Excellent.*

Roxanne surveyed the apartment with both eyes, though her left blinked erratically. It was her first good look around without multiple crazed vege-lanties threatening her. "Uh, where are we anyhow?"

"This is my special refuge I told you about. You know, away from the hustle and bustle of downtown Nashville." He looked around. Jason's living room suddenly seemed threatening. "Although I don't think I'll use this place any more. Too much weirdness out here in the sticks."

Roxanne wiggled her toes, glanced down at her right foot, and pointed. "Um, Kevin, what happened to my other shoe?"

****

With no further incident and remarkably little discussion among Bravo Team, Maria drove Sunny home and dropped her off.

Sunny was still jazzed — she'd had more excitement in that single night than she could recall in the past four years. Carefully she turned off her defectively reconditioned cell phone replica stun gun and slid it into a pocket of her sizeable purse. One never knows when even the lowest setting of 100,000 potential volts might come in handy... especially when a judicious dose of amperage is delivered along with it.

Maria drove herself home with an expectant tingle. Roger's shift at the fire station was over; hopefully he'd still be waiting at her apartment for her. She could practice her spying techniques again. If Roger wasn't there, perhaps she could be comforted with a margarita or two. Maybe three.

Her jaw still ached.

Chapter 52

As soon as the engine rumbled down to silence outside her duplex, Amanda reached for the car door handle.

But Christine grabbed her arm. "Bogey at six o'clock."

"Huh?" Amanda turned as close to 180 degrees as she could in a car seat. An athletic-looking woman walked toward the duplex door. "Oh, hairy hell! Do we have to kidnap this one, too?"

Christine's fingers tightened. "Better be ready for anything."

Amanda scrambled from the car with no idea what she'd do, only that she had to confront the unidentified female. Clearly startled, the woman nevertheless looked prepared to mount a defense.

"Stop!" A male appeared from the darkness behind her.

"Jason!" It was more shock than recognition — a lump in her throat and ice in her belly. Jason's approach had eluded the amateur sleuths. The confusion and mounting anger of the past week had blindsided her into breaking up with him. Amanda shivered, the cold stretching into her arms and legs and leaving her numb. *And now he's here to dump me.*

And in her next heartbeat, Amanda knew that if she could take a mulligan on the past week, she would totally ignore Christine's influence and ask Jason directly for answers.

Hustling alongside, Christine drew a quick breath and went directly to offense. "So *this* is the bimbo you've been bagging!"

"Let's take this inside." Jason's face was stern and his tone cold — it had obviously been a long week for him.

"Jason?" Amanda jerked her head at the unidentified woman, who hung back on the sidewalk. "What does this mean?"

"Inside. Your neighbors don't need to be involved."

Barely inside the still-open door, Jason turned on Amanda. "Your friends have been following me, linking stuff that didn't really connect at all, making things up from thin air, and building a *file* on me, dangit! Now it's my turn to finally clear things up. And this time you're going to listen."

"Who's she?" Christine pointed. "Your enforcer?"

Amanda was thinking bodyguard.

The mystery lady followed them inside. "Actually, assuming you're Christine Powers, I'm the private investigator you hired. Diane Cheney." She extended her hand. "Your lawyer and my boss worked it all out. Pleased to meet you finally."

For perhaps the first time in her life, Christine was totally speechless. She rather limply held Cheney's firm hand.

Amanda stared. "*This* is your private eye? I expected Phillip Marlowe."

If offended, the detective didn't show it. "Throughout this very short case there were numerous gaps in communication." Cheney looked pointedly at Amanda and then Christine.

In her early thirties and athletically attractive, Cheney

wore dark Dockers and comfortable black shoes. A six-button Henley revealed attractive upper proportions. Since both sleeves were pushed up to her elbows, a light tan glowed on her firm forearms.

"I've been following Mister Stewart, as you hired me to do." Cheney pulled out a small notepad but didn't refer to it. "But I could never find him doing anything wrong. Oh, he went to odd places, some of them at unusual times. But only one thing was the least bit compromising."

Jason winced.

Amanda couldn't look away from Jason. The numbing cold ate away at her anger, leaving her more confused than ever. *First he's guilty, then innocent, and now he's compromised. What next?* But beneath her emotions, an illogical part of Amanda didn't really care. He was still her Jason. Wasn't he? "Detective Jane better get back to that part."

"Diane," Cheney corrected. "What I did observe was a lot of unusual activity from a man I later realized was Jason's friend and colleague, and from a woman I later identified as Mizz Moore's sister," Cheney checked her notes, "Kaye Moore-Smith, from Indianapolis."

"Amanda's sister?" Jason's mouth hung open. "Diane, you didn't say anything about her sister."

Amanda clutched Christine. "How does he know her first name?"

Jason frowned at Amanda. "I never got to meet your sister. Don't even know what she looks like."

"Well, she's..." Amanda started a description but instead went to the bookcase and grabbed the small photo album. "Uh, here she is."

"That's your sister?" When astonished, Jason looked like a cross-eyed umpire had just called him out on strikes. "Hmm, if she has a bit of a belly, that might be the woman Kevin said was a hooker asking questions about me!"

Deep inside, Amanda smiled and wondered if she could find an opportunity to relate that vivid impression to their parents in Tempe. *Mom might not think so favorably about Sis with that info.*

Cheney leaned over and checked. "Yeah, she was the one talking to your friend after you gave him the money and left." Raspy voice. "He thought she was a hooker?" Cheney smiled.

As hostess, Amanda realized she was amiss — her guests were all standing in the small entryway where there was a single chair by the door. No self-respecting Tennessee lady would refuse to seat guests no matter how uninvited, so she motioned to the area near the television.

Cheney took the wooden rocker. "Plus, there were some other women skulking around who I assume are friends of at least one of you, and a lot of involvement from you, Mizz Powers, though it also took me a while to figure out who you were."

Christine pulled over a dining chair and finally found her voice. "We'd been texting and e-mailing back and forth for several days!"

"But we'd never met." Cheney shrugged. "You were apparently off doing your own amateur detective work. Which, I should add, I specifically asked you *not* to do."

"I was going to meet with you tomorrow for lunch."

"Yes. Well, that won't be necessary now." Cheney tapped her notepad. "Because you and your friends, unless they've already been arrested for something I heard on the scanner in downtown Nashville, have greatly accelerated things."

Christine sat up straighter, visibly offended. She didn't like the hired help telling her off.

"I still don't get it. Obviously *something* was going on." Amanda grimaced and shrugged at Jason. "Sorry." She sat on one end of the loveseat.

Cheney continued, "Jason can later explain the things he's

told me about his softball team, his work, the consultant interview, the performance evaluation, and his associate Kevin Haywood. But the key is, I never found Jason doing anything wrong."

Jason seemed suddenly ill at ease in a place which had become his second home. He scratched his head and took the obvious position — on the loveseat next to the hostess.

The touch of his hip to hers was their first contact in many days, yet it seemed less intimate than crowded. Amanda closed her eyes for a moment of misery. *Everything's ruined and I watched it happen.* She wanted the closeness back, the intimacy they'd lost. But it was too late. She'd helped drive him away and even if she could trust him again after Christine's allegations, he'd never be able to trust her.

"There've been some strange 9-1-1 calls from Jason's neighbors, so I gather there was a lot of unusual activity at his apartment tonight. But he wasn't even there." Cheney tapped her notepad again. "I located Jason at the downtown hotel."

"Yeah, what were all those calls from my neighbors about?" He glared at Christine.

Strained silence. Nobody explained.

"Hold on a second." Christine's face looked like someone had tugged on a rug beneath her. "So neither of you knew that Kevin was using Jason's place?"

"Kevin was doing what?" Jason gasped like a ref had blown a late whistle in his ear.

Christine eyed him levelly. "He's been bringing his floozies to your apartment, when you weren't there, of course. He admitted it. Three or four times, at least."

"That lousy creep!" Jason pointed to Cheney. "Did you know this part?"

"I didn't know Haywood was using your apartment, though it better explains certain elements."

Wheels clicked asymmetrically in Amanda's brain. "Why

on earth was Kevin using your apartment for his bimbos? It's so far from downtown Nashville."

Chapter 53

11:05 p.m.

"Okay." Jason cleared his throat. "Kevin's apartment lease is still in his wife's name and she has people watching. If Kevin shows up with a companion, her lawyer gouges him for even more in the settlement."

"Can they do that? I thought everything was already settled." Amanda frowned.

Christine smiled mysteriously but didn't speak. She was known to keep her lawyer digging in her ex's wallet.

"Kevin kept mentioning a favor. I guess that was it, using my apartment. Even though he never actually spit it out, obviously he took it for granted that I'd agree."

Christine had not spoken much. "How much of this did you know?" she asked Cheney.

"I just knew Jason wasn't bringing other women to his place," replied Cheney. "The only woman I saw there while Jason was present was you, Mizz Powers. By the way, I'm assuming you taped whatever happened… and that's illegal."

"Tape? You *taped* me?" Jason sputtered and growled, "You bugged my apartment?"

"Not exactly." Christine cleared her throat.

"Then how did you tape me?"

"She bugged her boobs, Jason." Amanda's reply had an edge. "There, I've said it. Now we can move on."

"You were shoving your boobs in my face because you had a mic hidden in there?" He took another look. True, said bosom offered sufficient cover and concealment to hide lots of objects. "But I thought..."

"That I had the hots for you? Ha! That'll be a cold day in Hades." Christine caught herself. "Uh, sorry, Jason. It's just I've concluded we're not exactly a good match, if you know what I mean."

He nodded. He knew exactly.

"Jason, when I learned tonight that Kevin's been using your place, I realized you had nothing to do with those incriminating things Christine found in your apartment." Amanda gulped. "And I'm sorry I even suspected you. But why didn't you explain them on the phone last night?"

"I had no idea what you were talking about." He shook his head. "And I didn't *know* the explanation! Not 'til just now. I'd find things missing, like cherries and, uh, magazines and stuff that was moved around..."

****

Amanda noticed Christine didn't mention her involvement with those anomalies.

"...but I couldn't figure what was going on," Jason continued. "It finally dawned on me that those unusual things might possibly have something to do with Kevin's big favor. You know, like maybe he was borrowing stuff. So I tried to reach him to see if he knew anything. But he doesn't carry his phone when he's hunting babes and I couldn't catch him this evening at his favorite hotel. That's how I ran into Diane here."

"Again with 'Diane'?" Amanda glared.

"Okay, Mizz Cheney." He gulped.

"Whatever." Christine waved her hand. *New subject.* "Exactly how or where did you and Jason hook up? Evidently it was tonight sometime."

Jason nodded. "I'd noticed a woman following me in the hotel lobby and thought she looked kind of familiar. Turned out she was the one drinking coffee at Wendy's, where we'd spoken briefly."

"You met her before?" Amanda punched his arm with bent knuckles. To Christine, "He met her before!"

Jason nodded again. "You had a mysterious, whispery voice that night, Diane."

"You met her at *night*?" Another slug to his arm. To Christine, "At night!"

Cheney placed two fingers to her throat. "Early summer cold. Touch of laryngitis."

"Anyway, I doubled back behind her and asked if she was."

"Was *what*?" Amanda glared again.

"Following me."

"Startled me, too," Cheney interjected. "Usually I'm pretty good about keeping the target in view, but I must have looked away as you made your move. Can't let that happen again."

"When she explained about being hired, but not really finding anything wrong — about me, that is — most everything kind of fell into place." When Jason faced Amanda on the loveseat, she had to turn away. Not only had she suspected him of everything the amateur detectives could dream up, but *he'd* spent the entire time stumbling in the dark trying to find his way back to her. "Except I didn't know about

Kevin using my apartment."

Cheney eased the rocking chair back and forth. "He convinced me to come here and help set it straight. Normally I wouldn't have, because my only obligation is to report to my client." She nodded toward Christine.

"On the way over here, we drove by my place, just in case you might be there." Jason pointed to the phone on his belt. "I tried to call you, but your phone isn't working."

Amanda didn't explain their stakeout phone blackout. Too embarrassing.

Jason looked around Amanda's small living space as if to see whether someone else had a question. "So, anyway, Diane and I pieced most everything together."

"Not everything." Christine squirmed in her seat like an anxious prosecutor watching her case fall to pieces. "And don't try to wiggle away so fast just because you've got a partial alibi. Amanda's sister heard you and a woman inside a hotel room on Tuesday night." Christine turned to Amanda. "Which room did she say?"

"Fifth floor... 537."

"I think I can straighten out this part," Cheney replied. "Jason got on the elevator with someone. I saw your sister following, but up the stairs, and she obviously got off on the wrong floor. I don't know who your sister listened to, but it was somebody else."

Amanda was not satisfied. "So exactly whose room did you go to, Jason?"

"It's confusing. And I knew you wouldn't believe it, which is why I didn't even try to explain it before. It was the counselor-trainer lady from Alabama. We'd had the interview that morning, but Grunion interrupted it to get me to cover lunch breaks, and that evening Erin bumped into me—"

Amanda interrupted: "Who the blistered butt-rash is Erin?"

"Erin Chester, the counselor, uh, trainer. Whatever."

"I checked her out with the desk clerk. The hotel staff said she's legit." Cheney nodded. "She and another trainer were here through Wednesday morning, but Mizz Chester is staying over another day or so."

Amanda motioned for Jason to continue.

"So we bumped into each other in the lobby of the hotel when I was looking for Kevin because I wanted to drag him over here to help me explain all this stuff to you. But Kevin was already gone, apparently, and I ran into Erin instead."

"Again with Erin." First names — especially female ones — really steamed her, no matter how badly she wanted him back.

"She had this razzle-dazzle article she insisted on giving me about the importance of couples communicating."

"Yeah, who needs that?" Amanda's irony was chilly and intentional.

Christine jumped back in. "And what floor was this female trainer on?"

"The hotel clerk gave me Mizz Chester's suite number — 686." Cheney turned to Amanda. "Different floor from whoever your sister listened to."

"Leave it to Kaye to eavesdrop on heated love-making and insist it was my boyfriend." Amanda's observation came out wrong and she blushed deeply.

Jason obviously didn't get it. But he evidently did remember something else. "And I finally think I know what you were talking about last night on the phone, when you asked about the woman pestering me at work. That was also Erin… uh, Mizz Chester. I'd been dodging her because I didn't want her picking my brain apart and she was asking questions about me all over Gee-keck."

"And I'd already figured out that the demanding woman in Gee-keck's lobby — the nasty one from Indiana — had to be my sister Kaye. Imagine her being pregnant with your baby."

At the word *pregnant,* Jason's eyes doubled in size.

Chapter 54

Jason was slowly calming from his elevated stress. As he scanned the faces in Amanda's living room, he wondered what else of the cluster of mysteries remained unresolved.

Christine resumed her attack. "Okay, let's say you can brush aside Kaye's eavesdropping in the hotel, the woman pursuing you at Gee-keck, and the Hoosier in the lobby demanding to see you. But you're not home free yet, Jason. I personally spotted you in two different places with two different women, during the week before all this broke out."

Jason's mind went blank. "Amanda, is this what you were fretting about on Monday, but wouldn't just spit it out?"

Amanda's shrug was partly a tremble. "I thought you knew what I was talking about. After all, you were *there* for the encounters in question."

"What encounters?" He glared at Christine. "Where did you see me and who were these alleged women?"

"Oh, they were women, all right. Mall food court — about, oh, ten days ago. Very attractive, business suit, nice legs, power shoes. You handed her something and she touched your arm."

Jason closed his eyes. "Legs?" *Would have remembered that.* "Food court?" He didn't recall ever meeting anyone at the food court besides Amanda or Kevin. *Hmm.* "Oh! My tax lady!" He opened his eyes wide. "You remember how I had to file an extension because I couldn't find one of my 1099s and some receipt she absolutely insisted on?"

Amanda nodded. "Kind of." She had actually proofread his IRS Form 4868.

"Well, she had filed Schedule Whatever because of those few bits of missing paperwork. And that bought us some time. So, anyhow, I finally located them and my CPA was on her way into Nashville for some big meeting with some rich muckety-mucks. All dressed up, too. I just had a few minutes to catch her and the mall was her most convenient place to meet."

Christine grudgingly nodded. "Okay, but what about the woman at the Verde Grocery a day or two before that? Snack aisle. Tight, tailored jeans and platform sandals. Low-cut tank top. Camo."

Jason sweated that one. He spent a lot of time on that snack aisle — this could be just about anybody. "Camo. Any other hints?"

"You cupped her."

"Did what?" He positioned his hand near his own chest. "You mean…" *Surely would've have remembered that.*

"No, not there — her elbow. Christine saw you." Amanda demonstrated on the crook of her own arm.

"It was right in front of the barbecue chips around late morning," added Christine.

"Eleven or twelve days ago?" That might not be solvable without replaying the grocery's surveillance tapes. "Dangit, I don't know. But what could I possibly do wrong in the snack aisle? I mean, unless I open the bags and eat samples or something." Jason shook his head. "Wait! Nearly two weeks back. Low-cut camo top, you said?"

Christine nodded.

"That's a little girl from my old neighborhood. Her folks still live not far from my Mom's house on Mayfield. We played together as kids — what a tomboy."

"She looked all girl to me, even without the five-inch platform heels." Clearly Christine hated learning a plausible solution to that well-documented sighting.

Cheney interjected data from her surveillance notes. "And I already texted you about Jason meeting a man and a woman at the mall on Sunday. The man later turned out to be Kevin Haywood."

"And like I tried to explain to you yesterday, that woman was Paula somebody from north Georgia who spent two nights with Kevin and he was so impressed with her intellect that he wanted me to see her as proof that he could bag a *smart* one. Remember?"

"Yeah, I remember hearing that tall tale, but I didn't believe it for a second."

"See? That's exactly why I didn't waste any more time trying to explain anything. You'd already decided that whatever I was going to say was automatically a lie, so there wasn't any point in saying anything at all. I would've been better off if I *had* told a lie that you might've believed, than telling a story that was true but sounded unbelievable." Jason's awkwardly phrased defense was heartfelt but barely understandable.

He was exhausted and everyone else looked it; his watch read 11:17. All the allegations had been refuted, the charges dismissed, and Jason stepped down from the dock — a free man.

****

In considerably less impassioned tones than before, Amanda asked why Jason hadn't tried harder to explain things earlier.

"That's exactly what Erin asked me."

"So, what did you tell this Erin person?"

Jason took a deep breath and needed every bit of it. "That I should've explained things I thought were so bizarre that you'd think I was lying and I didn't want you to think that so I somehow convinced myself it was almost better not to say anything and let you imagine whatever rather than tell you stuff that was so unbelievable that I didn't even think I could explain it without looking like an idiot, which, as it turns out I probably was, because I could've just told you outright, like I'm telling you now, instead of storing it up and letting it explode into a big brou-ha-ha with you thinking I'm messing around and me thinking you were just ticked because I was late and stuff, which is what Erin was trying to tell me in our conference at work once I finally got trapped into going in there when Grunion nabbed me."

Whew! Amanda had to take a breath for him. Jason's Faulknerian explanations were epic. "Well, we still need to work on the explanation part. But disclosure is the right idea, even if it is a bit murky." She'd need to know more about this Erin person.

"So you do believe me, finally?" Jason edged toward her on the love seat.

Amanda hesitated. "Well, *believe* isn't the most accurate word, because — like you said — the explanations are so unbelievably bizarre." She searched his face. "But I do trust you, again, and I accept your, uh, debriefings."

Jason grinned — his first time in days.

Amanda crushed into him and they squeezed. "Oh, Jason,

I'm so sorry. I knew you wouldn't be messing around. But everything everybody saw and heard just seemed so overwhelmingly suspicious."

"You mean all that stuff in my *file*?"

Eyes moistening, she nodded.

"So how come you went along with Christine even though you didn't really believe I was messing around?" He obviously didn't care that she sat four feet away.

Christine looked uncharacteristically uncomfortable.

Amanda thought a moment. "It's a bit like debating a tornado. Know what I mean?"

"Yeah, like arguing with a ref or an umpire."

Oddly, Christine didn't visibly object to the tornado imagery. It likely fit into her self-concept. She'd probably have to think about the sports metaphor.

Amanda hugged him again tightly. "I'm sorry, Jason."

His long arms enveloped her so intensely that she suddenly felt absorbed by him. Then he eased back and kissed her lips. "I'm sorry, too, Mandy." He only called her Mandy at certain times and this was the first occasion in over a week.

As Amanda looked into Jason's eyes, she addressed Christine and Cheney. "Look, you two… Jason and I are going to bed. Lock up when you leave."

Jason displayed his second grin in a week.

****

Christine's eyes grew large.

"I'd call that a hint." Cheney jabbed with an elbow. "Okay, Mizz Powers, shall we continue this out in the parking lot?"

In a bit of a daze, Christine led the way out the door. The apprentice investigator waved a quick goodbye to the couple retreating down the hallway, but they didn't notice. Cheney twisted the handle lock switch and closed the door until there was a satisfying click.

Chapter 55

Diane Cheney started along Walkway B toward her parked Bronco. "You want to cover any more material tonight? Or would you rather wait for my full report? After you pay the bill, of course."

Christine frowned. "Oh, I'll just read the dang report when it's ready." She was likely imagining an invoice for four figures. "I think I've got the broad strokes, but answer me two things."

"Shoot."

Christine followed. It likely felt unusual since she appeared accustomed to leading. "Why didn't you tell me you were a female investigator?"

Cheney tried to keep from smiling. "One, you didn't ask. Two, would it have made any difference in me getting the contract? Three, why does it matter now, since everything's evidently solved?"

"Okay, fair enough. I just assumed a detective would be a man, so shoot me for a sexist. And in my imagination, I pictured a young man with muscles and a scar across his cheek."

Cheney laughed. "Which cheek?"

Christine smiled ruefully. "I meant on the face."

"Sorry to disappoint you." She thought a moment. "Oh, I once dressed up as a male pirate for Halloween. Maybe you picked up that vibe. Ha."

Cheney stopped at the Bronco and looked over her notes one last time.

"Oh, my second question — what was that 'single compromising thing' you so briefly referred to?"

Cheney climbed in, slammed the door, and turned the key sufficiently to roll down the window. "You hired me, so I'm obligated to tell you. But I wish I didn't have to."

"Hold on. I might want to be sitting for this." Christine circled around the vehicle's front and got into Cheney's passenger seat. It was a lot higher off the ground than she'd thought. "Okay, go on."

Cheney cleared her throat, still painfully raw. "On Tuesday evening, Jason was in the hotel lobby looking for someone. I assumed he was looking for a girl, but he just now said he went after his friend. Anyway, this tall woman, the consultant, startled him. When she tapped his arm, he nearly jumped out of his skin."

Christine motioned for the story to proceed.

"So anyhow, Jason was still looking for Kevin — and suddenly this Mizz Chester was leading him by the arm."

Christine's eyes grew large.

"Very odd. He actually looked like he was helpless under her power."

"Hypnotized?"

"Well, glazed look… and she steered him right into the elevator."

"And you got her room number from the clerk, et cetera."

"Glad you mentioned that. The bribe for that clerk is listed on the bill under miscellaneous expenses."

Christine waggled her hand. *No matter.*

"I was right outside her door. They were in there at least twenty full minutes. Jason came out, looking exhausted, with an article in his hand. I figure it takes about two minutes to pick up an article from a trainer you've been dodging... unless you *want* it to take longer."

Christine nodded sagely. "So what do you figure happened in the other eighteen minutes?"

"Can't swear to this." Cheney swallowed and winced. Still painful. "But I think he and the consultant were doing some role-playing."

"What kind of role play? You mean like the rich witch and the cabana boy?"

"Couldn't hear all that much. I should've brought my electronic amplifier, but I'd left it in my vehicle since I figured to be mainly inside the lobby." Cheney scrunched her face. "And I don't think it was necessarily *sexual* roles. Heck, it might not have been role-playing at all."

"Just spit it out. What did you hear?"

"Bits and pieces that sounded like she was prepping him with what to say to his girlfriend."

Christine's mouth hung open. "Why would she do that?"

"Exactly. Didn't make sense, unless there was some reason an explanation was necessary."

"Explanation of what?"

"Don't know. Honestly, I don't." Cheney flipped back over her notes. "Look, I kind of wanted to catch him red-handed, so to speak, just because that was the gig and I like to produce what the client wants if I can. But those eighteen minutes were more significant for what I did *not* hear."

"Clear as mud." Christine rolled her eyes.

"Okay. What I'd expect in a situation like that is the

sound of clothes coming off, heavy breathing, maybe some giggling, various noises of bed springs, and the like. With the wilder ones, you might hear a headboard bang against the wall, or even elbows."

"Whew! Hold on, I think I need a cigarette."

Cheney kept going. "But I didn't hear any of that. Just low voices mainly. And I'd catch a few words here and there when I was in just the right spot at the door."

"So you don't think they *did* anything, after all?"

Cheney paused to consider her phrasing. "That's not what I said. I didn't *hear* anything that sounded incriminating. But his presence in that room seemed pretty damning. Eighteen minutes is a long time in the sense of urgent get togethers of a sexual nature, if you know what I mean."

Christine nodded again; she certainly knew. A fine sheen of sweat glowed on her forehead. "So what's your gut say?"

"I can only report what I saw and heard. But if you want my personal, uh, guesses, I can give you those separate from the formal report."

Christine rolled her hand. *Proceed.*

"Well, if two people were on the same page, you could have a lot of 'interaction' in eighteen minutes." Cheney made air quotes. "On one extreme, she could have *serviced* him during that amount of time."

Christine gasped.

"On the other end of the spectrum, they could have just been making out."

"Making out? But these aren't high school kids parked behind the gym!"

"You asked my gut reaction. I can't think of anything else that would produce so little detectable noise." Cheney paused. "But, remember, both of those are merely wild guesses, *assuming* they did anything at all."

Christine was stony silent.

"Look, I know very little about Jason Stewart beyond what you furnished to enable me to monitor his activity. You've known him, what, some two years or so? What do *you* think he was doing in that woman's room for twenty minutes, besides picking up an article he threw away before he left the lobby?"

"Well, if you'd asked me that before this evening, I would've sworn he was banging her brains out. But after learning all my carefully collected evidence has crumbled, I guess there's a possibility that maybe they just, uh, talked."

"That's kind of my gut feeling, too. But it's important for you to be settled on the matter."

"You say he tossed the article?"

Cheney nodded.

"What was it about?"

Cheney reached to the back seat for the folded and bagged article. "See for yourself."

Christine held it with fingertips. "Uh, it's 'Honest, Direct Communication: Why So Many Couples Break Up Without It'."

"Notice the author."

"Erin B. Chester!" Christine's mouth fell open. "That's *her*."

"Yep."

"Wonder why Jason tossed it."

"I was hoping you could tell me. But from that long winded paragraph-sentence we just heard, I'd say that boy can't express himself too well, so he doesn't try all that often."

"Which would suggest that he keeps the article and reads it."

"A smart guy would." Cheney nodded. "Is Jason pretty smart?"

"Not so much. He can play ball and fix things, and he's good at his job, as far as I know. But he's not female-smart at all." Christine chuckled. "In fact, as far as understanding women, I'd say he's about dumb as a mud fence."

Cheney whapped her own thigh with the notepad. "You know many men who *are* really bright in that area?"

Both laughed.

"That Jason is a bundle," said Christine with her tongue clucking in her cheek.

"Yeah. Amanda better hope he never gets sick."

"Oh, he already was. Had a sniffle in January, I think." Christine closed her eyes. "Yeah, January for a few days. But Amanda was endeared by all the attention he needed."

"I'll bet they'd only been together a couple of months by that point," said Cheney. "Right?"

"I believe so. From about Halloween to mid January."

"Well, if he ever gets a Man-Cold, it will shut down the whole town. She'll have to move him to the quarantine unit in Nashville."

"Man-Cold, huh?" Christine seemed to be thinking out loud. "Well, maybe I could help her with that."

"Best to stay out of it, Christine. When guys get a Man-Cold, the last place you want to be is between them and their woman."

"Whatever."

Cheney's eyes caught her notes about the truck stop, still unresolved. But her mouth wouldn't let her mention it. No need to interrupt the momentum so near closure. Besides, she'd decided to further investigate Exit 248, on her own time, to try to figure out its attraction.

****

Christine sighed. "So, happy ending."

"Well, it depends on how you use the information and supposition about those eighteen unexplained minutes."

"What do you mean?"

Cheney eyed her. "Do you plan to tell Amanda?"

"Of course!" Christine saw the immediate look of disapproval and realized she didn't appreciate even unspoken censure from the hired help. "So you think I should keep it secret?"

"If Amanda finds out about those missing minutes with the consultant, it should come from him, not you. Certainly not from those flakes you stationed across from the Nashvillage tonight. This is your friend's relationship at stake. That should never be meddled with."

"But wouldn't Amanda want to know?"

"Maybe, maybe not. But leave it to Jason whether she finds out." Cheney studied the photocopied pages on the seat between them. "The fact that he had an article on couples' communication suggests he's interested in making an effort."

"But he tossed the article."

"Maybe he scanned it. Is he a fast reader?"

"Only if it deals with sports."

Cheney cleared her raw throat. "Leave it lay. I mean, that's my formal recommendation."

Christine scrunched up her face. "So Jason wasn't doing *any*thing wrong? I mean, besides maybe some smooching for up to eighteen minutes."

Cheney shook her head. "Not as far as I can tell, not for these past five days and four nights. And I've been on him like a bad case of poison ivy."

"That's a plug saying you've earned the fee I'll see when the bill arrives."

"Actually, I've got the bill right here. Frank said the client is more *invested* when she handles the bill immediately." Cheney handed it over.

Christine gasped. "Yikes! I'm invested, all right."

"See any charges you disagree with?"

She glanced over it. "No. Looks valid. It's just unreal how

fast it adds up." Christine exhaled. "Whatever." She opened the Bronco's door and slid out. But the added height threw off her balance. When her right foot hit the pavement, the ankle buckled and she tumbled into a heap among the potholes. "What the…!"

Cheney hurried around and helped her up. "You okay?"

She moaned and cursed as she took inventory. "Twisted my ankle, tore my slacks and shirt, ruined my raincoat, banged my knee, did something to my elbow, and I think I'm dizzy." She'd also skinned the heel of her right hand.

"Sit back and let me see the ankle." Cheney slid up her sleeves. "I had first aid during my Air Force hitch."

Christine's bottom landed with a thump in a low spot, still damp from the last rainfall. Moisture seeped into her panties. She gritted her teeth. Hateful feeling. Christine moaned as she mentally tallied up her losses for the evening, including — as her nose just remembered — dog dung on her new butt-toning shoes. *Why do things always happen to me?* She studied the athletic detective and yawned — 11:50 p.m. "So, other than me paying this bill, what's next?"

"Your instructions were for me to follow Jason until I found him boinking his honey. Since we were just tossed out and those two lovebirds are going to bed, I'd say I've completed my assignment." Cheney nodded back toward Amanda's apartment. "However, in their case, I wouldn't use the term boinking. My guess is they're making love with passion and tenderness. Big difference."

"Yeah," she said, rubbing her aching and rapidly swelling ankle. "I remember."

****

Amanda asked only one question. "Do you still love me? Even after all this… whatever it was?"

Jason answered with a long, deep, urgent kiss.

No need for further discourse.

Their passion seemed like it had been pent up for weeks.

Chapter 56

Friday, May 29

"Oh, I've been wanting to ask you since my sister left." Amanda rested the nearly empty cup in her palm. It was just past 7:15 and they sat on her loveseat drinking their second coffees. She needed to leave her duplex by 7:40 to be on time at Coor Sup Fun, King Louie's madhouse. "What did that consultant lady look like? Kaye said she had stunning legs, even if she did select the wrong shoes to show them off."

Jason reached over and lightly stroked Amanda's bare legs, already showing an early summer tan. "Not as stunning as yours."

Good answer.

Jason surely knew he'd nailed that one. "And no trainer from Alabama can scratch my itch, either."

Amanda leaned over and gave his unshaven cheek a caffeine kiss. It wasn't fair, but he didn't have to be at work until eleven. As she settled back down on the cushion, a thought hit her like low-amp voltage. "I finally remembered!"

Startled, Jason spilled some coffee down his front. "What?"

"Christine's detective said you'd left the mall after meeting Kevin and his two-night floozy last Sunday and then you went somewhere six miles east of town. Later, she reported that it's a big truck stop at Exit 248. I've never even noticed it before." Her forefinger caressed the back of his hand. "Why'd you go all the way out there? More than once."

****

Jason frowned into his cup. *Leave it to a woman to dredge up old business after a new beginning.* "Do we have to talk about all that stuff again? So early in the morning?"

"Well, we never really discussed it before. It was left kind of hanging."

Hanging was a good place for it. No reply.

The smile she'd had when he'd walked in with the Hardee's egg sandwiches was fading quickly. Now her short nails pressed into his hand. "So how come?"

People were always riding Jason about his addictions and lack of willpower. He took a deep breath and held it. Silently.

"Okay, is gas so much cheaper out there that you can still save money even though you have to drive over twelve miles roundtrip for a tankful?"

He let his breath out. "Um…" *How to phrase it?* That was always the problem with his explanations.

Worry drove away the last of Amanda's smile. "Spit it out, Jason. Couples have to communicate. No matter how unbelievable it sounds, I'll accept your, uh, statement. I'm sure."

"Um…" He shook his head. "Things don't always come out right when I explain stuff. I always figured it was just some kind of verbal snafu, but Kevin says it's a gender divide."

"If you're quoting gender expert Kevin now, I can understand how explanations might go awry." She checked her watch. "I've still got a few minutes. Let's give it a shot." *Firm*.

Sometimes Jason had verbal constipation, but other times it was more like diarrhea. Worst thing was, he never knew in advance which it would be. He exhaled again. "You know how sometimes a man can't help but give in to cravings?"

Not the best beginning.

"Jason...?" Amanda looked close to tears, but her face flushed with the blood that accompanies anger.

He tried not to notice either and looked instead at his knees. Didn't like talking about himself, especially his weaknesses. But he struggled on. "And you want some so bad, you're willing to drop everything and drive six miles to get it?"

"Jason, who is *this* out-of-town skank?"

Her reaction startled him. "She's a distant cousin... on my mom's sister's side."

"You're boinking your distant cousin at a truck stop?" Amanda sputtered. "That's not only the epitome of gall, but it's illegal. Even in Tennessee!"

"What do you mean, *boinking*?"

"You just said so."

"Huh?" Jason looked around. She had to be talking to somebody else. "I didn't say anything about boinking. You asked who I usually saw when I went out there. Noreen's my cousin."

"That's what I just said."

"Look, I'm pretty sure she's still in high school. I don't think she's even old enough to be working there legally. That's why I don't like talking about her. You know, she might get into trouble."

Tears were forming. "Jason, this explanation of yours is getting worse and worse. If you don't say something I can comprehend in about one minute, I think I'll scream."

"Settle down. What's got you so riled up all of a sudden? You asked why I went to that truck stop and I just told you. I can't help myself."

"Some men do manage to control such cravings." *Icy*.

"But Noreen has the juiciest loins in middle Tennessee."

"Jason, I swear if I had a club, I'd just beat you senseless! I can't believe after all we went through this past week and all that making up we did last night — that you'd admit carrying on a tawdry affair with an under-aged relative."

"What affair?" His eyes felt like they'd fall out if they bulged any more.

"Will you stop talking in circles? The affair that gets your Mr. Baldy into her juicy loins!" She pointed angrily below his belt buckle.

"When did you start calling…?" Incredulous. "Amanda, which story are you listening to? This doesn't involve my so-called Mr. Baldy at all. I love those loins and just eat 'em up."

"Okay, I've had just about enough. You can take your kinky mouth and just get out of my apartment and I don't care if I ever see you again."

"What are you so crazy about? It's just a dozen miles and about seven bucks for a double."

"She gives you *two* pops for seven dollars? Cheap little hussy. What trash!"

"Amanda, she's a distant cousin. Just a kid. It's probably illegal for her to even work there at that age, but she's not trashy. Noreen's just trying to make a little money and get ahead, probably saving for college or something. I think her mother taught her the whole operation and then just turned it over to her."

"Jason, I'm about three seconds from calling the police to arrest you and the sheriff to rescue that poor girl and put her mother in jail. I can't believe you think you're helping her by purchasing her loins for seven dollars."

"How much do *you* think is fair for two juicy pork tenderloins on two warm, homemade biscuits?" His lips smacked as he said it. Couldn't help himself.

Amanda's jaw dropped. "Would you repeat that?"

"How much do you think is fair?"

"No, the last part."

It took him a moment to play the tape in his head. "Uh, pork tenderloin biscuits. You can spread jelly on the warm biscuits and they're scrumptious on their own. But the loins are so juicy, I usually already have most of them down in my belly by the time I hit the Verdeville ramp at Exit 242."

"You've been talking about pork chops on a biscuit?"

"Boneless loins, actually. The chops are a different cut, I think." He peered into her face. "What the creepin' crud did you think I was talking about? Everybody around here knows they're the juiciest loins in the county. All the guys go out there after games and get some loins and a few brewskis."

****

Though her tears ceased immediately, it took Amanda a while to regain her composure. *Why can't men just speak directly to the point of a matter?* After her heart rate finally leveled off, she asked, "Is this the kind of discussion you had with the trainer lady from Alabama?"

"You mean about the truck stop tenderloins?"

"Well, not that specifically. I mean, were you discussing with her how to explain things a little better?"

"Oh, yeah. She figured she ought to coach me on how to talk to you. As if."

As if. "No offense, Jason, but you may possibly be the worst explainer in the entire history of discourse."

He did not look offended. "Maybe that's why I never bothered too much."

Amanda paused and then patted his hand softly. "So when you rushed off last weekend to that truck stop, you were picking up a pork and biscuit sandwich, basically?"

"Exactly what I just said. Except I got a double that night." He smiled. "Sometimes one tenderloin just doesn't quite cut it."

Amanda exhaled audibly. "Jason, I swear, a relationship with you is always an adventure."

That observation seemed to puzzle Jason, but he clearly thought it best to drop the entire thread, if possible. "You want to go out there this evening after work? Loins and a brewski?"

"Will your cousin be there?"

"Uh, not sure. Wait, it's Friday night. Yeah, that's one of their busiest. She probably will. Why?"

"Nothing. Just wondering. I don't know many of your extended family." It would be difficult for Amanda to look at Noreen without the *juicy loins* image in her mind. "Okay, sure, it's a date. Tonight after work... juicy loins. On me."

Jason looked at her funny. "You know, when you say it that way, it sounds like something besides pork loin and biscuit." He grinned and kissed her cheek. "It sounds... sexy."

Amanda smiled slyly. In a perfect world, she could have explained to him that was how she'd gotten confused during his initial explanation. But in Verdeville's real life existence, she was better off not even mentioning it. *Leave it lay.*

"One more thing," he glanced over his shoulder as though someone might be nearby and lowered his voice, "where on earth did you get that Mr. Baldy reference? I've never heard that."

"I read. I get around." She stood with a wink. Almost time to leave for work. "Don't underestimate me, young man." Then she patted his lower belly for emphasis.

"I don't, Amanda. Oh, I don't."

Chapter 57

After work, Amanda was snoring softly on her loveseat when Jason used his key to let himself in quietly.

When she finally woke, Jason was sitting nearby smiling.

"Was I drooling?"

"No comment. But I love watching you when you're resting."

She sat up and hugged him closely. "That is so corny, but I love it anyway."

****

For supper Friday evening, Jason finally drove Amanda six miles east to the celebrated truck stop to meet cousin Noreen Spender and taste her juicy loins.

In the crowded and cluttered grill, Amanda watched the seemingly endless stream of customers. *Noreen must sell a truckload on a busy Friday night.* "You know, I'm not really a big fan of greasy boneless pork chops, but I will admit, these are the best I can remember tasting."

"What about the biscuit?" Jason wiped grease from his mouth. "Doesn't it make you want to slap your momma?"

"Well, maybe slap my sister." Amanda dabbed a napkin to her lips. "But seriously, they are delicious." She took in the surroundings. "But the ambience leaves something to be desired. Big rigs, smell of diesel fuel and gasoline, yucky cigarette smoke, plus all the gaudy merchandise over there in the store part." One of the chairs held an unidentifiable potted plant near the moderately grimy window. Jason had explained that Noreen wiped off the booth tops and tables once a day, whether they needed it or not.

"Everybody says the food is good where truckers stop."

"Maybe so, but there's something vaguely unappetizing about eating tenderloin that's prepared thirty feet from a men's shower room."

"Apparently the private detectives eat here too," Jason nodded at a corner booth, where Diane Cheney sat in mid-bite.

"Should we go say hello?"

"Not sure. What if she's on a stakeout?"

"Evidently not. She's waving." On the way to her table, Amanda stepped over a spill on the floor. She didn't extend her hand — unwritten law when eating greasy tenderloin. "Hi. Surprised to see you."

Cheney chewed rapidly and swallowed hard. "Oh, I've been wanting to come out here."

"So the atmosphere doesn't bother you?" asked Jason.

"Nah, I've seen a lot worse," said Cheney. "I've been to facilities where you could taste the diesel in the chicken skin. And sometimes you didn't even order chicken."

Jason's laugh was so loud and sudden that he surprised not only himself but most of the nearby diners. "Yeah, buddy. Been there."

"Well, we don't want to interrupt your meal," explained

Amanda. "Just wanted to say hello."

"Okay. Nice to see you two together finally." Cheney smiled and returned to her sandwich.

During their meal, Amanda hadn't said much about her job. A little birdie had called her at the office and explained that Jason was evidently experiencing some sort of conversational claustrophobia when she spoke of work problems. But on their way to his truck, Jason shared, "People at work today kept razzing me about the pregnant Hoosier woman demanding to see me."

"Why didn't you just tell them that was your girlfriend's domineering sister?"

"Somehow I think that could sound even worse." Jason shook his head. "Oh, and somebody started a rumor that Erin-the-trainer is coming back to pester me again."

"Don't you think a little of her coaching could do some good? You know, with the way you sometimes explain things so, um, circuitously."

Jason screwed up his face. That word had no place to land. "I just don't like women walking around inside my head." He reconsidered. "Except you, I mean."

"You don't mind me in your head?"

"Mandy, I want you all over me — inside and out, high and low, top and bottom."

She didn't precisely understand what he meant, but the sound of it made her *hot*.

****

Jason drove back to Amanda's duplex without saying much of anything. When he parked his truck and turned off the ignition, he sat still and stared down at the dark dashboard. "Did you really think I had the so-called seven-month itch?"

"No, I didn't. But Christine thought so. And I let her

convince me. After I accepted the possibility, it was easy for that to color all the so-called evidence Christine, Sunny, and Maria came up with."

"But everything is easily explained, once you get the right words in the game." He looked at her to turn his statement into a question.

"Pretty much. I mean, everything happened so quickly and it gathered up like a rain-swollen river overtaking a levee of 48,000 sandbags."

Was that a metaphor? Or had Amanda seen something on the news? "Well, did you ever listen to that tape Christine made while I thought she was seducing me?"

Amanda nodded. "Couldn't get much from it, actually. Too much static and a faint echo. Kind of like when you're in the mountains."

"Mountains. Yeah, that's the right image." Jason was relieved. All Christine's talk about keeping secrets from Amanda and prying secrets out of Jason would likely upset the beautiful woman sitting next to him.

****

Amanda started to pull on the door handle, but paused. "So you don't have the itch?"

"Well, not the one Christine built a file on. But I do have something that needs scratching." Faint cheesy smile.

"Plan to head down to happy hour and see if Kevin's found any smart ones?"

"No, I thought maybe we could handle things here." Jason grin looked a bit loopy. "My itch is just for you, Mandy."

"In that case, I just might scratch it. And I've got claws."

"Like a cougar?"

"Forget about cougars." *More like a wildcat.*

As they headed toward her duplex, Jason reached down

for her hand. His large, strong hands were warm and comforting. When Jason held any part of her, Amanda felt utterly safe. He pulled up their clasped hands and kissed the back of hers. Instinctively, Amanda wrapped her other arm around his neck, stood on her toes, and embraced him.

Jason slid his fingers from hers. Then he squeezed her tightly enough to remind them both of his strength, but not enough to hurt her. Amanda couldn't breathe until he relaxed his arms. When held that way, she felt warm and protected from anything and anybody — a tornado couldn't rip her from his safety. Nor could other domineering forces of nature... except possibly headstrong cougars.

His hands dropped to the small of her back, just above her derrière, and he sighed with a low growl.

Amanda lowered her heels to the pavement and her face to his chest. His heartbeat raced. "So are you still hungry?"

"Starving, as usual.

Ravenous less than an hour after supper? "Are you looking to satisfy your craving for juicy loins?"

Jason looked into her eyes and kissed her deeply. "You have any biscuits?"

"I've got warm buns."

"I can tell." His long fingers moved lower. "And they'll do just fine."

Postscript

By the end of the following week, pretty much everything had settled down in Verdeville, Tennessee.

Amanda Moore organized the entire effort for the public works department to test its flood disaster sandbag distribution. The T-shirt giveaway launched on Friday, June 12, after a single day of TV crawlers, provided gratis by the cable company, and massive radio PSAs. The PW counterpart from Greene County's northerly neighbor monitored the volume of response as well as traffic flow and management.

Having survived the GCEC seminar one week and the follow-up trainer interview, **Jason Stewart** found himself scheduled for Advanced Customer Service workshops on Wednesday of the next week following. Supervisor Grunion began scrutinizing him even more carefully because of the in-house rumors about the irrational and pregnant Hoosier. Grunion received a strange request from trainer Erin Chester.

Jason had his worst season ever in MLB Fantasy League, but he just blew it off.

Christine Powers paid the apprentice investigator's entire bill with a single check and didn't even have to transfer any funds. She threw away her ruined outfit from the big stakeout. Her elbow and knee still hurt, and her palm was still raw. She hobbled on crutches for three days with the twisted ankle.

From this experience, most people would have learned two important lessons: *things are often not what they seem* and *don't meddle in your friend's relationship*. Christine, however, perceived two quite different messages: *verify your evidence before you confront the betrayed woman* and *find a less obvious place to conceal your microphone*.

Kevin Haywood returned to his regular happy hour hunting and looked for a new hideaway, though he'd have to be more careful about picking up after the women he took there.

Maria Perry discovered that applying an extra bit of seduction with Roger made their love-making even more mutually enjoyable and the Mata Hari role-playing really liberated her passion.

Sunny Cannon found herself practicing radio code talk of her own making, in case she was ever needed again for a posse.

Diane Cheney hooked up with Nashville Police Department's Jack Blaine, because she wanted to meet the officer who'd refrained from arresting Maria and Sunny. Plus, she liked his voice on the police radio scanner band.

Kaye Moore-Smith returned home to Indianapolis and considered dropping her hyphen (along with *Smith*) from her surname. She friended her daughter on Facebook to better understand what made the hostile thirteen-year-old tick. Chelsea continued to post complaints about her life and her mother as though Kaye couldn't see them.

After two extra days seeing the sights of Nashville, **Erin Chester** drove home to Alabama. On the way she had a brainstorm about a series of articles on dysfunctional communication in unmarried couples. When Erin contacted Mrs. Grunion about another visit to speak with the employee who'd inspired this new series, the supervisor said, "You can have Jason any time you want him."

After a wonderful romantic weekend with no softball games for Jason and no calls from work for Amanda, the **happily reunited couple** resumed their regular schedule of dining out, watching DVDs, and making love. Except for the surf and turf buffet on Friday night, they both enjoyed the best juicy loins in the county.

— —

Mid-July

FEMA officials sent a team to interview Coor Sup Fun Director **Louis Erie** about his innovative testing and assessment matrix and hoped to adapt it to larger scale Homeland Security drills. At its massive monthly breakfast, the Greene County Chamber of Commerce planned to present Louis a special certificate recognizing his inspired T-shirt giveaway program's value in testing civil defense notification, response, and logistics.

However, Louis arrived late for the Chamber's breakfast — and covered with grease. On the night before, Amanda and Christine reactivated the Stealth League and deflated all four of King Louie's tires.

— —

Early May [11 months later]

After the heaviest Nashville rainfall (and worst Cumberland River flooding) since records had been kept, FEMA officials confiscated 47,988 of Greene County's prefilled sandbags to protect downtown businesses in the capital city.

A dozen sandbags had escaped with Mr. Withers, the evaluator, on the day of the exercise.

Author's Note

In the middle of drafting my screwball comedy, *Curing the Uncommon Man-Cold* in August and September of 2009, I had an idea for a scene that would not fit in the *Man-Cold* novel, but I thought could possibly become the basis for a different story with the same three main characters (Amanda, Jason, and meddlesome Christine). Plus their supporting cast (Kevin, Maria, Sunny, and Louis). But I had to put the notion of *Scratching the Seven-Month Itch* aside until I completed *Man-Cold*.

Though I composed notes and fragments for *Seven-Month* through that same autumn, it was actually January and February of 2010 when I wrote most of the first draft.

A partial genesis for the core plot of *Seven-Month* goes back to the summer of 2008 when I was talking with an attractive mid-twenties female who happened to comment that she'd helped one of her friends 'catch' a cheating boyfriend (though she didn't say how or where... or what they'd been doing). There was a particular gleam in her eye as she mentioned her role (unspecified) and their general approach to the caper, though without supplying any details (other than it involved a vehicle). I tried to capture that gleam as I wrote the supporting characters for *Seven-Month*.

Though written afterwards, this is actually the **prequel** to *Man-Cold* and is set roughly three months before *Man-Cold* begins. As this story opens, it has been about seven months since Amanda and Jason became an official *couple* (Halloween the previous year).

Acknowledgements

I'm extremely grateful to my friend, the talented author Gunnar Grey — owner of Dingbat Publishing — for letting me in on the ground floor of her developing company. And I must mention that Gunnar was also the editor for this novel. She held my hand through an exhausting round of *deep* edits which resulted in removal of some 28,000 words from my original completed manuscript. Folks, that's a lot of chopping! But I think we both agree the result is leaner, cleaner, and faster-paced getting to the main chase scenes of the story.

Thanks also to John Grey for his thorough proofing of the final draft... and to Elaina Lee, the creative artist, for this striking cover.

I am greatly indebted to my brother, Charles A. Salter, who read an early draft and provided very helpful feedback and follow-ups. And, years later, he assisted with the tagline, hook, and blurb. Special thanks to my wife, Denise W. Salter, who provided insights, suggestions, and other assistance for various aspects of particular scenes during the drafting phase... and also helped me proof the galleys.

Thanks also to author Leigh Verrill-Rhys, who graciously read the first 100 pages of an early draft and provided very useful comments. Other readers of early drafts were Sharon Pullen and Doris R. Salter.

Special appreciation to Betsy Moers, for allowing me to borrow her colorful and multi-purpose expression, "Shoot a monkey."

About the Author

Two screwball comedies — *Scratching the Seven-Month Itch* (September 2014) and *Curing the Uncommon Man-Cold* (December 2013) — have been released by Dingbat Publishing in the series we're calling **Amanda Moore or Less** ... and we have plans for additional episodes.

Other titles, released by Astraea Press, include *Hid Wounded Reb* (August 2014), *Called to Arms Again* (May 2013), *Rescued By That New Guy in Town* (October 2012), and *The Overnighter's Secrets* (May 2012). Also released through AP are the short novellas *Echo Taps* (June 2013) and *Don't Bet On It* (April 2014), and the short story "No Love, No Diamonds" in an anthology.

Screwball comedy, romantic comedy, and romantic suspense are among nine completed novel manuscripts. Many more are in the pipeline.

I'm co-author of two nonfiction monographs (about librarianship) with a royalty publisher, plus a signed chapter in another book and a signed article in a specialty encyclopedia. I've also published articles, book reviews, and over 120 poems; my writing has won nearly 40 awards, including several in national contests. As a newspaper photo-journalist, I published about 150 bylined newspaper articles, and some 100 bylined photos.

I worked nearly 30 years in the field of librarianship. I'm a decorated veteran of the U.S. Air Force (including a remote tour of duty in the Arctic, at Thule AB in N.W. Greenland).

I'm the married parent of two and grandparent of six.

Books by J.L. Salter

From Astraea Press
The Overnighter's Secrets
Rescued by That New Guy in Town
Called to Arms Again
Echo Taps
Hid Wounded Reb
Don't Bet On It

From Dingbat Publishing
Scratching the Seven-Month Itch
Curing the Uncommon-Man-Cold

Don't miss the hilarious sequel!

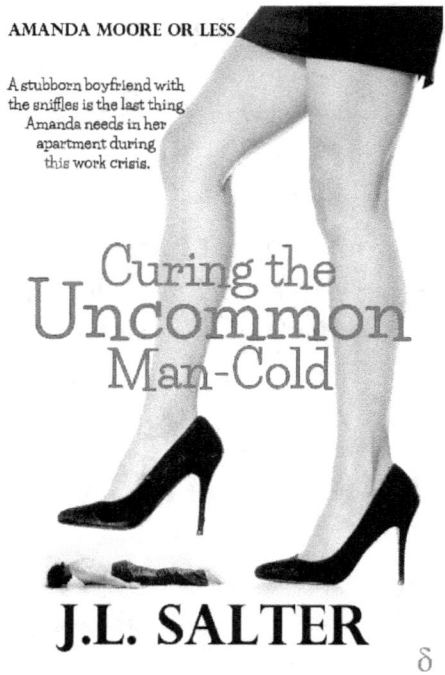

AMANDA MOORE OR LESS

A stubborn boyfriend with the sniffles is the last thing Amanda needs in her apartment during this work crisis.

Curing the
Uncommon
Man-Cold

J.L. SALTER

δ

Chapter 1
August 10 (Monday)

"I don't think I can hold up…" Amanda's eyes were full. "Jason just left the doctor." Her apartment suddenly felt smaller.

"What on earth is wrong?" Her friend Christine had just arrived and already plopped down on the small sofa. "Cancer? Paralysis?" She probably pictured even worse diagnoses because Christine zealously read supermarket tabloids.

Amanda groaned softly.

Christine grabbed her younger friend's shoulders. "You'll feel better if you talk about it." She moistened her lips slightly. Medical news was known to be among her favorites, along with stories about nasty divorces.

Amanda looked for her nearest tissue box. "It's... a... man-cold."

Christine sighed heavily. "Don't wind me up like that. I thought this was a real *situation*."

"It is!" Amanda had been home from work about twenty minutes and still had her heels on. "I don't know what I'm going to do."

"Just ship that basket case back to his momma." Christine snapped her fingers. "Let Margaret wait on him hand and foot for the next week."

"More likely two weeks. Remember when he was sick in January?"

"I thought he had triple-Nashville-man-ditis or something."

Amanda nodded. "Totally helpless. He could barely use the bathroom by himself."

"Look, Jason was overindulged from the get-go. I bet Margaret nursed him too long. Ship him back."

"I can't." Amanda closed her eyes. "She absolutely won't take him."

"His own momma?"

"The last time a sick Jason stayed at her place, it nearly put Margaret in the hospital." Amanda lowered her voice. "She said Jason moaned every waking hour. Hardly ever moved from her couch for over a week... and he *limped*, for cryin' out loud!" Amanda shook her head. "I can't live with that."

"You can't let him stay here! You won't survive two days with Jason's sick-over." Christine sputtered. "There's got to be somewhere else... somebody else. Maybe he can bunk with a buddy."

"A buddy? Just picture irresponsible Kevin trying to assist helpless Jason who's down with a deadly illness. Kevin would hightail it out of his own apartment so quick you'd think he just spotted a fumigation fog sliding under his door."

"Slow down and rethink this." Christine touched her friend's forearm. "Do you really know this person well enough to nurse him back from near-terminal man-sniffles?"

"Know him? We've been sleeping together since the Halloween party last year. My place *and* his!"

Christine leaned in closer, even though she should have remembered this development. "At his place too?"

"Three times." Amanda was prepared to list the dates.

"Hmm. That is serious, I guess." Christine waved her hand briefly. "Okay. So you do have an investment, so to speak. The issue is how to tend Jason enough that it even registers with him, yet not so much that the effort kills you."

"Now you understand why I'm freaking." Amanda moaned again. "Not to mention these are my Hell Weeks at work."

Verdeville was about twenty miles east of Nashville's Interstate loop. Amanda Moore's current crunch was reviewing applications from every Greene County agency seeking federal grants. Some thought she was too inexperienced, at age twenty-eight, for such a significant role and she was not taken very seriously in county government offices because of her shapely legs and hips.

"Okay, back up. Let's say you were in-the-bed ill, with doctor-ordered bed rest." Christine's hand went horizontal. "Would Jason take care of you at *his* apartment?"

"Are you kidding? He'd tell me he'd been evicted and show me a cell phone picture of a notice on his door."

"Okay, you're catching on. So, tit for tat." Christine

Powers crossed tanned arms beneath her augmented bosom. Divorced for about four years, she was financially secure because of her lucrative alimony settlement. Frankly, she had too much free time on her hands: brunette Christine had lots of urges and often followed up on them — she behaved more like a redhead. "In fact, if you were the one sick, I'll bet Jason wouldn't even help you here at *your* place."

Amanda merely shrugged.

"Of course not." Christine showed a satisfied smile. "I'm glad I was able to talk sense into you."

"You realize I've got to help Jason."

"Why? He's obviously not worth it."

"I do actually love him, you know." Amanda sighed.

"Give me one reason." Christine rolled her eyes. "And don't go way back to him rescuing you at that New Year's Eve party. Jason did real good in a scary situation, but you can't let him coast forever on a single night of good ole boy gallantry."

Actually, Jason had been Amanda's very chivalrous knight that memorable evening nineteen months ago, and his rescue was both literal and figurative. However, Amanda loved Jason more for the connection they'd made since then. "Well, right now I can only think of his eyes — they're deep and soulful... and loyal."

"A spaniel has interesting eyes and loyalty. Get a dog." Christine was uncommonly pragmatic at times. "And that's his most endearing quality?"

It was sometimes difficult to ignore Christine's negative attitude toward the man in Amanda's life. *Why does she have it in for Jason?*

Christine frowned. "So you actually intend to cancel your own home life for the next two weeks and baby Jason?"

"Don't really have a choice. I can't totally refuse to help my boyfriend. But I don't think I'll survive his sickness."

"Okay, the only workable option is he stays in his own

apartment and you bring deli soup each evening."

"You must be joking." Amanda bent forward until her face nearly met her knees. "He'll be on Facebook and e-mail telling everyone he's been abandoned to die. Somebody would probably start up a blog to raise donations for his cure."

"Yeah. He does tend toward the dramatic. Probably got that from his momma, too. When boy babies nurse that long, they suck in a lot of drama." Christine didn't explain her certainty that Jason had spent more than the typical phase at Margaret's breast. "Plus, I thought guys who played all those team sports didn't get sick. This is weird."

"You know, it is pretty suspicious that he fell ill during the one sliver of August when none of his leagues have any games scheduled."

Christine's mind obviously churned. "I still say there's got to be another solution."

"I've been pulling my hair out, looking for it." Amanda tugged on the longer front tresses of her inverted bob cut — honey brown coloring this year. "I hate guys getting man-sick. If you and I had a cold like that, we'd just keep on going." She moaned again. "I'm in for total misery with no escape. He'll sit around in his jammies all day, contemplating what's inside his jammies. Guess what he's thinking about while I'm at work all day."

"Sex... with you."

Amanda nodded and closed her expressive blue eyes. "One time in that January siege, I was up all night bringing water or pills... or just listening to him whimper. I dragged myself to work, put up with nine hours of B.S. from my boss, and then crawled home. There was Jason — a stupid smile on his face, sprawled on the couch in those ratty jammies."

"Just hand him the December *Cosmo* and tell him you've got a headache." Christine looked into her friend's tear-stained face. "You didn't fall for that old routine."

"I did, back then, but I've wised up. So it's mainly a matter of extra guilt." Amanda recalled the previous occasion. "Don't even get me started about the mucous and coughing… plus he hadn't showered in two days. Yuck."

Christine's expression clearly indicated she shared that characterization.

Amanda slowly toppled over onto the vacant cushion. "I feel sick myself. Maybe I'll go home to *my* mom."

"Arizona? In August?" Christine poked her friend's shoulder. "Just pull up your big-girl panties and tell him no. Jason cannot stay here with you, period. Just break the news quick and steel yourself against his whining."

"I can't. I've been trying to tell you: he's already on his way over. Right now."

Christine quickly began gathering her belongings. "You've got two choices…"

"Suicide is one. What's the other?"

"Seriously. This is the time to decide if Jason's going to remain part of your life. Because if he does, this ultra-high maintenance side of him is going to kill you."

"What's the second choice?" Amanda tried to look hopeful.

Christine shrugged. "Become his nurse, errand girl, and sex slave for the next two weeks."

Amanda's tears gathered again. "Well, there's one thing I won't do. Absolutely will not do."

Christine nodded solemnly. "I wouldn't do that, either, 'specially if he hadn't showered."

"No. I mean I'm not going to call in sick for him." Amanda clamped her jaw shut. "Jason can make his own calls every morning."

"Oh, I thought you meant the other thing." Christine held up her hand, signaling a new subject. "Well, if Jason does stay here, he sleeps on the couch."

"No, too much in my way out here. Back in my guestroom."

"You couldn't fit a sick hamster in there."

"I cleaned it up, a little." Amanda had not intended it to sound so defensive.

"Show me."

Amanda escorted her friend down the short hall to the guestroom. Boxes were stacked along one wall and a single bed occupied a corner. Extending from another wall was a treadmill with a long row of clothes hanging on each handrail.

"I didn't know you also had exercise equipment in here."

"Mom insisted on leaving it here when she and Dad moved to Tempe." Amanda shrugged. "I only use it for closet overflow."

"I did that with Daniel's treadmill for a few years. Works better if you stack bricks under each back corner." Christine pointed. "That helps level out the handrails so the clothes hangers won't slide down to this end."

Amanda fleetingly wondered where she could find some free bricks. "Well, anyway, a human can certainly fit in here."

"Okay, I guess so, since you've got that path through all those boxes. Might need a map, though." Christine obviously didn't approve. "Although now that I think about it, you don't really want him too comfortable. So maybe this hamster nest is a good idea after all."

"It doesn't matter where he stays, really. In this tiny apartment, he'll never be more than about twenty feet away. Coughing, whimpering, calling for whatever kind of attention."

They left the cluttered guestroom and returned to the living space. Amanda crumpled to the couch and curled into a crescent. She knew the dreaded uncommon man-cold was incurable — so nobody even tried. They just gritted their teeth and stuck it out... or they packed up and left. Not many options. "You've got to help me."

"Sorry, there's no cure." Christine started to leave, but stopped suddenly. Her eyes brightened and her fingers twitched slightly. "Unless…" She sat again. "Well, it's a long shot, but theoretically possible."

Amanda straightened slowly and pulled hair from her damp eyes. A few strands stuck in the corner of her mouth where drool had started to collect. "Do you have a plan?"

"Scare him."

"You mean, like… boo?"

"More subtle." Christine lowered her voice. "Remember that movie with Kathy Bates and James Caan in a remote cabin? He's a writer."

"*Misery*? You call that subtle? You want me to scare Jason with a sledgehammer and a stub of lumber?"

"No, I'm still on *subtle*. But you might need the hammer later." Christine nodded. "If this works, you'll get Jason out of your apartment and might even cure him of man-colds forever."

"Okay, I'm on board." No hesitation. "Tell me your plan."

"Fear is a powerful force if properly applied."

Amanda heard a noise outside. "He's here! What's your plan?"

"We're going to give Jason the Scare-Cure."

"The what?" Amanda looked out the window. "Hurry! He's nearly at the door."

"The Scare-Cure." Christine seemed to like its sound even though she obviously had no strategy yet developed to implement that devious term. "I've got some research to do."

"You're leaving me alone with Mister Sick?"

"I'll call you tomorrow at work." As the doorknob twisted, Christine whispered, "Don't feed him anything besides really thin soup and those nasty crackers your mom left last year. You have any other yucky food?"

"There's a soy hotdog leftover from July 4th."

"Perfect. That's Jason's lunch tomorrow. No bun. Hide everything else." Christine opened the door.

Jason Stewart was slumped over like he'd been at hard labor on a chain gang for weeks without food or water. He looked up pitifully, saw who it was, and waved lazily. "Hi, Christine. Where's Amanda?"

She turned her head to indicate the interior of Amanda's apartment. Christine moved down the walk — partly backwards and partly sideways. She noticed how much more debilitated Jason looked when Amanda came to the door.

Scare-Cure. This could be interesting.

Amanda took in the pitiful sight. Jason seemed like an abandoned kindergartener clutching his teddy bear as he looked for Mommy at the house next door. It might have been endearing, except her boyfriend was no longer in preschool. At 32, Jason seemed in no hurry for their serious relationship to grow deeper. He obviously adored Amanda and loved being with her, but his notion of commitment had some leftover adolescent one-sidedness. Could he become a responsible mate? Nobody knew, including Jason… apparently.

Good-looking and leaning toward handsome, Jason had a boyish face and thick, dark hair that would look better combed the other direction. His blue eyes, occasionally dark and soulful, were bright with zeal when he participated avidly in basketball, softball, soccer, and flag football. About average weight for his frame and medium height, Jason's strength and athleticism were belied by a slight paunch, due to his predilection for junk food, beer, and frequent snacks.

She remained in her doorway, blocking his entrance. "I'm sorry you're under the weather. But like I said on the phone, these are my most horrid work weeks all year. Already stretched to the limit. I simply can't deal with anyone staying here."

Jason looked puzzled at why he was still on her

threshold. "I won't be in the way. You won't even know I'm here."

"Trust me, I'll know." She frowned. "Even without the bell you auditioned in January."

"The concept was good; maybe the tone was off."

"If you'd rung that bell once more, I would've stuffed it up a... really... dark... place."

Jason's muscular shoulders slumped. "But I don't think I'm well enough to drive."

"You got here all right and your place was closer to the doctor's office."

"But I shouldn't be alone when I'm sick."

Whiny is quite unbecoming in a lover. "It's a cold, Jason. How bad could it be?"

"Doctors miss a lot. I have complications." He coughed to illustrate. "And fever."

"Well, I'm sure this is the worst cold in all of middle Tennessee." She sighed heavily and felt his forehead. No discernable warmth. "Okay. Wait right here and I'll get a thingy to check your temp."

When she returned from her bedroom, Jason was sprawled out on her couch and already had the TV on. She paused to consider *where* to insert the thermometer.

After an hour of channel surfing, Jason entered the hall bathroom. Moments later, he emerged wearing floppy socks, a very old tee-shirt with several holes, and pajama bottoms with a sprung-out waistband. He headed toward Amanda's bedroom.

"Hold on, Mister Germs! Not in *my* bed!"

"Huh?"

"These are my Hell Weeks. I can't get sick with all those grant apps stacked on my desk. The boss would bring files to my hospital room." Amanda ground her teeth slightly. *Why can't you wait 'til after Labor Day to get sick?*

"So where do I sleep?"

"Your own apartment."

No reply from Jason.

Amanda shrugged and pointed to the guestroom.

"All the way over there?"

"It's forty-two inches across this hallway."

Jason peered in. "That's not enough room for a five-year-old."

"Well, stop acting like a five-year-old." Amanda sighed. "You'll be safe enough if you stay on that path."

Supper was a few hours later. As per Christine's instructions, Jason's complete meal was a small mug of chicken-flavored consommé with one stale, generic rye crisp cracker.

It was a long night for Jason. Highlights included: loud groaning, coughing fits, sneezes like backfires from a rusted exhaust manifold, and snoring which rattled the inside wind chimes. On numerous trips to the bathroom he even managed to click the light switch with amplified noise. Beginning around 2:00 a.m., he spent another hour flipping through TV channels.

Amanda netted about three hours of sleep.

* * * *

Also from Dingbat Publishing

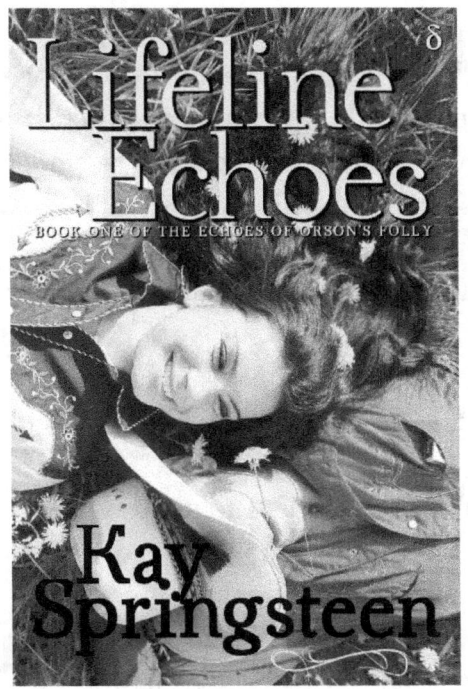

Prologue

There is no natural phenomenon which is held by all mankind in greater dread than earthquakes. Our ideas of permanence, solidity and strength are based upon the condition of the earth, as we daily see it; so that when the firm ground shakes under us, there naturally comes over the mind a feeling of abject helplessness. ~New York Times, April 9, 1872

Seven years earlier…

Splat.

"Son of a—"

Sandy glared down at her double chocolate iced mocha. Pale brown slush slid off the toe of one white shoe to form a sticky puddle on the blacktop.

A quick glance at her watch told her she'd have to hurry or she'd be late for her shift as a dispatcher for Los Angeles City Emergency Services. She kicked the melting mush from her shoe and stepped around the puddle of yuck and raced across the parking lot to the low brick building. Behind her, traffic on the packed freeway growled and honked.

Good morning, Los Angeles.

Sandy yanked on the heavy glass door and stepped into the coolness of the air conditioned building with a sigh.

"Morning, Alley Cat!" greeted Rose from behind the reception desk. "Lunch at Del Rio's today?"

"Hi, Rose. Yeah, lunch sounds great. Gotta run. I'm late." With a wave, Sandy hurried past the desk and into the ladies' restroom. She set her oversized purse on the counter and grabbed several paper towels. Crouching, she dabbed at the mush, noting with dismay that it had worked into the seams of her athletic shoes.

"Gross," she muttered. She'd be lucky if it didn't stink like sour milk at the end of her shift. After she mopped off the worst of it, she pushed to her feet and staggered sideways. Her hand hit the cool marble wall of the first stall as she fought to steady herself.

"What the hell?"

A low primeval rumble surrounded her, invaded her midsection and radiated up into her heart and throat. Sandy stumbled to the left then the right. The fluorescent light overhead became a flickering strobe.

Earthquake!

The word registered in the recesses of her mind, and spurred her toward the door. She had to get out of the enclosed space before the ceiling collapsed and buried her.

Sudden blackness swallowed her as the lights lost the battle to stay on. The grumble grew to a roar and then a scream. She lurched to the right, pushed off the wall, and careened through the bathroom door. The scream grew louder before she realized it came from her own mouth. The floor beneath her rolled and writhed as her cries were echoed by a half-dozen coworkers at their workstations. Shelves toppled, notebooks tumbled to the floor.

The roar dwindled to a dull grating, the heaving slowed and finally halted. Sandy lay on her side, her back jammed against the wall. Her insides still quivered and shook like jelly, the remnants of the quake continuing in her viscera. Chills washed over her as she sat up and took stock of the dispatch room. Her coworkers moved slowly, sitting and looking around, dazed expressions gracing their faces.

"Holy cow," murmured Rose, pushing to her feet and doing a three-sixty. "That felt like an eight or a nine."

Fluorescent lights overhead sputtered then half of them winked on. That would be the backup generator, running nonessentials at half power.

More operators pushed to their feet, their faces all wearing uniform dazed expressions. Jabbering filled the air as a dozen people seemed to find their voices at the same time. The cacophony crescendoed. Any second her head would explode. She closed her eyes and attempted to sort out what was being said.

"…my kids…"

"I think my arm's broken…"

"Maybe we should get…"

"Comm's down!" called out Albert Torres, IT wizard and

technical problem solving guru. "Switching to backup."

Phones began ringing. Frowning, Sandy oriented herself and located her desk. Someone had to answer the calls. And there would be calls.

She located her station and placed the headset over her ear, then punched the button. "Emergency services—"

A shrill scream came over the line and assaulted her ear. Forcing herself to speak calm words of reassurance as she wrestled open her desk drawer and pulled out an empty notebook and a black pen, Sandy managed to discern that the caller was an elderly woman who was merely disoriented and frightened.

The phone lines began to flash as more calls came in. Around her, more dispatchers followed Sandy's lead and began answering.

"Backup comms are on line," announced Albert, emerging from the computer room.

The first report of a fire came ninety seconds after Sandy started answering calls. The gas line alongside the Convention Center had burst and somehow ignited. Hell had erupted in Central Los Angeles.

Sandy couldn't stop the tremors running along the inner fault lines of her own neural pathways. *I'm a professional. People are depending on me.* She studied the older system that had just been replaced by a two million dollar upgrade, only months earlier, and re-familiarized herself with the buttons and switches. Then, in a voice that only barely trembled, she dispatched Fire Station Number 9 to the L.A. Convention Center.

The first shift after Sandy's vacation was off to a very rocky start. Before that shift was over, she would learn two important things. First, she was getting the hell out of L.A. Second, it was possible to fall in love with someone, sight unseen, in twenty-three hours and fifty-seven minutes.

Chapter One

Present day

Sunny and warm, the perfect day for mourning lost love. Maybe this would be the year she'd finally be ready to move on. Even as the thought teased her, Sandy suspected it might take another cataclysmic event to let go of the man she'd given her heart to in less than a day.

Summer was a handful of days off, but the mountain air was clean and brisk, nothing like the heavy smog of L.A., where she'd first met *him*. She had no memories of the man in this place except for the ones he'd painted into her mind while they'd talked. Yet Wyoming was where she felt his presence.

Her red roan colt pranced beneath her, needing to run off his teenage-intensity energy. Dry dirt kicked up by Domingo muffled the sound of his hoof-falls to dull scuffling *plunks*, which he punctuated with occasional impatient snorts.

As they traveled, the dusty ground became more firmed and flattened. Gray rocky outcroppings thrust upward amid a tan landscape dotted by the washed-out green of desert grasses. More of the same lay between them and the scrub pines along the swell of foothills in the distance.

Sandy pointed Domingo toward those hills, finally allowing the exuberant colt to set his own pace. He catapulted them across the plain, brawny muscles alternately flexing and contracting beneath her, racing at a full gallop. The denim jacket she hadn't bothered to fasten caught the wind and billowed behind her. Chilly air worked icy fingers along the exposed skin of her neck, bringing with it a wonderful ache.

They topped a gentle rise and a sea of yellow and purple wildflowers surprised her, God's own casually sown garden. The sky overhead was deep blue and cloudless. With the prairie behind her and the snow-covered peaks ahead, Sandy pulled Domingo up inside a cathedral of Ponderosa pines, closed her eyes, and inhaled the pungent scent. It was exactly as he had described it, which made it the perfect place to remember him.

Seven years had passed, yet her pain was an exquisite, fresh wound, probably owing to the fact that she revisited the memory once a year on the anniversary of that horrific day. In the hills of Wyoming that he had loved and missed so much, in the place he had brought her to with just his words, Sandy picked the scab off the wound she never quite allowed to heal.

* * *

The job was all that mattered now. Sandy made herself disregard the toppled shelves and scattered books. She blocked out all thoughts about the likely state of her own home. As she listened to the chatter on the official channels, she kept meticulous handwritten notes regarding the status of each unit checking in.

"Battalion 9-Alpha, this is Engine Squad 9-Bravo, do you copy?" The connection was filled with static and the voice was muffled, hard to hear.

Sandy waited for the response of the battalion chief on scene. None came.

The callout was repeated, the voice sounding a bit more urgent. "This is L.A. Engine Squad 9-Bravo, dispatched to the Convention Center—" Again static broke the transmission.

Following protocol, after the second unanswered call, Sandy intervened. "Copy you, ES-9-Bravo. This is central dispatch. Your transmission is breaking up."

She checked her watch and jotted the time in her notes: 0724 hours.

The response was drowned out by a loud burst of static in the earpiece.

"9-Bravo, be advised you are breaking up," she repeated.

More harsh squawks of static burst from the receiver. Sandy winced. If that kept up, her head might explode — or at least an eardrum. Then, amid the static, she clearly heard the code every dispatcher dreaded. "9-Bravo is 10-60, this location. Code three, code three, code three... trapped..."

The code for firefighter down!

Static filled the airwaves again as Sandy punched buttons on her console, frantically trying to boost the signal.

"Dispatch, are you there?" The voice was screaming. "Central! This is 9-Bravo in need of assist. The building's coming down around us!"

Afraid to switch over to relay, with the risk of losing contact altogether, she motioned to Ellen, the dispatcher sitting next to her. Quickly, Sandy wrote on her notepad in bold black ink: UNIT IN TROUBLE.

At the next desk, Ellen nodded and switched channels to contact the Battalion 9 squad leader over the comm.

"9-Bravo, this is Central Dispatch," Sandy acknowledged. Stomach-wrenching fear threatened to leak into her voice, so she bit the inside of her cheek. Dread shot out little tentacles of hopelessness to curl around her lungs, squeezing the breath out of her. "I'm reading you, sending help your way. What's your location?"

"Civic Center parking garage — A level. The building's coming apart! We need extraction." The voice was still urgent but the panic had faded.

She had to get her own terror under control and keep it that way, Sandy reminded herself, or she couldn't help anyone.

"Copy you, 9-Bravo. Who am I speaking with?"

"Mick-" More static, then, "Mic-key."

Sandy scribbled everything she could make out into her handwritten notes. "Mickey, you're breaking up badly. How many do you number? How long have you been trapped?"

"Two confirmed, dispatch, possibly three. I can feel my partner. He's not moving. I heard someone else moaning down here earlier. I

don't know how long it's been. I think I've been unconscious — I'm pinned — can't move. It's dark — can't see a thing."

Sandy passed off the information to Ellen so her coworker could convey it to the battalion chief. The sarcastic part of Sandy's mind registered the irony of having crossed into the twenty-first century and being reduced to the mockery of a child's game of telephone.

With a pointed shake of her head, Ellen caught Sandy's eye and handed her a message from the battalion chief. As she read, Sandy's heart fluttered in her chest before moving upward to stick in her throat. Her free hand rose of its own volition and covered her mouth, as if to prevent her from saying the words she was reading.

The Convention Center had collapsed with several men inside. Some of them were buried under four floors of rubble, while above them the fire from the gas main explosion burned fully involved and uncontained. Rescue efforts would be delayed and prospects for extraction were grim. A chaplain was en route.

God help them all! How could she tell the man on the other end of the comm that he wasn't going to be rescued? What could she say to someone when her words were likely to be the last he'd ever hear?

*   *   *

Ryan kicked in the clutch and rammed the gearshift into second to take yet another turn on the series of switchbacks through the mountains. The 1967 Corvette Sting Ray had been a mess when he'd bought her, but she'd been his mess. And a bargain at the price he'd wangled. It had taken almost every one of his days off over the past two years, but he had fully restored her from the engine up. The work had been a welcome distraction from other aspects of his life.

Currently, on his first long trip in her, he was enjoying the way she held fast to the road, caressing the pavement around the twists and turns through the mountains the way a woman caressed a lover.

The throaty growl of the engine wasn't quite drowned out by the whoosh of the wind over his face. It was early in the year to drive with the top down in the mountains, but Ryan didn't care. The bracing cold reminded him he was alive.

It had been too long, the guilty whisper nagged. He should never have let his life get so far out of hand. It shouldn't have taken an emergency letter from his baby brother for him to come home and make things right with the old man.

Tires squealed just a bit when he took the downward curve a little sharply. He was in the foothills now, only a few miles to go. He'd be able to open his baby up on the two-lane once the last hill was at his back. Soon the sun would drift down into the shadowy embrace of the mountains behind him, leaving him the stars for company. Damn, he'd missed the mountains of home.

Halfway through what he recognized as the last switchback, Ryan downshifted again and punched the gas. His mind registered the apparition blocking the road in front of him a bare second before reaction set in. He stood on the brake, sending the car into a slow sideways skid and stalling the engine.

"Holy hell!"

Darts of adrenaline screamed through his veins, sending his heart into a staccato rhythm as he stared at the horse and rider in the road.

Washed in the golden blush from the setting sun, the horse reared, angrily striking out at the air between them with menacing hooves, nearly unseating his rider. With a toss of his head, the startled horse reared again, baring his teeth and screaming defiance.

The red roan colt had excellent lines, but he was clearly too much for his rider. Though the horse responded to her steady touch, it was obvious any sense of control she had was an illusion. Ryan shoved the car door open and jumped to his feet, ready to pick up the pieces when the rider was thrown. But when she swung her gaze in his direction, fury blazed in eyes the color of chicory blossoms. Her face mirrored the horse's defiance.

Sparks of awareness replaced astonishment, and a grin pulled Ryan's lips upward as he lifted a hand in greeting.

"Jackass!" The rider shoved at the wild mass of dark hair falling across her face. The motion distracted her, giving her mount the opening to misbehave.

With a clatter of edgy hooves on asphalt, the big colt danced and circled, threatened to rear again, but she recovered quickly and held him down. Then she tugged on the reins, steering the agitated horse away from the road, and sidestepping him down the steep, gravel-covered incline. Upon reaching solid footing, the colt wheeled sharply around. The rider cast a scathing look over her shoulder as the horse erupted into a reckless gallop across the prairie.

Pain shot through Ryan's neck, and he realized he'd been clenching his jaw. Absently, he rubbed the back of one hand along his chin, but he kept his eyes on the horse and rider until they were no more than a speck in the distance.

"Well," he said to the early evening sky. "I've just been schooled."

He wasn't sure if he was going to shake things up with his return or get himself shaken up. But he sure as hell planned to find out who lived behind those haunting chicory blue eyes.

Shaking his head, he started to lower himself into the car when he froze. Why was it sitting at such an odd angle? He strode around to the passenger side and groaned at the sight of the front tire, rolled right off the rim from his sideways skid.

* * *

By the time she had encountered the stranger in the fast

car, Sandy's earlier upbeat mood had degraded, thanks to the dull heartache she'd given herself from lancing her old wound. Ordinarily she would have laughed off the incident and introduced herself once she'd realized no one was hurt. But the moron had just sat in his car staring in disapproval, apparently waiting for her to move out of his all-important way.

Wherever the aggravating stranger was going, she sincerely hoped he didn't so much as make a pit stop in Orson's Folly. She was pretty sure another meeting of that sort would result in her doing more than yelling at him. Pictures of strangling the shit-eating grin off his face popped into her mind.

Her heart raced with the need to dispel her jitters, and Sandy let the colt have his head again. Domingo calmed them both by doing what he loved most, streaking at breakneck pace over the plains of western Wyoming.

By the time they slowed to a walk alongside the fence leading to the stable yard, her ire at the stranger on the road had mellowed to a mildly bad memory. Whoever he was, it was likely he'd already hit Orson's Folly and driven on through. The sun rested in the cradle between the peaks of two mountains, sending lingering shafts of red to cast long shadows against the blue and white buildings. Sandy closed her eyes, bracing against the little pinprick of pain, and allowed herself to remember the reason she'd first come to Wyoming.

* * *

"You hang on, do you hear me?" she ordered. "I won't go anywhere until they have you, I swear. But you have to stay with me. Promise!"

"Okay... promise." His words were slurred, his voice weary.

Sandy struggled to think of something to talk about — to keep him speaking and alert. "Do I hear an accent, Mick?"

His laugh was slow and soft. "Yep, I'm afraid so. I can't seem to get the Wyoming out of my voice."

That worked! "Tell me about Wyoming."

He sighed. "There's nothing like a wild gallop across the plains on a fast horse. If you can be up on that horse at daybreak, you feel like you're flying up to meet the day. And to be in the Red Desert at sundown's even better. If you time it right, just a split second before the sun's gone, you feel like you're inside all that red and orange glow. Then in your next breath you're standing in pitch black. When you look up, the stars are already popping out. So many stars they blend together. And there's always shooting stars for making wishes." *He laughed softly.* "I guess I sound a little pathetic."

"No." *She wished she could touch him with more than her voice.* "More like a homesick cowboy."

He was quiet for a time, then, "I guess maybe I am, Angel. I am homesick."

His quiet admission brought tears to Sandy's eyes, and she prayed he'd see those sunrises and sunsets and stars again. "So you lived in the desert plains?"

"I had the best of both worlds," *he answered, his words filled with pride.* "Our ranch is in the middle of a finger of desert that's nestled between two legs of mountains and forest."

"Why did you leave?"

"That's a story for another time," *he said.* "I'll tell you when we're on our first date."

"Are you asking me out?"

"Oh, we'll go out." *His voice gave her visions of an easy cowboy grin.* "I was just making the plans."

Her lips twitched at his audacity.

* * *

Cooled and brushed, Domingo nickered a soft goodbye as Sandy left the comfort of the stable and walked into the cold night air.

Stars twinkled into view overhead, millions of glistening pinpoint lights fusing into a lacy curtain of soft illumination against the darkness. A trail of shimmery light tracked across the sky.

For the first time in seven years, her automatic wish wasn't for something impossible. "I want to feel alive again."

Emotionally and physically exhausted, she tore her eyes from the stars with a heavy sigh and climbed into the rusty Chevy pickup. It was older than she was by several years, so she counted her blessings it still ran. Driving past the main homestead, Sandy tossed a wave to Justin McGee, sitting on the wide front porch of the ranch house puffing on his nightly cigar. With a smile and a nod, the old rancher politely touched a forefinger to the brim of his battered tan Stetson.

Just as Sandy reached the cedar fenceposts marking the entrance to the ranch, a pair of headlights swung in from the main road. So, the McGee men were about to receive a caller. Maybe Sean had finally convinced Melanie Mitchell to drop by after her shift at the bar.

The two sets of headlights collided, the bright beams briefly joining forces and splitting the darkness. Then the moment was gone, leaving Sandy with a vague impression of something low and fast before she was engulfed by the cloud of dust chasing behind.

Nope. She coughed against the sting in her throat. Definitely not Mel, who tended to drive her ancient economy car with the caution of a grandmother. Tough break for Sean.

* * *

Ryan braked in front of the old ranch house and killed the engine. He popped open the door but took some deep breaths before climbing out of the car.

Though the land slumbered beneath a blanket of darkness, the nighttime couldn't mask his memories. He knew just beyond the edge of the light lay open spaces, fields of green and gold dotted by brown-and-white cattle and rolls of cut hay, all in the protective embrace of the Rocky Mountains to the west.

Closing his eyes, Ryan inhaled deeply, intoxicating himself on the aromatic blend of cow manure, freshly mown hay, and mountain wildflowers that hung in the air. The sweet, somewhat earthy scent of home.

Overhead, a shooting star blazed a fiery arc through the myriad visible stars. Ryan thought of a time, so long ago, when he and Sean had lain next to their mother on a sleeping bag, watching the stars overhead. Every time she saw a shooting star, she had urged them to make a wish.

The memory faded as suddenly as it had come. What the heck was he doing, coming back to Wyoming?

"Not much call for such a fancy machine on a ranch," admonished a gravelly voice from the porch's shadows. "But you always did love speed, didn't you, boy?"

Ryan stiffened as Justin took a step forward into the light cast by the moon.

"Hello, Dad." Ryan kept his response respectful and reserved. Leave it to his father to act like this was just another homecoming after a night in town. "You look good."

Justin chuckled. "Still spreading it thick, I see." But fondness had crept into his voice. "What I look is old." He nodded in the direction of the huge barns that had been standing since before Ryan was born. "Your brother's out there locking up... if you want to go find him, let him know you're here."

The statement startled Ryan. "Since when do McGee barns need locking?"

The old man leaned against the porch railing and

examined the tip of his cigar.

Ryan waited. It was maddening, but no amount of pushing would get his father to talk before he was ready.

Finally Justin shrugged, fixed Ryan with a pointed stare. "A boy goes away for sixteen years, he's bound to see some changes when he comes back a man."

Same old shit with you, isn't, Dad? But Ryan held his tongue and acknowledged the well-deserved punch straight to the heart with a nod and a wry smile. Then he turned and strode toward the barns.

Strong floodlights, mounted at the corners of each building, lit the yard. Sean was clearly visible as he slid the barn door closed and set the lock. He walked toward the stable, a black-and-white dog at his heels.

Ryan stood just outside the light's edge watching his brother, looking for a trace of the kid he'd left behind.

The skinny boy's frame had become lean and muscular. Glow-in-the-dark blond hair had toned down some, but Ryan noticed it still had a tendency to curl at the ends even though his brother kept it cut short. Sean had been thirteen when Ryan had left. He'd grown into a man.

When Sean emerged from the stable, he ordered the dog to stay inside. Then with a flexing of his muscles, he slid the door closed. Ryan raised an eyebrow. His little brother had developed some broad shoulders and strong arms. While setting the latch, Sean's hands stilled. He eased around, his body tense, ready for anything. It had always been uncanny, the way the kid had been so acutely aware of his surroundings; it still was.

Ryan stepped into the light. Green eyes identical to his own met and held his gaze. Ryan marshalled his expression and waited, unmoving.

Sean's tension visibly drained. His smile started slowly, in his eyes first, then spreading to his mouth, where it bloomed into a full grin.

"Ry!" In two long-legged strides, Sean was in front of him. "Oh, man, it's good to see you!"

In a move too sudden for Ryan to dodge, Sean folded him into a bear hug and lifted him off his feet, his carefree laughter driving out the last vestiges of Ryan's uncertainty.

Welcome home, Ryan McGee.

* * * *

Thanks for reading! Dingbat Publishing strives to bring you quality entertainment that doesn't take itself too seriously. I mean honestly, with a name like that, our books have to be good or we're going to be laughed at. Or maybe both.

If you enjoyed this book, the best thing you can do is buy a million more copies and give them to all your friends... erm, leave a review on the readers' website of your preference. All authors love feedback and we take reviews from readers like you seriously.

Oh, and c'mon over to our website:
www.DingbatPublishing.Weebly.com

Who knows what other books you'll find there?

Cheers,

Gunnar Grey,
publisher, author, and Chief Dingbat

δ

Dingbat Publishing